RELEASED
VAGABOND CIRCUS → BOOK THREE

SARAH NOFFKE

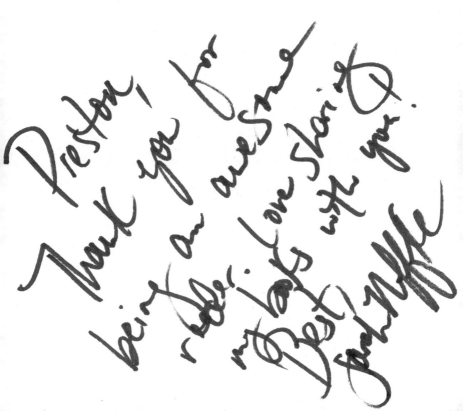

Preston,
Thank you for
being an awesome
reader. I love sharing
my books with you.
Best,
Sarah Noffke

One-Twenty-Six Press.
Released
Sarah Noffke

Summary: To some, death isn't the worst case scenario. Living in an
inescapable world ransacked by unspeakable evil, that's much worse.

Published in the United States by One-Twenty-Six Press
ISBN-13: 978-1530394418

Praise for Works:

"There are so many layers, so many twists and turns, betrayals and reveals. Loves and losses. And they are orchestrated beautifully, coming when you least expected and yet in just the right place. Leaving you a little breathless and a lot anxious. There were quite a few moments throughout where I found myself thinking that was not what I was expecting at all. And loving that."
-Mike, Amazon

"The writing in this story was some of the best I've read in a long time because the story was so well-crafted, all the little pieces fitting together perfectly."
-The Tale Temptress

"There are no words. Like literally. NO WORDS. This book killed me and then revived me and then killed me some more. But in the end I was born anew, better."
-Catalina, Goodreads

"Love this series! Perfect ending to an incredible series! The author has done this series right."
-Kelly at Nerd Girl

"What has really made these books stand out is how much emotion they evoke from me as a reader, and I love how it comes from a combination of both characters and plot together. Everything is so intricately woven that I have to commend Sarah Noffke on her skills as a writer."
-Anna at Enchanted by YA

Also by the author:
Awoken
Stunned
Revived
Defects
Rebels
Warriors
Ren: The Man Behind the Monster
Suspended
Paralyzed

For Stephanie Colman.
Because of your support.
And because you scare me.

Table of Contents

RELEASED

VAGABOND CIRCUS → BOOK THREE

SARAH NOFFKE

Chapter One

*T*he temperature in the miniature big top seemed to have dropped suddenly. Zuma's teeth chattered against each other as she stared at Finley beside her. She hardly recognized him suddenly. Everything that made him him had shifted. His confidence had drained in a single second. The fierceness in his greenish-hazel eyes was somehow stolen by Knight's presence. Now Finley stood in Titus's office motionless beside her, his eyes on the dirt ground, his pulse beating wildly in his neck.

Titus still had his head cradled in his hands, defeat oozing off his slumped shoulders. He reminded Zuma of an ostrich right then. The fact that Knight, the man responsible for Dave Raydon's death, now owned the majority share of Vagabond Circus was the worst-case scenario. The man was dangerous and cruel and Titus was burying his head and pretending that it wasn't happening.

Jack, who sat in his wheelchair beside Zuma, hadn't shifted his reaction since setting his eyes on Knight. Zuma could see, using her combat sense, that Jack was in pure shock. His mouth had fallen open, his pulse had slowed. And besides these observations, Zuma's telepathy told her that the thoughts streaming through his head were mostly unintelligible. *Broke me. Bad man. Not happening. Nowhere to go.*

Knight's dark eyes looked all too pleased as they rested on Finley. He seemed to almost regard the boy with fondness, as if he'd missed him in the long three months since Finley'd escaped Knight's compound. The man who stood before her wasn't intimidating just because of all she knew of his cruelty or the fact that he, like Finley, could lock her out of his head. Knight's very height made him appear like a monster to her. He was impossibly tall, maybe close to seven feet. His skin was the color of copy paper, and just as translucent. This made it easy to see the tiny expressions going on within him that told Zuma he was the only calm person inside the miniature big top.

"Now Finley," Knight began, saying his name with a certain degree of power and conviction, like he owned the word, "this is what's going to hap—"

"You're the one who murdered Dave," Zuma said, cutting him off and stepping forward, her eyes like sharp blades aiming to cut Knight.

NO! she heard Finley say in her mind. He briefly had opened a telepathic link, but as soon as she spun to look at him she knew it was closed. And Finley's eyes were still locked on the ground, a hollow expression in them. Nothing about him communicated the urgent message he'd just sent to her.

Knight revolved his gaze on Zuma with a nonchalant expression. "I do believe my poor brother died from a heart attack. That's what the coroner's report stated," he said, a smile in his voice, which reminded her of a bear's growl.

"We all know it was you," she said, vibrating with a hostility she'd never known before. "You and your kid—"

And then something else new happened to Zuma, cutting off her words. It wasn't a telepathic message from Finley. It wasn't a telepathic message from Titus or Jack, who hadn't changed from their prior states. It felt as though a hammer had crashed onto the top of her head. Then blinding pain shot down her brain, all the way to the base of her skull, and radiated out until her entire head felt close to exploding. She clapped both her hands to her ears as the scream she couldn't stop shot out of her mouth. Tears raced down her eyes and she fell to the ground. She'd buckled over from the pain. Lost the ability to hold herself up as the all-encompassing stabbing in her head stole her attention.

Over her she felt someone move but her senses weren't operating right. The pain was too great for her to do anything but convulse from the tremors now raking through her body, which was simultaneously shivering and sweating.

"Oh, poor girl seems to have grown suddenly ill," Knight said. "Titus, you should really take better care of your performers. They are your bread and butter, you know? Well, actually now they are mine, since I own Vagabond Circus."

Zuma's teeth were locked down right against each other when the pain finally melted into something manageable. She felt a hand under her arm. It sought to pull her up from the ground where she lay. Shaking, she rose as Titus's arm slid around her shoulder to steady the girl. "It's all right," he said in her ear, a new gentle tone to his usually serious voice. "I'll help you."

She blinked the stars from her eyes to discover Finley was just staring at the ground, his hands lifeless by his side. At first she'd thought he was the one helping her, but he looked helpless now.

"I'm taking you and Jack to see Fanny," Titus said, his back to Knight, his eyes on Zuma. "Can you walk so that I can push Jack?"

She slid her gaze to Jack, whose eyes on his pale face were bemused, like he was stuck in a nightmare. Zuma nodded. "Yes, let's go," she said, not daring to look directly at the man holding his arms across his chest with a satisfied expression written on his face. Knight, she knew, was responsible for the headache still making her feel close to exploding with pain. This was what he could do. This was how he maintained control. This had been why Finley had dared, for just a split second, to take down his shield to warn her. She knew it wouldn't be safe for him to keep down the wall as it was the only thing that protected him from Knight. Zuma saw Knight in her peripheral, still not daring to look straight at the new owner of Vagabond Circus. Something in Zuma told her that she should never again look at him directly, if she wanted her head to remain pain free.

Chapter Two

A chill slid over the backs of Finley's hands and inched over his arms, raising every hair as it took its path to his bunched up shoulders. He hadn't followed Titus, Jack, and Zuma out of the office tent. He knew better. You didn't leave Knight's presence until he dismissed you unless you wanted to be punished at the next meeting.

A morbid laugh almost spilled from Finley's mouth as his current reality sunk in. How had he thought he could beat Knight? Finley stupidly had believed at the compound that he could teleport into Knight's quarters and negotiate for Zuma's happiness, for the curse to be lifted. Not only had he been unrealistic, but he'd been unwise not to see all this coming. He cursed himself for not seeing that Knight would come after Vagabond Circus. Of course that's what he'd been after. That had been the other motivation behind Knight's revenge. And now Knight had won. He'd killed Dave, taken his circus and with it any chance Finley ever had of freedom or happiness.

Finley sensed the two figures approach behind him and he knew immediately that even if he wanted to teleport, he couldn't. If he wanted to move at super speed, he couldn't. Power-Stopper was behind him, in close enough proximity that she was robbing him of his dream travel skills. What Finley didn't know was that Power-Stopper had graduated and now was named Gwendolyn. What Finley *did* know was that if he did try to run, Sebastian, the other person behind him, had every chance of catching him. Touching him. Killing him with a single hand clasped to his arm. As he had been his entire life, Finley was trapped. Again, he laughed to himself, this one also reeking of no humor. How did he think he could escape? Knight would never have let him get away for good. Now the only advantage Finley had was that Knight couldn't get into his head to create mind-numbing headaches. But Knight didn't know that, which was also in Finley's advantage.

"Tell me, Finley," Knight said, his gravelly voice bringing that familiar dread to the acrobat's mind. "You escaped from my compound. But I don't understand why. I brought you into this world. I fed you. Taught you. Gave you everything you ever HAD!" Knight boomed on the last word. Finley knew from his peripheral that the older man's face had suddenly blossomed into a fire engine red but he didn't dare look at him directly. He knew better. "And you left me," Knight said now in an urgent whisper. Oddly he sounded almost hurt.

"How long?" Finley said, his voice even quieter than Knight's.

"Excuse me?" Knight said.

"How long do you plan to make me serve you, Master?" Finley asked, his chin nearly touching his chest.

Knight's loud laugh was soon joined by smaller ones behind Finley. "We are a family. Family is forever. What we do is a family business. And you have your name. You have a rank. Why would you want to leave that?"

"That's why I escaped. You were never going to let me go, Master," Finley dared to say, all the while his eyes on the ground.

"Where did you want to go when you left me?" Knight asked, but Finley knew he wasn't supposed to answer. "You went to Vagabond Circus. I was about to take you there, as you can see now since I'm the majority owner. When are you going to see that I'm always a step ahead of you? I've always known what you wanted. And I'm now in the position to give my kids whatever they desire for serving me. Sebastian and Gwendolyn, tell me what you two want."

"Power," Gwendolyn said without hesitation.

"Power and freedom," Sebastian said.

"And guess who now has the privilege to run freely and do whatever they want at Vagabond Circus," Knight said to the kids at Finley's back.

"We do, Master," they said in unison.

The idea that Sebastian could run around and *do* whatever he wanted terrified Finley. He didn't know the boy well, but knew he was obsessed with creating pain.

"And Finley. You wanted to be a star in this circus and if you would have just been patient you would have known I was about to give that to you. But your haste and show of disrespect has earned you my forever contempt. Sebastian tells me that you seem to care for these people at Vagabond Circus. The ones who now work for me." The threat was as heavy as lead in Knight's tone.

"Master, punish me," Finley said, his voice a raspy plea.

"I've always respected you, Finley," Knight said, ignoring his request. "You were my first named kid. The one who was relentless, always doing what I asked. You were so strong you never went any further than round one of the punishments. I've always found this strange because usually the pain I create inside my kids' heads makes them pee their pants before any physical threats start, but you weren't ever weakened. Strange really." And the insinuation flanked the last two words, bringing instant panic to Finley's mind.

"Master, I can explain," Finley said, his voice an urgent whisper now.

"Can you? CAN YOU?" Knight said too loud. "Sebastian?"

"Yes, Master?" the younger boy said.

"Tell me how this feels," Knight said.

A deep guttural scream ripped from the boy's mouth. Finley didn't dare turn around. The groan dissipated over a long few seconds.

"And Gwendolyn?" Knight said when Sebastian had quieted.

"Yes, Master?" the girl said.

Again a wail of pain filled the tent, this one high-pitched.

"And Finley?" Knight said when he'd apparently released Gwendolyn from the torture. "Do you want to fake a yelp of pain as you always have? Because I targeted the pain at you when that girl made her accusations since I saw you holding her hand when I came in. I thought torturing you would be a better punishment for her since I know assaulting the people others care about is most effective. However, you didn't even flinch. And now I'm targeted on you but there's no effect. For how long has my mind torture not worked on you?" Some of Knight's words were quick and others drawn out, like he was alternating his delivery for amusement.

"Always, Master," Finley said in a low voice.

A chuckle that sounded nothing like one slipped out of Knight's mouth. "Then you've given me no choice but to give your punishment to the ones you care about."

"But Master—" Finley almost jerked his head up.

"Silence! You want to hurt them and also be cursed? Do you, Finley? Oh, and I realize you figured out you can dream travel. So do it. Escape again, but note that I will find you and when I do I will destroy you after I've cursed or murdered every last person at this circus. IS THAT CLEAR?"

Finley nodded, unable to manage anything else.

"You are a part of *this* family whether you like it or not. You will stay, you will serve, and you will be an example to my kids and the people of Vagabond Circus or next time I won't let up on the girl with the pink stripe in her hair. I'll make her head hurt until it hemorrhages."

"Yes, Master," Finley said on the tails of Knight's words, hoping to cut him off, to make him stop. Finley couldn't believe how flawed he'd been in thinking he could save Zuma from the curse. That was impossible. And now he was going to have an incredibly difficult time just keeping her alive. His only hope was that she'd leave Vagabond Circus and that hope was worthless. The girl would never abandon Dave's circus. Especially now that it was in drastic need of saving.

Chapter Three

*T*he stuffy air in Ian's truck was starting to make him feel like he
was suffocating. He'd been sitting in the old teal Chevy for three
long hours with the windows sealed shut. He'd been in the truck's
passenger seat when Zuma, Finley, and Jack had arrived. She had
cast a relieved glance at the truck, but since it was dark she hadn't
noticed him in there. He was grateful she looked relieved to see the
truck, grateful she felt better knowing he was still there at Vagabond
Circus. Ian had no disillusions. He actually was the one person at
Vagabond Circus, and one of the few in the world, who really saw
things for what they were. His divination and clairvoyance made his
realities always clear. Ian's heart was only lightened that someone
with a spark as pure as Zuma's cared about him. He went unnoticed
by most by choice, but he wanted to be thought fondly of by the girl,
especially once he was gone.

Ian hadn't been surprised to see Jack's legs stretched in front of
him, hadn't been surprised to see him in a wheelchair. He'd known
that if Finley and Zuma had followed his directions, they would save
Jack, but not from his fall. Some futures were unavoidable. And in
the case of Jack's paralysis, it wasn't the worst-case scenario. In
truth, Jack living his life without the challenges he was going to face
would have delivered him a much worse future. Now Jack had the
chance at real happiness.

Ian opened the glove box and stared at the blackness inside it.
He knew what was in there, although he couldn't see it directly. He'd
bought the item last week. Now he sat in the passenger seat wishing
he would have run away from Vagabond Circus last week instead.
That's one reason he'd chosen to sit in the passenger side instead of
the driver's side of his truck. His constant visions of the future made
him feel like a passenger to what was going to happen to Vagabond
Circus. He would have little involvement in the things Knight would
do to his people, but still he'd be forced to watch one way or another,
either in person or in his head. And that's why he hadn't run away.
One way or another he'd be cursed with the visions of the future.

Ian would always see the horrible no matter where he was. So he didn't run even though he wanted to. Soon most at Vagabond Circus would want to run away too, but none of them would. For most, they would stay with the faith that they were in the right place at the moment, or that they were protecting Dave's circus. For those who didn't instinctively believe this, they would once Ian spread his well-crafted rumor.

He threw his hand through his light-colored curly hair. He didn't like to lie. The man had never had a reason to lie before; withholding information was as close as Ian ever came. But now he'd have to tell the Vagabond Circus members that if they stayed and endured the torture Knight would put them through, then they would overthrow his leadership and run him away. He would also tell them that if they ran away then Knight would ruin Vagabond Circus, forever tarnishing everything Dave sought to do. Knight would make all those who believed in magic, believe in something sinister. Knight would spread evil if the Vagabond Circus members left the big top. That's what Ian would tell them.

This actually wasn't the future that Ian saw. Not at all. What he saw had forced him to lock himself away in his truck, almost hoping to suffocate in the small compartment. However, Ian knew he couldn't give up yet. Except with the first vision he ever saw, he never tried to change the vision in his head. But now Ian had to. If his gift was to be considered that at all, then in this case it had to be employed to make things right. And after he'd told his lies and set up a different path for Vagabond Circus members then he'd finally be done. He would free himself of the torture of being a prisoner to the unrelenting tragedies of the future playing in his vision.

Ian reached into the dark glove box and removed the pistol he had bought last week. He had no doubt that when the time came he could raise the gun to his head and fire. No doubt at all. Ian had already seen himself doing just that in a vision of the future.

Chapter Four

"*H*e can't get away with this," Zuma said to Titus in a hush. Her head was still pressed between her palms as she walked beside the older man.

Titus pushed Jack's wheelchair. The acrobat seemed to be in a silent state of shock. He hadn't said a word since he'd confronted Knight. Now Jack just stared at his outstretched legs like he didn't believe they were real. It was his current reality he was doubting. It didn't compute and he regretted that he hadn't said more. Charged Knight. Confronted him. Accused him. Attacked him. But how could he? He was powerless. And trying to convict Knight of attempting to murder him was ridiculous. Jack had jumped through a skylight. That's how the authorities would see it. He'd broken and entered. Trespassers had no rights. Finley had once said that Knight's crimes were untraceable. Now Jack fully understood why.

In the background Jack heard muttering. Titus and Zuma were talking. To decipher their words would take more focus than his shocked state would allow so he just stayed locked on the unmoving legs in front of him.

"Titus, what is he doing here? How can we stop him? We have to do something," Zuma said, her voice low, her tone frantic.

Titus halted and spun to face the girl. "Don't you think I know that?" Just as Zuma pulled her hands from her still aching head Titus had her face cupped in his fingers. It was an urgent gesture, but still full of gentleness. It spoke so eloquently of the fear inside of Titus. For him to reach out, to grab her, meant he was bursting with panic. "Zuma, get this straight, we are doomed. There's nothing we can do. And therefore you have to leave Vagabond Circus. You and Jack and everyone have to leave. Without you all here, Knight has no circus."

Zuma's dark eyes narrowed and she stepped back out of Titus's hold. "No." She said that one word sharp enough it could cut. "I'm not letting him have Dave's circus. I'm—"

"It's *his* circus now," Titus said. "He has a legitimate claim to Dave's share of fifty-one percent. That's why you all have to leave.

10

There's nothing we can do and Knight will destroy Vagabond Circus now and turn it into something sinister."

"That's exactly why we have to stay and take it back," Zuma said, wanting to stomp her feet into the earth.

Titus was already shaking his head before she was done speaking. "No, Zuma, you don't get it. There's no beating Knight. Even Dave knew that. That's why he only banished him from Vagabond Circus using a curse. He knew he could never get rid of him, although I'm not sure he would have tried."

"So what? You're just going to allow him to have your shares and abandon everything you've worked for for twenty years?" Zuma asked, shaking with anger.

"What choice do I have?" Titus said, and the defeat in his voice attempted to crawl into Zuma's heart and hibernate there.

She shook this off, rose up higher on her long legs. Stared up at the creative director. "You can stay with me and figure out a way to save things. This can't be over. Because if we leave then Knight will just find new performers. He'll enslave his kids to perform. At least if we stay we can protect people. At least if we stay we have a chance of taking Vagabond Circus back," Zuma said.

Titus shook his head and looked away from the girl, off into the dark where he could see nothing. But when Titus spoke, he was talking to Zuma. "So you won't leave then?"

"Not even if my life is at stake," she said, her voice full of conviction.

"Well, if you stay that's exactly what's at stake, Zuma. I want you to know that."

"Titus please," she said, reaching out and taking the creative director's hand. He'd known Zuma her whole life. Had been there when she was born in the big top. And like Dave he knew she carried a special magic in her, a power to change things. "Please, Titus. You have to believe we are strong enough to stop this. You have to believe you're strong enough," she added.

"Okay," he said, his eyes on the petite hand clutching his.

Before he could say more the phone in Zuma's pocket rang, clanging like the loudest sound in the world inside the silent dark circus grounds. Zuma shuffled hastily for the phone. With a quick glance at the screen she turned and rushed for Fanny's trailer. "It's

Dr. Chang," she called over her shoulder. "Bring Jack," she said to Titus. "Hurry."

Chapter Five

*F*anny had been trudging the same path out in front of her darkened trailer when she heard the approaching footsteps. Her three charges were finally asleep inside. Fanny had tried to lie down, knowing if she was exhausted tomorrow she wouldn't be able to care for the kids with the affection they deserved. However, the multiple attempts at rest had been met with defeat. A nervous hum buzzed in the older woman's chest and the only thing that made it bearable was pacing. Back and forth. Again and again.

She turned at the sound of the racing feet. A dark figure moved swiftly across the grounds in her direction. Could it be more heartbreak? Fanny almost considered running into her trailer and locking the door. Locking herself away from the potentially approaching bad news. Then Fanny spotted the unmistakable, almost white hair flying back behind Zuma's face as she ran. Something glowing was pressed to the girl's head. She was ten feet away when Fanny heard her speak into what she now realized was a phone. "Yes, we got here safely. And Fanny is right here. I'll turn the phone over to her now," the young girl said.

Zuma arrived with a graceful halt in front of the bewildered woman. The girl's hair hung in strings around her reddened face, and her chest vibrated, not from running, but rather from adrenaline. Before Fanny could praise God for bringing the acrobat back to Vagabond Circus safely she took the cell phone from Zuma's outstretched hand.

"It's Dr. Chang," Zuma said in response to the confused look on Fanny's face. "He's Jack's doctor and he only released him because he knew Jack would be under your care. You have to speak to him and prove that you're nurse Fanny."

The woman closed her swollen fingers around the cell phone. "Jack's doctor?" she said, trying to remember the last news she'd heard about Jack. He'd broken his legs in a fall in Knight's compound. That's what Titus had told her. She drew in a long breath and nodded a high chin at Zuma. "Of course." She slid the cell phone to her ear.

"Nurse Fanny Swedlund speaking," the woman said at once into the phone.

A man on the other side of the line cleared his throat. "Nurse Fanny, I can hardly believe this could be you. I'm Dr. Chang," a man said, a subtle Chinese accent to his words.

"Hello, Doctor," Fanny said, trying to understand why she was talking on the phone with a stranger at this late hour.

"I've studied your cases extensively," Dr. Chang said. "And I released Jack early into your care because I believe his future is best in hands like yours. However, for my peace of mind, I have to know you're the world renowned nurse I've heard of."

Fanny nodded, although the man on the other side of the phone couldn't see this response. "If you've studied my cases," she began in a confident tone, "then you know that in over ten years I oversaw the care of six hundred seventy-five cancer patients, two hundred thirty-four injury patients, and eight hundred ninety patients with viral infection. Seventy-five percent of my patients were considered terminal and yet only twelve patients passed away from their conditions."

Silence on the line. Something bristled against the receiver. Then Dr. Chang said, "Well, there's no doubt now, only the real Nurse Fanny would know those numbers without hesitation."

"Exactly," she said. "Now, you said that Jack's future rested in my hands. What is his prognosis?" Fanny said, her curious eyes on an anxious Zuma in front of her; then her eyes tightened on someone else approaching in the dark between the trailers in the distance.

"Wait," Dr. Chang said. "You don't know? Haven't you seen Jack yet?"

"He just arrived," Fanny said, now seeing it was two figures approaching, Titus pushing Jack in a wheelchair.

"Oh, well, you'll want to check his legs to ensure the travel didn't open any of the incisions," Dr. Chang said. "And then you and I should plan to discuss his physical therapy treatment and how you intend to approach his healing. You see, I discharged Jack, but I still feel invested in his care. Turning him over to you was a special case and I'd like you to loop me into his recovery."

"Of course, Dr. Chang," Fanny said. "And I appreciate your confidence in me. I know Jack must have been anxious to return to his home."

"He was. You were a big factor in allowing him early discharge with his condition," the doctor said.

"And again, you haven't answered my earlier question. What is Jack's condition?" Fanny asked.

There was another pause. "He's paralyzed," Dr. Chang said just as Jack and Titus made it to a portion of light, illuminating the defeated look on the young man's face, and the bandages on his legs which stretched out before him.

"Right," Fanny said, feeling something like a stone fall to the bottom of her stomach.

Chapter Six

"Oh, in heaven's name," Fanny said, pushing the phone into Zuma's hand and hurrying toward Jack. She didn't completely register the exhaustion dripping off his face before she flung her arms around his shoulders. Fanny's embrace had the effect on Jack that it had on most: it opened him up. Gave him a silent validation to allow his emotions to spill out of him. He clapped a hand around the older woman's back and squeezed his eyes shut. Unlike most at Vagabond Circus he hadn't been raised by Fanny. He had come to the circus at the age of fifteen as a performer. But still he knew why all of her kids would do anything for the caregiver, because she gave herself to them. Loved them with all she had. Such was the capacity of Fanny Swedlund.

When the healer pulled back she dropped into a kneeled position so she was looking at Jack straight on, not down at him.

"What has happened to you, Jack?" she said, her eyes on his, not on his legs.

"I met Charles Knight," he said dryly.

She nodded, a knowing expression in her eyes marked by lines. "But you lived and most who have trespassed into his territory cannot say that."

"Was that…?" Jack trailed away, pointing to the phone clutched in Zuma's hand. He hoped it was Dr. Chang, and not his brother Dr. Fuller. The brother who, like the rest of his brothers, was better than him. The one who, like his parents, disapproved of Jack.

"Yes, that was Dr. Chang," Fanny said, rising to a standing position, her knee popping as she did. "I've assured him that you're under my care now, and he did relay his prognosis. However, Jack, these things are never set in stone." She tapped two fingers to the side of her head. "We are only ever a thought away from changing a would-be destiny."

Titus now moved around from his place behind the wheelchair. "What is this would-be prognosis?"

Fanny waved her hand dismissively at the tall man. "Nothing for you to concern yourself with now. You have other concerns and Jack will be mine."

"Fanny, please remember that as the creative director for Vagabond Circus I need to be informed. Lord knows I'm already at a serious disadvantage now, I don't need you keeping things from me," Titus said in a tone he reserved solely for Fanny. He spoke to her like he was pleading.

She turned sharply to Titus. "Relaying this information to you or anyone else will only make the idea more powerful. Half of my power as a healer is making people forget there was anything wrong in the first place. When a thought has no power it can no longer control a person. And that's mostly what an ailment is. A thought. So why don't you forget this for the time being and help me figure out how we're getting Jack into my trailer," Fanny said with the authority of an army general.

Chapter Seven

*F*rom Fanny's trailer window Benjamin had the curtain peeled back just enough so he could spy the events going on outside. The healer had thought he was asleep when she left to pace just in front of the trailer. She'd been doing a lot of pacing the last couple of days. It worried the ten-year-old boy. He didn't like seeing Fanny so stressed. It made his chest vibrate with worry, his palms sweat, his tummy hurt. What would have Fanny so stressed? After Dave's death she was sad. Everyone was still so sad. They always would be. But then the black trucks pulled up to Vagabond Circus and Fanny's sadness turned into pure fear. Benjamin knew that look although he'd never seen it on his caregiver's face. She had shuffled Benjamin, Tiffany, and Emily into the trailer, not allowing the kids to see what was in the black trucks, or who. They looked just like the white semis which held various compartments where the crew members had living quarters in sleeper row. However, these trucks were black and didn't look like they had cozy compartments.

Benjamin squinted through the window. Truth be told, Benjamin as a young boy had perfect vision. However, at that moment he wasn't in his little boy form. Rarely since he came into his dream travel gift was he himself anymore, which had been another reason that Fanny had ordered him in the trailer. She also wouldn't allow him to tell anyone but the other kids or Titus what his gift was. The caregiver had ordered him to only use his skill when inside her trailer. And then she said, "This is a gift we protect by hiding it."

Benjamin shook his head now at the strangeness of that thought. He believed that everyone should know he was a shape shifter. He couldn't wait to announce it to the world of Vagabond Circus. But he trusted Fanny more than anyone he'd ever known and would never betray her order.

Benjamin had trouble seeing up close with his current eyes but as they were able to focus he realized that he could see better in the dark than usual. Where things usually were shades of black and gray at night, now through the window he could see the pink strip in Zuma's hair. He could see the blue of Fanny's eyes as they widened when Jack was wheeled forward by Titus. Benjamin could see the details of the group that told him bad news was being relayed. It wasn't something that he would be able to see with his own eyes. His own eyes would have only seen dark figures congregating. However, *these* eyes could see in high definition in the dark of night.

Then the boy reflexively straightened when Fanny picked up her long skirt like she always did when she was about to climb the steps into the trailer. Benjamin backed up to the far wall, blinking rapidly. He needed to switch back into his normal form but the sudden nervousness made it impossible to concentrate. His mind was a blur of commotion as he realized the group was about to enter the trailer. He looked to the bedroom at the back, where the younger girls were sleeping. He could race for that space but it was unlikely he'd make it in time. This body didn't move fast, not like he did when in his ten-year-old body.

The door handle jiggled. Benjamin's eyes stayed focused on it. Then when Fanny swung it open he realized her eyes and Zuma's weren't on him, but rather on the people trying to negotiate their way into the trailer. It was a sight to see. Titus had Jack cradled in his arms, the older man's face red from the exhausting task. Jack's face was a grimace of lines too, his bandaged legs held firm in Titus's arms.

Benjamin watched as orders were given and people moved. He was so entranced by the strange scene in front of him that he forgot his prior concern and fear. And it wasn't until Zuma turned around and saw him that he remembered what she was seeing. The girl screamed and that's precisely when Benjamin covered his face with his gloved hands.

Chapter Eight

Zuma clapped her hand over her mouth, muffling the scream that burst out of her without her permission. She backed up suddenly, colliding with Fanny, who was already reaching out and grabbing the girl by the shoulders.

"It's okay, Zuma," Fanny said, her voice stern, her fingers pressing into the girl's skin firmly.

Zuma shook her head widely and coughed on the remaining piece of the scream lodged in her throat. She tried to say something but it was Jack in Titus's arms who whispered the one word she'd been trying to say. "Dave?" he said in a hush.

"No," Titus said at once and turned and gently laid the acrobat on the couch. "It's not Dave."

Jack flinched from the pain of being moved and handled. Too much was going on at once. He moved the best he could to see around Titus and at the man who stood in the corner. He in fact looked exactly like Dave Raydon, dressed in his teal blue suit, complete with the top hat that had killed him.

"Then who is that?" Zuma said, stepping forward and studying the now cowering figure.

The man didn't move like Dave. Didn't have his confidence or smile. Zuma's combat sense told her this much. She reached out, holding her hand a foot away from the man. Her approach was tentative. The man widened his eyes, which looked so much like the ringmaster's. Light blue, outlined with a darker navy blue.

"It's a real person," Fanny said behind her. "But it isn't Dave. I'm sorry." The healer remembered her own disenfranchised state when she saw the figure of the man she thought was dead. Hope and confusion had blanketed her mind then, until she learned who was really inside the body of Dave.

The man lifted his gloved hand, a look of heart-wrenching regret on his face. "I'm not Dave," he said, using the ringmaster's voice but without any of its usual merriment. "I'm sorry," he said and reached forward and clasped his hand around Zuma's.

She squealed with shock, jumping back a foot into Fanny again, who was watching all of this with pain in her eyes. Titus and Jack watched too. Jack in awe and Titus with a haunted expression laced with bitter disappointment.

"What are you?" Zuma stuttered out.

"Who, you mean," Fanny said, her voice calm. "I apologize you found out this way," she said, looking at Zuma and then Jack. "This must be quite the rude shock." She then turned and looked at the imposter. Fanny stepped forward and placed a hand on not-Dave's shoulder and looked down at him. "I understand you're scared," she said in a voice she reserved for her kids. It was a higher pitch than her normal voice. Not one she ever used with Dr. Raydon. "It's okay. You're not in trouble for this. It's not your fault they found out your secret, and I dare say Zuma and Jack can be trusted with the knowledge. So take a few deep breaths and then you should be able to change back."

She was right too, Benjamin realized. He had no control over his shape-shifting when frightened. He'd have to learn to control that. It would do him no good. He sucked in a short breath, followed by a couple of deeper ones. When he let them out Zuma thought that the long drive was making her hallucinate. The colors on the teal blue suit swayed and blurred. The hat flickered and disappeared and then all at once in front of her Dave vanished. He seemed to melt into something smaller and only her combat sense explained to her the complex shifting that was happening all at once. Dave's form had molded until he was in the shape of a little brown-haired and wide-eyed boy.

"Benjamin?" she said, covering her mouth for a second time.

"Hi," he squeaked, throwing his chin to his chest, his eyes to the ground. That didn't last long because suddenly arms were around him, the acrobat's body pressed to his.

"Congrats," Zuma said, total astonishment in her voice. She pulled back, looking him over. "You came into your gift early?" she said, looking at him and then to Fanny for confirmation when all he did was bite his lip from the nervousness of the girl's hands still gripping onto his arms.

Fanny nodded proudly. "Yes, and what an incredible gift to be bestowed with so early in life."

"Indeed," Titus said, his voice heavy.

21

Chapter Nine

Sunshine stared at the handful of hair ends pressed between her fingers. From only three inches away her eyes could spy the split ends and breaks in her long black strands. She snapped them or split them depending on the damaged thread. It was a nervous habit she'd broken herself of years ago, but now all her bad habits had surged to the surface, a series of comforts in the midst of her newest tragedy. Titus had assured the people of Vagabond Circus at Dave's eulogy that things would get easier with time. He was wrong and didn't know it. When Titus gave that speech he had no idea that the next day a truck carrying a lot more problems was about to unload itself on Vagabond Circus.

Morning sunlight had been greeting the rousing members of Vagabond Circus when the first black truck had appeared. Most people were milling about trying to find a normal activity on another day that felt extremely abnormal without Dave's presence. Sunshine had been staring at her scrambled eggs with a strange hostility like the pile of protein had made a personal insult at the girl. That's when she had heard a commotion of crew members' voices. They were busy prepping the big top for the first show the next day. Sunshine felt the embers of frustration from the rig crew members using her empathesis. She was so attuned to the emotions around the circus grounds that she felt new ones pretty acutely, especially a flood of them from a dozen crew members.

Sunshine raced in the direction of the noise and that's when she spied the first truck parked right in front of the main entrance of the big top, the one where patrons entered. Then a second black semi pulled up, blocking the side entrance, and then two more. They didn't stop negotiating themselves into place until they formed a wall of sorts around Vagabond Circus grounds. She expected that Ian, who was in charge of rig crew, would be charging toward the driver of the first truck and telling him to move off their grounds, that they were blocking their loading zones. She caught Ian's stocky figure standing in front of the grille of the first semi, six feet from it. The man shook his curly head, his lip pressed between his teeth which were covered in braces. And although she knew he was furious from reading his emotions, Ian only balled up his fists and turned and marched away. Marched away from the trespassing trucks. The ones blocking him from doing his job. Nothing was more important to Ian than his job. And he had marched away. Sunshine couldn't make sense of it.

The door to the first semi opened and Sunshine squinted through the morning light to see who had gotten out. Around her most of Vagabond Circus stood, also staring with confused expressions. From the cab of the truck a man who was both too tall and too thin exited. He had to be close to seven feet tall. His pale head was bald and she realized there was something else strange about the man. He had no eyebrows. His snow-white complexion seemed to glow in contrast to his black shirt and pants.

Sunshine sucked in a sudden breath and then choked on it. She almost thought she'd been slapped across the back but no, she'd been assaulted by the emotions of this invader. It was the weirdest experience she'd ever had. For ten years she'd read people's emotions. Hundreds of thousands of emotions. But this was the first time she'd ever met someone who had emotions that made her shiver. She looked down at her arms and realized she'd absentmindedly been clawing at her skin. Bile rose in her mouth. Never before had she felt such hatred in a person. The man in front of her was pure evil and there was something else. Something she hadn't quite figured out at that point.

The man climbed out of the truck and pretended not to notice that most of the circus was staring at him. To Sunshine's right she spied Titus materialize from the crowd. He was tall but not in comparison to the strange man. The creative director stepped forward. "Knight? What are you doing here? You know you aren't allowed here," Titus said, his voice attempting to be strong, but Sunshine spied the cracks in it.

And still the man didn't look at Titus or the various Vagabond Circus members gawking at him. The man named Knight seemed to have his attention focused on the other trucks. From his high vantage point he could probably spy them well. Finally his narrow eyes brightened as a boy and girl joined him on either side. The girl had orangey red hair and wore an expression of entitlement. The boy had shoulder-length black hair and when he turned to face the crowd Sunshine again felt assaulted. It was Sebastian. The boy who had been under Fanny's care but ran away from Vagabond Circus. That had always seemed strange to Sunshine. Who would willingly leave the circus?

Only when joined on either side by the girl and Sebastian did the man turn and face Titus, who now stood only a few feet from him. "Well, hello, Titus. It has been too long, hasn't it?" the man said and his voice sounded like it was running over sandpaper to get out of his throat.

"What are you doing here?" Titus said through clenched teeth, his face already pinched red from his fear and frustration. "You know you aren't allowed here."

"Things have changed, haven't they? Dave is dead." Then the man dropped his bald head and shook it with pretend grief, but Sunshine felt his emotions and knew that there was no remorse in him. Actually there was pure glee. Sunshine fought the urge to tear forward and attack the man. Her eyes scanned Sebastian and then the redheaded girl. They were protectors. That was what she felt from them. More than just that actually, but mainly that they wanted to protect the man. She knew then that attacking him would never work. But why? Who was Sebastian and who was this man?

The stranger raised his head, a sharp smile in his dark eyes. "Now Titus, if you'll step aside I'd like to briefly address the circus, *my* circus," he added. His voice was scratchy and raw and his words all wrong.

"No! What are you—" Titus began.

The man held up his hand. "I will explain. Step aside."

And to Sunshine's horror Titus did step to the side, a fear like she'd never seen in his eyes.

The tall man raised his long arms, holding them out in a greeting fashion. "My name is Charles Knight," he said in the most unwelcoming voice she'd ever heard. "Dave, your dearly departed ringmaster, was my brother. What a tragedy his loss was," he said, shaking his head, but inside him Sunshine felt a giddy excitement. "I was shocked when I learned of my brother's passing. And even more so I was shocked to learn that as his only living relative I am now the majority owner of Vagabond Circus."

"No!" Titus said, stepping forward.

24

Charles Knight snapped his menacing eyes on Titus. "Oh, yes," he growled. And then Titus's hands shot to his head. Sunshine knew he was feeling pain. Horribly distracting pain. With his head pinned between his hands Titus snuck back into the crowd, instant defeat on his face.

Sunshine had no idea why Titus, who although fearful at times, appeared completely cowardly in front of this man. And Dave had a brother? Where had he been for the ten years she'd lived at Vagabond Circus? Dave never mentioned him. And why were there trucks? What was in them?

Sunshine couldn't understand any of what had happened. However, she did know two things with ultimate certainty. First: there were dozens of new, unique emotions at Vagabond Circus. Emotions that felt raw and were best labeled as neglect. And second: she knew Titus had withheld information from Vagabond Circus. Dave didn't die of natural causes. He was murdered. She felt it blast her like a missile at the mention of Dave's death, but not from Charles Knight. She felt it from Sebastian. Pure and selfish pride. When Knight spoke of Dave's death, Sebastian was bathed in a gleeful satisfaction. He'd murdered Dave. And the night the ringmaster died had been the night the boy disappeared. Sunshine knew there was more to unravel here and she would. She would undoubtedly stay and find out what happened to Dave. And if Sebastian had in fact killed him as she suspected, then she'd strangle the boy with her own hands. Happily.

Chapter Ten

*S*ince seeing Dave's figure standing in Fanny's trailer, Zuma had found it impossible to fully catch her breath. Each attempt to fill her lungs with oxygen was cut short by an ache in her chest, leaving her lightheaded. Yes, she knew that the extremely real form wasn't Dave. It could talk like him, looked like him, but inside that body was Benjamin's soul and not Dave's. His had vanished. Moved on. Still, she kept seeing Dave in her head. Wondering how many ways he lived on in the people of Vagabond Circus. That was the gift and curse of the circus. Anything could happen. The impossible didn't apply to Vagabond Circus.

After Fanny heavily asserted she be alone to examine Jack, Titus had insisted on chaperoning Zuma to her trailer. On the quiet trip to her place, the creative director kept jerking his head over his shoulder looking for a lurking figure in the dark.

"You think we could be attacked?" she finally asked.

"I don't know what to expect. Knight can't be trusted. You've already seen that," Titus said, his voice low.

"Why is he here? Why did he take his inheritance? Why would he want it?" Zuma asked.

"Because Knight once loved Vagabond Circus," Titus said, his eyes scanning the grounds continuously. "Well, as much as he is capable of loving anything. Anyway, I know when Dave forced Knight to leave the circus that's when he really broke. Became pure evil."

"And is that why Knight cursed the circus?" Zuma said. "Because Dave forced him to leave?"

Titus stopped with eyes so wide she could see too much of their white in the dark night. "How do you know about the curse?"

"Finley told me," she said, studying the new nervousness that covered him.

"He told you?" Titus said, sounding almost angry.

"Well, not what the curse was, but just that Knight had done it. You know what the curse is? Tell me," Zuma said.

Titus looked around, unable to see much in the dark grounds. Finally he grabbed Zuma's hand and dragged her toward her trailer. "Not right now. Let's get you to safety."

"Titus..." she said, frustrated and confused.

"Not right now, Zuma," Titus said and there was a rare authority in his voice she didn't question. She wanted more of that to come out of Titus. If Titus was going to protect Vagabond Circus from Knight then he'd have to be stronger than he'd ever been.

At Zuma's trailer Titus stood looking around, scanning for hidden dangers. "There's a meeting first thing tomorrow morning. Knight called it. Be there and then we will figure out what we're doing next."

Zuma felt so sorry for Titus. He wanted to protect his people. To get them as far away from danger as possible, but to do that he'd have to give up an empire worth more than anything he'd ever had. The torn look in his eyes made her breath fully catch in her lungs. "Okay," she said.

"Now get inside there and lock the door. Call me if you need anything, got it?" Titus said.

She nodded and did as she was told, pushing the latch closed as soon as she entered the space. However, Zuma didn't move away from the wall. She stayed there for a long minute. Then she pushed back the curtain of the window beside her. Titus had gone. Zuma realized she was shaking when she pulled the lock back open. She didn't like defying Titus's orders. If he were Dave then the thought wouldn't have even occurred to her, but Titus had never held as much authority as the ringmaster.

Zuma searched the dark but the grounds were quiet. Gloomy. Still. There was one light on, two trailers over. She snuck past Jasmine's trailer. How confused her fellow acrobat must have been when Jack, Finley, and Zuma disappeared. She'd have to explain so much to her friend tomorrow, Zuma thought.

The light in the trailer beside Jasmine's was dim, probably just the light over the stove or one in the bathroom. He probably only turned it on briefly, but it was enough for Zuma to know that Finley was inside his trailer. That light hadn't been on when she'd run past there an hour ago with Titus and Jack following her to Fanny's trailer.

Zuma brought in a full breath, grateful she could finally breathe properly. Soon she'd be with Finley and have his comfort. His protection. That was the only ray of hope in the current dismal circumstances.

Her fist paused before quietly rapping on the metal door to his trailer. Inside she heard something stir. Her combat sense caught the blinds move quickly. Most would have never seen it. She knew he'd used his super speed to see who was outside his door. Zuma expected that she'd hear the door unlock and pulled back. Then she'd walk forward into Finley's arms, the only place she'd feel safe. And yet she realized that nothing was happening. She stood for a full thirty seconds when she realized maybe Finley wasn't about to open the door. But why? Another thirty seconds passed. Zuma knocked again. Quite possibly Finley hadn't seen her. Couldn't see his visitor in the dark.

"Finley, it's me. Open up," Zuma whispered, her lips an inch from the crack in his door. Her hands pressed into it.

She then felt a weight press against the other side of the door. Something firm. And then Zuma heard a rustling as something slid down the door and landed on the floor. *Was Finley sitting with his back against the door? Keeping her out?*

Again she knocked. Louder this time. "Finley, what are you doing? Let me in," Zuma said, then looked over her shoulder spying a movement. Then there was a sound. A twig breaking underfoot. She spied through the dark for Sebastian or Power-Stopper or whoever else could be prowling in the grounds of Vagabond Circus.

She thought she saw something in the distance. Her eyes focused until she saw two green beads in the dark. The light from a nearby streetlight reflected off them. Yes, it was a pair of eyes. She was certain of that. *Maybe the eyes of a raccoon or opossum?* But then she realized the two reflections in the blackness were too high off the ground to belong to a rodent. The eyes were roughly twenty yards away down a row of trailers and hovered at the height of a person. At Sebastian's height. However, humans' eyes weren't supposed to reflect light, Zuma remembered. Eye shine occurs in nocturnal animals, mostly carnivores who hunt at night. And still this not quite animal, not quite human, moved and the outline of their frame took shape. It was a person. A boy. And then everything but their green eyes went dark. Disappeared. The person's body was bathed in dark. She was sure it was Sebastian. Sure, although the dark was robbing her senses of so much. And Zuma realized all he had to do was touch her, touch her and she'd be dead. She turned back to the door with a new urgency. "Damn it, Finley, open up," she said, her voice a hush. "There's someone out here."

She felt a thump on the other side of the door like something banged back into it. Finley's head maybe.

"Go back to your trailer, Zuma. You're not safe out there," he said from the other side of the door.

"Finley," Zuma said, her voice catching in her throat. *He was in there!* "Let me in then," she said, whipping her head over her shoulder. The eyes were gone. Had moved.

"You're not safe in here either," Finley said, his voice breaking the veil holding Zuma's emotions back.

"What?" she half croaked out through threatening tears.

"Go away, Zuma," Finley said, a new sternness in his voice.

From her peripheral Zuma's combat sense noticed movement behind her, still a bit of distance, but someone was there. Now she knew it.

Zuma turned, putting her back to Finley's door and scanning the darkness. Whatever had moved was hidden now. "Finley," Zuma said, her head to the side, pulse racing, "I need your help now. Please." She said the last word with a begging urgency.

"Then listen to me and do exactly what I say," Finley said.

Zuma pressed herself into the door, almost sensing she could feel Finley pressed into the other side of the door.

"You're fast," he said, his words hard. "Much faster than *him.* Take off running now and don't stop until you're locked inside your trailer. Okay?"

"But Finley," Zuma almost cried, panic taking over her once steady heart.

"No," he said in a harsh whisper. "You can't come in here. Just stay away from me."

Tears rattled in Zuma's throat. Her combat sense spied the figure move out into the dark open. Fifteen yards in the opposite direction of her trailer.

"Please," she said through a bottleneck of tears.

"Go now, Zuma!" Finley yelled, his voice angry and urgent.

She caught the movement in front of her a second before the figure started in her direction. Zuma shot in the other direction, racing for her trailer, using her acrobatic grace to manage the distance ahead of her with precise efficiency. She felt the figure rushing behind her. Heard him moving, not as fast or graceful as her. Zuma's hand reached for her door before she was there. She whipped it open and shut and locked it in one single movement, like a morbid dance move. She backed away from the door shaking, her eyes pinned on it, realizing how flimsy the divider was from her and the person on the other side. Zuma reached for her cell phone in her pocket when Sebastian's voice came through her door.

"The night belongs to me, Zuma," he said in a voice that slithered through her mind, echoing its dark intent. "Let's play a game from now on, shall we? During the day you're safe, but watch your back when night comes. Tag, you're it." And then a laugh so wrong and sick slipped through the crack. "I'm dying to put hands on you. I've always wanted to, but now I have permission." Another laugh, but this one faded as its owner moved away from the trailer.

Chapter Eleven

*T*itus checked to ensure the ringer on his mobile phone was on and at full volume. Everyone at Vagabond Circus had his number. They all knew to call for any reason. As he stood motionless in the center of his own trailer his conversation with Zuma sped through his mind, different parts of it all at once, like several tracks playing over each other, inundating his brain.

Titus stared at the door of his trailer. What dangers did he expect to hurt Vagabond Circus members? Besides from what Knight did to Zuma in the office tent and to Titus when he arrived, there had been no other threats, but that was just the thing about Knight. He did things so they were impossible to link to him. Got into people's heads to create mysterious headaches. Used a boy with poison in the oils of his skin to murder. Commanded Gwendolyn to stop Dream Travelers' powers so they couldn't fight back. And suffocated innocent babies when no one was around.

Knight hadn't made any threats yet, but Titus knew there was still something to be feared. When Knight had been at Vagabond Circus before, in the early years, his presence made everything tense. His precise tone of speaking to people set everyone on edge. And yet he was Dave's brother so no one said anything about the sinister stares Knight gave them or the things he said which seemed to insinuate threats.

Titus folded his gaze down to the worn carpet of his trailer. He should move. Do something. Eat something. But he felt paralyzed by the thoughts still streaming wildly across his mind. Zuma wouldn't leave the circus, but maybe others would if it looked like things were getting worse. Titus wanted to save Dave's circus from his crazy brother but he didn't know how. The very man responsible for the ringmaster's death was now running the show. How was this venture even worth doing anymore? But Titus knew Zuma was right. They couldn't just run. However, the coward in Titus had been so close. So close to never confronting Knight when he climbed out of that truck upon arriving at Vagabond Circus. He would admit only to himself that once he saw Knight he almost turned and ran the opposite direction, abandoning the circus and its people. He wasn't a strong man, but he was starting to realize that fate was trying to make him into one. Would fate win or would Titus be defeated? Murdered. Made nameless and forgotten like so many who confronted Knight or opposed him.

And still Titus felt that twitch in his legs to get in his car and drive as far away as possible. He had always run from conflict. Cowered when confronted by bullies. The only time he'd ever been brave was when Knight had come to fight Dave. Knight had just killed his own child. Dave didn't know when his brother confronted him on the day Dave's wife, Cynthia, gave birth that the child wasn't his. And Dave also didn't know that Knight had just found out he'd murdered his own son. But all was revealed as Knight smashed his fist again and again into the ringmaster's face. With each swing of Knight's arm he told a piece of the story. And Titus had watched from a distance, thinking he was going to witness Knight beat his best friend to death. Just watch. Unable to build up the courage to stop it. And he almost did.

But then somehow something took possession of him. Titus remembered moving with an urgency, his hands not hesitating when he neared Knight. He grabbed his arm, which was in the process of throwing another punch into Dave's bloody face. Knight, who knew Titus was a coward, turned with a look of pure shock when he discovered the creative director was the one stopping him. When people act in ways incongruent to their usual behavior they have the most advantages. That's how Titus gained the advantage on Knight that day. While the assailant was momentarily beset with shock, Titus threw his own punch into Knight's face. Forty years of repressed anger rocketed out of Titus's fist, breaking Knight's nose and sending him to the ground where he was quickly restrained by two crew members.

It was soon after that that Fanny appeared to reveal Cynthia, Dave's wife, was dead, as well as Knight's son. That's when Knight cursed the circus. Titus had only ever known two people strong enough to lace the right words together with the right amount of intention to create a true curse: Dave Raydon and Charles Knight.

Still restrained by the heavily motivated crew members Knight had drilled his gaze at the teal blue and neon green big top. He then said, "With the life force within me I curse any child ever born at Vagabond Circus to be unable to ever experience happiness. Since my child was stolen from me through lies and deceit none shall ever have what I cannot."

This curse was in essence the reason that Dave had instituted rule number two: no dating among circus members, and therefore no breeding. Dave hadn't looked afraid by the words his brother spoke which had felt as tangible to Titus as the hard ground under his feet. He'd never witnessed a curse, but felt this one's magic lacing itself around everything that belonged to Vagabond Circus and knew it was real and to be feared. Dave, who had just lost his wife and learned his dead child was really not his, simply wiped a white handkerchief across his face until the fabric was all red with blood. Not an ounce of emotion slipped from the short man's demeanor. It was in stressful scenarios that Dave was always the calmest.

"And I vow that as long as I live, you, Charles Knight, my once beloved brother, shall never step foot on the grounds of Vagabond Circus without experiencing your own mind-numbing torture," Dave said, producing his own curse. And again Titus felt those words like a monumental gust of wind and knew that they carried a power not to be ignored.

And if that wasn't enough, then Knight changed. First there was a twitch at the side of his face, then a grimace, and then his legs dropped under him, making it so the crew members restraining him were suddenly holding him up. He let out a loud yelp of pain. "Stop this!" he yelled to his brother.

"You know exactly how to stop it," Dave said and then directed his eyes to the crew members on either side of Knight. "You can release him. My brother will no longer be a threat to anyone at Vagabond Circus."

And they did release the man, who almost fell to the ground. Knight caught himself with one hand, the other hand clamped onto his head. Pain shot out of him in the form of a groan.

"Now you feel what it is you do to others," Dave said, head held high. "You will be punished by it the longer you stay here."

Knight looked up at his brother, murder in his eyes, blood covering his shattered nose. Then he pushed himself up and gradually, painstakingly, turned and walked with great effort in the opposite direction. Each step seemed to get easier for him as he neared the edges of the circus grounds. Titus and Fanny had exchanged bemused expressions, both wondering if what they'd seen had been real. Neither knew curses really existed until that day, but after that day neither would ever doubt it.

Titus turned to Dave, and he still appeared calm as he watched his brother retreat. But it wasn't the cool expression in Dave's face that gave Titus pause. Dave's face, which Titus knew well, was now different, aged. It wasn't just the dried blood. There were new wrinkles, more grays in his light brown hair. The curse had taken years from him, his very life force. But Dave had cast the curse to protect Vagabond Circus. Knight had cast his curse to punish the circus.

Titus then turned and realized Knight had finally disappeared from view. He wouldn't see that man again for almost twenty years. But Dave's curse had been very clear. *As long as I'm alive you shall not set foot on Vagabond Circus grounds.* And now Dave was dead and Knight had nothing stopping him from taking what he always wanted. He'd always wanted what Dave had: his wife, his child, and his circus.

"I will not run," Titus said out loud, in his empty trailer. He still stood in the center of the main room, but now a little straighter. "I will face this. I won't cower. I won't be defeated. I will bring Knight down." Then he looked up to the ceiling, but in his mind's eye he saw the heavens. "For you, old friend, I'll take your brother down."

Chapter Twelve

*I*t had been silent since Nabhi and his brother, Haady, had lain down for bed. Not even the usual sounds of the crew members working late in the big top echoed from the tent, which sat close to the triplets' trailer. Nabhi lay on his back on the sofa staring at the ceiling. Haady lay beside him on the trundle bed. Padmal had closed the door to her room an hour before her brothers decided to finally retire. They had spent the whole night discussing the new owner, Charles Knight. The brothers had postulated on what was in the trucks. Equipment? Furniture? Supplies? Four long semis had to contain a whole lot of something. Haady had visibly shivered when he talked about the new owner, Dave's strange brother.

"There's just something not right about the whole thing. I don't trust that man," Haady said.

"Well, I do," Padmal said as she marched out of her room. She'd been listening to the conversation from her room. She took the last bottle of water from the refrigerator, not caring to ask her brothers if they minded. She unscrewed the top and turned her dark brown eyes on the pair sitting on the sofa. "I think he'll be good for the circus," she said and then downed half the water. "You notice that effect he had on Titus? The man looked afraid of him. What a coward. We need a real man running this show for once."

Nabhi narrowed his eyes at his sister, but Haady simply said, "Does that mean you're staying? You aren't still planning to leave Vagabond Circus?"

This had been Padmal's threat for years now. It was what she held over her brothers' heads if they didn't comply with all of her demands. She didn't care if her leaving ruined their juggling act. Padmal hardly cared about anything. "I guess I'm staying for now. I'm curious to see how things change at the stupid circus. And what's the point in leaving now that I know my mom is dead."

"Our mom," Nabhi reminded his sister.

"Whatever," she had said before walking back to her room and disappearing for the night.

That conversation still made Nabhi burn with anger. He knew
he should love his sister the way Haady did, with such unending
patience, but he wanted to strangle her at times. The idea actually
made him smile and for that he felt simply awful. Nabhi turned his
head and checked on his brother. Haady had drifted off on some
dream travel adventure an hour ago. He was probably in Glasgow or
Mexico City. Those were his two favorite cities. Nabhi had declined
to join him. He needed to think on his own. The younger brother
needed to calm his thoughts and then dream travel to Portland,
Maine. That was his favorite place. He had just closed his eyes to
focus his thoughts when a series of cries and screams interrupted the
silence. He shot into a sitting position. Listened. The sounds were
muffled but they were in fact a cry of sorts. Nabhi just knew it.
Several voices made a stifled chorus of noise. He pushed back the
curtain to the window next to the sofa. The night was black but
Nabhi could plainly see what stood just beside his trailer. One of the
black semis.

Chapter Thirteen

The big top began to fill with Vagabond Circus members ten minutes before the meeting time Knight had announced. Performers and crew members were anxious to learn more. Some like Haady and Nabhi were automatically suspicious of the new owner of the circus. Some like Bill, the circus chef, were withholding judgment until they had more information. And then there was Ian, who knew the truth. He had already started to spread the rumors that staying at Vagabond Circus was the best option for everyone's future. No one doubted these instructions, once told to them from the "never wrong" Ian. Now he sat on the back row watching various people as they entered the big top.

Padmal entered smiling beside an extremely unhappy Oliver. She went to reach for his hand, to pull him toward a certain row of seats, but he pulled away, although he still followed. Oliver's eyes had been on Sunshine, who was giving the couple a cautious stare. The empath wanted to uphold Dave's rules of no dating out of respect for the deceased ringmaster, but also because she'd finally allowed herself to loathe Padmal and wanted a reason to punish her. However, what only Ian knew was that Padmal's true punishment would only come once she openly disobeyed the rules. And Sunshine too would soon break Dave's rules, but not with Oliver. They were only friends.

Ian pressed his head into his large hands. The visions never stopped. Actually they had started to play on top of each other. Futures of everyone he knew constantly looping in his cramped head. If he had been looking up he would have seen Zuma enter the tent a few seconds later. But he already knew what was about to happen to her, and the vision had broken his heart the first time he'd seen it. She rushed into the tent seeming to be looking for someone and then also scanning the crowd with a fearful gaze. All eyes shot to Zuma when the girl entered but she didn't notice.

"You're back!" an eager crew member said.

"Zuma!" another said, waving.

She smiled politely and waved but had spotted the person she'd been looking for. To most he would have been impossible to find in the back corner of the big top, head down and partially hidden behind Bill's large figure. But Zuma's eidetic memory made it easy for her to take a snapshot of something as complicated as a few dozen people and find exactly what she was looking for.

Zuma marched past the people who all wanted her attention, performers and crew members. She marched past Titus, who had looked relieved to see her and had been scribbling notes on a pad in the front row. Zuma marched straight over to Finley, who stood in the corner, arms crossed. He didn't lift his head when she paused right in front of him, sliding into the space between him and Bill in the back row.

"What the hell is going on? What was that about last night?" she demanded in a harsh whisper.

"What do you mean?" he said, his voice cold, eyes on the ground.

"Finley, I was nearly killed last night," she said in a hush. "By Sebastian. He made threats."

Finley looked up then and his eyes were different. "And why do you think he came after *you*, Zuma?" he asked, his tone insinuating.

She put her hand on his chest and encouraged him back a few feet farther from the crowd. "Because he's a freaking psychopath," she said up close to him, careful to keep her voice low.

"No, because you came to *my* trailer. Stay away from me, Zuma. Better yet, leave Vagabond Circus." Finley knew Zuma would be a target if associated with him, not just by Knight but also by Sebastian. He and the boy had a past. One where Sebastian went to great lengths to sabotage him. Finley had been the first kid named and Knight's best thief. Sebastian loved two things in life: power and Knight's recognition. He would take down anything Finley loved just as he had so many times in the past. The kids Finley had cared for. The ones he dared to almost love. They'd all died by Sebastian's hand without explanation.

"No, Finley. This is ridiculous." She gripped his shirt and stared deep into his eyes, all her anger and hurt showing. Some people in the crowd turned to stare, but most couldn't see past Bill, who couldn't care less what the acrobats were doing in the back of the tent. "You could have protected me last night and instead you left me to fend for myself. I could have been killed."

Finley wrapped his hand around Zuma's wrist. "You weren't because you followed my directions. And you'll stay alive if you keep listening to me. Stay away from me for good, Zuma." He then ripped her hand off his shirt and threw it to the side with a new ferocity he'd never used when touching her. Finley moved around her, knocking her shoulder hard as he stalked to the other side of the tent. Away from the heartbroken girl.

Chapter Fourteen

"*F*inley!?" Zuma heard Jasmine's voice. "What the hell? Where you been? Where's Zuma?"

There wasn't an answer from Finley. And then Zuma heard her friend say, "What, you're not even going to say hi to me? Where you going?"

Zuma then moved back to the front of the crowd. Her eyes couldn't focus and inside her chest her heart thumped with long painful beats. Her throat had tightened with tears and she wanted to tear across the grounds and assault Knight. He'd taken so much from her. Dave, Vagabond Circus, Jack's ability to walk, and now Finley. How could she feel so much pain and anger at once? It felt impossible that so much emotion could live in her at the same time. Still, Zuma approached the front of the crowd feeling like a smaller version of herself. When she materialized at the front, Jasmine shrieked and ran for the girl. She had been staring with bewilderment at the exit where Finley had just passed through, ignoring her as he went. Jasmine sprinted across the space and threw her arms around Zuma, knocking her back a few feet. Often Jasmine forgot that her super strength could bulldoze people if she wasn't careful.

"Oh my god!" she said, pressing Zuma so firmly into her it hurt.

And then the tears Zuma had been holding in, the ones created by Finley's rejection of her, slipped to the surface and down her cheeks. When Jasmine released Zuma, tears were also glistening on her brown face. "Where have you all been? I've been so worried," she said, pushing the tears back from her bright green eyes.

Realizing they'd attracted quite a bit of attention, Zuma pulled her friend back to where she and Finley had been, a place where they could see the ring and the crowd but couldn't be seen themselves.

"We've got to talk," Zuma said.

"You're telling me," Jasmine said, her hands pressed tightly into Zuma's like she was afraid her friend would disappear if she let go of her.

"But not right now," Zuma said as a line of kids began filing into the big top.

Chapter Fifteen

A line of kids filed silently in to the big top in two separate rows. They were all dressed in black T-shirts and black pants. To Zuma they looked to be between the ages of eight and fifteen. Nothing was distinguishable about them. They were like soldiers, all with the same determined expression on their pale faces. They did vary in skin and hair color, but they all had the same lean build, similar to Finley, although he was definitely older than any of Knight's Kids. Eighteen or nineteen she'd always guessed, although he didn't know for sure.

Zuma noticed Finley had slid back into the tent on the other side next to the entrance to the practice tent. His eyes were undoubtedly on her, burning with that intensity he always reserved for Zuma. But now the expression had that hostility he used to regard her with before they built bridges, the one he stared at her with when he first came to the circus. And she instinctively knew that now, and also then, the anger wasn't at her but at himself and his regretful predicament.

Zuma didn't hide her gaze on him or her own regret. But then the two lines of kids split and she was forced to watch the strange formation they made. One line went to the right, one to the left, circling the perimeter of the ring. They each moved like Finley, with such precision. All eyes were on them, no circus member commenting on the strangeness of this all. They stopped when the first kid in each line met the other on the other side of the forty-eight-foot-diameter ring. They lined it creating a half circle. Roughly forty kids. Zuma looked back at Finley to see his eyes still on her. She pressed her mouth together, wishing just this once he'd open a telepathic link for her. She needed to know what was going on. What to expect. How to protect her people. What the abilities of these kids were and who was most dangerous. And then two figures entered side by side and Zuma reflexively straightened.

Jasmine caught the sudden intake of air Zuma sucked in and she looked at her friend. "What?" she said.

Zuma only shook her head. Sebastian looked as she remembered, long scraggly black hair and cold green eyes. He was short for his age of fifteen at just under five feet. This was why Fanny believed the boy was twelve and didn't have his Dream Traveler gift yet. She was wrong and Dave was dead because of Sebastian.

A girl a few inches taller marched beside him. The look on her freckled face made something feel like it was crawling on the inside of Zuma's skin. Power-Stopper had straight, chin-length red hair and the same cold green eyes as Sebastian. In truth, the two were siblings, born from the same Dream Traveler's sperm and surrogate's eggs, but they were a year apart.

The siblings stopped in the center of the ring, leaving three feet between them. They halted in unison and pivoted to face the crowd. And then Zuma felt the blast of wind that surged through the big top when the impossibly tall man she'd met the night before stormed down the center aisle and took the spot in the middle of the ring. She had realized he was impossibly tall when she first saw him, but now towering over the kids beside him he seemed like a giant. Knight turned and faced the crowd, his small dark eyes not bothering to hide their cruelty. He spread his arms wide. They were like the wings of a giant hawk. It reminded her of the welcoming motion Dave made when he entered the big top at the beginning of each show, but there was nothing welcoming in Knight's gesture. "I am Charles Knight and I'm the new owner of Vagabond Circus."

Chapter Sixteen

*K*night swung his gaze over the crowd in front of him. Zuma's eyes moved to Titus on the other side of Jasmine. He didn't look tense like she expected, but rather pissed. Then Zuma noticed every one of the Vagabond Circus members were present with the exception of Jack, Fanny, and her kids.

"You all knew my brother," Knight began, his voice deep, matter of fact. "You knew him as your ringmaster. You probably judged him as a good man. He did run a successful circus, I'll give him that. I bet he rescued many of you, am I right?"

There was a murmur of yeses from the crowd.

Knight nodded. "Oh, my dear brother. So kind." Again he held his arms out wide, indicating the kids half circling him at his back. "These are my kids, and I have rescued them."

Zuma clenched her teeth together. Her combat sense told her Knight was lying, but she already knew that and didn't need to read the micro-expressions on his long face. "I have rescued many an orphan and now I run a school of sorts. I have done as my brother had and have taken in those at a disadvantage and given back to them. Isn't that right, kids?"

"Yes, Master," the kids said in unison.

"And are you happy under my guidance?" Knight asked the kids behind him, his gaze forward.

"Yes, Master," they answered.

"And I," Knight said to the Vagabond Circus crowd, "I have rescued more than my brother, taken more risks to save and care for more. My brother tried but was always limited."

Zuma couldn't believe that the people of Vagabond Circus would stand for this manipulative talk but when she scanned the crowd she saw no disgruntled faces, so slight were the remarks Knight was making.

"Now my kids are fragile based on the circumstances I've rescued them from," Knight continued. "Furthermore, they have strict regimens. And therefore none of you"—he pointed to the crowd and brought his finger across them—"will under any circumstances speak or interact with them. I do not allow unknown influences around my kids and as far as I'm concerned you all are unknown. And I WILL NOT STAND for anyone hurting my kids." The sudden yell in his voice made several people jump. "Is that clear?" he said in a soft voice.

The people of Vagabond Circus agreed with startled nods.

"Now if you want proof of the types of genius talent my school produces then just look at your star performer, Finley," Knight said, throwing an unexpected hand in Finley's direction. Finley straightened suddenly, coming to attention. The people of Vagabond Circus all gasped in surprise. Some exchanged whispers.

"That's right, once he graduated I arranged with Dave that he work with him. Isn't that right, Finley?" Knight said, an edge in his voice.

"Yes, Master," Finley said at once, not missing a beat, although Zuma spied the lie in him, the resistance.

"Isn't that wonderful?" Knight said to the crowd. "Now you see how great my school is for its kids."

There were more murmurs from the crowd but now they sounded like impressed exclamations.

"And Sebastian was a kid that Dave elected to transfer to my program. My brother had failed to meet the boy's needs for a higher degree of training due to his brilliant nature, isn't that right?" Knight said to the boy on his right.

"Yes, Master," Sebastian said and his voice ran over Zuma's skin like a Brillo pad, reminding her of their encounter last night.

"And to my left, please meet Gwendolyn," Knight said, indicating the girl Zuma believed to be Power-Stopper. "If you need anything from me I must insist that you never approach me directly but rather one of my three graduates, Finley, Sebastian, or Gwendolyn."

Zuma noticed the resentment flowing through Finley. He was being forced into this situation and what was worse, anything he did would make him look dishonest. He had been manipulated into this position and there was no way out for him.

"Now we discuss why you all are in such a blessed position to be a part of the circus I now run, Vagabond Circus," Knight said.

Chapter Seventeen

"Things have indeed changed," Knight began, strolling to the front of the ring. "Your old ringmaster has died. You naturally have doubts about your new ringmaster." He pressed his long-fingered hand to his chest. "And I hope you've all deduced that will be me. Owner and ringmaster of Vagabond Circus. These doubts of yours are normal. And I will not force any of you to work for me as Dave once did."

Oliver noticed Padmal slightly smile beside him. She was eating this speech up like a decadent dessert. He wanted to stamp his foot down on her toe, but then quickly admonished himself for such a thought.

"Like my kids, you will always have a choice," Knight said and then jammed a finger in the direction of the crowd. "But if you want to be a part of a show greater than one you've ever known, then I suggest you stick around."

And just then Oliver noticed the tall man's expression shift. It was a strange arrangement on his crooked face and then the illusionist realized that Charles Knight was trying to smile. It looked like a grin adorned by a lizard, all wrong.

"Now if you want to perform in the greatest circus ever then you will firstly not speak to my kids. We've established that. And secondly, you'll always do everything that I tell you. No questions asked. These are not hard requests to follow, but follow them you will. None of you are so good that you won't be booted from your spot and replaced. But those compliant will perform in a circus world renowned. You thought Vagabond Circus was good before but under my leadership it will be magnificent. Those who follow me will perform for the President of the United States in San Francisco." There were gasps from the crowd. "And when we cruise into Santa Barbara we will be doing a private show for dozens and dozens of the most A-list stars in Hollywood. And in Los Angeles we will perform another private show, not for powerless stars, but rather for the most influential directors and producers in the world. Stick with me and you won't just stay with me, you'll go on to rule the world with your stardom." And then Knight went silent and raised a slow hand at the exit. "If you don't like my rules then you won't perform in my circus. This will always be YOUR choice. Decide. The first show starts tonight."

Chapter Eighteen

*K*night didn't stay to take questions. He didn't offer a closing to his speech. He merely walked out of the big top, Sebastian and Gwendolyn behind him and his kids marching in formation.

"What in the hell is going on?" Jasmine said, turning to Zuma and slapping a firm hand on her forearm. The heavy pressure of the girl's small hand made Zuma's arm sting from the unintentional assault.

Zuma pulled her arm away. "Please remember that you have the strength to break my neck with two fingers, so ease up," she said to her friend.

"I'm not that far from doing just that. Where have you been? Who is that guy? And what the hell was that about Finley?" she said, flinging her arm in his direction. "Oh, and don't tell me you don't know, since you disappeared with him and Jack. And now I just find out Finley is one of that strange guy's graduates."

"Jaz," Zuma said in a whisper, hoping that would encourage her friend to do the same. They probably couldn't be heard over the commotion in the tent. Everyone was turned discussing the newest events with their neighbor. Several were lined up to speak to Titus, but he was bent over his notepad making notes with a strange intensity.

"And why the hell is Finley standing over there staring at you like that?" Jasmine said, her eyes straight on the acrobat.

Finley just shook his head and turned to the practice tent and disappeared in there.

"Zuma, I want some answers and I want them now," her friend said, her hands brushing her wiry brown curls back from her narrow face.

"Look, Jaz, I'll tell you everything but not here," Zuma said.

All of Knight's kids had filed out of the tent. Zuma stood and Jasmine followed.

Just then Titus said, "Zuma and Jasmine, I want your attention first. Then I'll be meeting with the rest of you."

Zuma stopped and turned. Titus had his reading glasses low on his nose and was standing now, his notepad in his hand. "We need to discuss changes to the act with Jack's absence."

"Yeah, where is Jack?" Jasmine said, scanning the tent.

Titus held up his hand to pause her. "Girls, follow me, we need to discuss all the changes to the circus acts. Then you will rehearse nonstop until we have mastered the performance." He didn't wait for the two girls to agree before turning to the performers and crew members lined up behind him, most wearing confused expressions. "I'll be back in a minute and will have attention for each of you then." Titus held his chin high and Zuma realized something else different about the creative director. He wasn't slouched, but rather standing straight, unlike his normal posture. "To the practice tent," he said, marching in that direction. Zuma and Jasmine followed him.

Chapter Nineteen

"*P*aralyzed?" Jasmine said before slamming her hands across her mouth like she'd said a dirty word. "How?" She looked at Zuma and then at Titus, who had divulged the information.

"It was—"

"An accident," Titus said, cutting Zuma off.

If you tell her the truth she will be too angry to practice and perform, Titus said in Zuma's head. *You know how emotional she is. I need her focused. Tell her the truth, but not now. Wait until after the first show.*

The brief pause in the conversation made Jasmine grow even more flustered. "What's going on? An accident? Are you two speaking telepathically and leaving me out?"

"No," Titus said firmly. "It's just that the whole thing is hard to discuss. It's hard in light of everything to describe." He looked at Zuma and then back at Jasmine. "Jack fell."

"What? While you three were gone?" Jasmine said, looking at Zuma.

"Yes," she said.

"Where did you go? Why did you leave me?" Jasmine said, real hurt in her voice.

"We went to…" Zuma trailed away, unable to think of a lie that wouldn't hurt her friend more.

"I asked them to run an errand for me," Titus said at once. Zuma, and only she, recognized the micro-expressions that made it clear that this was a lie.

"An errand?" Jasmine said, her tone unconvinced.

"We don't have time to go into this right now. We have to figure out how you're replacing Jack. Finley, get over here," Titus said, waving him over.

He'd been propped up against some equipment, watching the interaction from a distance. Finley strutted over, his eyes firmly on Zuma. She couldn't force her eyes to look at him any longer and busied herself pulling her long, almost-white and pink hair into a high bun. It was the way she wore it for practices, which she guessed they were going to be doing nonstop until it was show time that evening.

"All right," Titus began when Finley had joined the circle. "Finley, replacing Jack will fall mostly on you. Can you take over his part in the globe act?"

"Yeah," he said without much thought. In the second act of the show, a large globe was lowered from the forty-foot ceiling of the big top. It spun on an axis, supported by wires, and it was where Jack spun and flipped. He maintained balance using his levitation, but Finley could rely on his teleporting to keep him safe.

"Are you sure you can take on the extra performances? I fear that having the extra acts will burn you out. And I need you to be rested enough that you can pull off the finale with Zuma, because that duo can't be cut," Titus said.

Finley looked at Zuma, who refused to look back at him. "Nothing will stop me from doing that act," he said, and the conviction in his voice made her insides burn like lava had been injected into her veins.

"Good," Titus said, not picking up on the tension. "And for the flying trapeze I'm thinking you, Finley, make the natural choice—"

"No," Jasmine said, stepping forward, aggression on her face. "I'm the natural choice. I'm stronger than Finley. Not only that, but a girl catcher isn't just interesting, it's unheard of, which goes in line with Dave's mission for Vagabond Circus."

"True," Titus said, "but are you sure—"

"I have the strength to throw Finley across the big top, so yes, I think I can catch his skinny ass on the flying trapeze," Jasmine said.

A minuscule smile wrapped around Finley's mouth. "I think she's right. And that way I can still perform the quadruple."

"Excellent point," Titus said, relief making his brow finally go slack. "Okay, well, you three rehearse and I want to know immediately if there's a concern. I'm asking a lot of you, more than Dave would have allowed on your shoulders, but—"

"He's dead," Zuma said, cutting him off. It wasn't a heartless statement, but rather one meant to encourage. "Dave is dead, Jack is paralyzed, and we are going to do anything it takes to ensure Vagabond Circus stays successful."

51

"Yes," Titus said, his voice strained. "Exactly. Thank you." He looked at each of the acrobats briefly and turned for the exit.

Jasmine turned to the chalk station and the mats where she planned to stretch.

Zuma didn't waste a second before stepping straight up to Finley. "Stop doing what you're doing, please," she said, finally locking her eyes on him. She reached for him but he stepped back. "Finley, please don't push me—"

"Oh, and a 'congrats' is in order," he said at full volume, cutting off her whispered, tortured words.

Jasmine turned to the couple. Titus paused, having made it to the exit. He turned as well.

"Congratulations? For what?" Titus asked.

"Oh, haven't you heard?" Finley said, his scarred eyes burning a hole in Zuma. "Zuma and Jack are engaged. They're going to be married."

Chapter Twenty

*A*n excited shriek ripped through the practice tent. Zuma's eyes widened, but no one saw them before Jasmine threw her arms around her friend's shoulders.

"You and Jack are what?" Titus said, walking back in their direction.

"Engaged," Finley answered.

There was another pleased shriek from Jasmine before she released Zuma, whose eyes were pinned on Finley and smoldering.

"It was really special to see. Very sweet," Finley said, his voice flat. "I was there. Saw the whole thing. Zuma said yes before the accident and then after Jack was declared paralyzed she vowed to always stay by his side and never leave him."

"Finley..." Zuma said, her voice a warning.

"And since Jack isn't in the circus anymore due to his condition, there shouldn't be any rules against it, right, Titus?" Finley said, turning to the creative director.

Titus scratched his head with the other side of his pen. He doubted with Jack's condition that the two would be breeding any time soon, so they were safe in that regard. And the idea that the acrobats had fallen in love despite everything gave him hope. A hope he needed. "Yeah, I don't see anything wrong with it. Congratulations to you both," Titus said and then almost smiled.

Zuma hardly noticed the pleased smile since her lips were pressed together, her eyes heavy on Finley, her hand pressed into Jasmine's, which was vibrating with excitement.

"I knew you two would end up together," Jasmine said. "What a sweet story. I can't wait to see my boy Jack and congratulate him." She then turned to Zuma. "Oh, girl, I hope you know I'm your maid of honor."

Zuma didn't respond. Didn't look capable of it.

"I can't wait to tell everyone!" Jasmine then said.

"But wait," Zuma finally stuttered out, trying to figure out how to undo this mess Finley had created to keep her away from him. "I don't think we want to go public about this. With Dave's death and the rules it would be a mess for the circus."

"Actually I'm not announcing Dave's passing publicly," Titus said.

"You're not?" Zuma and Jasmine said in unison.

"No, I don't want the bad press," Titus said. "But actually, Zuma, I think that announcing your engagement to Jack, the once star of Vagabond Circus who is now paralyzed, would make for a great press release. And I think Vagabond Circus members won't be upset about you two obviously breaking the rules. How would anyone be mad at Jack given his prognosis?"

"Yeah, right..." Zuma said, realizing exactly how ingenious Finley's reveal had been. He knew Zuma wouldn't leave him alone but now she had no choice. She was engaged to Jack.

"Then it's settled. I'll draw up a press release. This is just the thing we needed," Titus said, actually sounding hopeful. Then he turned and left, leaving Finley and Zuma staring at each other, both overflowing with regret.

Chapter Twenty-One

Redding Record Searchlight

Acrobat Paralyzed, But Hope Remains

Performing the stunts that entertain audiences isn't always safe but the performers at Vagabond Circus know the risks they face. They take every precaution to ensure the safety of all, but accidents are in some cases unavoidable. The creative director for the circus, Titus Rogers, states that one of those accidents has happened to the beloved star of the flying trapeze act, Mr. Jack Fuller. The acrobat was in rehearsal last week when his harness was discovered to be loose during the famous globe act. By the time the glitch was discovered it was too late for adjustments and the discovery led the acrobat to lose concentration and that's when he fell from the top of the tent, a forty-foot fall.

"We are grateful Jack survived the fall," Rogers reported. "However, he has a long road to recovery and it's unknown if the star of Vagabond Circus will be able to ever walk again. At Vagabond Circus we are all reminded of how small things can change the course of our lives irrevocably. Jack is actually in high spirits though for many reasons. One is that the acrobat, who has amazed millions with his grace and stunts, has a resilient nature. Also he has his Vagabond Circus family supporting him. The last reason," Rogers continued, "is that prior to the accident his co-star, Ms. Zuma Zanders, accepted his proposal for marriage. The young female acrobat will still be performing in the show during her fiancé's recovery and she stated she will stand beside him no matter what because their love is that strong." It appears that the people of Vagabond Circus are as magical as their performances and have the capacity to bring true inspiration to our hearts no matter what they do.

Chapter Twenty-Two

*W*armth spread through Jack's lower legs as Fanny's hands hovered an inch from the bandages. "I'm really not certain of our odds here," she said, an almost apology in her voice.

"It can't hurt though, right?" Jack asked, sitting up a bit in the bed Titus had brought in and had set up in the living area of Fanny's trailer.

"Oh no, not at all," Fanny said, her eyes closed so her mind could seek focus. "It's just that my healing ability doesn't mend bones."

"Oh," Jack said, the defeat strong in his tone.

Fanny popped her light blue eyes open. "Now you don't worry there, Jack. Just because I can't mend bones it shouldn't give you such a bleak perspective. I can mend ligaments and encourage your body to do its own healing. I'm thinking there's lots of repairs going on in that miraculous body of yours. If I can take those repairs off your body's agendas then it can devote all its resources to fusing the bones back together the proper way."

"So I can use them to one day to walk again?" Jack asked. He had already tired of skirting the obvious concern and was speaking plainly now.

"Exactly," Fanny said. "And once your bones seem strong enough then we can talk about physical therapy, which is where my work takes a backseat and you'll really be in the driver's seat. Attitude will be crucial to your success."

"I am going to walk again," Jack said in a voice full of confidence. No mock conviction to his tone, only pure determination.

"I know you will," Fanny said, a sensitive smile on her smoothly wrinkled face. She stood from her seated place on the edge of his bed. "Now I'm going to go rest up. Healing wipes me out but I'll be back in a couple of hours to do another round. Call if you need anything else."

"I'll be fine," he said, looking up at the woman.

"No you won't. If we left you here then you'd starve and wet yourself. So here's how it's going to go: when you need something you call. I'm just here in the back," she said, indicating her room at the back. "Now you need rest too, so close those beautiful brown eyes of yours and sleep. No dream traveling until you're strong enough."

"Okay," he said, feeling the exhaustion heavy in just the effort it took to say that one word. Fanny was still regarding Jack with a sweet sincerity when an unstoppable force shut his eyelids and he drifted away to a place where he could walk and move and seek the revenge he coveted in his heart.

Chapter Twenty-Three

*S*nap. *Snap.*

Jack's eyelids fluttered but didn't open. He was on the edge between waking and falling back into sleep.

Snap. Snap.

He felt the presence, but couldn't bring his attention to a wakeful state. Sleep had him hostage and he tugged at the chains they bound him with, but to no effect.

A piercing whistle hooked into his brain, helping to saw through the chains. It was right up against his ear. Whoever this person was they didn't smell like Fanny. Lilac and honey laced through his nostrils.

The whistle again and this time he felt the breath tickle his ear. Jack brought his hand up to cover his head but found himself too clumsy to successfully complete the task. His hands ended up knocking into his chest. It was only then that his eyes actually broke the seal that had been imprisoning him in sleep. The images before him swam in a series of blurs before turning crisp.

"Well, hey there, Jacky, did I wake you?" Sunshine said, wearing a cunning look. "Oops," she said, no remorse in the word. She held a tray of food in front of her. The girl slid it onto the table next to his bed. Then she motioned him forward. "Go ahead and sit up."

Jack regarded her like she was a new species who had just materialized for only him to see. Sunshine's long black hair hung next to her pale face and she was wearing her costume for her pyrokinesis act. It was a sleeveless teal blue leotard and a skirt that was made of neon green chiffon pieces that hung unevenly, some ending at mid-thigh and others trailing to the ground in the back.

"Sunshine?" Jack said, doing as he was told and putting his hands under him to drag his legs back with him as he sat up.

"Oh good, pretty-boy-hot-shot actually knows my name. Afraid there for a second you were going to call me Rain or Windy." She grabbed a pillow from the couch beside his bed and slid it behind his back as he made to lean forward. "Here, this will help."

Jack pressed back into the pillow. It did help to support his sitting position. "Of course I know your name. We've been in the circus together for three years."

Sunshine had the tray back in her hands and didn't ask permission before laying it on Jack's lap. "I've been told to feed you," she said like she'd been assigned a torturous chore.

"I thought I was supposed to sleep."

Sunshine rolled her green eyes. "Yes, smart guy, to survive we're supposed to sleep. However, humans also eat and drink, and pretty soon you'll need to piss, but that's not in my new job description so don't get your hopes up. I'm not helping you with little Jack."

Jack looked at the quinoa and curried vegetables in front of him. He wasn't at all hungry.

"New job description?" he said, picking up the fork

"Yeah, on top of being absolutely incredible, but also a reluctant performer in this circus that has been accosted by the devil himself, I'm also Fanny's new helper." Sunshine said all this in a monotone voice. "I'll watch the kiddos when she's caring for you and then I'll watch her big kiddo"—she indicated to Jack—"when she's doing their lessons and other things she prefers to do for them. Fanny apparently doesn't want to spend too much time away from her rugrats even though healing you is time consuming and draining for her."

Jack deposited the fork back on the tray. He dropped his gaze as well.

"Oh no, now I've gone and made you feel like a burden. Oops," Sunshine said, again no inflection in her voice.

Jack looked up at her. "No, it's not that. It's just…"

"It's exactly that. I'm an empath, you know."

"I do know that," Jack said, irritation now in his tone. He shoved the tray a few inches. "Will you take this please? I'm not hungry."

"I won't actually. I was told to make you eat something and I take my job quite seriously. If it's cold I can heat it up," she said, circling her finger in the air, an amused look on her usually blank face.

"But I'm not hungry," Jack said.

"Well, you haven't eaten all day and it's almost evening, so stop arguing about it."

"It's almost show time then?" Jack said, trying to turn to see the clock on the back wall but his bed was angled away from it.

"It is, and don't make me late for my performance. Eat," Sunshine said, pointing at the plate. "My act is third in the lineup, which is in about fifteen minutes."

"I know that," Jack said, pulling the tray back to his waist. "I know your act is after ours, that's the way it's been for three years, Sunshine." He slid the fork under the pile of fluffy rice and brought it to his mouth and to his relief he didn't have any trouble with the small task. He'd been afraid his hand would shake or miss his mouth.

"Oh good, I wasn't sure when I said 'performance' if you would connect we were in the same circus together," Sunshine said.

Jack dropped his fork on the plate and again pushed the tray away. "Why do you keep making those insinuations like I don't know who you are?"

"Because I realize there's a real possibility that you might not."

Jack's brow knitted together and his head tilted to the side. "What? Why would you say that?"

"When was the last time you ever said anything to me?" Sunshine said, pinning both her hands on her hips. She was built a lot like a young Fanny, tall with voluptuous curves.

Jack blanked on the question. "I don't know."

"Exactly, because you and the acrobats are too good to spend time with the freaks."

Jack sat up higher, knocking the tray further on his lap. "Ouch," he said, reaching for the tray which now rested on a sensitive incision.

Sunshine picked up the tray, a look of actual concern on her face. "Are you okay? That hurt you." She stated rather than asked the last part.

Jack pressed his eyelids together until the throbbing receded. When he finally opened them his expression had shifted entirely. "If you can't tell, I'm not an acrobat anymore. I don't know why you think now is the perfect opportunity to berate me for not running in the same Vagabond Circus circle with you, but if you wouldn't mind now isn't a good time."

Sunshine slid the tray onto the table. "Right. Yeah, I guess that wasn't very thoughtful of me," she said, but it was more of an observation than an apology.

Jack pressed his eyes back closed and then after a few seconds cracked one eye and looked sideways at a stoic Sunshine. "Why are you still standing there?"

"Because you still haven't eaten."

Jack looked down at the plate and then back to Sunshine's determined face.

"Fine, but don't put that thing back on my lap."

"What if"—Sunshine lifted the tray and unfolded the two legs from underneath—"it didn't have to rest on your lap."

Jack nodded. "Yeah, thanks. That will work." He realized that was probably Fanny's intention for the tray all along, but Sunshine had been too insensitive to allow it. She set the tray over his legs. "There, does that work?"

He nodded. "I'll eat. I promise. Go get ready for your performance."

She nodded and there under the girl's usually melancholy eyes was something new. A real thread of remorse.

"Thanks for bringing my food," Jack said, picking up the fork again.

"No problem." Sunshine turned to leave and then spun back. "I'm sorry this has happened to you, Jacky."

He blew out a long breath. "I'm not," he said, meaning it.

"Yeah, I know. And that's kind of cool," Sunshine said before turning to go, her skirt dragging behind her.

Chapter Twenty-Four

Zuma had always coveted the ten minutes before the Vagabond Circus show started. Those were sacred minutes that held so many possibilities. The patrons finding their seats were about to be changed. They'd walked into the big top with doubts or average expectations. Maybe they had seen the Vagabond Circus show before, but it just kept getting better. And therefore Zuma knew every individual who left Vagabond Circus was going to leave a different person. When they left through the same way they entered they'd believe in magic, maybe for the first time or maybe their faith would be renewed. The patrons of Vagabond Circus would use that newfound belief to spread a love so pervasive Zuma was sure it was saving the very earth where she stood.

Dave's circus brought miracles. It healed. But it was no longer Dave's circus and now dread filled Zuma's being. How would Knight's presence change the vibe, the end result that the circus created? Would people still leave changed for the better? If that rested solely on Zuma's shoulders then she'd bear that weight. Vagabond Circus had to bring good to the world. It had to.

She absentmindedly ran her fingers over her braid. It was arranged down the back of her head and fashioned with pearls and diamonds. She was slightly chilly in the teal and neon green full body leotard she wore for the first act with Jasmine and Finley. She rubbed her hands over her arms and shivered. Zuma could step into the practice tent at her back and instantly be warm and surrounded by her circus family. But she needed some space to get her bearings before the show. The girl wished she still had her fortune-telling booth. At least when she read fortunes she could distract herself from the dread circling her thoughts. However, that booth had permanently been reassigned to Ian in light of the amount of changes she was responsible for in order to replace Jack.

The flap at the back of the practice tent swished as someone stormed out. She blinked as Finley's figure slowed. He'd obviously been in a hurry to get out of the tent if he was using his super speed.

He halted twelve feet in front of her, his back to her, his chin lifted to the sky, his being vibrating with frustration. She could have sworn she heard a silent scream rip out of him.

The three acrobats had worked nonstop all afternoon. And Jasmine and Zuma were exhausted from the endurance it took to get the arrangements perfect. But Finley wasn't exhausted. He hardly ever was. She guessed he was emotionally exhausted, or so it looked from the way he held his shoulders. He raised his hands to his head and pressed like a vise grip. He was also dressed for the show in his teal blue and neon green leotard, but he didn't look cold, like her. Actually Zuma thought that she could feel the heat pouring off him. He lowered his hands, took a few steadying breaths, and turned, his gaze finding her at once.

Finley's eyes narrowed, punishing her with a single look for watching him. He crossed his arms and lowered his chin, eyes still burning into her. "Why didn't you tell me you were there?"

"Why did you tell a big fat lie about Jack and I being engaged?" she said.

He stepped forward a few paces, his long stride bringing them closer. Finley looked down at her. "You know why." His dark hair looked almost black with the gel holding it back away from of his angular face.

"So you're just going to push me away in an effort to protect me?" she said, her voice higher and louder than she intended. Zuma couldn't help it. All her barriers were cracked and straining increasingly with every moment.

"Yes," Finley said through clenched teeth.

She reached out for his arms tied across his chest and he didn't move to block her, although that's exactly what he knew he needed to do.

"Please don't do this," Zuma said, cinching on to him, pressing her fingers into Finley. "Stand beside me if you want to protect me. Stand in front of me. But don't abandon me."

"You don't get it, Zuma," Finley said, ripping his arms down to his side and out of Zuma's reach.

"I do though. Knight is here and he's a threat, but pushing me away won't accomplish a damn thing," she said.

He shook his head. "No, you obviously don't get it. You've lived in your perfect world where you haven't been happy, but you were always safe and the biggest danger was falling to the springy net below. The world you're in now is actually dangerous," he said, his face red, his words carrying heat, his finger pointed to the ground under Zuma. "You seem to think I can save you or protect you. I can't. There's no net now, Zuma."

"Finley, just because I didn't grow up like you doesn't mean I don't know how to negotiate this turn of events. Maybe you're too colored by your experiences. If you'd listen to me then maybe we could work together. We could figure out how to take Knight down. Don't push me away. Partner with me."

Finley regarded her for a long few seconds, studying the soft curves of her face, the way her brown eyes looked sharp and warm at the same time. She felt he was considering her words, and that gave her hope. But then he shook his head. "Zuma, I don't discount you because you didn't grow up like me. Hell, I know you're smart and strategic, but in this you have no clue. Knight can't be beaten. That's where the flaws in your reasoning begin."

"Finley, stop—"

"And you think we can partner together to beat him?" he said with a morbid laugh. "Zuma, you're my greatest liability."

"No, I'm not. We could protect each other," she said, growing more frustrated than she thought possible.

"Zuma," Finley said quietly, "Knight uses information to his advantage. There's a reason I never formed relationships with any of the kids after the ones in my initial group all died. Anyone I ever cared about never lasted." Finley raised his hand and paused it an inch from her face. She shivered out a breath just before he brought his fingers across her cheek. "The day Knight finds out I love you *will* be your last."

Chapter Twenty-Five

The big top was cast in black. Then low techno music started and with it a red rope of lights around the ring grew in intensity. Kids leaned forward. Smoke filled the big top, covering the neon green rug which made up the forty-eight-foot diameter ring. The rope of light cast an eerie glow through the smoke as the music shifted to one with low notes and a haunting rhythm. Then through the smoke a crouched figure rose from the center of the ring. A dim spotlight rained down on Knight, who stood in a red suit with tails that almost touched the ground and a matching top hat. His head was down as he rose to his full height, his long arms by his side. The music faded to nothing. The tent fell silent. A laugh that sounded like it must be projected from a microphone but wasn't shot out of Knight's mouth, making several kids and some adults startle.

"Have you ever wanted to be bad?" he said, his face still down, top hat shielding him.

No one answered.

"You came for a show, but I'm giving you something more." Knight then raised his head and looked out at the crowd. His face was painted with black and red flames. "I'm giving you permission to be bad," he said in his gravelly voice that made him sound like he needed to clear his throat.

No one made a single noise. Women grabbed their children's arms. Fathers leaned forward, squinting at the demonic-looking creature in the red smoky ring.

Knight spun around, holding his arms out over his head and up to the sky. "Here at Vagabond Circus you get to be bad. Don't you want to join us?" Knight stopped and faced the silent and mesmerized crowd. "Looks like you'll need some encouragement. As your new ringmaster I'm happy to do that," he said, pressing his hand to his chest. "Mister," he said, pointing at an elderly gentleman in the front row. The man wore an old tweed suit and his best shoes. He sat beside his wife and grandson. The man startled to attention.

"Me?" he said, pointing to himself.

"Oh yes, you," Knight said and took off at a sprint around the ring in the opposite direction of the gentleman. Then when he'd made the circle he grabbed the metal cane sitting just in front of the man. Knight didn't ask permission before plucking the cane up and spinning it in his hand as he strolled back to the center of the ring. "Is this your cane?"

"Why yes, it is," the man said, looking at his wife and then back to Knight, a giddy smile on the old man's face. He was excited to have been chosen. To be a part of the act. Knight strolled to the other side of the ring. He paused in front of a young man. "Tell me, sir," Knight said, "is this cane in fact real, meaning it doesn't appear fake in any way?" He tossed the cane through the air and the man caught it but only barely, surprise written on his face. The young man stared at the cane in his hands, dumbstruck.

"Well, is it?" Knight said. "Go ahead and inspect it. I've never seen it before this moment but I need you to confirm to the crowd that it's real. That there's no tricks up my sleeve."

The man slid his hands over the metal and plastic cane. "Yes, it looks real in every way. Feels real too."

"Strange then," Knight said. "Why are you bending that poor gentleman's cane, that he no doubt needs for walking?"

And then in the stranger's hand the cane bent, not once, but again and again until the metal was formed into an almost perfect circle. The young man dropped the bending metal in front of him and stared at it in shock. "I'm not doing that!" the patron yelled.

Knight strolled forward and picked up the complete circle of metal. "No, *you're* not."

He then turned and tossed the cane at the feet of the old man. "But if you want to do something bad, then you should." Knight held up his arms wide and he spun as he spoke, talking to the entire crowd. "Welcome to Vagabond Circus, where we embrace your inner child, who we all know wants to be mischievous. Here you can be BAD!" Then the crowd erupted into applause and laughter. Because this crowd, who had started off shocked and intrigued, was now enlivened, they believed that the old man and his cane were a prop. But the elderly gentleman stared at his cane in angered shock. No one noticed this though.

The crowd's attention was on the center of the ring where two poles were being lowered. "And I don't just give you permission to be bad. I want you also to be bold," Knight said and then threw his hand at the first pole. It molded like the cane into a large ring about five feet wide. The crowd gasped. Some whipped around to evaluate their neighbor's response. But none of them looked away for too long.

When the first pole was a perfect circle, Knight shot his hand at the other and it did the same thing, seeming to manipulate itself on its own. When both poles hung now as perfect rings Knight laughed loud enough it hurt some children's ears, making them clap their hands to them.

"I don't just want you to stand in the face of danger, I want you to leave Vagabond Circus commanding it!" Knight said. And then two giant lions that were Oliver's illusions appeared on the far side of the ring. The crowd gasped at their sudden appearance. Knight stood between the two large rings and turned to face the two lions, who both growled angrily at the ringmaster. "Silence," Knight said and the lions both cowered. "Now give these good people a show," Knight sang to the beasts.

The lions raised their large heads.

"NOW!" Knight boomed and the lions lurched into a sprint aimed straight in his direction. The crowd gasped in unison. But Knight didn't flinch. Then in perfect chorography the lions sprung off the ground and jumped through the metal rings. They landed two feet from the crowd, making the front row jump back, fearing they were about to be mauled.

"Good boys," Knight said and the lions nonchalantly turned and sauntered until they stood on either side of the ringmaster, like guard dogs. "Ladies and gentlemen, you came here to restore your hope in magic, to be inspired. And I do want to spark something in you." Knight crouched down low and jumped up and spun around, kicking up the tails of his jacket as he did. "Your bad side!" Knight said and winked, making the flames on his face appear even more sinister. Loud music and smoke filled the air as Knight pulled his top hat off his head. "Welcome to Vagabond Circus." And the lights blossomed into a sinister red before burning out completely, leaving the crowd in black.

Chapter Twenty-Six

*F*inley grabbed a plate of eggs and polenta filled with spinach and cheese from the food truck with a swift but sincere "thank you" to Bill the circus chef. He looked a bit overwhelmed and Finley was positive that Knight had made certain demands on the chef to prepare extra food for his kids. Not something delicious like what was on Finley's plate presently. Knight usually fed his kids things that didn't require chewing—oatmeal, soups, and protein shakes. Inexpensive and filling options.

Finley found an empty table at the back of the food area and sat. The slice of polenta looked like an impossibility to eat, but he knew he had to. After last night's performance he had to fill his reserves, but still the idea of ingesting anything was met with nausea. The crowd at Vagabond Circus had stood with applause no less than half a dozen times. Knight had sprinkled nuances into the show that kept the crowd gasping, usually in fear, but then sighing with relief. And the new ringmaster had strongly encouraged Sunshine to cast her fire act closer to the audience, to ensure the front row felt the heat. During rehearsal Sunshine had declined the suggestion and then she'd mysteriously been assaulted by the same headache that Zuma had when she met Knight. The circus owner then stated he thought the remedy to get rid of headaches would be compliance. When Sunshine finally agreed to the idea regarding her act, her headache magically disappeared.

Finley hated watching the manipulation on Vagabond Circus members that he feared would only worsen, but more than that he despised that the show Knight led had actually been a success. People loved horror movies, but it didn't mean they were good for them. Drugs ran the world and yet they weren't always healthy for young or old minds and bodies. And that's how Finley felt about the show and the way it affected its patrons.

When the performance was over, boys ran for the exit, knocking into each other and wrestling fiercely once in the parking lot. The bickering of little girls could be heard from the practice tent. In less than two hours the young girls had turned socially aggressive, making catty remarks to the best friend with whom they'd entered the big top while holding hands. Men and women didn't leave the big top with a renewed belief in magic, but rather with the inclination to entertain naughty ideas they hadn't allowed themselves to give that much consideration to in the past. Knight had, like Dave, changed the people who watched his show, but not for the better. He'd planted a seed that would grow into a noxious weed and kill every healthy idea in that community. The only consolation for Finley was that at least they were leaving Medford later that afternoon, once the big top was packed up.

That job of dissembling the big top was supposed to be done the night before, as it always was, but Knight had presented the crew with a keg at the after-party. The crew was now all sleeping off hangovers and therefore the whole schedule was off. They'd have to work double time to transport the caravan down to Redding, California, and be ready for tomorrow night's show.

Finley was still staring at his food when he felt a presence slide into the picnic table beside him. He looked up to find Sunshine's always melancholy face staring back at him. Now there was a new expression. Her black arched eyebrows were nearly touching. Her eyes red. Regret and frustration written on every part of her face.

"Don't sit with me," Finley said, putting his eyes back on his untouched food.

"Nope," she said, popping her lips together with the one word.

"Association with me is a bad idea," Finley said. "Don't press your luck."

"I singed the hairs off a four-year-old girl's arm last night. I think I got the market cornered on bad luck."

"You've been warned," Finley said with a defeated sigh.

Sunshine turned so she was facing Finley. "I knew something was up with you since the beginning. Now we learn you were transferred from this school to a circus."

Finley didn't nod in agreement. He just stayed focused on the now cold eggs.

"But you know, Fin, I'm not buying that bullshit so how about you pony up with the truth?"

"I'm not answering any questions. Burn off my hair. Rifle through my emotions. Just stop with the questions," Finley said.

"Here's how this will work. I'm pretty brilliant, if I say so myself. I think I've figured out what's going on here. But you can confirm. I'm going to ask yes or no questions. Tap once on the table for yes and two for no. Then you've told me nothing. How does that sound?"

Silence met Sunshine's ears, but she didn't adorn a defeated expression. "Here, this will help," she said, handing Finley a fork. "Now eat and tap."

"Thanks," he said, taking it.

"Knight can create headaches in people, can't he?" Sunshine said in a whisper. "That's what he did to me yesterday, wasn't it?" She then paused and stared not at Finley but at the hand holding the fork just over his plate.

He looked at the girl for a long moment. Since the beginning he had trusted Sunshine but now he was torn if more information would help or harm her. Finley recognized the pain in her longing gaze. It was the same detail he spied in his own eyes. So quickly Knight had brought that grief upon her. And he sensed it would worsen. He tapped the twines of the fork once against the plate before lifting it back and sliding the fork under the food. The bite tasted cold and chewy in his mouth. Sunshine looked back at him with a confident knowing.

"Next question," she said. "There's no school, is there?"

Finley set the fork down. Eating just wasn't in his near future. He then tapped his finger once on the wooden table.

Sunshine's eyes widened.

"They're slaves then," she said, no question in her tone. Then she looked out at the crowd filing to tables. Some were sluggish crew members who had none of their usual cheer in their eyes. "That means you weren't transferred," she stated again and turned to face Finley. "You escaped from Knight, didn't you?"

Finley pressed his lips together. He too had noticed the abused bodies grabbing food and sliding into tables. The crew were now a danger to themselves, working after a night of binge drinking which had been highly encouraged by Knight.

Finley turned back to Sunshine and then slid his gaze to his hand on the table. With one finger he tapped again.

"Oh shit. This is as dark as I feared then, which means we are in trouble," Sunshine said.

"You can leave," Finley said. "Go join another circus. Go to college. Go live your life. Go save yourself from this."

"Screw that. And allow that madman to take over Dave's circus? Also, Ian says that if we stay and do what Knight says that soon something will happen that will run the man away."

"He said that?" Finley said, his chin down, mouth hardly parting for those words.

"Yeah, he's been talking way more than usual. He was whispering that to the performers last night during the after-party, while his crew was getting drunk."

"Hmmm..." Finley said, not making sense of the idea that anything could run Knight away. "Ian said you should do what Knight said?"

"Yeah," she said, nodding. "He told us that otherwise things will get worse faster."

"I can't argue with that statement."

Sunshine then noticed "the freaks" headed in their direction, Nabhi in the lead and Oliver looking less than happy to be bringing up the rear behind Padmal. "One more question," she said, scooting in closer to Finley, her voice low. "Is Knight responsible for Dave's death?"

Finley straightened, unprepared for the direct question. Nabhi and Haady slid onto the bench opposite of them, forced smiles on their always pleasant faces. Everyone at the table reeked with a negative emotion. Sunshine knew this using her empathesis and Finley knew from plain observation. This was Knight's doing. In less than a day.

Finley looked straight at Sunshine and then balled his hand on the table and knocked once.

Chapter Twenty-Seven

Sunshine's green eyes widened, showing too much white as the triplets and Oliver took their seats at the table. *Knight was responsible for Dave's death.* Finley had confirmed it.

"But that means—" she said, but Finley knocked on the surface of the table twice sharply indicating "no."

"That means we have to be careful," he said in a low voice that only she could hear.

Oliver arched one of his black eyebrows at Sunshine and then Finley. "Well, you all are keeping up with the status quo of the rest of the circus members." He indicated over his shoulder at the carefully moving crew members, two of whom were actually arguing at the food truck. "Chuck and Corey are fighting over line order and you two look like you haven't yet resolved an argument. Everyone seems to have woken up on the wrong side of the circus," Ian said.

"Well, everyone but Paddy," Sunshine said, shoving the repulsion of learning Knight, and probably Sebastian, murdered Dave to the corner of her being. The girl was used to hiding things, being privy to everyone's emotions. "What's with the wide grin on your usually sour face? You look like a freaking jack-o'-lantern, Paddy."

Padmal didn't answer, just gave a snobbish grimace to the other girl.

"We just had a meeting with Knight and he's okayed for us to replace the knives in our juggling act with real icicles," Haady said, his usually cheerful voice subdued.

"That's not accurate. He demanded that we up the danger aspect of our act," Nabhi said, not hiding his usual frustration. "He said it wasn't enough. That's when Padmal supplied our earlier idea of using icicles."

"I don't see what the big deal is," the middle triplet said. "I was just giving a suggestion we'd already considered."

Nabhi spun to his sister on his left. "The problem," he said through clenched teeth, "is that Dave wouldn't approve using the

73

icicles because they're too dangerous. And it blurs the line of what is believable, and you know that. People are going to think the icicles are fake. Doing something like this puts us at risk, as well as the reputation of the circus."

"Well, the old ringmaster is dead and I'm just trying to be helpful to the new one," Padmal said.

"Since when were you ever helpful?" Nabhi said, pulling the rubber band off his wrist and absentmindedly tying his brown shoulder-length hair into a bun. He did it with a practiced finesse. Now he matched his brother, Haady, who had his hair the same. They could usually pass for identical twins but they weren't since they were triplets with a girl.

"I think that Knight actually has some bold ideas and therefore I'm willing to be helpful to him," Padmal said, looking to Oliver for support. "Don't you think he's going to take Vagabond Circus to better places?"

"More dangerous places," Sunshine said, spite heavy in her voice.

"I'm not sure of anything," Oliver said, his voice slow due to exhaustion. And what made him feel worse was having Padmal's cinnamon-colored eyes still pinned on him, a certain expectation in them. "He had me double my illusion output last night. That lion opening act nearly wiped me out for the rest of the show."

"You'll just have to be stronger," Padmal said, no sympathy in her tone.

Finley watched this interaction with a stone expression. He had seen all this coming. This was how Knight worked. He created divides because friendships could turn into alliances and that would be dangerous to the new ringmaster's rule. And he worked people past the point of exhaustion, encouraged bad habits, and made people go against the direction of their moral compass. Over time, it forced individuals who were strong into a position to follow blindly. In six months the members of Vagabond Circus wouldn't even recognize themselves. Finley knew he had to stop this but he was powerless. He couldn't leave, and watching was torture.

"We will try practicing with the icicles, but if they don't work we aren't using them," Haady offered, always the voice of reason.

"They will work," Padmal said. She was even more intimidating since she'd learned that her mother had died. She wasn't silent about her hate for Dave anymore. And she'd spoken of it so much recently that Oliver was truly questioning his choices. He didn't want to leave Vagabond Circus, but he was the one person truly considering the idea. It seemed like the ideal solution to all his problems. He looked up right then to find the one person he'd been looking for. The one person who could help him decide what to do next.

"I'll be right back," Oliver said, rising from the table.

Chapter Twenty-Eight

*I*an, for as bulky as he was, moved quite swiftly. He had almost jostled out of the food area by the time Oliver caught up with him. The illusionist called out to the clairvoyant but his voice couldn't be heard over the bickering of the crew members. Oliver reached out for Ian's arm when he was close enough. The large man paused but didn't turn immediately. One way his divination gift worked was that he could sense things and futures by touching someone. It was one reason he'd never had a romantic relationship. Seeing a lover's ending, even if decades into the future, spoiled any intimacy.

Finally, Ian swiveled his head, which was angled down since he knew he was going to turn to find Oliver, who was a foot shorter than him. He looked into the boy's eyes, one brown and the other green. "Are you quite certain you want to know?" Ian said.

The question hung mysteriously in the air, but Oliver didn't have to wonder long. Ian would have sensed that Oliver wanted to have his future read. And if Ian was reluctant to share it then it meant his future included tragedy. "I think so," Oliver said, suddenly feeling small looking up at the overburdened eyes of the man in front of him.

"You need to be certain, because you can't unknow your future. And if you think you can do something to avoid it, then that will surely be the act that causes it." With a humorless laugh Ian then said, "The universe plays games, but not by the rules."

Oliver wanted to shiver from the look in Ian's eyes. The man had always been strange to him. He was burly in his features, but had the demeanor of a koala bear. However, now he seemed brimming with a craziness, like it was scratching to escape him.

"How about you *not* tell me my future. Really what I need to know…the thing is… I need to make a decision…" Oliver ran his hand over his Mohawk, making it go flatter.

"And you want me to tell you what decision to make?" Ian said, that hint of sensitivity always in his voice, just partnered with madness now. "To stay or leave? Is that right? The answer to that is easy, Oliver. You must stay. Everyone must. But let's talk about what sparked the idea in the first place. You want to leave because you don't know how to exist at the circus with her."

The *her* was obviously Padmal. Oliver had tried to break up with her, but she'd sensed it. Made threats about how she'd make his life hell if he abandoned her after everything she'd been through. He wasn't sure if he could believe the threats but something told him that Padmal was crazy enough to do a lot of unthinkable things. And now she had someone like Knight to encourage her bad behavior. There would be no repercussions. So Oliver had played with the idea of leaving Vagabond Circus to rid himself of her. But this had been the only place he'd ever called home. He consoled himself by thinking he could find a job as a magician at another circus. Not as successful as Vagabond Circus, but still he'd be free.

"My advice to you is to break things off with her, but not quite yet," Ian said. "You'll have to endure her a little longer. And when you do break things off, you have to break her spirits in order to stay safe."

"And then she won't retaliate?" Oliver said.

"Oh, she will, but it will backfire on her," Ian said, and his eyes lost focus, like he was studying something in his mind. It was almost the look of a blind person.

"And I'll be safe? Her brothers will be? She won't do anything to punish us?"

"She won't be able to," Ian said.

Oliver considered this strange bit of information. It was always like this with Ian, but he was never wrong. "Okay, so when do I do it?"

"When you absolutely can't put up with her anymore, because you need to be properly motivated to deliver the final blow."

"How will I know when that is?" Oliver said, realizing there would be a riddle of sorts to Ian's instructions.

"You know how right now you can grit and bear it when she says disrespectful things?"

Oliver nodded.

"Well, you won't have that restraint. It will rocket out of you."

"What will?"

"The secret I'm about to tell you." And Ian leaned down and whispered three sentences in Oliver's ear.

Chapter Twenty-Nine

"*H*ey, fortune teller!" It was Sunshine calling to Ian from her table. She waved him and Oliver over to their area. The girl sensed now that Ian knew about the cause of the ringmaster's death. She could feel it in him and so much more. However, Sunshine was going to figure out exactly what was going on at Vagabond Circus before she made any plans, which would involve bringing down the people responsible for Dave's death.

Ian strode over to the table, Oliver behind him.

"Hello, Sunshine," Ian said, not quite meeting the girl's eyes. They'd been at Vagabond Circus the same number of years, ten. They'd politely avoided each other as their skills intimidated the other. Sunshine never wanted to know the future and Ian didn't like that Sunshine could feel the burden and pain he harbored.

"You notice that your crew is in a rare, despicable state?" Sunshine said, pointing at the people behind him.

Ian turned and studied the crew members, who were all looking to still be drunk. One grabbed for Zuma as she strode through the crowd. Ian flinched but soon his fears were relieved when Jasmine stepped in. In a quick movement the tall girl had the guy pinned to the wall of the food truck with barely three fingers. Jasmine whispered something in the man's ear and then turned and joined her friend, who didn't look startled, only a little frustrated. Zuma stared around at the crew members all adorning large bags under their eyes and irritated expressions as though the normal sounds of Vagabond Circus were deafening to them.

Ian turned back to the table and caught the crazed look of worry on Finley's face. The acrobat had raced forward at the first sign that Zuma was in trouble and he now stood on the other side of the table. Ian smiled at him. Nodded in approval. "I think she's safe," he said to Finley, just to him. "I don't see any future where Zuma is endangered for a little while."

"A little while?" Finley said, irritation in his voice.

Ian tilted his head to the side with an expression that said "what do you expect?"

"Thanks. I'll sleep so much better now," Finley said and took his seat again next to Sunshine. He was intent on forcing the breakfast down his throat one way or another.

Ian turned his attention back on Sunshine. "I have, in fact, noticed my crew isn't acting up to the standards I've usually held them to."

"Well, aren't you going to do something about it? Punish them for getting drunk? Tell Knight not to get them intoxicated?" Sunshine asked incredulously.

Ian swung his gaze over his shoulder at his crew. Twenty men and women who he respected and had worked alongside for years sat in various states of disarray. He blinked back to the present, letting the flashes of their futures fade away. Then he turned back to Sunshine. "You know, I'm not going to do a damn thing about it."

"But why? If you don't then things aren't going to get done. Things are going to go to hell," Sunshine said, her face suddenly flaming red.

"You know as well as I do that only those who have been through hell know how to withstand fire, Sunshine," he said and then winked at her. "No pun intended."

"Ian, you've obviously seen a future connected to the crew," Haady said in his pleasant peace-making voice. "Can you shine a light on this situation for us?"

"He's just going to give us some dumb puzzle that hardly helps and only confuses us," Sunshine said, tying her arms across her chest, all emotions suddenly rising to the surface as she realized how complex this was going to be.

Ian didn't look at her with offense, but rather a sensitive thoughtfulness. "I can guarantee what I tell you all will help, even if it's also confusing."

"Ian, don't you get there's no guarantees," Sunshine said, suddenly standing and pressing both hands into the table top. She leaned forward in Ian's direction, menace in her stance. No one attempted to calm her, especially not Finley, who had his eyes locked on Zuma, a quiet wanting radiating in the gaze.

Zuma looked just then and caught Finley's stare, his undeniable expression. She threw him a look of contempt before stabbing a potato with vengeance. Then she turned to pretend to give all her attention to Jasmine.

"You're right, Sunshine," Ian said. "No guarantees, but there's certain things I can rely on. Unfortunately, I see the complex arrangements that create futures. In most cases, I know exactly what will produce a future, but I also know that giving you all the information is more detrimental than helpful. However, I know three things that I can share with you all."

Everyone, including Padmal, who had been looking bored, perked up and gave their full attention to the fortune teller.

"The first is that things aren't getting better. Not before they get a whole lot worse," Ian said.

"What? Well, tell us how to change that," Sunshine said, still standing and looking like she was about to hurl fire across the table at Ian.

"There are no options to create that future," Ian said with a defeated shrug. His shoulders were the size of a linebacker's and therefore the gesture carried much movement with it. "I've tried. It appears that tragedy is necessary to bring the Vagabond Circus back to a place of peace. Not even peace, but to a higher place than it's ever been. I've seen it for a while now."

"That's why you allowed Dave to die," Sunshine said, her tone on fire with anger.

"Yes," Ian said matter-of-factly.

"And that's why you're standing idly by while your crew sabotages the circus?" And it was Finley who said this. But there was no anger in his voice; rather a calculated tone, like he was piecing this all together in his strategic mind.

"Yes, avoiding chaos usually only puts us on a quicker train to that destination," Ian said.

"Again with the damn riddles," Sunshine said, slamming her palm onto the table top.

"Remember when you asked me why I hadn't confronted my crew about their behavior?" Ian said.

"Yes," she said with a growl.

"Well, the second thing I know is why be the bad guy when I can let *that* man be it," Ian said and angled his head over his shoulder at the crowd behind them. It was parting like oil being poured into water. High above other people's heads a tall bald figure could be seen moving forward. Everyone at the table turned and watched as Knight stalked until he was standing right in front of the crew, all hunched over at several tables. He stood appraising the crew members, some aware of his presence and others too absorbed in their headaches or quenching their thirsts.

"What in the hell is going on here?" Knight said in a voice so quiet the table by Ian could hardly hear him. "The big top is still UP!" he said, screaming out the last word, startling people all around.

Zuma remained cool, Finley noticed. And she spied the change coming in Knight's vocal cords.

"I do something nice to celebrate the first show and what do you all do?" Knight said. "You get wasted and take us off schedule. This is unacceptable."

What everyone knew and no one was saying was Knight kept betting crew members that they couldn't down another drink. And when they did, he flicked them a devilish smile and commented on how impressed he was. Now all the people who he said impressed him the most had eyes more bloodshot than all the rest.

"You will all have the big top down by noon," Knight said. "I don't care if you have to kill yourself to do it. Every crew member's pay has been docked for one week, and if you don't have the big top loaded and on the road by noon then it's another week. If you want to increase your wages tenfold then you will be a part of this circus, but as long as you derail our schedule then you will get nothing. Is that clear?"

No one answered. They were all too stunned by the punishment which seemed strange and fitting, and also so different from the kind of treatment they were used to. However, in Dave's day there was no drinking. Things always ran smoothly.

"I'll repeat that one more time since you all appear to be deaf," Knight said in a quiet voice. "Is that CLEAR?"

The crew all nodded their heads. Some answered with a short "Yes sir."

Knight did not greet anyone else or offer compliments on the performance the night before to the acrobats. He just turned and strode off, Gwendolyn and Sebastian at his back.

Ian faced the freaks again, his face neutral. "It's a shame, but these things must happen."

"Why? Why do we have to go through hell to get to some other fate?" Sunshine said.

"Because the alternative is that we all stay imprisoned in hell," Ian said, and those words were like cold beats being played down everyone's spines.

"So you said you knew three things," Nabhi said to Ian. "Bad things have to happen," he said, holding up a finger and thinking before holding up another one. "And that we should allow Knight to be the bad guy, not us. And then what else?"

Ian nodded, giving Nabhi a look of pride. "Yes, the third is the most important and the one I know with absolute certainty. No matter how bad things get you all can't leave Vagabond Circus. No one can. If any of you leave then things will grow exponentially worse for everyone Vagabond Circus touches. You all are keeping the balance, but leave and the evil he promotes will reign."

"But how are we supposed to stay, knowing that things will get worse?" It was Oliver's raspy voice asking the question this time.

"If you stay, if you weather the storm, then I can guarantee Knight will leave," Ian said.

They all stared at Ian in awe, hope surfacing in their faces for the first time all morning. However, it was only Zuma, who had been listening from her table, who knew Ian was lying. She'd spied it even from that sideways angle in his micro-expressions. But now she'd have to wait to find out *why*.

Chapter Thirty

*T*he crew worked faster than ever, some putting their fatigued and dehydrated bodies under incredible stress. There were multiple crew members with strained muscles, two with fractured bones and several who sustained injuries in the process of taking down the big top at record speed. Fanny would have a long line of patients once the caravan stopped to set up camp in the new location. And still the crew wouldn't have long to break since they were expected to work through the night to have the big top up by morning. That wouldn't normally be too big a problem since they could dream travel to put up the big top, but these tired and drained bodies needed good old-fashioned sleep and that wasn't in the cards for the crew.

The newspapers hit the press just as the Vagabond Circus trailers pulled on to the I-5, heading out of town. The circus would be set up and ready for three shows a day by the time the *Mail Tribune* was dispersed in Medford, Oregon.

Lots of Changes for Vagabond Circus

For at least a decade I've been sitting front row at Vagabond Circus when it comes to town. I was a little disappointed when almost all the shows were canceled in Medford except for one. Apparently the circus had an accident involving one of my favorite performers. I was worried that losing Jack Fuller from the cast would change the show I've grown to look forward to all year. Still I did everything I could to ensure I saw the circus. And the show has changed. However, I cannot confirm the change is due to the loss of this beloved trapeze artist. For one, the infamous Dave Raydon, the ringmaster for Vagabond Circus, has been replaced. I suspect this is only temporary, since no press release has crossed my desk about it. However, because of casting changes or other changes it appears the entire tone of the circus has shifted from dreamy to more nightmarish. The Vagabond Circus shows in Seattle and Portland all sold out before coming to Southern Oregon and I wondered what the change had been. The critics stated there was a new acrobat, a Finley Anders, but again there's more than a few role changes that have affected the feel of this show.

Now I love the fantastical dreamy tone of the old show. However, as a young girl I was banned from watching scary movies, and now I feel like I've been given the opportunity to sit front row on the set of a horror film. Was this the same show I used to watch on my father's knee and dream about? No. But it's just as good and has stayed with me in different ways. I left that show feeling something creepy lurking behind me, like I was being watched. And days later I still find myself waking up in the middle of the night, worried that there's something hiding under my bed. However, the few times I've made myself peer under my bed, I just see vivid flashes of the scenes from that show. It takes something incredible to linger in the backs of our minds after the circus has long rolled out of town. I will definitely be in the crowd again the next time Vagabond Circus comes through Medford, but this time I won't be in the front row, for fear of being eaten or burned alive.

Chapter Thirty-One

Once Zuma had her trailer parked in the new Vagabond Circus grounds in Redding, California, she hesitated at the door. Usually she'd spring out after arriving in a new place to check that everyone else at Vagabond Circus had made the journey safely. The trip had carried less exhilaration in comparison to most of the journeys between locations. Two of Knight's black semis led the long caravan and two brought up the end. It didn't feel like they were accompanying the circus, as much as guarding it with their solid black exteriors and dark tinted cab windows. Zuma had only caught a glimpse of one of the drivers, an older man. She guessed this was one of the supervisors Finley had told her about. They were people with no power useful to Knight, but they followed his orders and kept the kids in line. Now Zuma was beginning to understand Knight's power and how his influence worked. She'd watched as he *managed* the crew members at the after-party. She wanted to stop them from drinking, but before she could Jasmine had intervened. Her speech had been cut short by the same headache that hit Zuma when she first confronted Knight about murdering Dave.

How would the people of Vagabond Circus overthrow a man who could kill them with a headache for their incompliance? The key was in something Ian had said. He didn't want the circus members to leave, but he lied about his guarantee. Zuma would have to confront the lead crew member, but not right then. He would have his workload full trying to get the big top up in time for tomorrow's shows.

Zuma's hand had been hovering above her door handle for over a minute. This fear was ridiculous. She was safe during the day, and it was midafternoon. She opened the door to find the sky gray and an autumn wind seeking to bury itself inside her chest. Zuma zipped up her jacket and pulled her sleeves over her hands as she shivered from the sudden cold.

"Congrats, girl," Bill, the circus chef, called to Zuma as he passed carrying a crate of carrots.

She smiled meekly. The press release of her engagement to Jack had been a shimmer of light in the bleakness of Knight's arrival. Most at Vagabond Circus were unclear about what was going on. Most had doubts about the story that Jack broke his legs because of a faulty harness since he actually never wore one. His levitation gift protected him from falls, most falls. Still, Titus was staying quite secretive, deflecting questions and again urging Zuma to keep the truth from her people, even Jasmine. He promised that a time would come when divulging the truth would be allowed, but for now it would create chaos and kill the show. Zuma agreed and therefore didn't even disclose to Titus that the engagement was a sham.

"Well, there's the beautiful bride-to-be." It was Fanny who greeted Zuma this time. She had Emily in one hand and Tiffany in the other and was leading the young girls in the opposite direction. The healer paused and offered Zuma a warm smile. The girls paused beside their caretaker and looked up with wide eyes directed at the acrobat. "Are you on your way to see your fiancé?" Fanny asked.

"I was," Zuma said. "I thought I'd check to see how he made the journey."

"So sweet," Fanny said, squeezing the little hands in hers. "You know, to find love in spite of all that's happened is a true gift. I hope, well...never mind..." Fanny said, looking to almost blush.

"What?" Zuma said, curious about the shifty look in the usually honest woman's face.

"Well, you two were breaking rules by falling in love, but I think that's a beautiful way to do it and..." Again she trailed away, her eyes pretending to look over her girls, who were both staring at Zuma like she was the finest doll in a store window.

"What?" Zuma asked again.

"I...well, I just hope that your marriage to Jack brings you some comfort," Fanny said, every part of her filled with hesitation. What she wasn't saying was she wished it would bring Zuma happiness, but that was an impossibility for the cursed girl.

"Uh, yeah, me too," Zuma said, not understanding the conversation she was having with the older woman. Fanny wasn't saying something but she hadn't lied, Zuma knew that.

Fanny raised the two hands in hers and pressed them fondly into her hips. "Well, I must be getting the girls off to their lessons. Feel free to go into my trailer. Jack is in there."

"Thanks," Zuma said, not keeping the bewilderment out of her tone.

Chapter Thirty-Two

Of course Zuma wanted to check on Jack. She'd hardly seen him since they had come back to Vagabond Circus. But she also needed to discuss everything from the fake engagement to how they were going to manage the Knight situation. Jack was protected, locked away in Fanny's trailer. But Zuma hoped he'd have ideas for how to protect the people of Vagabond Circus who weren't shut away. And she also wanted to talk to Benjamin if she could get a chance. Fanny had forbid them from telling anyone about his shape-shifting abilities and Zuma thought she knew why. The healer was protecting the ten-year-old boy, but what if he could protect the people of Vagabond Circus? Zuma would have to get him alone, which right then was the perfect time.

Zuma rapped on the door to the trailer, expecting Jack to call her in. Instead Sunshine answered the door, her usual unwelcoming look on her face. "Oh, good, now it's an acrobat party," she said. "Pink streak is here," she called behind her. "Just need Jazzy-Afro-head and the party will be complete," she said in a monotone voice.

"Hey, Sunshine," Zuma said, not even showing any offense. She was used to this from the girl. "How are you? I know you and Dave were close, I'm so sorry." And there was genuine sympathy in Zuma's voice. She knew how heartbroken Dave's death had made Zuma herself, and could only imagine how it affected the girl in front of her whom Dave adopted at age ten.

Standing in the doorway, Sunshine stared down at Zuma, who still hadn't entered the trailer and was two steps down. "Why are you apologizing? You didn't kill him," she said, narrowing her eyes, and a quick trip into Sunshine's thoughts told Zuma she knew exactly who *had* murdered Dave.

"No, I didn't and that means maybe we should start working together to protect Vagabond Circus," Zuma said, taking one step up.

"Me work with you?" Sunshine said and almost smiled with amusement. "That might have been a possibility before I learned you broke Dave's second cardinal rule." She then stepped past Zuma and out of the trailer. "Guess it doesn't matter since your fiancé isn't even in the circus anymore. Nice planning," Sunshine said.

"Sunshine, listen," Zuma said.

"No, you listen. I don't have time to deal with you right now, Pinky. I've got to go find Benjamin, who's currently prowling around this place in the form of Oliver."

"Why is he doing that?" Zuma asked.

"Because he's a little boy who can and besides, he's curious what's going on around here."

"Oh," Zuma said, looking up at the trailer and realizing she probably wouldn't be able to talk to Benjamin on this visit. "Well, good luck," she said in another attempt to be pleasant to the girl she'd only ever ignored.

"Yeah, luck, that's not what I freaking need," Sunshine said with a grunt and a sigh. "Do you know what's going to happen if Oliver runs into himself? Or if someone sees the two together?"

"Or what Knight would use Benjamin for if he knew his gift," Zuma said, the idea dawning.

"Exactly, brainiac. Why don't you go into the trailer and make your damn fiancé eat something. I'm tired of having that job. Should be yours anyway," Sunshine said and marched away.

Zuma just shook her head and turned for the door.

Chapter Thirty-Three

"*H*ey, yoohoo," Zuma called, knocking on the door frame as she entered the trailer. "Jack, it's me," she said and froze when she entered the trailer to find Finley sitting tensely beside Jack's bed. She straightened, not expecting to find him there. Jack's bed was angled away from the entrance, but he still managed to turn a bit to peek around the bed at her.

"Oh, hey," she said, shifting her eyes to the right of Finley. "You're here. That's what Sunshine meant by an acrobat party."

"Yeah," Finley said, standing. "I was just leaving."

"You don't have to leave because I'm here," Zuma said.

And then Jack turned back and threw his head hard into his pillow. "Does everything here have to be a mess?" he said.

Zuma strolled forward until she was just beside Jack's bed; just beside Finley. "What do you mean?"

"Oh, I don't know, the engagement, now you and Finley being awkward, and how about the killers prancing around the circus and none of us can do a damn thing about any of it," Jack almost yelled, his fists clenching into his covers.

Zuma leaned forward and hugged him, sliding her arms around his shoulders. She was careful not to shift him or press into his legs as she did, although he looked more comfortable than she'd seen him. Zuma pulled back. "You're not supposed to be frustrated like this. You're supposed to be calm so you and I can strategize on how to deal with what you so appropriately deemed 'a mess,' although 'disaster' is a better term."

Jack smiled at her. "Sorry. I needed to have that outburst. I've actually been saving it for you, fiancée," he said fondly at her. It had always been easy between these two.

"Thanks, that was kind of you," she said, leaning forward and kissing his cheek, conscious that Finley was behind them, awkwardly watching since he hadn't had a chance to dismiss himself.

Zuma then sat on the bed. She took Jack's hand, doing a great job, she thought, of ignoring Finley beside her. "How are you feeling, Jack?"

"I should be going," Finley said, his eyes on the space between Jack and Zuma.

"I'm good," Jack lied in a clipped tone to Zuma and then swiveled his head up to Finley. "No, you can't go. Strategize. Didn't you hear Zuma? We've got to figure out some things and you are our best resource."

Zuma swung her head over her shoulder at Finley. It hurt to look at him when his eyes weren't on her. That pain was excruciating when they were. Now that tortured gaze was on the floor, his hands pressed in his pockets.

"Oh, he's no help to us," Zuma said, still forcing herself to look at him. "Finley doesn't want to fight. He's given up. Pretty much decided to cower to Knight's rule."

"Zuma, that's not fair," Finley said through clenched teeth, his chin low as if he was speaking to Knight.

"No, it's not, and announcing that Jack and I are engaged and pushing me away, well what's that?" she said in retaliation.

"Necessary," he said.

Jack tugged on Zuma's hand to gain her attention. "What's been going on while I've been trapped in here?"

Zuma shook her head. "Well, I didn't think it could be done, but in only a few days' time and with one show Knight has made a mess of the circus. He's instigated so much trouble in such a short period of time that we'll be cutting each other's throats in a week. So keep doing what you're doing, Finley," she said, throwing her head back over her shoulder in his direction. "This 'ignore and comply' strategy sure seems to be working."

"It could be worse, Zuma," Finley said.

"Right, worse. Like the best man in the world is murdered and my best friend is paral... Oh wait," Zuma said dryly.

Finley brought his gaze to finally look at Zuma. It expressed his own frustration and disappointment in how she was punishing him in that moment. "Right, well, I'll leave you two love birds," he said, the humor not really registering in the dark joke. "That will give you a chance to discuss privately what a failure and coward I am."

Jack shot a disappointed look at Zuma. "Finley, I don't think that about you. If it wasn't for you I'd be dead. You saved my life by showing up and carrying me out of Knight's warehouse."

"Actually"—Zuma spun around—"Finley abandoned me right when we found you." She stood and narrowed her eyes at him. "I'd forgotten all about that until now."

"He what?" Jack asked behind her.

"Well, he showed back up a few minutes later, but *you*," she said to Finley, an accusation getting loaded into her speech, "you acted like you weren't coming back. Like you'd left me for good." She sized him up, taking her time. "Where exactly did you go and what were you doing?"

"Nowhere, Zuma," he said, frustrated.

"You're lying. Tell me."

He didn't know how to respond to this confrontation. It seemed like a good idea to run but there was no getting away from Zuma for too long.

"Damn it, Finley! Tell me!" Zuma yelled.

He slowly brought his gaze to hers. "You don't want to know."

"Stop saying stuff like that. You're not the only one sentenced to be punished endlessly anymore. We are in this together."

"No, Zuma, what you don't realize is that you're in your own private hell," Finley said. "And I've been trying to pull you out of it."

"What? What does that mean? Where did you go and what did you do?" Zuma asked.

He looked at her, really looked at her, so that she sucked in a painful breath. "I'll tell you if you really want to know," Finley said, "but please note you've been warned."

Chapter Thirty-Four

Zuma stared at Finley, unsure, as she'd been many times since she met him, if she could trust the acrobat. He *had* been a thief for most of his life. And she could always tell when someone lied, but that didn't mean they couldn't hold back information. Or, as in Finley's case, take Zuma's heart and hold it in his hands and crush it. No one had ever had an effect on her, and then Finley strolled into Vagabond Circus, looking very much the way he did now: lean, dark, and mysterious.

Zuma looked back at Jack for reassurance.

"Find out what he knows that you obviously don't know," Jack said in response to the unsure look she gave her friend. "Zuma, you will never conquer a challenge unless you have all the information and it sounds like there's more to know."

She nodded at Jack and then turned and took two steps toward Finley. And she knew immediately that her sudden closeness made him nervous. It put the restrictions he'd been placing on himself in danger of being frayed. "Tell me what you know. And Finley," she said, reaching out and touching his arm, gripping it. She waited until he returned his attention back to her and not to the hand pressed into his bicep. "Don't leave out a single thing. I want to know it all."

He nodded, but simultaneously stepped back out of her reach. Finley cleared his throat and forced himself to keep his eyes pinned on Zuma's, although the anger and desire radiating from them were making his soul ache. "You know how you told me you've never been happy?" he said and paused.

Zuma squinted at him, like she'd misheard. "What does that have to do with anything?"

"It has everything to do with everything. Your lack of happiness is why the circus is the way it is. It's why Dave made arrangements with your parents for you to come to Vagabond Circus. Your happiness, or rather lack thereof, has shaped so much," Finley said.

"How?" Zuma said, almost wanting to laugh at the ridiculous notions Finley was spouting. However, he wasn't laughing.

93

"Zuma, you have never felt real happiness not because there's something wrong with you or because you have a chemical imbalance," Finley said, slipping his hand through his dark brown hair. This was harder than he imagined.

"Then why?" she said, baffled why he would know anything about her inability to feel pure happiness. And yet he seemed to.

"Zuma, you remain in mostly a state of indifference because since you were born you were cursed," Finley said.

Zuma did laugh now. "Finley, are you listening to yourself?"

"Yes, and am I lying?" he asked, knowing her combat sense would support his claims.

"Well, no," Zuma said, scratching her head. "Which means you believe this bullshit and *that* makes you crazy."

Behind her Jack laughed. She'd almost forgotten he was there.

Zuma turned to him, more to share the stupidity of the moment than anything else. However, when she looked at Jack he was shaking his head. "Finley's probably the sanest person in this freak show, Zuma. Give him a chance to explain his case."

She shook her head at Jack and turned back to Finley. "Okay," she said, drawing out the word. "Pony up with a reasonable explanation for this bullshit."

"Remember I told you that Knight cursed Vagabond Circus?" Finley said.

"Yes, because he murdered Dave's baby, and then discovered the child was actually his because he'd been having an affair with Dave's wife." Zuma said the whole thing with only a brief hesitation, as she recalled the details.

"Whoa!" Jack said behind them. "Rewind, say what?"

Zuma held up her hand. "You'll get details after I get the whole truth."

Jack gave a frustrated sigh but remained silent.

"Yes, that's when Knight cursed the circus," Finley said. "Cynthia, Dave's wife, was dead and so was Knight's child. It made Knight go crazy."

"Because he wasn't already, having suffocated an infant?" Zuma asked.

"Anyway, you may not believe someone can curse people but—"

"I do," Zuma cut Finley off. "I heard details of it in some of Dave's private thoughts. He had the ability to curse people or places but he rarely used the gift." She had heard the thought by accident once when Dave allowed the wall in his mind to come down.

"Right, yes, Dave possessed and Knight *possesses* the ability to curse people. They have to use the right words and focus. And in return for the curse to work their power is stolen, taking years off their lives."

"That's crazy," Jack said, astonished and also disbelieving.

"Just ask Titus. He was there the day Knight cursed Vagabond Circus and then Dave cursed Knight right back," Finley said.

"Wait, how do you know all this?" Jack asked.

"I dream traveled back in time to witness this specific event. I needed to confirm the things Fanny told me," Finley said.

"That's right, Fanny was there. She told you this?" Zuma asked.

"Yes, she told me that after Dave's wife committed suicide and Knight found out he murdered his own child, he made a curse that's almost impossible to break," Finley said.

"What is it, Finley?" Zuma said, his words sucking out her breath

"Zuma, Knight cursed that any child born at Vagabond Circus could never be happy," Finley said, his eyes heavy with regret.

Zuma sucked in a sharp gasp as her hands slapped over her mouth. She stuttered out a moan, but quickly tried to cover it with something less weak sounding. Finley moved, only a fraction but she spied it. He'd almost reached for her. Almost wrapped his arms around her, but even in unveiling this tragedy and being behind closed doors he wouldn't tempt himself. Finley knew if he took off his restraints, he couldn't put them back on.

"Zuma, it—"

"I was born under the big top eighteen years ago," she said, interrupting Finley.

"And I know from time traveling that Knight cursed the circus one year before your birth. I checked," Finley said.

"You time traveled to the day I was born? You witnessed it?" she said in disbelief.

He smiled a little, but real smiles shouldn't adorn that much pain. The gesture cut at Zuma's heart. "Yeah, it was a beautiful moment." He shook his head, like he was seeing the memory then.

"The day you were born… Fanny delivered you, and Dave held you before your own father. He whispered in your ear two words and that's what confirmed the curse for me," Finley said.

"What were the words?" Zuma asked, her hands in her hair.

Finley pressed his lips together. "He said, 'I'm sorry.'"

And now Zuma did cry, a soft gasp of tears and a fresh pain seeping to her usually stone surface.

Finley didn't budge this time, but the look in his greenish eyes communicated perfectly the regret he had for her pain.

Zuma slid the back of her arm across her wet eyes, drying them on her sleeve. "You said this was why Dave arranged with my parents to have me come to Vagabond Circus?"

Finley nodded. "He thought that he owed you a life with the highs of a performer, since you could never experience the best thing, happiness."

"And my parents know?" she asked.

Another nod.

"But you said this impacted the success of the circus," Zuma said, confused now.

"Zuma, two things happen when a curse is made that robs," Finley said. "The first is that it steals years of life from the caster, like I said before. But then, because the curse, in your case, takes from you, then the happiness you should have had goes into a bank of sorts. It's funneled into a place. Like when it rains and the water evaporates and gathers in the clouds. Everything has to have an exchange."

"So, where did my happiness go?" she asked.

"To the only place named in the curse, the circus. Your stolen happiness has fueled the success of the circus," Finley said.

"What?"

Finley held up his hand. "It would be successful no matter what, but everyone who comes to the circus is gifted with a piece of what you lost. It's the law of return. Every one of Knight's curses works that way, since he uses them to take. If he curses a kid to lose a dream travel ability then their power is showered on his other kids to make them stronger. Everything goes somewhere."

"Oh," Zuma said, her mind angered and then also honored that the emotion she never felt had been such a gift to Vagabond Circus.

"But this is the reason you abandoned me at the compound? Why? I don't get it."

Finley now looked away. "I went into Knight's chamber to confront him, but as we now know he wasn't there. He had already left."

"Why would you confront him?" Zuma said.

"Because the only person who can lift a curse, according to Fanny, is the person who casts it," Finley said.

"And you were going to what? Demand he lift the curse from the circus?" she said in disbelief. And the look in Finley's eyes confirmed that this had indeed been his plan. She was enraged and also incredibly touched. How could she want to slap him and also kiss him at the same time?

"Zuma, I've never had a chance at a life, but you, if you could just experience real happiness…well you'd shine even brighter. That would fuel the circus for eternity. I just—"

But he didn't get a chance to finish his words because she rushed into his arms. Finley made to move but she sensed this and outmaneuvered him. And once he felt Zuma's arms around him, he crumbled into a thousand pieces of defeat. Finley didn't hesitate before wrenching her into him and holding her close. "I can't believe you'd do that for me," she whispered against his cheek.

"I'd do anything for you, I already told you that," Finley said. "And I've been trying to keep you alive by keeping you away from me, but you're making it incredibly difficult."

"No one can see us right now," she said and slid her nose across his cheek, her lips pausing in front of his.

A sharp cough behind them. "I don't really like being called 'no one,'" Jack said. "And if you're going to kiss my fiancée, will you get it over with so I can ask my questions."

"Damn it, Jack," Zuma said, pulling swiftly away from Finley. The girl was unable to kiss him now that she knew Jack was watching and waiting. "You ruin everything," she said, turning but keeping one of Finley's hands in hers. "What're your questions?" she asked.

"Well, Finley, you said Knight cursed the circus and Dave cursed Knight right back. What was it? Did you witness that too?"

"Yes," Finley said. "But unlike Knight's curse, Dave's wasn't one that robbed, but rather protected, so its energy has only worked to do the one thing for which it was intended."

"Which was?" Zuma asked.

"Dave's curse stated that as long as he was alive Knight could never set foot on the grounds of Vagabond Circus," Finley said.

"And now Dave is dead," Jack said.

"The word construction of a curse is key," Finley said, squeezing Zuma's hand once before forcing himself to let her go.

Chapter Thirty-Five

"You're not even trying," Padmal shrieked, her face dark with anger.

"I am," Nabhi said, throwing his hands in the air. "It's a freaking icicle. It melts. It's undergoing a chemical reaction which makes it incredibly difficult to control."

For hours the triplets had been practicing their juggling act, trying out the idea of using sharp icicles instead of their usual knives. The triplets started off their act by individually juggling using their hands but as things sped up and they began juggling together they used only their telekinesis. Each was responsible for three knives for a total of nine. Now those had been replaced by eight-inch-long icicles, which were sharp as knives but so cold they froze their hands in the first part of the juggling act. Padmal and Haady had both dropped several icicles. But due to the items' changing natures and Nabhi's growing frustration at his sister, his icicles flew dangerously close to himself and his brother and sister.

"Nabhi, maybe you need to sit out from this part of the act, since you can't hack it. You could join us when we move onto juggling easier objects," Padmal said.

Nabhi, who was increasingly having trouble quelling his anger, marched straight over to his sister. Since the girl was tiny compared to her lanky brother, he towered over her, but still she appeared like a bull looking a mouse straight on.

"What? You want to say something to me? Maybe you want to hit me?" she said, stepping up on her tiptoes and then pressing two fingers into his chest. "Go ahead. Hit a girl," she taunted, her cinnamon brown eyes laughing, but she wore no accompanying smile on her wide lips.

"Nab…" Haady warned from behind his brother. "Take ten to cool off, okay."

Nabhi kept his hands frozen by his side, although the urge to reach out and strangle his sister was spiraling through him, growing with intensity.

"Nab…" Haady said again, his calm voice seeking to talk Nabhi down from doing something that he'd regret. Nabhi, the youngest triplet, turned and nodded sharply to his brother. "Why don't you talk to your sister, because when I get back I won't be spoken to with disrespect," he said to Haady.

"I agree," Haady said, slapping Nabhi on the shoulder as he passed on his way to Padmal. "Little sister, you're really not being productive."

Nabhi had almost left the yard in front of their trailer, intent on making a few laps around the grounds to burn off his anger, when Padmal yelled, "Productive? I'm not the one being productive? Without me you two worthless telekinetics would have no show. You'd settle for juggling golf balls, but I'm the one who pushes us to take actual risks."

"That's simply not true. It was Titus who created our show," Haady said, his voice steady.

Nabhi turned, his eyes blazing in his sister's direction. *She really has no boundaries,* he thought.

"And I kept pushing Titus for more. If we are going to do child labor, we might as well go big," she said. "But I get that you two don't have the skill to keep up with me."

Nabhi was just about to scream back across the yard calling his sister the worst name he could think of, when between the rows of trailers something materialized. It took his eyes a second to process the man who didn't move like a man, but rather like a lizard, smooth and jerky at the same time. Knight stepped until he was in their yard, Sebastian and Gwendolyn flanking him on either side.

The triplets fell silent. Nabhi looked at Haady, who was looking at Padmal, who was looking straight at Knight.

"Sir, we were just—" Padmal began, but Knight held up his hand and she stopped.

"First of all, don't ever look at me directly. Is that clear?" Knight said in the voice that Nabhi thought also reminded him of a reptile, slippery and with a slight hiss.

"Yes, of course," Padmal said, looking down at the ground immediately. It was weird for her to appear subservient, but there it was. Padmal's usually scowling eyes pinned down low with zero hesitation.

"Very good," Knight said, and then crossed his arms. "You see, I've found my leadership to be more effective when my kids listen, which usually takes great focus. And I've been told I'm quite distracting to look at," he said, a smile in his voice. "Now am I right in thinking that you're all having an argument?"

"Sir, I can explain," Padmal said, her eyes on the grass.

"I don't want you to explain," Knight said. "I simply love conflict. I've been bored all day and could use some entertainment." He waved his hand in the air; the triplets all noticed the gesture from their peripheral. "Please continue. Argue away. I'd love to watch."

"Sir," and it was Haady this time. "Honestly, we need to resolve this conflict. Things just got heated and Nab was going to take a break. Go ahead and leave," he said, looking at his brother, waving him away.

"Freeze, Nabhi," Knight said. "You don't go anywhere unless dismissed by *me*." The circus owner then looked at Padmal. "What was this argument about?"

"We were practicing, trying to incorporate the icicles into the juggling act. However, Nabhi, who has a lesser skill than my brother and me, kept messing up," Padmal said.

"Which is why there's a bunch of melting icicles ruining the grass right now?" Knight said.

"Yes, sir," Padmal said.

"Do you think that this circus wants to go bankrupt funding your faulty ideas?" Knight said on the verge of yelling.

"Well, sir—"

"Do YOU?" Knight yelled, cutting off Padmal.

"No, sir," she said at once.

"And this was *your* idea, Padmal," Knight said. "So blame this on your brother, but whether this is a success or not rests on *your* shoulders."

"Sir, if you just listened—"

"I'm not the listening type, Padmal," Knight said.

"The act would work if my brother just tried harder," she said.

"You do realize a single person juggling isn't very entertaining. It's been done a trillion times," Knight said.

"I'm not sure why that's relevant," Padmal said.

"Because you are a trio," the man said. "And if you're going to work together then you better get your act organized. We have a show tomorrow and you promised me you all could increase the danger aspect. If you can't do that—"

"I appreciate what you're saying but it's not my fault if Nabhi sucks at using his telekinesis," Padmal said.

Knight tightened his eyes on the girl who had dared to cut him off but made no comment about it. "Pick up your knives."

"What?" she said.

"Padmal, I don't like to repeat myself. Pick up the knives you use in the act." They were sitting on top of their case, a few feet from Padmal, as they had used them to warm up before switching to icicles.

Hesitantly the girl walked over and picked up the knives she'd handled a thousand times. She almost looked up at Knight for further direction but caught herself. "Now what, sir?"

He gave an annoyed sigh. "Juggle."

"By myself?"

"Yes," he said with a growl.

Padmal gave a reluctant look to her brother, Haady, who nodded, encouraging her. He sensed Knight was not a man one questioned.

Padmal threw one knife, then less than a second later another, and then the third. They formed a rotation as she tossed them through the air, grabbing each by their rosewood handle and keeping her eyes on the blades as they flew.

"Faster," Knight ordered.

The knives picked up in speed, the slapping of her tiny hands making rhythmic music as they clapped onto the handles.

"Now use your telekinesis to juggle," Knight said.

Padmal was practiced with this as it was the first part of their act. Once she used her telekinesis then she just made a show of her hands touching the handles, but they were now moving so fast few could tell they never touched her. The knives were a blur though the air, Padmal's hands moving with a practiced grace.

"*Now*, Gwendolyn," Knight said to the girl beside him. That's all he had to say. The girl who could stop a Dream Traveler's power from working knew what he wanted done.

And then quite suddenly the gift that Padmal had owned for a few years now was stolen away. Disappeared. And she realized that with no telekinesis to hold the blades up, they were headed in one direction. She jumped back as three blades moving at a blinding speed raced for the ground. One ripped through the side of her finger. One stuck into the ground. And the third came down stabbing through her shoe and straight into her foot. A scream shot out of the girl's mouth, as she stood frozen, staring at the knife pinning her foot to the earth. Haady and Nabhi sprinted forward, Nabhi grabbing his sister's bleeding finger and wrapping it in the shirt he'd pulled off his body. And Haady went to work freeing Padmal's foot.

"Oh, it looks like you're just as faulty with your telekinesis as your brother, Padmal," Knight said, not having moved. "Maybe you shouldn't act so full of yourself in the future. You are a triplet after all." He then turned and walked away coolly, Sebastian and Gwendolyn behind him.

"We will get you to Fanny. Just hold on," Nabhi said, kneeling down to offer his sister a sensitive look.

She was silently crying, her face overflowing with tears of pain and shock. "You," she stuttered out to him. "This is all your fault!" she screamed, a moan in the words.

Chapter Thirty-Six

Zuma watched from behind a semi-truck in sleeper row until Ian had disappeared into another semi a few trucks over. He closed the door behind him after he entered the workshop semi. It's where the crew repaired parts of the big top or crafted new parts. It also served as Ian's office when he wasn't working on the oversized tent.

Zuma sprinted across the space between her and the truck and checked over her shoulder for anyone watching. The fewer people who knew she was on the hunt for information, the better. In a series of quick movements she whipped open the door and slipped inside, shutting the metal door behind her.

Ian had his back toward her and he stood at the workbench on the other side of the truck. It was set up into multiple stations, stocked with different equipment. Ian didn't straighten or turn at the sound of the door being closed. In front of him there was a clinking noise, like metal on metal. He was working something with his hands, but Zuma couldn't tell what.

"You know, Zuma, I get flashes of everyone's future," he said, his voice slow like he was working to get out the words while also concentrating on the project in his hands. "Everyone's future has been static but yours. Yours keeps changing."

Zuma took several steps until she was flush with the workstation. She pinned her back to it and looked up at Ian. "Why? Why does my future keep shifting?"

"The answer to that is the reason you came here," he stated, no question in his tone.

Zuma's eyes narrowed. "If you weren't so damn likable then your riddle talk would make me punch you."

A warm smile spread on the clairvoyant's face, showing his silver braces. "Likable. I'll settle for that in this lifetime."

"What are you gunning for in the next lifetime?" she asked, her angry expression morphing to one that was more amused.

He gave a dry chuckle. "Well, it's no use, but if I was the wishing type I'd want you to find me lovable in the next lifetime."

Ian fiddled with a large bolt which looked to have a ring cross threaded on it. "However, I know better than to wish and I also believe in soulmates and I'm definitely not yours. Too bad really," he said matter-of-factly.

Zuma's throat tightened, making it impossible to speak. Ian was so sensitive and had always spoken of his affection for her. But he also stated he wasn't unique in his desires, only more deserving of the affection he would never receive from the acrobat. It was heartbreaking to continuously watch Ian bathe in his case of unrequited love.

He turned and set his troubled eyes on the acrobat. "You came here to find out why I didn't say anything to Dave about his approaching death?"

"Yes," she said.

"Zuma, you're not going to understand all this at first, but now that you know about the curse you will assimilate the information much better."

"You know that I know I'm cursed to never be happy?"

He gave her a look that said "duh."

"Right, of course you do," she said. Zuma pinned her hands on the workstation behind her and then hoisted herself up until she was seated on the surface. "All right, tell me why you didn't warn anyone about Dave's death."

"This might come as a shock, but I did," Ian said, regarding Zuma with a quiet thoughtfulness.

"You what?"

"I couldn't explain this to you before because you didn't have all the information," Ian said. "Before, I made you believe I didn't warn Dave about his death. I actually did. I went to Dave after I got the vision of him dying. I didn't tell him who murdered him or how because I knew telling too much information could be dangerous. I just asked him if he wanted to know his future and he said yes. I told him he'd die soon, be murdered, and needed to be extra careful to avoid it."

"What? He didn't ask for more information, like exactly how to avoid it?" Zuma said.

"He did and so I told him," Ian said.

"So he knew not to put on the poisoned top hat? He knew it was Sebastian?" Zuma asked.

"No, not who. Only how," Ian said.

"Wait, then why did he put on the hat? Was it a mistake?"

Ian shook his head. "No. After I told Dave about his death, then your future shifted. Before that it had shown you in the distant future and it was beautiful. You were happy, Zuma, unlike you've never been granted before."

"Wait...before Dave knew about his death, I had a potential future to have the curse broken?"

"Yes," Ian said. "And Dave knew that since he was extremely invested in your happiness and you obtaining it. Dave actually had me make him aware of everyone's future. That's how he was able to make plans and change them to ensure his people had the best life."

"That's crazy," Zuma said with a breathless gasp.

Ian nodded in agreement. "But the thing is that after Dave knew about his own death your future shifted. The future where you were happy disappeared and instead you grew old and died never experiencing real happiness."

"But Dave lived in that future, right?" Zuma asked.

Ian nodded again. "And as Dave ordered I informed him when your fortune shifted. We both discussed it at length and decided it was his death that triggered the potential of your happiness. It was Knight taking over Vagabond Circus. It was everything happening after Dave's death that made a happy future a possibility for you."

"What? My happiness was hinged on Dave dying?" Zuma said, her stomach suddenly aching.

"Yes. I'm sure that's a hard piece of the history for you to digest."

"So that means..." And Zuma choked out a sharp painful tear and covered her face from the sudden shock. She rocked with three convulsions and dry tears burned her throat. Ian wrapped his thick arms around her. He pressed her to him and she pushed her face deeper into her hands and firm into his chest.

"Yes," he whispered just above her head. "That's right. Dave willingly put on the top hat knowing it would kill him. He allowed himself to be murdered so you could one day be happy."

Chapter Thirty-Seven

*F*or ten long minutes Ian comforted Zuma while she cried and shook and convulsed with confused tears. Finally she slid her hands out from in front of her face to show her reddened skin. Ian stepped back, feeling drained by how much he'd seen and felt in the girl, his divination stronger when he touched someone.

"Why?" she said through the tattered tears that had shredded her throat. "Why couldn't Dave find another way to bring the future of my happiness about? Why was him dying the only option?"

Ian nodded, having expected this question and having talked it over with Dave at length. "He couldn't risk it," he said. "Yes, he could go after Knight but he'd already tried that and he hadn't been successful. The man has been in hiding for all these years. Dave's death lured him out and made him exposed. Knight had to take over the circus."

"Dave died knowing Knight would come, paralyze Jack, and create havoc?" Zuma's head felt like it would explode from learning this strange history.

Ian nodded. "But Dave also knew that tragedies bring about great fortunes sometimes."

"That doesn't make sense," Zuma said.

"Did I ever tell you about the first vision I saw?" Ian asked.

"The girl at your synagogue. You held her hand and saw she was going to step off a curb, making a car swerve and go off the road," she said slowly as the story came back to her mind.

"Yes, and the driver would die," Ian said, finishing that part of the story for her.

"But she didn't because you told her."

"And the driver went home and murdered his wife," Ian said.

A chill ran over Zuma's shoulders. "So you messed with reality and a woman died?"

"That woman, I later found out, was the lead scientist at a private firm who was studying the cure for cancer," Ian said. "I interviewed her team a few years ago because I was trying to unravel how much I changed by telling that girl not to step into the road that day. They told me the woman who was murdered was the closest anyone has ever been to finding a cure for the disease. However, none of her notes made sense to them. That cure may have died with her."

"So her husband *was* supposed to die?" Zuma said.

"Yes, to bring about a better future. Dave knew this. He knew how the universe operates. Sometimes I can give information to assist, but intervening is usually a problem. Creates worse futures."

"Then why the other day did you tell the circus members that if they stayed then they could beat Knight? That was a lie," Zuma said.

Ian slid his large calloused hand through the loose curls on his head. "Because of you," he said in a heavy voice. "Your future keeps changing in my head."

"What?"

"Now it's gone back to you never being happy," Ian said. "You die without ever knowing that emotion. The curse is never lifted."

"But Dave died to bring about the other future," Zuma said, her voice shaking.

"Dave died for many reasons. He died because Jack being paralyzed was a better future for him. Knight taking over the circus was better for Titus. And Dave dying was better for your future. And although all those futures have stayed mostly static, yours has changed. You still aren't ever going to be happy. Something isn't right and I can't figure out what changed or what I need to do to get things to go back to the way I saw before. I did see a future where people left and that was the future before that meant you didn't get your happiness. So I told everyone to stay to see if I could change things."

"And?" Zuma asked, her nerves making her breathless.

"No change yet," he said. "I'm sorry."

"Ian..."

"I know," he said, reading the look of concern on her face.

"You're playing with futures...for me. That can't be safe."

"It isn't. It's a huge risk, but I have to," Ian said. "Right now the future I see isn't just bleak for you. It's bleak for so many others. Everything's gotten worse. Dave died for this and I have to make it work out."

"But you said that Dave dying was going to help Titus and Jack and others," Zuma said.

"It does, but not like it did before. I think everything shifted based on your future. The key to their extremely good fortune is centered on yours. If you get to be happy, then everyone also gets a truly happy ending."

Zuma threaded her hands into her hair and clenched her fingers shut, pulling at her roots. "This is so complicated."

Ian nodded with a heavy sigh.

"So what are you going to do now?" she asked.

"Something I have only done twice. I'm going to tell someone really important to your future how they die. Maybe if they avoid it then things will shift again."

"Is that really possible? To avoid death?" Zuma said.

He shrugged his large shoulders, burdened by the potential futures playing in his head. "I don't know. Avoiding death could also bring it about. That's what I've always thought. I've never tried anything quite like this."

"So if this works then I'll get my future where I'm happy? And everyone will be happy? And Vagabond Circus will be saved?" Zuma asked each question faster than the previous.

"Yes, but I'm not answering your next question. You can't know who it is that I'm going to save. I've told you enough."

Zuma closed her heavy eyelids and took a breath. *Who was the person that her happiness was hinged on?* Before, it had been Dave's death that brought her happiness. And now it was the saving of another person that created a positive future for her.

Chapter Thirty-Eight

The knock on Zuma's door caused her to jump, making the book hiccup in her hands. Her startled eyes skipped to the clock on the wall. Eight o'clock at night. She sat frozen staring at the door, wishing her super power was that she could see through walls. Was Sebastian on the other side of the door, trying to tempt her to open it so he could "tag" her? During the day she constantly turned to find him stalking her. And then in the distance behind him Zuma often saw Finley, a protective look on his face.

Again the knock.

"I see your light on," Jasmine's voice rang through the door. "And I totally just peeped through the crack in your drapes and saw you sitting on the couch. Open up already."

Zuma sighed with relief before getting up and answering the door. "You realize that makes you a freak, don't you? Peeping at me," she said to her friend upon opening the door.

"Do I look like the type Sunshine would induct into her group?" Jasmine said with a wide smile. Her large white teeth shone in the dark and in contrast to her light brown skin.

"Get your ass in here," Zuma said, reaching for her friend's hand and pulling her into the trailer before glancing around the dark circus grounds. Her eyes caught him two trailers over, propped against a tree. Sebastian, as she feared, was stationed outside her trailer just waiting for her to slip up and exit it at night.

"Well, that settles it," Zuma said, slamming the door and throwing her back against it. Her blood thundered suddenly in her head just from seeing the figure lurking in the dark. The cut of his hair gave him away, shoulder length and longer in the front.

"Settles what?" Jasmine said, plopping down on the couch along with half a dozen wedding magazines she'd been carrying.

"You're sleeping here tonight," Zuma said.

Jasmine arched an eyebrow and gave Zuma a flirtatious look. "Is this your way of telling me my greatest dream has come true and you're actually gay?"

Zuma shook her head, unable to even laugh at her friend. "No, Sebastian is out there. You're not safe traveling back to your trailer."

"You do remember that I can break his spine with the tiniest of efforts?"

"Doesn't matter," Zuma said, moving away from the door. Again she wasn't laughing at Jasmine's light manner. "Sebastian has the advantage over you."

"I have the strength of ten men and you think that scrawny boy could best me?" she said with a laugh.

"Yes, it's his gift," Zuma said.

"Gift? I didn't know he'd gotten one," Jasmine said.

"He has and Sebastian isn't as young as he led us to believe. He's fifteen."

"Wait? What? The kid looks twelve, for sure."

"I know, but he only pretended."

"Wait, Z, you aren't making sense. Why would he pretend to be younger?"

"So he could stay with Fanny undetected and hide his ability," Zuma said.

"You mean when he was here, before he was transferred to Knight's school?"

"Exactly," Zuma said, taking a seat on the sofa beside her friend.

"So what's this gift he's hiding?"

Zuma looked at Jasmine sideways. Titus had told her to keep what she knew a secret so the circus members could focus and didn't revolt early; however, she was tired of keeping one of her best friends in the dark. "Jaz, he can kill through touch. It's something about the oils in his skin."

"Wait, that's his gift? That sounds like a curse," Jasmine said, almost laughing.

"Not to someone who wants to use it for their own evil purposes."

Jasmine blinked at her friend. "When you were gone, did you bump your head, like really hard?"

Zuma shook her head and grabbed Jasmine's hand. "No, and I have so much to tell you about where I've been and why."

Just then Zuma heard a clawing sound on her trailer wall. She looked up and through that crack in the drapes Jasmine had peeped through, Zuma saw one green eye staring at her, inches from her window. She jumped as a scream shot out of her.

Jasmine turned around but the sliver of Sebastian's appearance disappeared.

"What?" Jasmine said, looking at the window and then Zuma.

"Sebastian was there," she said in a whisper. "Looking through the crack."

"Why would he do that?" Jasmine said.

"Because he threatened me the other day. Told me that if he caught me at night then he'd touch my skin, which would kill me."

"No way," Jasmine said, sitting back on the couch. "Come on, Z, please be real with me."

"Jaz, do you remember when you recently passed out from a mysterious virus and almost died? You remember that Fanny brought you back, but only barely? It was after you intercepted a note for Dave. Remember that?"

"Yeah," she said, her mind trailing back to the recent memory.

"That was Sebastian's doing," Zuma said.

"Wait, what?" Jasmine said, anger flaring on her face suddenly. "That shithead was trying to murder me?"

"No, not you…"

"Well, then who?"

"Do you remember who the letter was for?" Zuma said.

"Z, you're telling me Sebastian was trying to murder Dave?"

"Not trying. He did," the girl said in a haunted whisper.

***

"You do realize that this makes you sound crazy? Knight is a slave owner? Created Finley? Trained him to steal? Uses kids? Paralyzed Jack? Killed Dave?" Jasmine said, ticking off each of the revolting ideas on a long finger.

"But it all fits, doesn't it?" Zuma had told Jasmine everything, except about the curse on her. She wasn't ready to talk about that with anyone. She hadn't come to terms with everything Ian had told her. About Dave. About what he sacrificed. About the person who wouldn't die and their life would somehow save Zuma's. Maybe…according to Ian.

"No, it actually makes perfect sense and explains all of my concerns," Jasmine said, her eyes looking, but not seeing. "I actually wanted to discuss Knight with you but was thinking I was insane for having suspicions."

Zuma's head flipped up at once. "What suspicions do you have?"

"Well, it's just me being sensitive after Dave's death so I'm trying not to read too much into it," Jasmine said.

"What?" Zuma asked, not liking how serious Jasmine, who was never serious, was acting.

"Knight pulled me aside today while you and Finley were practicing. I looked right at him and again he warned me to never do that."

"Yeah, you know you're not supposed to do that."

Jasmine gave her a frustrated look. "And you know that I don't like being told what do. I might have told him that."

"And then you got a headache, right?" Zuma said, hardly a question in her voice.

"Yeah, how did you guess?"

"It's one of Knight's gifts," Zuma said, remembering the stabbing sensation in her head she'd gotten after meeting Knight.

"Killing by touch. Ability to produce headaches. These aren't gifts."

"I know."

"Zuma..." Jasmine said, her voice careful.

"Yes," Zuma said, looking at her, sensing the dread in her friend.

"My ears were ringing from the headache and I could hardly hold my head up. I thought I was going to crumble to the ground," Jasmine said.

"I know. I've been there. It's horrible."

"Thing is that I could have sworn I heard Knight say that he wasn't sure if he liked the idea of having someone as strong as me around."

Zuma's breath skipped in her throat. "Oh no."

"Yeah, I told you I had suspicions. Before I thought that meant he was cutting me from the act, but now..."

"You've got to be careful, Jaz. Keep your distance from Knight."

"Are you kidding me? I just found out he's responsible for Dave's death. I'm going to kill that man. I'm going to snap his neck with a tiny flick of my wrist."

Zuma jumped to sitting on her knees. "No, Jaz, you can't even try. Knight will have his guards. Or he'll disable you with a headache."

Jasmine shook her head, a stubborn expression on her face. "We were alone today. I sensed he fears me. And I told him off for telling me that I couldn't look at him. Told him I would never be marginalized by a man. And I realize now he's intimidated by me. He should be too. I'm going to sneak up on him during a practice and take him out. This has gone on too long. Titus is too much of a coward and there's nothing anyone else can do. You're right, the man is crafty and well protected but an opportunity will present itself and then he'll be gone and we will be free."

Zuma sat back, throwing her head into the cushions. If Jasmine was quick, which was an acrobat's specialty, then she could take him out with little effort. Zuma's mind inflated with the excitement that her friend could take out Knight thereby making all their problems disappear. "Okay, but be careful and don't even attempt it if Gwendolyn is around."

Jasmine nodded, a burning anger on her face. She then stood and walked for the door.

"What are you doing?" Zuma said, suddenly panicked.

"Well, I came to plan the wedding but since you've informed me that's a scam then there's no need. I'm going to go run a few laps. I need to burn off some of this revolting anger."

"No, you can't. Sebastian could still be out there," Zuma said, considering plastering herself in front of the exit.

"We've been talking for hours. There's no way that prick stuck around. And I'm much faster than him."

"Jaz, I don't like the idea."

"Z." Jasmine came back and grabbed her friend's hand. "We've been through a lot, but everything's going to be fine. If my daddies taught me anything it is that you don't hide when there's a threat. You fight. You stand up to the bully. You bring them down with your pure unyielding spirit. And you *never* allow them to hold you down."

Zuma smiled a little at Jasmine. How had she kept any of this from her? Now that Jasmine knew the truth Zuma felt the first bit of hope. "You're right," she said.

"Girl, of course I'm right." She winked at Zuma before leaving. "Catch you tomorrow," she said and then laughed at her own pun, since she was the new catcher in the flying trapeze act.

Chapter Thirty-Nine

The next day, morning light illuminated the big top, the dew on the roofs of the trailers and Jasmine's lean body. The acrobat was laid out in the yard between Zuma's and her trailer. It appeared the virus she'd contracted the week prior had finally taken her out. She was dead.

Chapter Forty

Sacramento Bee

Vagabond Circus Suffers Another Tragedy

Vagabond Circus, which has had many changes and tragedies this year, has yet another to add to the list. This month the star of the circus, Jack Fuller, fell during rehearsal causing him to be paralyzed. Now another tragedy has befallen an acrobat. Jasmine Reynolds-Underwood suffered from cardiac arrest yesterday, Titus Rogers, the creative director, reported. She had apparently contracted a virus and it appears to have not been cured. Complications due to the untreated mystery virus caused the young girl's heart to go into cardiac arrest and she was found too late. The nineteen-year-old performer was a beloved star of the circus and will be missed. Her parents, Joseph Underwood and Trent Reynolds, are extremely grieved by the loss of their only daughter. Vagabond Circus, which has brought love and happiness to so many, appears to be having a tragic year. We send our prayers and condolences to the members of Vagabond Circus who definitely have a long road of healing in front of them.

PART II

Chapter Forty-One

$\mathcal{B}$y the time Vagabond Circus reached Santa Barbara, winter had transformed everything brown. Knight had transformed a once happy circus into a dysfunctional conglomeration of lost souls. It only took three months for him to steal the fire out of the eyes of Fanny's young girls, Emily and Tiffany. Ninety days was more than enough time for him to turn the rig crew against one another. The once happy staff fought so often that they were always behind schedule, which meant their wages were constantly docked. Injuries were up. Crime among Vagabond Circus members was an actual phenomenon. Morale was at a record low. And yet no one had abandoned the circus. The show still received reviews complimenting it on delivering a thrilling performance. However, fewer children and non-believers were in the crowd. It was mostly full of teens looking to be spooked or rebels who dared to sit in the front row. However, by the end of the show the front was usually abandoned. Most patrons left after being singed or were scared so much by the idea of being attacked by a lion that they knocked out the row behind them trying to get away. The circus, once reminiscent of a midsummer night's dream, was now a nightmare sought out by those looking for a year-round haunted house experience.

Zuma hadn't given up on the circus. She didn't abandon it after Jasmine's death. The girl of stone simply nodded when the news was told to her. Zuma had been practicing with Finley when she'd been interrupted and then those three words matter-of-factly spoken to her.

"Jasmine is dead."

Inside Zuma, she screamed. Something felt as though it sliced through her chest, making it impossible to breathe. Her mind shook with torturous grief. However, on the outside Zuma was unchanged. A true girl of stone. She then held her chin up and commenced her routine, practicing with Finley. For a brief second, Finley's appearance gave something away. It told her he was sorry. The sharp angles of his face softened and his expression seemed to say, "you're lying to pretend you don't care." But what could she do? The news had been delivered by Knight himself, Sebastian standing at his back. If she cried or showed any emotion at all then she'd give them both what they wanted. Her pain. Her remorse. She'd show them that they'd won. Instead she bolted her emotions in a storm shelter, away from her grief which had the power of a hurricane. Then Zuma looked down at the ground, her words directed to Knight. "Finley and I will get the changes made pronto to replace Jaz," she said, her voice cold and removed from her body.

From her peripheral she spied the twitch on Knight's face. He hadn't gotten the response he'd wanted. The ringmaster hadn't gotten a response at all to this devastating news. That was unacceptable.

"There is a memorial service," Knight said, drawing out the last two words, almost singing them. "But I can't permit you to go, since you have much work to do replacing Jasmine."

Inside Zuma's inner child was throwing a fit. A pure tantrum where each tear brought a torrent of more uncontrollable tears. Ones that made it hard to breathe. That burn. Inside she was hyperventilating. On the outside she was a marble statue of poise. "I don't want to go," Zuma said, her words quiet, dead.

"It's being held here on the grounds. Should only be a short service, since I think that best. And still it is better for you to devote your time to practice," Knight said.

And Zuma felt too acutely what he was doing. Knight had worked for this moment and didn't like to be deprived of the pain he caused. He'd had Jasmine murdered and he knew Zuma knew that. She was supposed to cry. To scream. To convict him and Sebastian of a crime she couldn't prove. And then he would punish her. But now Zuma's worst-case scenario had somehow gotten even worse. This didn't weaken the girl. It hollowed her out and made her more motivated than ever. She wouldn't be defeated.

"I understand," she said, and then turned her cold, flat expression on Finley. "That means we should get to work right away."

He nodded, his expression also trained into something emotionless.

Finley wouldn't comfort Zuma. There would be no talk about Jasmine. Not a single look would be exchanged that spoke of the great sadness this loss meant for the two acrobats. They were soldiers. And that's how Zuma stayed at Vagabond Circus. A quiet, calculating soldier.

For the three long months after Jasmine's death, Zuma kept her head down, her words full of compliance. Ian had promised Zuma that he was tweaking the future and she must only hold on for a solution. She knew they needed a way to fight because resisting Knight was a death wish. Many at the circus had tried it, had simply disagreed with the ringmaster. It never turned out well for them. Over the last ninety days pain killers had become a desperately sought after commodity. Headaches beset the Vagabond Circus members and spread like lice in a nursery school.

Zuma had been fortunate not to have too many headaches; only when on a rare occasion Knight caught her eyes on him. Her combat sense could teach her so much about the man, but not when she wasn't permitted to study him. After being caught several times she trained herself not to look at the impossibly tall man. Zuma forced herself to practice. To keep to herself. To telepathically encourage Titus. To keep things with Finley brief.

The acrobats worked together, both restrained by their marionette strings. They spoke in a script. Looked at each other with mostly sideway glances. Zuma had figured out how to survive when most people at Vagabond Circus were withering away, physically and mentally. But it was easier for Zuma. She'd never known happiness. Zuma was different from the others who had experienced joy from being a part of the magic of the big top. Those who have yet to taste the sweetness of life can endure its bitter moments much longer.

Chapter Forty-Two

Charles Knight was not a man who gave up anything easily. Not grudges. Not possessions. And not people. However, he had to finally admit that it was getting too difficult to maintain control of his kids with the circus all around them. When they traveled, patrons asked questions about the strange kids they saw, the ones the surrogates failed to hide in the semis fast enough. And the same kids, who had been easy to manage inside the compound, were now adorning shifty expressions. They saw what freedom looked like when observing the Vagabond Circus members. They smelled popcorn. They realized there was a life they could have and they were hungry for it. Knight's kids, who he knew would one day help him to get Vagabond Circus, were now a liability. They had served their purpose though. They had stolen enough that he was worth millions, and three prodigies had come up through their ranks. Finley, Sebastian, and Gwendolyn. The rest weren't necessary anymore.

"You know what to do?" Knight said to a man he'd almost come to like.

Riley nodded. "Yes, Master." This man, a bum, had been digging through a dumpster behind the compound when Knight first took possession of the property. Knight already had the plan to breed an army of thieves, but he knew he'd have to find the right people to assist him. Riley was a Middling and had a desperate look in his eyes. Knight loved that look. That's how he found all his supervisors and surrogates. He sought out those who were destitute and in need of saving. The bum was thin then, with a head full of black, dirty hair, but now he had muscle and his shaved head had wrinkles in the back and extra folds of skin. Since Riley was a Middling, Knight knew he would do him no good in building his army since he needed Dream Traveler sperm. However, the homeless man was perfect for keeping the kids in line and supervising them on jobs. To ensure Riley's compliance, Knight gave him room and board and manipulated him with his words, alternating between being nice and then cruel. Knight also opened a bank account for the man and deposited funds every year; however, he never granted him access to it.

"I told you the day would come when I gave you everything you wanted if you followed my orders. You've served me well." Knight then handed Riley an envelope with all the information regarding his untouched bank account which now held eighteen thousand dollars. A thousand dollars a year for each one he served Knight. It wasn't a livable wage, but the people who served Knight didn't know any better. "Here, you've earned this," Knight said. "Now finish your last job for me and then you can sell the truck or keep it. Your call."

"So kind, Master. Thank you for saving me," Riley said, his eyes to the side.

Knight didn't respond. He just roamed his gaze over the closed up semi where the sounds of kids shuffling emanated. He wouldn't say goodbye to them. Knight had brought all of them into this world using surrogates, and trained them, and yet he felt no attachment to the kids. He was ready to move on.

"Be sure to drop them off one at a time, one hundred miles apart. And warn each one not to talk or we *will* hunt them down," Knight said.

"They're getting what they think they want, the ungrateful little bastards," Riley said with a sneer, several of his gold teeth showing. "They won't talk. They all think they want to be free, but soon they'll learn how hard it is without you to take care of them, Master."

"I suspect you're right," Knight said.

"I'll be on my way then," Riley said, a fond look in his one good eye. And then he climbed in his truck to finish his last job. He was about to give the kids crammed in the semi the same fate as he had before Knight found him. He was about to make them all homeless.

Knight watched the truck pull away. All the kids were packed in that one vehicle. The other two semis were empty now and living quarters for Gwendolyn, and Sebastian. Before they had been living with the other kids. But now the two had their own places, a real treat for them and a testament to their rank. Gwendolyn and Sebastian were test tube babies as well, but Knight felt almost an affection for those two. Actually the only one who wasn't born from a test tube was the one kid Knight admired the most, and the one who he suspected despised him the most.

Chapter Forty-Three

"*U*nbelievable," Dr. Chang said on the other side of the phone.

"Is it?" Fanny said, trying to keep the smile out of her voice. "Why is that?"

"Bones mending after the kinds of breaks Jack endured takes several months. I expected him not to be ready to start physical therapy for a good while longer," he said.

"Well, there you go, our expectations were different," Fanny said into the mobile she had pressed to her cheek.

"What were your expectations?" the doctor asked.

"That I'd be amazed by something miraculous," Fanny said, her Louisiana accent bringing more conviction to her words.

"Is that what makes you such a successful nurse? Is it because you bring a bit of faith to the art of medicine?"

"I think I'd like you if we ever met, Doctor," she said. "Few doctors would refer to what we do as an art. And yes, I do rely on my faith. I dare say it was God who bestowed my talents on me." Fanny thought fondly of the warmth she felt tingle from her fingertips when she used her gift of healing.

"So Jack's bones appear to have healed in all the places where major breakage occurred?" Dr. Chang asked.

"Yes, we had X-rays done here in Santa Barbara. Now what we are hoping to see is regeneration of the bone loss in places."

"That's what he'll need if those bones of the legs are going to be able to support him for standing and maybe walking," Dr. Chang said.

"I have every hope they will be strong enough one day to do more than just that," Fanny said.

"More?"

"Jack is an acrobat. He's anxious to get back on trapeze."

"Nurse Fanny," Dr. Chang said and she spied the disapproval in his tone. "I support your methods and mind set but I hope you aren't giving Jack the false impression he will have that sort of mobility in the future. We are being hopeful to believe he will walk."

"Again you and I are divided by our expectations," Fanny said, sounding almost amused.

"It's simply that I'm applying logic and experience to the expectations I have set."

"And I'm simply not restricting outcomes. Why should history dictate Jack's result?" Fanny said, knowing this was the opposite thought of most conventional doctors.

There was an exasperated sigh on the other side of the line.

"Look, Doctor," Fanny continued. "You asked me to keep you in the loop on Jack's recovery and I'm happy to do that. Now that we enter the physical therapy portion of his healing I ask that since your consciousness impacts his future that you have positive expectations, whatever they might be. I won't dictate what you believe will occur and you shouldn't dictate that for me."

"Very well. I must say your methods, whatever they involve, are incredibly successful. I wish you'd consider coming out of retirement. I would be happy to employ you in my private practice," Dr. Chang said, hope in his tone.

"Thank you, but my place is here, with my family. My days of treating the public are over."

There was a pause that Fanny felt reeked of Dr. Chang's hidden disappointment. "Well, then I must ask you, your methods were always considered mysterious. There was hardly any documentation on how you treated most of your cases that were considered terminal and yet made full recovery. Nurse Fanny, would you do me the honor of sharing with me how you do it? How are you so brilliant with your care?"

Fanny smiled, although no one could see it since she was alone in her room. "Magic, Dr. Chang. What I do is done by magic."

Chapter Forty-Four

"*W*hat you believe is what you experience." Jack heard Fanny's words echo in his head. She'd repeatedly said that statement to him over the last three months.

Jack had weaned himself off the pain meds pretty early on in his recovery, knowing they were preventing him from dream traveling. One must be totally lucid in order to instruct their consciousness to travel to a specific location and time. Jack had been incredibly excited to dream travel. However, Fanny had told him he had to wait until a month after the accident since his body needed the nourishing power of good old-fashioned sleep.

It is important to note that most things behave similarly in the dream travel realm as they do in the physical world, although laws can be flexed. Just as in dreams the imagination makes many things possible. The day the drugs wore off and the very same hour that Fanny gave Jack a thumbs-up to dream travel, he closed his eyes with the intention to "escape." To escape his imprisonment from inside the tiny trailer, with children who were never quiet. And to escape his legs, which imprisoned him in a bed that always smelled of sweat and dead skin. The acrobat *almost* believed when his consciousness landed on Division Street in Nashville, Tennessee, that he'd be standing on his legs, able to walk on them. However, he found himself lying on the pavement, his legs stretched motionless before him. There was a brief moment where Jack wanted to cry from the unfairness of it all. It was only his consciousness, not his physical body, in Nashville, so he should be able to walk. *Hell, he should be able to fly if he wanted,* he thought. And although the things that happen in dream travel really affected the physical body, the physical body wasn't as much impacted in the dream travel form. At least that's what Jack thought from years of practicing stunts in the dream travel realm. It was always easier to practice in that realm, muscles not hampered by soreness or the stress of the day.

After that first failed dream travel Jack returned to his body and called for Fanny. She gave him a knowing look when he explained what he'd experienced.

"How was I just lying on the sidewalk?" he said, his hand in his hair, which she'd just washed that morning.

She clapped a warm hand on his. "Because you believe you're paralyzed. Your body, whether in the physical or dream travel realm, acts based on your expectations. If you don't expect your legs to function properly right here and now then they aren't going to allow you to walk around in your dreams. You are always confined or enlivened by your beliefs."

"So I can't walk in my dreams as long as I can't walk in my waking life?"

"Try it the other way around," Fanny had said. "You can't walk on the physical earth until you can make your mind believe it can do it in your dreams. Healing is less about mending bones and ligaments and more about changing thoughts that inhibit."

Since that conversation months prior with Fanny, Jack hadn't dared to dream travel. Instead he meditated like never before, really exploring all his limiting thoughts and changing them once discovered. It hadn't been easy to clean all the negative thoughts from his mind. This was because his first few attempts to merely stand were met with defeat. Fanny was strong but it had been difficult for her to maintain his weight when his legs refused to bear it. Walkers and devices had been brought in, filling Fanny's trailer so it was hard for others to negotiate the space with their perfectly healthy legs. Jack looked at the devices and bitterly remembered his attempts to stand. How could he replace the idea that he couldn't walk with the one that he could when there so many reminders of the accident that changed him?

Two more months passed before he looked at the walker and said to himself, "I don't really need that." Soon his physical therapy would begin and he was expected to spend several hours a day building the muscles that had atrophied along with the skill that he once had to walk. He was a baby gearing up to take his first step. And although the X-rays reported he was finally ready to start physical therapy, Fanny refused to allow him. The healer had said he couldn't begin therapy until he achieved one important goal: walking in dream travel form.

Jack pressed his eyes closed and focused his attention on the location. He hadn't dream traveled in months, not since Nashville. He'd used all usual dream travel sessions to meditate. Like the last time he dream traveled Jack landed in a lying position on the grass of the stadium of Olympia. He was resting on the site of the first Olympics in Olympia, Greece. It was a location he and Zuma and Jasmine had practiced in many times. It had been Dave's idea. "To be an athlete you must practice in the place where the greatest people made inspirations we still follow to this day. To be great, practice where the great practiced." The memory of Dave's words and the experience of Jasmine in that place tightened Jack's heart. He wasn't going to be another victim. Knight's abuse had to stop. He would no longer be walked upon.

Jack looked not at his outstretched legs but rather at the heavens. "Dave, you believed in me in a way I couldn't understand before, but now I get it. I am like the gods the athletes first competed for. I'm great! I'm powerful. I can do anything," he said aloud to the sky. Then Jack pressed his hands behind him into the sandy ground. He pushed up, pushing his legs underneath him the way he practiced with Fanny. She had him do this from the floor, knowing he had to get up before he could move forward, both in a literal and metaphorical sense.

Jack took a breath and felt his knees bend. That had always been the easy part. It wasn't the movement of the legs, but rather their structure that had prevented them from supporting Jack's weight. That was not the thought Jack had in that moment. He wasn't thinking of the past. Jack's thoughts were firmly hinged on a reality that hadn't come to pass yet. One that he saw clearly.

"This is possible. This is easy," he said through gritted teeth. His foot slipped under his weight, making his rear end fall back on the earth. He drew in a heavy motivated breath.

"I can do this." And again Jack saw himself doing it. Saw in his mind his legs easily negotiating under him until he stood. Jack pressed his eyes shut, pressing the visual firmer into his cortex. His hands ached beside him from the exertion of putting so much of his weight under them. He pulled his feet in close and decided to make a fast attempt. *Not an attempt,* he corrected himself. *I will stand. I can.*

And then his feet bore more weight than he'd managed since the accident. He pressed his hands under him until he felt steady on his legs and pushed up to a standing position. Jack wanted to look down at the legs under him that held him up, but he knew that would reek of his astonishment. Instead, he looked out at the stadium where athletes performed great feats for the gods. Competed, showing their incredible speed and agility.

"I can walk. Nothing is stopping me," Jack said and like a bolt falling into place, opening a door, a new pathway fully opened inside his mind. A new neural network had been paved and it operated with a clear flow, electrifying the potentials that had died before. Jack's foot rose only an inch, but it was all he had intended. He brought it forward another inch and set it down. Again he didn't act surprised by this reality within the dream travel realm. Instead he said to himself, *Just as I suspected, I can walk.* But a smile did join that thought.

The next movement was bolder; his other foot rose higher, reaching further. And it was followed by another step, not graceful, but a step nonetheless. And then Jack was walking in his dreams, not because his muscles could physically support him. That would take much effort in the physical world. Jack was walking in his dreams because he believed without a single doubt that it was possible. He looked out at the grounds. Clamped his feet together as he had done so many times before in practice. And then in a firm standing position he made himself levitate off the ground until he was five feet in the air. Jack also hadn't been able to use his dream travel gift because he was so scarred by the pain of not walking, but now the acrobat hovered off the ground, higher than he usually dared to rise from the earth. He then lifted his arms out and spun like a ballerina on top of a music box, all grace and control. Then the acrobat raised his eyes to the sky. "For you, Jasmine. For you, Dave. For me. I won't give up. I am a god," he said with pure conviction. No longer a victim to pity, Jack felt something he had never known. He felt his own worth. He finally felt equal to the greatest of beings. No longer did he think of himself as "less than" in comparison to his brothers. He was Jack Fuller, the guy who would walk again.

Chapter Forty-Five

Titus's head lay cradled in his hands when Fanny entered his office tent. This was now known as the "Titus is frustrated" stance, and his back and neck ached from constantly taking the position.

"You know I've never told you how to do your job, Titus," Fanny said, a look of disapproval written on her usually accepting face.

"Does this mean you're about to start?" he said, his voice muffled due to his mouth being obstructed by his hands.

"Really, how much more are you going to wallow in this self-pity? You bucked up when Knight first showed up. I even thought you might make a stand, but now you're looking incredibly defeated," Fanny said, the drawl of her words lengthening due to her emotion.

Titus slowly brought his head up, his eyes carrying a sobering expression. "He killed Jasmine." The *he* didn't have to be detailed. They both knew Sebastian did it, under Knight's orders. "I can't even protect my circus members. Ian says we can't give up. That we defeat him by staying, but how many more are going to die first?"

"I know," Fanny said, fretting her hands in the tail of her button up shirt. "It was a senseless death."

"And I can't prove a thing. All I have is Zuma's testimony that Knight made a threat and she saw Sebastian outside her trailer that night," Titus said.

"But you can't release that without putting Zuma in jeopardy," Fanny said. They'd been through this dozens of times over the last few months, never finding a solution.

"I know!" Titus said too loud and then grabbed the back of his neck which spasmed. "Ouch," he said with a grimace.

"Oh, look at what you're doing to yourself," Fanny said, stalking around the table dividing them. "Let me work on that for you." The healer didn't ask permission before laying her hands on Titus's long neck. He instantly let out a groan of relief.

"There's so much abuse that the circus is having to endure. And he's so good at his manipulation that I can't prove anything. I even called the authorities about Knight's kids," Titus said, rolling his head around as Fanny massaged him from behind.

Fanny's hands paused on Titus's neck. "You did what?"

"I thought I could prove he'd kidnapped or enslaved them."

"What happened?"

"The sheriff couldn't find anything. The semis are all suitable living quarters now," Titus said.

"Where did those kids go?" Fanny asked, bemused.

"I don't know. They just disappeared one day."

Fanny shook her head before pressing her hands into Titus's neck, massaging away the tension with the pressure and her healing ability. "Oh, I tried to help those kids. To get close to them, but the supervisors and surrogates kept them well-guarded."

"Well, they're all gone now," Titus said, blowing out a long breath, like the tension released from his neck was torture to let go of. "Only Knight, Sebastian, and Gwendolyn remain. And they keep creating problems I can't fix. And the circus is doing well. Bringing in enough profits to flourish and yet the show we put on doesn't promote the message Dave wanted."

"No, it doesn't."

Titus tilted his neck to the side, allowing Fanny to work deeper into the muscles, his eyes closed. "If you want to start telling me how to do my job, then go ahead."

"Titus, we have to outmaneuver Knight and the only way to do that is to actually get one step ahead of him."

"How do I do that?"

"You start by facing these fears. By summoning the strength I know resides in you," Fanny said, her usually sweet words demanding.

Titus reached up and laid his hand over Fanny's, making her pause. "Thank you for believing in me. I don't know where I'd be without you."

She looked down from her position standing behind Titus and smiled affectionately. "Well, I can believe in you all day long, but that does you no good if you don't also believe in yourself."

Titus released her hand and swiveled the chair around so he was facing Fanny. She took a step back so they weren't so close. "I'm working on it, Fanny. I'm not deserting the circus. I promise."

"Good."

"So I summon the strength to bring Knight down and then what?"

"We make a plan," Fanny said plainly, like it was as easy as making a grocery list. "One where we systematically take him down."

Titus sputtered out a long breath. "I'm a bit at a loss for what that will look like."

"Well, I might be able to help with that."

Titus, who had averted his eyes, looked up at Fanny. "Oh really? Do tell."

She shook her head of soft graying curls. "It's better if I wait. Ian's given me instructions on the most effective way to disperse this information."

"Fanny, you're going to start keeping secrets from me?" Titus said, looking hurt.

"I'm sorry to say, but I've been keeping this particular secret from you for a long time. Soon though, I'll make things right by telling it," Fanny said.

"I hope you do. I hope Ian is setting this up right," Titus said, stretching his back and neck.

Fanny's face fell with worry; it didn't look right on her, like an angel crying. "Oh, me too. Everyone's life is in that crew member's hands."

Chapter Forty-Six

*P*admal narrowed her eyes toward the top of her foot before slipping a sock on it. The two-inch-long scar made her pulse with anger for the man who did it to her. The fibrous scar tissue was waxy in places and too thick in other places. Fanny had said healing the knife wound evenly was too tricky since the sharp knife struck through Padmal's shoe. The speed and assault of the knife had forced the soft fabric of the sneaker into the wound, widening it. And Padmal was certain Nabhi only made the wound worse when he pulled the knife from her foot, although Fanny said that there was no right way to do it in that scenario. Now the girl was never going to be able to wear sandals without seeing the gross remains of her encounter with Knight.

Padmal had thought she was going to come to respect Knight, but this just proved that there were no good men in the world. Even Oliver, who had once made her heart flutter at times, had lost favor with her. During the three weeks she'd been laid up in her bed, unable to walk properly, he hadn't visited often enough for her liking. Only once every few days. He had used the excuse that reworking the circus to replace Jasmine had been taxing on him. And that he also had to replace Padmal in his magician act, which meant Sunshine was his new lovely assistant who he made disappear and reappear multiple times in multiple places inside the ring. Padmal didn't like the idea that Sunshine was spending so much time with *her* Oliver. She saw the way the girl watched him. And on every occasion he visited he had little to say, always making the excuse that Jasmine's death and all the negative events at the circus were weighing on him.

"She was a stupid acrobat," Padmal had said to him one time.

"We are a circus family and she was a part of it," he said, his strange eyes not on her.

"We aren't a family," she said through clenched teeth. "And why should you care about the Afro?"

"A girl died, Padmal. Mysteriously. Doesn't that bother you?"

"She was sick," Padmal said, disinterested.

"It still doesn't feel right," Oliver said, shaking his head at her.

"Look at me," she ordered and he complied, pulling his heavy eyes to stare at her lying in her bed. She glared at his eyes, one green and the other brown. "Leave the circus with me. Let's run away."

He narrowed his gaze at her. "I can't. The people here need me. I can't believe you'd abandon them after everything they've been through."

"My brothers seem to have no problem replacing me in the act so why should I care?" she said angrily.

"Padmal, they *had* to. You're on bed rest until you're healed. Do you think they want to do a two-person juggling act when the crowd expects three people?"

"Get out," she said, pointing to the door. "As long as you're going to make excuses for other people I don't want to speak to you."

Oliver shook his head at her and turned to leave, not even caring to argue.

He had only been gone for a few minutes when Sebastian showed up. Padmal had startled at the sight of the kid.

"What are you doing here?" she said with a sneer, remembering he'd stood by watching when Knight maimed her by having Gwendolyn take her powers. Before that moment no one knew that was her power. Now everyone kept a distance from the redhead.

"I just came to check on you to see how you were doing," Sebastian said, pinning his straight black hair behind one of his Dumbo ears.

"Why do you care how I'm doing?"

He shrugged, his eyes on her foot. "Can I see your wound?"

"What? Why?"

"I wanted to see if it was healing all right." He dropped his eyes with a rehearsed look. "I was worried about you when you were stabbed," Sebastian lied.

"Yeah, you had a funny way to show it."

"So can I see your foot?" he said, bringing his eyes up to meet hers. There was a piercing quality in the way he looked at her, something dangerous. Padmal instantly realized she liked it. Liked the adrenaline that shot through her, telling her he was a bad boy not to be messed with.

136

"Sure," she said, leaning forward and pulling the tape from the bandage back to show a red gash sutured with black thread. It was black and blue in places and swollen around the stitches.

Sebastian leaned forward, his eyes lighting up when they connected with the wound. He looked at Padmal and tilted his head to the side. "That must have hurt a lot," he said, a tiny ounce of delight in his voice.

"It did," she said, almost shivering from the way he looked at her.

"Well, I hope you heal fast," he said and then licked his thin lips and turned and left without a goodbye.

Padmal slipped the bandage back into place, feeling goose bumps from her encounter with Sebastian. She was mistaking the crawling sensation on her skin for attraction and she was also mistaking his check-up on her as kindness. The truth was, on the long list of demented things about Sebastian, he had an obsession with looking at fresh wounds.

Chapter Forty-Seven

The Pacific Ocean had always been just a few miles from Finley's back, and yet he'd never had a real opportunity to study the magnificent body of water. A rare chance had presented itself to Finley and he stole it for himself, indulging in selfishness for the first time ever. He had one solid hour where he wasn't required to practice with Zuma or run an "errand" for Knight or to serve his own needs. Finley's long legs carried him farther and farther, a distance that most would consider driving, and then he found himself face to face with the navy blue waters of the Pacific Ocean. The clouds in Santa Barbara were low on that winter's afternoon, reflecting back the water's dark blue appearance.

Finley kicked off his shoes once the pavement ended and the sand began. His feet sunk down two inches, the granules of soft earth bathing his skin in a cool warmth. He almost smiled at the feeling. To feel cool and warm at the same time. To feel smothered and also comforted. To feel planted firmly to the earth and also like he was sinking. And then Finley realized something and it made him stare down at his feet with a strange reverence. *He'd never had his feet in the sand.* Ever. He hadn't been given the type of life where one indulges in weekend trips to the beach or pops over for a picnic. Finley was born a slave and had lived that life, without the experiences that so many people took for granted. His evenings had been spent lying on the pad in his cell, watching other children cry themselves to sleep. He had spent his free time doing strength training. And that time had been rare since Knight monopolized most of his time with teaching him everything he now knew.

The acrobat walked until the tide was only a few feet away. Finley considered going to the edge and allowing the ocean to lap up on his feet. He shook his head. *Not today.* Today he wanted to remember as the day he met the sand. Another day would maybe be reserved for meeting the waters of the Pacific. He shouldn't overwhelm his senses or overwhelm the memories he was creating.

Finley took a seat in the sand and immediately realized the stuff was going to be all over him. Such was sand. It found its way into every spot and liked to be carried away from the ocean, hiding in places to be discovered later. He looked down at the cuff of his jeans and realized sand had already adhered into the fabric and folds and would travel back to Vagabond Circus with him.

The acrobat hadn't been seated for more than a minute when a man came and sat next to him. A bit off put by the closeness of the sudden stranger, Finley turned and then realized it wasn't an unknown person at all.

"Did you follow me here?" he said to Ian, who had his long legs in front of him, his arms resting on them.

Ian's gaze was fixed on the waves rising and falling in front of him. He simply shook his head.

"Well, how did you know to find me here?" Finley said, studying Ian's face. The man had a round face and reddish stubble had formed on his usually clean shaven chin. He was half Jewish and half Irish, which was where he got his curly blond hair and large build. Now he hardly remembered the mother who his appearance took after so much. Really he'd only gotten his once crooked teeth and wide nose from his father.

Ian gave a dry laugh. "How did I know to find you here?" Another laugh. "I realize we haven't known each other long, but unfortunately for you, I know you better than you'd like. I know everybody better than they'd like usually."

"So what, you saw a future where I came to this spot?" Finley said, crossing his legs tailor style in front of him. He hadn't even known he was going to end up in that spot until he did.

"Yes, and I know what you're eating for dinner and that you'll accidentally stub your toe in the morning. Move that chair away from the side of your bed to avoid that," Ian said, lisping through his braces.

"Hmm," Finley said, directing his gaze out to the ocean. It seemed to go on and on, like time itself, each second endlessly ticking by.

"So, I'm sorry to interrupt your first real break in…well, forever, but I needed to tell you something," Ian said.

"You really do know everyone. Is that from seeing people's futures?"

"I now see the past too. The past and future of everyone I'm connected to," Ian said, his voice carrying stress in it.

"What do you mean 'now'? You didn't used to?"

Ian nodded and squinted as his eyes swerved up, following the flight of a seagull. "My visions are increasing. Lacing together."

"I wonder why?"

"It's just the evolution of my type," he said, thinking of his dead mother. Her visions had overwhelmed her at the end. However, it had taken longer for that to happen to her, since she knew fewer people than Ian. His involvement with Vagabond Circus had been a blessing and a curse. It had gotten him away from his Middling father, who never took the time to understand his son, the Dream Traveler. However, it had given Ian dozens and dozens of people to be connected to and therefore he was overwhelmed by the visions of their lives. His mother, who was mostly a recluse, didn't take her life until she was thirty-five. Ian didn't think he could wait another decade.

"What do you have to tell me?" Finley said, not sure he wanted to know.

"I have to share your fate with you. I've only ever shared *this* type of fate with other people twice and in each instance the results had assorted effects."

"Why are you making this sound like something major?" Finley said and took his eyes off the mesmerizing ocean to stare at the clairvoyant beside him.

Ian only shrugged his shoulders. "It very well could be major. But for me to tell it to you I want your permission. I can't share a future of this magnitude with someone without first being granted that."

"Look, maybe you got it wrong this time. You're acting like what you have to tell me can make a huge impact. If you've seen my past and my future then you know that I'm not some great hero with the ability to make changes. I'm going to live and I'm going to die, and unlike Dave or most people at Vagabond Circus, I'm not full of some greatness," Finley said, and realized he had directed a fair amount of the anger he'd harbored recently at the guy beside him.

"Most people aren't destined for greatness, Finley," Ian said, irritation in his voice. His once pleasant manner was gone, washed away by the ever-increasing visions of other people's futures. "Most people aren't going to go on to live great lives. They are just mediocre. They will love and be loved, but do nothing of significance. Still they are important in their mere role to just survive life." Ian realized this was different than what most people had been taught. Not Finley, as he'd only been taught how to survive with a beautiful agility. However, most people are told they are special. That they are unique and adding something special to the world. And in Finley's case this was actually true. "But *you,*" he said, pointing directly at Finley, "*you,* I believe could actually be destined for greatness."

Finley regarded him with a skeptical glare. "Then why do you say it like it's a curse?"

"Because usually greatness is achieved alone and takes an incredible sacrifice. Those who achieve greatness lose much in the process, which is why few actually obtain it," Ian said.

"And you see a future where I obtain greatness? Where I do great things?"

"No," Ian said, his tone dropping into one of regret. "I actually see one where you fail. Where you stop just short of your goals. Where you die."

"What? Why?"

"Because you're unwilling to make the ultimate sacrifice," Ian said, and the last two words he said with a strange bit of drama.

"What? How is dying not the ultimate sacrifice?"

Ian gave a small sadistic smile. "Oh, that's no sacrifice at all. Leaving this world is usually a relief, I believe."

"Then what's the ultimate sacrifice?" Finley asked.

"Love, of course."

"What? You mean like giving your heart to someone?"

"No, I mean the opposite," Ian said. "It is usually easy for people to love a person. Natural. We are born to love one another. A sacrifice is made when we turn our backs on love. When we deprive ourselves and others of what we need to thrive."

"I *have* been depriving myself," Finley said through clenched teeth, thinking of how many times he'd looked at Zuma with scornful eyes and a burning desire in his heart.

"Oh yes, I'm fully aware," Ian said, his mind spinning with too many futures. They were shifting though. But would what he was about to say change them enough? Would it bring about the future he told to Dave, the one where Zuma was actually given happiness? "However, in the future you aren't so restrained. You do something to protect her, because your love is so strong for her."

"You mean Zuma? I protect her? And it gets me killed?" Finley said, looking without seeing, his mind blanketed by the idea of this future.

"Exactly," Ian said. His eyes also weren't focused on the physical world, but rather watching the visions streaming through his head.

"But if I don't protect her, then what happens to her?" Finley said.

"That is something I don't know since it's not what you do in the future. All I know is that if you step in, then you die."

"And if I don't then I leave her to fend for herself, don't I? I leave her in danger," Finley said.

"Yes, the ultimate sacrifice for you will be to turn your back on her when she needs you most," Ian said.

"Why are you telling me this? I didn't think you told people how to avoid death."

"I'm telling you because if you die, then the greatness you could do will too," Ian said and then leaned in close, too close, to Finley. "I fear if you die, then Vagabond Circus does too. That is what I see as of now."

"Okay, tell me what I must do then," Finley said.

Chapter Forty-Eight

*J*ack's hands were white under the weight of his body. Both were pinned on either rail beside him.

"Come on pretty boy. It's fairly simple. Babies can do it, put one foot in front the other," Sunshine said, standing at the far end of the rails.

Jack bit down on his lip and willed his foot to rise the same way he had in his dream travel.

The foot remained cemented to the ground. "I-I-I," Jack stuttered.

"Say you can't and I'm going to push you down and walk away. You'll remain there until you figure out how to get up or wait for Fanny to return," she said.

"Seriously, Sunny, I'm never going to do this if you're so soft on me," he said through tattered breaths, his face red with focus.

And then something ever so slight sprung to Sunshine's face but she corrected herself before it fully developed. How stupid she would have felt if that smile had fully unfurled. "Look, I only signed up to help you with this physical therapy because watching an acrobat struggle seems like a brilliant way to spend my time."

"That's sweet, but I think I prefer Fanny a bit more for these PT sessions," Jack said.

"And she'd be here if the crew wasn't killing each other with fist fights."

Jack grimaced. "This is all Knight's damn fault," he said, and his foot floated up an inch. The space below it felt like a million miles from earth. He looked up at Sunshine with astonishment and then lost his balance on the unsteady supporting foot. His weight shifted and his leg buckled under him and Jack slipped down, his arm catching the rail as his tail bone hit the ground. "Dammit!" he said, looking up at Sunshine as he untangled his arms from the railing.

"That was pretty ungraceful, Mr. Trapeze. At this pace you won't be catching Finley doing the quadruple in this lifetime. But don't worry. He's taken over catching since Jaz was murdered. He and pink streak are quite romantic as a flying trapeze act. Does it bother you that he catches your fiancée while you lie around?"

Jack narrowed his eyes at the girl, feeling lame looking up at her. "Don't joke about Jaz."

"I'm not joking, Jack. I'm angry as hell about it. That could have been me or you or Oliver. And it still could be. The man has to be stopped."

"How do we do that when he has Sebastian mysteriously kill people who resist his power?" Jack said.

From the doorway, Zuma said, "I've got some ideas." She'd been there longer than she was going to admit. The two had been so focused on each other that they didn't notice her there.

"Well, speaking of your sweetie," Sunshine said, crossing her arms in front of her and lowering her chin.

"How long were you going to let him sit there?" Zuma said, walking over to Jack and taking the spot behind him. "On the count of three," she said and hooked her arms under his armpits. "One. Two. Three." And then she pulled him up using his help until he was standing again. She didn't release him until he had his hands firmly pinned on the rails.

Sunshine watched all this with a quiet hostility. "I actually had no plan of helping him up. That will teach him not to fall in the future."

Zuma shook her head at the girl and then came around to face Jack. "Are you all right?" she said.

He nodded, his forehead beaded with sweat. "Mostly," he said.

"Well, I can take over, Sunshine," Zuma said, not looking at the girl, her eyes firmly on Jack, who was building up his confidence again.

"Thought you had practice with Fin," Sunshine said, not having moved.

"He cut it short," Zuma said.

Sunshine didn't leave, but rather kept her curious eyes on Zuma's back. "Say, Z, why don't you tell me something else about Finley, like what you all did while you were rescuing Jack?" Sunshine said. Between sessions with Jack and meals with Finley she knew most of what happened after Dave's death. And she knew what they weren't telling her too. What the three acrobats were lying about.

Zuma whipped around, her eyes red. "I don't think that's your business and right now I'm trying to work with Jack." Zuma paused her gaze on Sunshine. The empath had a cunning look on her face. "What?" Zuma said. "Why are you looking at me like that?"

"Oh, no reason," Sunshine said with a nonchalant shrug. "And please continue. I want to watch Jack fall again."

"You're a real sweetheart," he said and blew out a breath.

"You can do this, Jack," Zuma said.

He nodded and then closed his eyes to visualize. "Give me a minute, please."

"You know he's only mean to you to keep you at a distance," Sunshine said to Zuma.

"What?" she said. "Jack isn't mean to me."

Sunshine rolled her eyes. "No, blondie, I wasn't talking about Jack. By cut your practice short did you mean Fin was tired of giving you the cold shoulder?"

"Sunshine, don't," Zuma said, realizing Sunshine was rummaging through her emotions which were sitting on the surface, fresh and raw from stifling too many tears related to Jasmine and Finley and everything that was wrong at Vagabond Circus.

"He doesn't hate you," Sunshine said when Zuma turned back to look at Jack, who still had his eyes closed and seemed to have tuned the girls out.

"I know that!" Zuma snapped. "Would you shut up?"

"He's in love with you," Sunshine said, a teasing tone in her voice.

Zuma spun around fully and faced Sunshine. "Stop it," she said, tears on the edge of her voice, but this reaction made Sunshine appear way too pleased to consider stopping.

"And you're in love with Finley," Sunshine stated.

"I am not. I'm in love with Jack," Zuma said.

"Oh, you and Jack care about each other, but you aren't in love," Sunshine said and turned her gaze to Jack, whose eyes had just sprung open. "That's right, lover boy, I know you two are faking it. So now I want to know why."

Zuma looked at Jack, whose arms were slightly shaking from the effort of supporting most of his body weight. She then turned back to Sunshine. "It was a lie that got out of control."

"Oh, well how much longer are you both going along with it?" Sunshine asked.

"It doesn't really matter right now!" Zuma yelled. "There's other bigger concerns, like helping Jack walk. So if you wouldn't mind…"

Sunshine waved her off. "Please continue. I'll shush for the moment."

"Thank God." Zuma turned back to Jack. "You ready?"

He shook his head. "No, I need a break actually."

Zuma nodded and grabbed the wheelchair to the side and placed it behind Jack and then hooked her hands under his armpits again, helping him to sit back into the chair.

"Quitter," Sunshine said, giving him a repulsed look before stalking out of the trailer.

Jack looked up at Zuma standing behind him. "Thanks, Z."

"Anytime," she said and leaned down and kissed his sweaty forehead.

He then looked at the door which had just closed. "She's delightful, isn't she?"

"Yeah, a real ray of sunshine," Zuma said dryly.

He laughed at this as Zuma came to rest her elbows on the railing beside Jack. "So I've been putting a plan together for taking Knight and his minions down."

Jack raised a cautious eyebrow at his friend. "Zuma, you can't be serious?"

"Of course I am," she said.

"You know how dangerous that is. What if he finds out? He will have you murdered too."

"Then what's the alternative? Just allow him to control us? Ruin us?"

Jack slipped his hand on Zuma's arm. "I can't lose you too. The circus can't lose you."

She picked up her other hand and placed it over Jack's as a tear peeked out of her eye. "I'm not going anywhere but I have to do something."

"Let Titus do it."

Zuma then looked up from where her haunted eyes were resting on their clasped hands. "We are working on it together." And there was a hint of pride in her voice. "We don't know how it will all work but Ian is helping."

Jack nodded, his eyes distant. "I want to do more."

"And you will."

"Is that what Ian says? Am I going to walk again?" Jack hadn't had a chance to speak to the crew member.

Zuma gave him a remorseful look. "I don't know. He won't say."

"Oh," Jack said, disappointment oozing from his tone.

"But you need to keep trying. And there's something else I want you to work on."

"What's that?" he said with a sideways look.

"Drawing out your other dream travel gift that you have."

He blew out a sigh. "I've tried, Z. Maybe Dave was wrong and I'm not electrokinetic."

"When was Dave ever wrong?" she challenged. "If he thought that skill was dormant within you then he had to be right. And I think it could come in handy."

"Handy? Like a pair of pliers? Great, I'll be handy in the battle to take Knight down," Jack said.

She shook her head at him but smiled still. "I mean handy like a Taser gun."

"Now you're talking," he said.

"Just promise me you'll work on it."

"Yeah, sure," he said as the door at her back opened.

A kind face poked in and paused. Benjamin's brown eyes brightened at the sight of Zuma. "Am I interrupting? Fanny sent me back to grab some books but told me not to interrupt your PT session, Mr. Fuller."

Jack waved the boy in. "Not at all. Grab your books."

Benjamin's face lightened with a smile that was without a single restriction.

"Actually, Benjamin, I'm glad you came in when you did," Zuma said.

"You are?" he said and his freckled face flushed red.

"Yes," Zuma said, also waving him in and over. "We were discussing a plan for getting the bad guys away from Vagabond Circus."

147

"You mean that mean man, the new ringmaster?" Benjamin said, his smile falling.

"Yes," Zuma said. "And I want you to help, but to do so you're going to have to keep a lot of secrets. Can you do that?"

Benjamin looked at Jack and then Zuma. "Will what I do make Fanny happy again? Take that worried look off her face?"

Zuma nodded confidently. "It will help everyone. It will save Vagabond Circus."

"Then absolutely!" the boy said.

Chapter Forty-Nine

"*I* hear this show gets into your bones," Gretchen Roberts said to her companion. They sat in the front row in the big top. "Oh, look," she said, pointing at the entrance. "Liam Williams is here." That actor, Mr. Williams, had won the Academy Award for Best Actor the year prior.

The entire tent was quickly filling with actors and actresses and their husbands or wives. Children were hardly in attendance since Vagabond Circus was quickly getting the reputation for being un-kid-friendly.

"My agent saw this circus in San Francisco. He said the show gave him nightmares for a whole week," Doris Flanagan said from three rows from the front. She had just finished an acclaimed role where she played Margaret Thatcher.

Never before had the circus performed for so many well-known people at once. Even the last show in San Francisco, which was performed for the President of the United States and the First Man, didn't have the anticipation that this one did. Zuma watched from the back curtain as the tent filled, her eidetic memory cataloging the faces. She was fine with performing for whomever, but she didn't like how this elite feel was taking the circus away from the very people it was originally supposed to entertain: the non-believers. It had been months since an overworked middle-class cynic sat in their audience. *These* people were thrill seekers, not ones who had lost their faith in magic and needed it restored.

Zuma turned from the curtain to find Finley a few feet away, watching her. The show had been rearranged due to Jack's absence and Jasmine's death. The duo now performed six times in each show. Double what they used to do. But they did it without complaint and also without speaking. The pair had mastered the art of working silently, reading each other's movements and making the alterations they judged necessary. Their muscles spoke to each other. Their eyes wrestled with one another's. But they hardly ever had reason to speak. Finley held his hand out to her and Zuma knew he was urging her to take their place for the first act. Just then she heard Knight announcing the circus.

After the lions charged the front row, Zuma and Finley would make their first appearance of the night. She laid her hand in his, softly, so they were barely touching. Finley directed her to the area by the side curtain. Zuma relied on him since it was pitch black, but Finley could always see fine no matter how much light. Zuma felt her long white train brushing the ground behind her. The story for the circus was still the same: she was still a girl unable to experience the night at her father's insistence, but one evening she escaped and met the monsters of the dark. However, Knight had made it more nightmarish and less of a love story. In the end, she falls for Finley, the diabolical monster, but just when she gives her heart to him he does the unspeakable.

Finley paused at the crack in the curtain just as Oliver made the lions appear in the center of the ring. The crowd of famous people gasped. One screamed. Finley gave Zuma a look she could barely see in the dark; she could only make out the whites of his lonely eyes. Then he pulled down the horned mask that covered half his face and she turned her gaze away, knowing she couldn't really see him anyway, not when he wore the mask.

***

By the finale of the show everyone in the crowd was perched on the edge of their cushioned seat. Some had left the show early, unable to deal with the dark images Oliver was forced to conjure, or they were afraid they'd feel the heat of Sunshine's flame. Those who remained were mesmerized by the show, like a car accident they couldn't look away from.

The greenish lights illuminated, showing Zuma crouched in the middle of the ring. She and Finley had already performed the duo on the wire, which involved flips and leaps that had threatened each acrobat with too many potential life-altering falls. Still they landed with a practiced grace. Then Finley had disappeared. Teleported out of the ring, leaving Zuma's character alone. She searched the ring, which was decorated like a haunted forest, for the monster she believed she loved. Finley then appeared wearing a neon green body suit lined with sequins that made him resemble a serpent. He sped

150

forward as Zuma's ballet-slippered feet brought her backwards. As rehearsed, she stumbled and just as she fell back he slipped a hand behind her, catching the girl, then he slung her into his arms and spun her around. It was a beautiful blur of movements. The couple fell into an alluring tango of actions. And just as he went to shove her away from him Zuma slipped a hand across his cheek, making the monster straighten, fear oozing off his masked face. Then he disappeared again, teleporting to the back stage.

Several times during the final act Finley disappeared, leaving Zuma to spin and leap around the forest. And then she grabbed the silver rings hanging from the ceiling, the ones Knight had bent from a pole before the audience's eyes. She gripped one and pulled herself up, manipulating her body into a series of graceful poses. But never did she stay in a position long because the bolts of fire Sunshine sent in her direction always made it necessary to seek refuge in another place in the ring.

And then at long last, when most audience members' adrenal glands were ready to explode, Finley appeared behind a tree made by a crew member. He caught Zuma from behind. She spun to face him, desire and longing radiating off her. He spun her around like a prize he had finally allowed himself to have as the eerie music grew in intensity. He tossed her in the air and teleported in time to catch the girl as she leaped. He spun her around against him, then as the pair faced each other he withdrew something from his back. She stood staring at him, her character vibrating with anticipation of the kiss she knew was about to grace her. Finley slid his leg behind her, encouraging her back into a low dip. The tip of his mask sunk down low close to Zuma's face. Her arms flung back like the wings of a bird, her position communicating to the audience her complete submission to the monster.

Once, twice, three times he slid the long tip of the nose of his mask against her face. Every eye in the big top was large. And everyone's heart beat with a strange foreboding. Zuma then grabbed his face to encourage the kiss she knew was about to happen. And just then Finley reared back, holding the long silver dagger high in the air directed at his partner's chest. And the lights faded to black.

There was never a standing ovation after the finale like there used to be. The acrobats didn't bow to a crowd of glistening faces and large smiles. With Finley directing them through the dark, they disappeared behind the curtain. Then the audience straggled out, speechless and changed by the show they witnessed.

Chapter Fifty

The Vagabond Circus didn't have a party after the performance for the movie stars in Santa Barbara. They stopped having those parties a month ago. No one really saw the reason for celebrating. Yes, they performed in a successful show. One that was sold out in every city. One that stunned audiences. However, it didn't serve the purpose that it used to. Knight said they were free to leave or do as they pleased, and although they knew they were prisoners as long as they stayed, no one left.

"There they are," a man said as Zuma and Finley exited the big top after the show, both side by side and also a million miles apart. They were still in costume. Finley gave the man who approached them a protective stare. The man was dressed in a black suit with a blue tie. Beside him was Titus, who had an unusually positive look on his face.

"Hello, my name is—"

"Robert Johnson," Zuma said, cutting the man off. Everyone knew the actor. He had starred in hundreds of movies and was now also a film producer.

"Exactly," he said, shaking Finley's hand. Then he took Zuma's and kissed it softly.

"Mr. Johnson was extremely impressed with your performances tonight," Titus said, a glint of pride in his eyes. He wore his hands clasped behind his back.

"I was," the man said, letting Zuma's hand go. Finley was afraid that the attention of this star would make Zuma blush, as it would with most girls. He was relieved to find her face impassive. She seemed to be studying the man's slicked back black hair and full features like a detective, no attraction on her face. "I have a film series I'm looking to produce. A six-part series actually," Mr. Johnson said. "And I was thinking the two of you would be perfect for the lead roles. You have an incredible chemistry and the right athletic skills."

"We aren't actors," Zuma said in response to this.

"You could have fooled me," the man said with a laugh, looking at Titus, who laughed too. "That was an incredible show of acting. And to be able to communicate words and emotions like you two did without saying a word, well, there are few in Hollywood as skilled as you."

"I'm not sure I understand what you're offering us," Finley said, and Zuma then felt something catch inside her chest. She realized it was the first time she'd heard him speak in a long time. Too long. His voice was fresh water to her parched throat. She looked at him then and realized he had his tentative eyes on her, sensing her tension mount. He could always read Zuma.

"I'm offering you a chance in my movie," the producer said with a smile in his voice. "I mean there's a process and if you got the part, then the other movies wouldn't be guaranteed, but they might."

Zuma shook her head, which was heavy with braids and the jewels fastened in various places. "But we'd have to leave Vagabond Circus."

The man nodded. "I'm afraid you would, but you might find it worth your departure from such a great organization. I think I could make it worth your while."

"But we can't—"

"Zuma," Titus said, an influencing tone in his voice, "Mr. Johnson is offering you a chance to audition for major Hollywood parts. For the both of you, Finley and yourself, to star in up to six films."

"And who knows the opportunities available to you after that," Mr. Johnson said, reaching into his breast pocket and withdrawing two cards.

"But we'd have to leave Dave's circus and our family here," Zuma said to Titus.

"But you and Finley would be away from here. Jack could go with you when he's strong enough. Think of the influence you could make on the big screen. That's what you want to do, to inspire, right? And you'd be safe," Titus said.

The Hollywood producer gave a curious look at the mention of safety, but before he could offer any more encouragement Knight appeared from seemingly nowhere. The night was dark and Zuma had sensed a person approaching. Finley, who could see well in the dark, knew it was Knight. But the other two men appeared almost startled when the tall man invaded the circle, his frame towering over the group. Robert Johnson was startled because that was the effect Knight had with his strange appearance. Titus was startled because he knew Knight and what he would think of this conversation.

"Robert, thank you for accepting my invitation tonight," Knight said, offering the man his hand. "I hope you enjoyed the show."

He took his hand and shook it, smiling. "I did indeed. Thank you."

Knight then turned his attention on Finley and then Zuma; both had their gazes on the ground, knowing better than to look at the ringmaster. "Two things," he said, hissing on the last word. "The first is Zuma, I do believe I just heard you refer to this as Dave's circus."

"I misspoke," she said. "What I meant to say—"

"I think you said exactly what you meant to say, but wouldn't have dared to speak so plainly if you knew I was listening," Knight said, the menace heavy in his tone.

"I'm sure Ms. Zanders meant no harm," Robert dared to speak up, to protect Zuma, sensing she was about to be punished in some way.

Knight revolved slowly, like a cobra finding a better source for its attention, until he was facing Robert. "And secondly, Robert, I did not invite you to my circus so you could pilfer and steal my best performers. I invited you here so you could help promote my circus through your channels."

"But Knight," Titus said, his voice almost a whisper, his eyes on Robert. "You said that if the performers stuck with you that there would be opportunities. You said that in Los Angeles you'd help by showing them off to directors and producers, like Robert."

"I did," Knight said, looking at Titus with a sinister stare, his voice much louder. "And I meant it." He turned to the actor. "Recruit the jugglers, the magician, the other stars in the show, but these two aren't up for grabs." He then looked at Finley. "Ever," he said, drawing out the word.

"Shouldn't that be their decision to make? Titus tells me they aren't under contract," Robert said.

"Yes, it should be," Knight said, his seething stare flipping to Titus before turning back to Finley and then Zuma. "Tell me, acrobats, do you want to go off together, abandoning your commitment to Vagabond Circus to make movies? Or would you rather stay here where you know you will be safe and with the people you care for and therefore want to keep safe and healthy?"

Finley only nodded. But Zuma, realizing the threat and instantly worried for her circus family, said, "Yes, I want to stay." She then looked at the outsider. "Thank you for your offer but we aren't interested in leaving, Mr. Johnson."

Robert gave a discouraged look to Titus before nodding to the girl. "Very well," he said and handed a thick ivory white business card to her. "In case you change your mind."

She took the card, her eyes low. He then offered it to Finley, but the acrobat knew better and simply shook his head.

"Well, I think that settles it," Knight said, his eyes on the card in Zuma's fingers, seeming to burn it with his gaze. "Robert, why don't I escort you to the exit," he said and turned and strode in the opposite direction.

Chapter Fifty-One

*T*he day after Vagabond Circus performed for the A-list celebrities there was no change in morale. Padmal was well enough to perform with her brothers but the boys still hung their heads low, depression heavy in their every move. At lunch the next day, Oliver pushed his tofu and penne around in its Alfredo sauce with no interest in actually eating the overly abused morsels of food. Sunshine was absent as she was most days, spending her extra hours to relieve Fanny or work with Jack.

"If everyone is miserable then why are we sticking around to endure this abuse?" Padmal said from her place next to Oliver.

He turned to her, irritation in his every movement. "Ian told us we shouldn't leave."

"Who cares what that idiot said," Padmal griped. "Have you seen that guy? He looks awful these days. I wouldn't follow his advice."

"Ian is under as much stress as the rest of us. Look around, Padmal, everyone looks awful," Nabhi said.

"None of you were stabbed in the foot," she said, leaning across the table. "You all have nothing to complain about."

"Oh, that's right, your woes are worse than everyone else's, I completely forgot," Nabhi said, not backing down but rather leaning in, creating a stare-off with his sister.

"Nab," Haady said, placing his hand on his brother's shoulder.

To everyone's surprise Nabhi shrugged him off with a sharp movement. "No, this little princess once again thinks she suffers more than the rest of us, and I'm about tired of it. Look, Padmal, we all get the headaches. While you were lying around recovering for months, we all were performing in this demonic circus. We've seen firsthand and continuously the cruelty, and we aren't going anywhere. But if you want to leave, then by all means. Haady and I can obviously handle the act without you."

Padmal whipped around and faced Oliver, who had his head down and almost no attention on the argument going on in front of him. His mind was preoccupied with Ian's advice. Was now the time to break things off with Padmal? Ian said he'd know. That he wouldn't be able to take it any longer.

"Oliver," Padmal said, her tone demanding.

Like a sloth moving, he lifted his gaze to meet hers. "What?" he said, pushing his loose black hair off his forehead. His Mohawk wasn't stiff and sticking straight up like usual. It did have streaks of green in it now though.

"Leave this stupid circus with me. I can't take being here any longer," she said.

Oliver ran his tired eyes over Padmal's beige skin. She was like the desert, beautifully smooth and elegant and also harsh. *No*, he wasn't at the breaking point yet. He actually looked at her and still felt the initial draw. Maybe he even still loved her.

"No," he said in his scratchy voice. "I don't want to leave."

"Are you freaking kidding me?" she said, banging her tiny fist on the table in front of them.
"You're overworked, doing three times as many illusions each show. How can you want to keep doing this?"

"Because I believe Ian. He's never been wrong. And if he says us staying saves Dave's circus, then I'm staying. I have to…that man rescued me from the streets," Oliver said, still remembering the day so clearly in his head. After that day Oliver was never hungry. Never cold. Never lonely.

Padmal blew out an annoyed breath. "He cursed you. He cursed us all."

"You know nothing about being cursed," Finley said from his place at the end of the table. He sat there at every meal and most of the time the freaks forgot he was present. He was always silent. So to hear Finley speak then brought everyone's attention at the table to him. His eyes were on the plate in front of him.

"Oh, and you do?" Padmal said. "You're Knight's prodigy and you didn't even tell us."

"He owes us nothing," Haady said.

"Whatever. I don't care if you all want to stay and support this nightmare of a circus. I'm leaving. I'm getting as far away from this corrupt organization as possible," Padmal said.

"What was that?" Sebastian's voice was heard first and then he materialized between Nabhi and Haady, standing dangerously close behind them. "You're not planning on leaving, are you, Padmal?" the boy said, a crazed look in his dark eyes.

"Well, actually I was," Padmal said.

"That would make Knight very unhappy. He doesn't like it when people leave him. You realize I will have to share this with him," Sebastian said.

"Why will he care what I do? He had Gwendolyn nearly kill me," Padmal said.

Sebastian clicked his tongue. "No, if he wanted you dead, well...I don't sense he has that kind of ill will toward you. But I really think you should stay at the circus."

"Why is that?" she said.

"Because your act involves knives and they are dangerous. The idea that one could slip and cut one of you creating a nasty wound..." Then Sebastian shook his head like shaking away the fantasy. "Well, that would be simply awful. But the element of danger. That's nice. So don't leave, Padmal."

She half smiled at the boy who stood a lethal distance from her brothers. Padmal was certain Sebastian enjoyed her act and was impressed with how skilled she was to juggle with knives. Sebastian in actuality was looking forward to one of the three slipping up again and being impaled by a blade. He could hardly wait to see the nasty wound it caused.

Chapter Fifty-Two

"*Y*ou know what's the most boring thing in the world?" Sunshine said, twirling her long black hair around her finger until it reached the black polished nail.

"I'm sure it has something to with watching my attempts to walk," Jack said as sweat trickled into his eyes. He pushed his head into his shoulder to blot the dampness. His arms were the only thing holding him upright. His hands were again pressed against the rails on either side of him. Their length five long feet. Five feet he wanted to walk. Needed to.

"Actually it's not, but that just proves how inflated your ego is," Sunshine said with an indignant sigh. "The most boring thing in the world is counting objects, which is why people do it to fall asleep. Sheep, stars, leprechauns, you know."

"Who counts leprechauns to drift off?" Jack asked, sucking in a deep breath and focusing on lifting his foot off the ground.

Sunshine shrugged from her place in front of Jack. "I don't know, people. But watching your poor attempt at walking is definitely the second most boring thing."

"Thanks, Sunshine," Jack said. Every day he had multiple PT sessions and at least once a day Sunshine commented on his insufficient attempts to walk. It was actually only in sessions with her that he raised his foot off the ground, and he was guessing it was because he wanted to thrust it at her.

"You know, if a foal doesn't walk minutes after birth it's considered worthless," Sunshine said matter-of-factly.

Jack brought his focus up to Sunshine. Narrowed his eyes. "I guess that makes me worthless."

Again she shrugged. "Your words, not mine." Her long finger was wrapped in her black hair, making it look like a finger puppet. He regarded her for a long few seconds. She had such an exotic look. One he never thought he'd appreciate but many things in his life had shifted. He wasn't the star of a circus anymore. He also didn't pity himself anymore or spend hours consumed with anxiety due to the constant comparisons he made of himself to his brothers. Jack spent his hours training as he had done before the accident but every moment was a humble beginning. Each hour was an observation of his thoughts with a deliberate focus to hunt for the ones that didn't serve him and destroy them. Then he thought new thoughts. Powerful thoughts. Positive ones. Ones that he swore the last time he looked in the mirror had changed his eyes. Now he looked like a new version of himself. A better one.

"You do realize that foals aren't broken at birth? They are designed to walk," he said.

"I'm sorry, did I just hear an excuse for why you can't take a silly step?" Sunshine said.

"No," Jack said, clenching his jaw as he took in a breath. *I don't make excuses anymore*, he thought to himself.

Sunshine blew out a bored breath and gave her attention to the tangle now arranged on her finger. She tugged and her hair caught in several places. "Well, don't fall now, looks like I'm all tied up and won't be able to catch you if you do," she said.

"You never catch me," Jack said, his head filling with heat. Air brushed under his foot as it hovered a foot off the ground. He didn't take that moment to celebrate but rather kept his motivation going. "You only ever let me fall," he said and brought the foot forward and then down.

Sunshine's eyes flew up like she wasn't sure what she'd just seen out of the corner of her vision. And she *wasn't* sure but she knew Jack had moved. She froze and kept her posture unaffected. "Why would I catch you? That won't teach you a damn thing," she said, her eyes on Jack's other foot. The left had risen in the air but not quite enough. Still it shuffled forward, his hands moving down the railing as he did.

"I don't need you to teach me anything, Sunshine," Jack said, a warm ferocity in his voice. Again his right leg, stronger than the left, lifted his foot and this time he took a proper stride forward.

"Oh yeah?" Sunshine said, her eyes wide on Jack's legs, her voice sounding bored.

"Yeah," he said, real conviction in the one word. "I already know how..." He took a step. Ever so small with the left. "To," he sputtered out, his breath hot. Jack took another step, this one almost strong. "Walk," he said, completing the sentence. And this last step brought him to the end of the railing so he was inches from Sunshine.

A smile like no one had ever seen blossomed on her face. Sunshine beamed at Jack, a real excitement finally spilling out of her. "I see that you do," she said and felt the muscles in her face do something she was so unaccustomed to. But looking at the awed look on Jack's face only made the smile widen. His expression spoke beautifully of his struggle and pride at conquering those five feet.

"Sunshine," he said, breathless, his hands shaking.

She thought he'd say something like "I did it!"

Instead he said, "When you smile..."

"Yes?" she said.

Jack's arms went wobbly under him.

Sunshine found her arms reaching out but wouldn't allow herself to connect with him to actually be his support. And then Jack slipped down, landing on his bottom as he had so many times before. He looked up at Sunshine.

"Well, that was a hell of a way to end that," she said dryly.

He shook his head at her. "Thanks."

She looked down at him, the smile gone but still lingering in her green eyes. "Nice job, Jack. That was actually quite the sight to see."

"Are you afraid you're going to explode now?" he said, breathless.

"From giving you that one compliment?" She shrugged. "Yeah, I might." She reached out her hands to him and he wrapped his fingers around them.

"You know what, Sunshine?"

She hauled him upright, directing his hands to the rails on either side of him. When he was in place she looked at him. "What?"

He took a deep breath and brought his hopeful eyes up. "When you smile, you're radiant."

Chapter Fifty-Three

*W*ordlessly Zuma and Finley practiced in the middle of the ring. It had come to be known by some of the other performers and crew members of Vagabond Circus as a beautiful arrangement. Their silence was poetic and mysterious. Some assumed that Finley had opened a telepathic link in his head and that's how he and Zuma communicated. Others rumored that the girl was so pained by the loss of her acrobat friend Jaz that she refused to get close to another ever again. Still all were struck by how they worked together silently, seeming to communicate without saying a word. When Zuma showed up, they rehearsed, their bodies seeming to talk as they danced beside one another. She might shake her head at something and then they would pause and reconvene. Finley might nod and they would continue with that same rehearsed movement. And when he walked away, the practice was over. No "goodbye." No "good job." Just two broken hearts forced to work together, while also drifting apart.

Sunshine watched from the practice tent. She and she alone knew exactly how the acrobats felt about each other. It almost made her feel sorry for them, but she knew that pity was never helpful. Fanny's kids, Benjamin, Tiffany, and Emily, didn't feel sorry for Zuma and Finley at all. They watched from the bleachers in awe. The girls wanted to be Zuma and Benjamin wanted to be Finley. The naïve children had no idea they were witnessing scorned hearts; they thought it was the magic of Vagabond Circus and that's why they couldn't look away.

"We aren't going to be able to do lessons in here if you three won't pay attention," Fanny said from her place sitting in front of the three kids. They usually did their lessons outside to give Jack a quiet place to rest when he needed it. However, it was raining in Santa Barbara, which was why they found themselves under the big top where distractions abounded. "Benjamin, I want you to read the paragraph on page one-twenty-six out loud for us all to hear," Fanny said.

Benjamin found it difficult to pull his eyes off the dancing duo, but managed, bringing his gaze down to the history book nestled in his lap. Actually, all over the big top it was difficult for crew members and practicing performers not to devote some of their attention to Finley and Zuma, since they exuded magic. It was real, intoxicating, and it made Charles Knight utterly livid.

The owner of Vagabond Circus sat in the front row staring at the practicing duo. He hardly left them alone during their practices, as he was constantly making alterations to their act, making it more dangerous, more provocative. Sebastian sat on Knight's right, his eyes cast down low. The boy didn't like spending hours watching the acrobats. It made his head burn with fire. Gwendolyn, on Knight's left, enjoyed it very much. She wanted to be Zuma in the act, to drift closer and further away from Finley with her graceful movements. She wanted to feel his hands on her waist as he effortlessly lifted her in the air. She'd arch her back like a swan, and he'd flow all around her like a pond.

"Stop," Knight said, and immediately Zuma and Finley froze in mid-step, knowing he was speaking to them. However, everyone else in the big top momentarily halted as well, giving as much attention as would be allowed to Knight and his acrobats. "Zuma, you need to move faster. You're slowing down that part of the act with your inefficient movements."

The girl's eyes were cast down low, although she was facing Knight. She didn't say a word, merely nodded.

Knight stood and said, "Look at me."

Zuma, having been reprimanded and punished multiple times for looking at Knight, didn't comply. No one in the circus was allowed to look at him directly. She was afraid this was a trick.

"I said look at ME!" Knight said, booming on the last word.

Slowly, hesitantly, she brought her large brown eyes up to stare at the chalk white man who towered in front of her, some fifteen feet away. "Good girl. In this instance and only this instance you are allowed, as I can't teach you precision of movement without providing a superior example. Now I want you to use your combat skill to observe. Watch me walk."

She nodded, her adrenaline making her chest ache.

Then Knight took six steps in her direction until he was standing in front of her. "Now look away," he commanded, and

Zuma instantly complied. To Finley, she hadn't lost her spirit, but Knight had for sure frayed it. This was one of the hardest things for him to endure during his time at the circus.

"What did you observe, and don't say me walking," Knight said.

Zuma cleared her tight throat. "You moved deliberately. Each of your steps was an equal distance apart. Your weight was evenly balanced on each of the strides and you had your core reinforced the entire time, so as to move with each muscle group right on top of the other."

Knight drew in a long breath and from Zuma's peripheral it appeared that he might have smiled. The man had short teeth and too much gums; she had noticed this once when he didn't know she was watching. He appeared to have baby teeth. "That's right. You might not be worthless after all," Knight said, and this statement made a crew member to the side who was installing a lightbulb drop his toolbox from the top of the ladder, creating an awful commotion. Knight squeezed his eyes together from the loud racket. "That will be one week's pay docked, Cliff," he said to the crew member, not looking in his direction, his eyes still on Zuma.

Cliff, the crew member, dropped his head and hurried to pick up his tools. He knew better than to argue with the ringmaster. It would only leave him with a debilitating headache and even less money. Cliff sorely hoped Ian was right about staying, because he wasn't sure how much longer he could endure the stress at Vagabond Circus.

"Now Zuma, what you just witnessed is me moving using efficiency, precision, and deliberate thought. It's how all my kids are taught to move. And your act will be better if you do this," Knight said.

She nodded. "I will work on it. I will try."

A loud, overly exaggerated sigh rode over Knight's lips. "Trying is what weak people do. I want you to do it. Is that CLEAR?"

Zuma nodded again, this time with force. "Yes, sir," she said.

"Master," Knight corrected. "You will call me Master. I am your master of ceremonies. I am your ringmaster. That is what you will call me. Do you understand?"

Many people were pretending to work, to practice, to do their history lesson, but everyone's attention was actually on this exchange.

Zuma hesitated. She had given up so much to stay at Vagabond Circus. Was there a limit to what she could take? she started to wonder. This was feeling like too much. *Maybe I should have left after Jaz died.*

"Do you understand?" Knight said again.

Beside her she felt and spied Finley tense. It was as if that one movement was an attempt to encourage her to comply. Finally she nodded. "Yes, Master. Of course," she said.

Knight turned and walked two steps before seeming to think of something else he wanted to say. He turned back to the girl. "You took Robert Johnson's card. Do you still have it?"

Zuma blinked at the ground, unprepared for this change in the conversation. "Yes, I still have it."

"Master," Knight reminded.

"Yes, I still have it, Master," Zuma said.

"Quick to answer that question, weren't you? I bet you still look at that card. Consider his offer. You probably hold it in your hands every single day, thinking that would be your big break. Your means to get away from me, the ringmaster who has made you the star so great a producer would actually want you. Is all that correct?"

There were too many questions there. The answers were yes, yes, yes, no, and yes. But Zuma only said, "No, Master. I'm staying here at Vagabond Circus." And now she remembered why she gave up and called Knight Master and stayed when she wanted to leave. At first it had been for Dave, but now it was because she knew how he would punish her if she left. Knight had all but said that he would harm her circus family if she took Mr. Johnson's offer.

"That's exactly right. You are staying because you belong to this circus. The others can leave. Hell, half of them, like the incompetent crew, I want to leave. But you, I would rather you and Finley die than abandon me. Call me sick. Call me demented. But like a crazed lover, if I can't have you two in my circus then no one will."

All noises in the big top were sucked into a vacuum. Then Fanny stood, the entire movement surprising even her. It had been a reflexive movement, one done out of her need to protect. After

166

standing, she merely stood though, staring at the three in the center of the ring. Finley wasn't moving, only clenching his jaw. Zuma was white, not as white as Knight, but still all blood had gone to her feet.

"Finley understands this, but you, Zuma, apparently need to have it stated plainly. Isn't that right, Finley? That's why you didn't take the business card, am I correct?" Knight said, his eyes shifting to a stoic Finley.

"Yes, Master," Finley said.

"See there, Zuma. So do I make myself clear?" Knight said.

"Yes, Master. I leave and you kill me," she said, and knew at once it was too bold of a statement, but she couldn't help herself. It was die or lose her spirit entirely and who would she be then? Would it be worth living?

If she was looking at him then she would have seen the all-wrong smile on his face. "Oh, but the thing is you can stay and the very same thing could happen. I cannot protect you. This all reminds me of the unfortunate accident that happened to Jasmine. Poor girl. I cannot protect your health and well-being and it is by no means guaranteed if you stay. You may be a star in this circus, but you can be replaced."

"What happened to Jaz wasn't an accident," Zuma said before she could stop herself.

"How dare you?" Knight said and then snapped his fingers over his shoulder. "Sebastian, come here."

The boy with greasy black hair stood at once and walked, copying the movements Knight had just displayed. He stopped beside Knight, his eyes lingering on Zuma, who wore her practice leotard.

"Remember how I told you Zuma was off limits during the day, but to do as you wished during the night?"

"Yes, Master," Sebastian said.

"Well, since she apparently has some fears about things not being accidents I want you to keep an eye on our acrobat all the time. Whenever she's alone, day or night, as long as no one else is around, keep her safe. Lend her your hand to assure her she's all right," Knight said.

Zuma backed up, as Sebastian took the same number of steps in her direction. "It would be my honor, Master," the boy said.

"Only when she's alone, Sebastian. Only when she dares to leave the safety of her trailer alone," Knight said. "That way she sleeps better at night."

Zuma was shaking her head now, furiously. "No. You stay away from me," she said, her words frantic.

"I only want to help you," Sebastian said and Fanny had now moved in closer, but was still watching. "Just know that if you need a hand, I'm here." And then he raised his poison-ridden fingers and directed them at Zuma.

Beside her, Finley turned and balled up his fists but didn't say a word.

Sebastian's hand was outstretched, moving ever closer to Zuma, who looked frozen, like she wasn't sure if she should run or challenge the murderer in front of her. If she ran, Knight would probably knock her down with a headache and then she'd be a real target for Sebastian. But he didn't look close to stopping and she hated the power he had over her. With a wicked smile Sebastian's hand closed the distance between them until his hand hovered an inch from her exposed forearm. Zuma felt the heat of his body close to hers.

"All I have to do is touch you once," he said, too much glee in his voice.

Finley was vibrating with a raging force. It was almost too encompassing. It was about to overwhelm him. Tear him apart. Take over. Force him to do something deadly. Then he reminded himself of what Ian said and he turned his back on Zuma and Sebastian, pretending to have his attention stolen by something on the other side of the big top. He squeezed his eyes shut. Whatever happened now was a new future. Zuma may die now, but Finley would live.

"Do you like or disapprove of this arrangement?" Knight said to Finley.

The acrobat turned and faced his master, but kept his gaze low. "It doesn't matter what I think."

"Oh, but you must have some sort of feelings on the matter. Does it make you uncomfortable that Sebastian will be watching your partner? Worried, perhaps?"

"I don't care," Finley said, the words feeling so wrong coming out of him. But this was what Ian had told him to do. This was him changing the future. This was him not tackling Sebastian and

168

pushing him away, earning him death. "It doesn't matter to me if Sebastian watches or touches Zuma."

"Sebastian, sit down," Knight ordered. "And you, Finley, are infuriating. You obviously care for the girl, but are trying to make a show of not, to take away my power."

"I don't give a damn about Zuma," Finley said, and then turned and looked away from her.

Chapter Fifty-Four

*F*inley's head thundered with anger and shame. His eyes were all too aware of Zuma's shocked face. She'd come so close to death and he had stood by and allowed it. This was different than his usual passive nature. This was Finley being heartless. And his words. *I don't give a damn about Zuma.* They were lightning in his being, scorching his insides.

"You think you can fool me?" Knight said to Finley. Everyone could feel the anger in his voice; it was a new anger, one born from Finley taking away his power by not reacting. "I know you better than anyone. And I know you're lying."

Knight's advantage lay in his ability to threaten the people Finley cared about. That had always been the way. And now he didn't have that. Finley was supposed to be dead now. In the future Ian saw, Finley protected Zuma. He did what Knight would have expected, but Ian had figured out how to outmaneuver Knight. And what happened next was all new. "I'm not lying. I care about no one and nothing," Finley said in a dead voice.

Knight tightened his beady eyes at Finley. He had to have a way to hurt the guy. "Do you know, all of my kids were produced using surrogates. All of them," he said, and now there was a smile in his snake-like voice. "All of them but one."

Finley's eyes almost gave away his surprise, but quickly he covered it with a blank expression.

"You see, Finley," Knight said, "I got the idea of creating an army of thieves from my dear brother, who had saved lost souls and made a fortune using them to create his circus. But I didn't want kids who had baggage, and that's why I used surrogates, so I could mold the children from the beginning."

Everyone in the big top, not even caring if they would be punished, stopped and focused on this exchange. Most had sensed there was something nefarious about the kids who had been there in the beginning and now were gone. *But thieves? Surrogates?* The cast and crew could hardly fathom this reality. And the fact that Knight was stating this so plainly meant what they all feared: he had total power. He wasn't even making a show of not being a dictator anymore.

"However," Knight continued, his eyes only on Finley, "I knew that breeding this army would take time and so I decided I needed one child to start with, while the surrogates were being inseminated and hatching my first children. You, Finley, will remember you were a year older than the children in your set and that's because you weren't born from a surrogate. You, my boy, were an orphan I adopted."

Finley's face did give something away then, and that was mostly Zuma's fault. He felt her look directly at him. Felt the fear in her vibrating. And the shock of this reveal was not something he knew how to assimilate. He had always thought of himself as manufactured. But he was born...from parents. The idea felt wrong, and also like a dream come true.

"Yes, that's right," Knight said, almost laughing at this secret. "I took a page out of my brother's book and went to orphanages."

Knight only gave information away to manipulate. To hurt. And Finley knew this and knew he had to be careful. "Why are you telling me this, Master?" he asked boldly.

And Knight did laugh now, one that reeked of his sinister glee. "When I adopted you, you were an infant. Extremely adoptable. You could have had a normal life. Just imagine it. Things could have gone differently for you, Finley. You could have had the life you've mistakenly thought you wanted."

Fanny watched from her place just in front of her kids. She was hinged on this exchange, her eyes daring to look directly at Knight. She wanted to step in right then. To take over and tear away the pain that was second by second overwhelming Finley's face. *Not yet,* she told herself.

"No, that's not true," Finley finally managed out through clenched teeth, his eyes blurring. His head dizzy.

"Nothing was ever truer," Knight said, a pleased tone in his voice. "Oh, and let me tell you, I had to compete for you. There was this really nice couple who wanted you. Picture perfect. But your would-be mother kept getting these awful headaches and the administrator didn't think they were the best fit seeing as how she seemed fragile," he said with a laugh. "My fake-wife, one of the surrogates, and I were chosen as the right family to take you."

And Finley now couldn't control the devastating heartbreak that covered his face. It oozed off him, and he knew it was the best present he could give to Knight. His pain. "No," Finley said with a growl.

"Oh, yes," Knight said, drawing out the last word into multiple syllables.

Finley was at the point of not caring. He'd explode on Knight and then teleport away. Run. Run until he couldn't anymore, until he reached the east coast. He had to get away. He almost didn't care if everyone else suffered because of this. Finley was normal. He was born from people who were real and not manufactured. And he could have had a life. He could have been free…

Finley was just about to raise his eyes to look at Knight when he felt a presence materialize beside him. Distracted, he looked up to find Fanny. She'd stepped forward. Not stepped. Raced.

"Charles, I know what you're doing here," she said in a voice that almost made the gigantic man seem small.

"Stay out of this," Knight said, his tone sounding dangerous.

"Oh, how about I fill in a bit of the history that even you, Charles, aren't aware of? And once I tell you where Finley came from then I'll happily stay out of this. You can even punish me with a headache if you like," she said and no one in the big top had ever heard the commanding tone the healer was using. It made Benjamin nervous. It almost made him proud.

"Go ahead, woman," Knight said, and now he sounded intrigued. "Tell me what you think you know."

"I know that Finley did deserve a normal life but our Lord obviously has a mission for him," Fanny began.

"Oh, shut up, woman, what do you know of this?" Knight said.

"I know everything about this. I was the one who dropped Finley at that orphanage," Fanny said, and she pinned her hands on her hips as the entire big top went silent.

"What?" Finley said, turning to the older woman, his eyes connecting with hers. It felt strange to look directly at someone.

"I dropped Finley at that orphanage's doorstep nineteen years ago. I told them I was his mother. I told them I couldn't care for him," Fanny said, realizing this story was going to have to be told the right way in order to be effective.

"So *you're* my mother?" Finley said, and now he felt Zuma at his side. She was his security in this moment. He had abandoned her when she needed him most and yet she was next to him now, silently loaning him her strength.

Fanny shook her head, indicating that she wasn't Finley's mother. None of this made sense to him, or to any of the people listening.

"Why would you do that?" Finley asked the healer.

She reached out and touched his chin. He hadn't realized she'd been close enough to do that. "To keep you safe, Finley," Fanny said.

Knight blew out an angry breath. He stood next to Fanny, his fists locked by his sides. "This is absurd, woman. How would you know the child you dropped off was Finley?"

Fanny smiled, her face pure and confident. "Because my healing ability acquaints me with a person's energy. I never forget someone and I know Finley's energy is the same as the baby I healed and dropped off all those years ago."

"What? You healed me? From what?" Finley said.

And now the smile faded from Fanny's face and was replaced by a haunted expression. "I healed you from your father's attempt to kill you," she said, and then her honest eyes dared to drift to Knight. She looked at him without regard for any punishment.

"WHAT!?" Knight said so loud it filled the big top, making most people jump. "No!"

"Oh yes, Charles. Finley is your son," Fanny said, and now she had the demeanor of a disciplinarian lecturing her charges. It was a rare role for her. She was strength and authority. Fanny was unlike anyone had ever seen her. "You thought you killed that baby, but while you were beating up Dave, while Cynthia was killing herself, I saved the child. You had been banished from the circus and Dave had a wife to grieve and a betrayal to deal with. So I decided to take the child to an orphanage. I didn't want Dave to have the burden of raising the child his wife had through infidelity. His brother's son. But then the Lord did something strange by making that the place you visited a month later. By making it so you adopted and ended up with your own son, turning him into your prisoner."

Knight laughed now, but it wasn't his normal laugh. This one was coated in worry. "This is ridiculous and you have zero proof."

"So you didn't adopt Finley from St. Paul's Orphanage?" Fanny said, all confidence.

Only she spied Knight's eyes widen. "I did, but that still proves nothing," he said, almost sounding on the verge of stuttering.

"Well, the child I delivered from Cynthia—your child—he had a crescent-shaped birthmark on his left hip. I know that. I remember it because I studied that child that I saved from your attempt at murder," Fanny said. She turned to Finley for confirmation. And in a daze he dropped his chin to his chest. This was all too much, and the implications made his head swell with heat.

"What? Finley, tell me this isn't true," Knight said, more worry in his tone.

"It must be," Finley said in a hush. "She's right about the birthmark and there's no other way she'd know that." He spoke like he was talking to himself.

Then a voice beside Finley shattered his world. It was the one person who could confirm the reality unfolding before him. "Everything Fanny has said is true," Zuma said in confirmation, having used her combat sense. "She isn't lying."

"Then...th-th-that..." And Knight did stutter then. "That means you're my son."

And to Finley's horror the man before him reached out. From his low cast eyes he spied a hand reaching for his shoulder. And a second before it connected with him he sprung back using his super speed. "Don't touch me," he dared to say.

Around the big top everyone was so still and quiet that it was as if they'd all vanished. Finley was only aware of the wrongness of all of this. Fanny was only focused on the acrobat she had saved almost two decades ago. Zuma had her eyes on Finley too. And Knight felt like he'd been transported into a nightmare, one where he was somehow not in control. He sucked in a breath and looked at his son.

"Finley," Knight said in a whisper, as everything dawned on him at once, "this explains why I can't get in your head. I couldn't get in Dave's either. It's our family connection. This explains so much."

"Dave," Finley said, his eyes unfocused as everything dawned on him as well. "You killed Dave, who was my uncle. You killed me, or tried to, you're the reason my mother committed suicide. You've enslaved kids. You're, you're, you're..." Finley, who had never gone against Knight before, now felt that he could. He should. He should say what he wanted to Knight. "You're the devil."

Knight blinked at Finley. He wanted his son to look back at him. To really see him. He wanted so much from Finley, especially now. "I did it for you. To avenge your death. Don't you see that? Everything I ever did was because I lost you. After that I went insane. I lost it."

For all of Finley's life he'd been afraid of the man before him. Not just afraid, but at times paralyzed by what Knight could do to him if he wasn't compliant. And now that boy who feared Knight was gone. Finley didn't care. There was nothing worse than being Charles Knight's son. To know his blood ran in Finley's veins. This was his absolute worst-case scenario. Finley could only manage to shake his head at Knight. Everything about the man disgusted him. It always had. And now that he knew Knight was his father, he felt disgusted by himself.

Fanny, sensing his burning hostility, put her arm around Finley's shoulder. "It's all right, child," she said, her tone placating a bit of his pain.

Knight was visibly shaking. To have his son. For it to be Finley. Everything was right and wrong about this for Knight. "Finley, I'm only a monster because I lost you and your mother."

"No, you're a monster because that's who you chose to be," Finley said and then for the first time in all his life he turned, putting his back to Knight, and then he left without being dismissed.

Chapter Fifty-Five

*F*inley heard the steps behind him, felt her approach. It wasn't just that her energy registered in him in the most primal way. He also knew the way she thought. She'd know he was a second away from exploding. An inch from the fuse inside him detonating. Zuma was the girl who would want to be there for that. She would endure the shrapnel if she could just be there to hold him up when he finally let it all out and then collapsed. Finley slowed but didn't turn. The other thing about Zuma was she was careless and kept putting herself so close to death because she'd quit caring. Why should the girl who couldn't be happy care if she died? She was diabolical.

"Leave me alone, Zuma," he said just loud enough for her to hear over the wind kicking up leaves and making branches clamber together.

She came to stand in front of him but he kept his eyes high. Off the girl he loved and couldn't have, especially now. "I know you, Finley. You don't want me to comfort you right now. You want to be left alone. I get it. And against everything I want I'm going to give you space. I'll keep giving you space. I'll keep not talking to you. Forever and ever I'll allow you to burn the bridges between us if that's what you want."

"Then what are you doing here?" he said, his eyes on the gray sky behind her.

"The keys to my car are in the glove box. Take it. You probably want to get as far from this place as possible," she said.

Finley nodded. She did know what he needed. Knew he couldn't be on Vagabond Circus grounds right then. He was so close to tearing it apart, to destroying everything that belonged to the man he now knew was his father.

Finley expected Zuma to say one more thing. But as she'd done for all these months, she did the one thing he asked for. The one thing that was also little by little turning his heart brittle. She turned and walked away.

"Zuma," he called out.

She paused and hesitated before turning to face Finley, almost like she didn't want to. Like looking at him without the freedom to love him had taken her brittle heart and flaked it until almost nothing remained. When Zuma faced him he finally brought his eyes down to look at her. She was more beautiful than he remembered since he hadn't allowed himself to really focus on her in a long few months. It was easier if they didn't speak, if he moved beside her without really looking at her.

"Do I resemble him? In any way? Am I a monster?" Finley asked.

"You resemble the soldier he created, but that's all. You are no monster. I've been in your head and I would know." A sliver of a smile made her pink lips spread slightly. "Actually, you think like your uncle, with concern for others. You have his eyes too. Maybe that's what first drew me to you."

Finley then found his feet had brought him to Zuma without his consent. He stood inches from her. His hands felt like magnets drawn to her but he found that closing his eyes overrode that instinct. His hands remained by his side. His eyes pressed closed. Inside his head he opened a telepathic link to Zuma.

Thank you, he said and then he opened his eyes, careful to keep them low. Finley stepped back twice before turning and leaving Zuma standing alone.

Chapter Fifty-Six

*A*ll night Finley drove through the Santa Ynez Valley, hoping with each mile he'd think a thought that didn't make him feel at a loss for ever having a satisfying life. After two hundred miles he found himself back at the grounds of Vagabond Circus. His round trip had only brought him exhaustion. Yes, he could have kept driving. Never returned. Taken the Audi as far as it would drive him and forget he was born to a murderer. But Finley could never live a real life knowing he'd abandoned the people of Vagabond Circus and left them to suffer under Knight's cruelty. His father would hunt for him. He knew that. And the longer Knight went without finding him, the angrier he'd become. Finley would never be able to stay gone for good. His conscience would drag him back, maybe in a month or a year, but then he'd learn that too many had died as a punishment for his leaving.

And Ian...Ian had said he held the key. That's the reason he couldn't step in to save Zuma from the bullying. Finley was supposed to die that day, but now he was alive and had returned to the once-doomed circus. Would things change now that Finley hadn't died?

He returned to his trailer well after midnight. The next performance would suffer if he didn't dream travel or go to sleep right then. The acrobat flipped on the light beside the door and would have startled but caught himself before he allowed the reaction to slip out of him. There, sitting on Finley's couch, his long arms resting on his spider-like legs, was Charles Knight. His bald head was slumped down low, in a way Finley had never seen the man before. Defeat was strong in his demeanor, like a cologne he'd bathed in.

Ever so slowly Knight pulled his head up until his eyes were resting firmly on Finley. Automatically Finley switched his gaze to the carpet. So automatic was the response he didn't even realize he did it anymore. Looked away. Cowered at the presence of the man in front of him. The man who he'd known his entire life and yet had never truly seen. From his peripheral yes, he'd seen Knight. In dream travels he'd seen him. And yet, Finley didn't truly know the man who spent the majority of his life training him with a strange pride.

"Look at me, Finley," Knight said.

"No," Finley said. And it wasn't because he was afraid it was a trap but rather because he didn't want to. He was angry. Irate. Unable to deal completely with the events that had been unveiled.

"You think I'm bad. You despise me. You always have, even when the other kids worshipped me. Do you know I wasn't always this way? She fell in love with me, your mother, Cynthia. Could she have really done that if I was pure evil?"

"I saw the past," Finley said, using a confident voice he never dared to direct at Knight.

"What does that mean?"

"I saw you suffocate that baby. It was wrong before, but now it's personal, now that I know that baby was me," Finley said. "And I saw that crazy look in your eyes. I saw you go to my mother after you thought you'd murdered me. I saw you tell her she was free because you'd lifted her of her obligation to Dave. You'd gotten rid of his child. And I saw that she loved you in the heartbreak that crossed her face, but not until then did she realize she loved a demon."

"That's NOT true. Losing her. Losing you. Losing the circus broke me. That's why I've become who you know. And I'll be the first to admit that my ways are unorthodox, but—"

"You created an army of Dream Traveler children to steal," Finley dared to say.

"Don't you forget your place, boy," Knight said.

"Why? What if I do? Will you have Sebastian kill me? Will you curse me? Take more from me? You stole my life. Imprisoned me. Enslaved me. What worse can you do?" Finley said, his voice bold, startling him.

"I did what I did because I'd lost you. I'd lost my child. And decided all others would be born to be great and serve. That I'd teach them and do what Dave never did. I would make them flawless."

"Are you listening to yourself?" Finley said. Who was this guy standing up to Knight? It didn't feel like him anymore.

"Are you not incredible, Finley? You move like the winds blows. You are more intelligent than those with a dozen collegiate degrees. I did that for you. I did that for all my kids. Yes, I made you steal but only so I could continue to help you to thrive. And now there's forty prodigies making waves out there. They may hate me. You may hate me, but you can't discount that I made you a super human. Can't you see what Gwendolyn and Sebastian see? That I break away your weaknesses and make you great."

Finley couldn't argue with Knight. He did discipline children until they had superior skills, but he did it in the worst ways. Since he couldn't argue against this he said, "And what are you doing to Vagabond Circus? Slowly killing it like you did to me when I was an hour old." And just then, for the first time ever, Finley pulled his gaze up and looked his father in the eyes. "You're suffocating this circus. You should leave it. Let us be free of you."

Knight shook his head. "That's never going to happen. Here is the only place I feel close to her. And look, it brought you back to me. This place is my destiny."

"Then if you are going to stay, lift the curse," Finley said.

Knight narrowed his small eyes. "Why?"

"Because your child didn't die. I'm right here. Don't steal the happiness of others anymore."

"You mean Zuma's?" Knight said, sounding satisfied. He had in fact found his son's weakness.

Finley only stared at his father with a vengeance he couldn't so blatantly show before.

"No, Finley. There's some curses that need to remain. My child was still stolen from me through lies and deceit." And then a laugh that sounded more like tools rattling in a toolbox echoed from Knight's chest. "To think the child that was my star student all these years is actually my son. I should have known." Finley, who hadn't watched his father speak before, never realized how strange the man looked. Knight had traits that mirrored an extraterrestrial being, or so Finley thought. The ones with the long narrow heads, willowy builds, and white, almost transparent skin. He was so similar to the aliens that were reported to have crashed at Area 51. This Martian-looking man was Finley's father and this made him feel more like a freak than ever before.

"And to think you could have killed me a second time. You did kill the other kids I was raised with," Finley said.

"They killed themselves. The weak don't survive. You did because you're my son. You were my first named kid. My most valued kid. I should have seen before now that my blood runs in your veins."

"The very same blood of mine you've spilled so many times," Finley said, thinking of the long scars that ran the length of his back.

"Finley, I only ever sought to make you stronger."

"Yes, I realize that, Master," Finley said, a cold irony in his words.

Knight stood and when he did he was taller than Finley but not by as much as he was with other people since Finley was well over six feet tall. "You cannot hate me. I have worked too hard to rectify your death. Now that I know you're alive—"

"Are you finally going to give me my freedom? Not punish me if I leave?"

Knight stepped forward. "I have only just found you. My punishments will be far worse if you leave me now."

"I wish you weren't my father," was all Finley said.

"Finley, you realize that I'm forcing you to stay because I know you and I belong together. That's why I found you at that orphanage. Don't leave. Don't make me do things I don't want to do. Don't make me punish the ones you chose to love instead of me."

Regarding the man in front of him, Finley stood for a long silent moment. He knew what Knight was capable of. He knew that he would find ways to punish him that would scar his soul. And Finley knew he couldn't withstand living with those scars. As he was since birth, Finley was cursed, cursed by the father he never wanted.

Chapter Fifty-Seven

Unable to focus enough to dream travel and too overwhelmed to sleep, Finley was exhausted when he walked into the big top the next morning. Word had spread and now everyone knew he was the spawn of the evil circus owner. Almost all of the performers and crew were in the big top getting ready for the show that afternoon. It would be the last one in Santa Barbara and then Vagabond Circus would load up and caravan south to the next city on the tour, Oxnard, California.

Most looked up when Finley walked into the big top. Those who didn't were elbowed by their neighbor and before too long every single eye in the tent was focused on the acrobat. Some whispered. Some pretended not to be staring at him as they tried to pinpoint exactly the resemblance he shared with his father. Knight's features were too sharp, his jaw looking to be cut from stone. And Finley, although angular, had a softness to the curves of his face. Where Knight was too tall, too thin, and too pale, Finley was perfect. The acrobat was the perfect height, had a healthy build and an olive tone to his skin. And unlike Knight, he had a full head of dark brown hair.

Finley paused and regarded the people around him with a cold stare. Then he sighed and trudged passed all the polite people who had a hundred questions for him and none of the gall to ask them. The lack of sleep made Finley feel on the brink of insanity. He wanted to laugh hysterically at the elephant in the room and then also throw a fit. He wished he could stomp around the big top and tell everyone off. Instead he only muttered under his breath on his way to the practice tent at the back.

"Finley." It was Knight's voice, and it made the chatter around him pause.

Finley halted too, taking several seconds before he turned around to face his father. The owner of the circus sat in his usual place in the front row, Sebastian on his right, Gwendolyn on his left.

"Get over here," Knight said, his scratchy voice low but easy to hear from the far side of the big top due to the silent crowd.

Finley, as he had done last night, looked directly at the ringmaster. The sight of his father made his stomach churn with unease. "I have to go warm up," he said, his voice flat.

Around the tent there were several startled gasps from performers and crew members. Sebastian narrowed his eyes at Finley.

Finley had only stated a fact, but he had in essence told Knight no. And no one knew that Knight had given Finley permission to look at him, had asked him to, so to everyone in the big top he looked like a guy who wanted to die. And what no one knew was Finley didn't really care if he did.

"You can warm up later," Knight said. "You and Zuma don't need to practice for a couple more hours because firstly, you look like shit. And secondly, I told her to stay in her trailer since her headaches seem to keep getting worse."

Finley narrowed his eyes at his father. He desperately wanted to go check on Zuma. The headaches would be his fault. Knight was going to keep punishing Finley until he fully complied with everything he wanted. And Finley was afraid the list of demands would grow now that he was his son. It had been what Knight wanted most and the reason he'd bred children. To find the perfect heir. To replace the son he thought he killed. *And this fate wasn't ironic*, Finley thought, *it was downright morbid.*

"Sebastian, get up," Knight said.

The boy didn't hesitate, so engrained in him was his training. Each of his movements was precise as he stood and then froze in front of Knight.

"Now move," Knight said.

"Where, Master?" Sebastian said.

"I don't care," Knight said with a frustrated growl. "Patrol the big top. Just get out of that seat. Now Finley, take the seat on my right. I want you beside me while we review the horrid acts for tonight's show."

"I'm fine," Finley said, staring straight at his father.

Knight's almost nonexistent lip curled into a half smile, half snarl. "That's cute," he said. And in the tent people moved but everyone's attention was on the father and son exchange. "You think

that your blood connection relieves you of your obligations to me."
A laugh that sounded more like scissors cutting cardboard flew out
of Knight's mouth. "Don't you see you are more obligated to me
than ever before? Believe me when I tell you that you can't sever the
ties to your parents or family. Even when they're dead."

"I'm not interested in being your right-hand soldier. Sebastian,
take your place," Finley said, switching his gaze to the boy still
standing beside Knight.

"How dare you defy him? How dare you give me orders?"
Sebastian said and stepped three times until he was right in front of
Finley. "I should put my hands on you right now."

"We both know you can't catch me," Finley said and in a blur
of movement he relocated so he was behind Sebastian, speaking over
his shoulder. The boy turned, murder written on his face. With his
hand outstretched, he stepped forward as Finley took quick super
speed steps backwards, a cruel smile on his face.

"Stop this," Knight said.

Sebastian brought his gaze down, but Finley simply crossed his
arms and regarded his father with the contempt he deserved.

"Sebastian, get away from my son. And if I ever find you close
to him then your head will explode. Do I make myself CLEAR?"
Knight said.

Sebastian's eyes grew into slits but he nodded. "Yes, Master."

"Now, go patrol, boy," Knight said. "And Finley, take the seat
next to me or you will be performing solo tonight."

The threat was so clear in his words that Finley's throat froze
mid-swallow. In his mind he was screaming, furious and cursed and
frantic with worry for the girl he couldn't save no matter how hard
he tried. However, he didn't show any of this emotion, only turned
and took the seat on the other side of Knight. He hadn't been seated
for more than a second when the smell of something acidic, like a
cleaning chemical, knocked into his nostrils. A shadow fell down on
Finley from overhead as Knight leaned over him, blocking the bright
lights of the big top.

"You are my son," Knight said, his breath colliding into the side
of Finley's head. "You already perform as he should. But now you
need to start acting like him. I'll be patient training you, but just
know your stubbornness will mean others suffer. If I make myself
clear then answer in a way that proves it."

Finley knew how to move using efficiency. He had the observation skills that made him an incredible detective. And he could deduce the solution to a problem with little thought. He could do all this because he'd been taught how to think by Knight. He'd been taught how to think *like* Knight.

Finley stared straight ahead. And very deliberately he said, "Yes, Father."

"Very good," Knight said, leaning back in his seat.

Chapter Fifty-Eight

Sebastian's gaze was focused on Finley and his master. *How had he served so loyally for all these years only to be shoved to the side so easily?* he wondered angrily. Finley had run away. He was always the kid to challenge Knight, and he was hardly ever punished for it. Knight seemed to find his rebellious attitude entertaining at times. He had punished him growing up, whipped him, taken away kids he got along with, but he never did what Sebastian thought was necessary. Any other kid behaving like Finley did would be cursed, or worse, Sebastian would be turned loose on them. And now Finley was Knight's son. It deflated any hope Sebastian had for standing beside Knight as he further built his legacy. And worst of all he'd been threatened by Knight. It made his head thump with a deliberate force. Still he couldn't go against his master's orders. He might be angry, and feel shoved aside, but Sebastian was loyal. This, in truth, was his only redeeming quality, even if he gave that loyalty to the wrong person.

Sebastian patrolled the perimeter as he was ordered to do, all the while keeping half his focus on his master. Different groups whispered as he walked by. Crew members exchanged opinions on the changes going on at the circus. Half were encouraged by Finley's show of disrespect to his father. "He looked straight at him," people whispered in awed disbelief. "He talked back to him," others said, both excited and fearful for the acrobat. And then there was the other half of the circus who thought that it was only a matter of time before Finley switched sides and became a sadist like his evil father. Then most would have to ignore Ian's orders and finally abandon the circus.

"You still think this piece of shit circus is worth wasting your time on?" Padmal said to Oliver. She was flexing and stretching her hands, getting ready to practice her juggling act with her brothers.

Nabhi and Haady stood close, pretending not to hear her insults. The brothers were practiced at ignoring her.

"Yes, Padmal," Oliver said, keeping his eyes low as he studied Finley sitting next to Knight. "Don't you see that Finley stands a chance of helping us rid the circus of Knight? He obviously hates the guy, probably more than we do. Did you hear what Knight did to him when he was a baby?"

"He tried to suffocate him, thinking he was Dave's child. Yeah, I heard the rumor," Padmal said. Then she smiled, but there was no happiness to the gesture, just demented lust. "I would totally suffocate that damn dead man's baby too. It would serve him right for enslaving us kids."

Oliver's eyes widened with repulsed shock. Nabhi and Haady even turned to stare at their sister with disgust.

"You can't be serious," Oliver said.

"Of course I am," Padmal said. "And it's too bad Knight wasn't successful. The last thing we need is people with Dave's DNA running around. Even if Finley is only Dave's nephew he should be dead. Even Knight should be dead. Anyone related to that horrible, slave-driving, manipulative man who ruined my life should be dead." She then laughed. "You know I wish I would have been there to watch Dave die. That would make me feel better about him keeping the secret of my mother's death from me."

"That's the worst thing you could ever say. Dave was a good man," Oliver said.

"Dave wasn't a man at all," Padmal said. "He was a pompous ass and anyone who followed him is a manipulated dumbass. Is that you, Oliver? Are you a dumbass? Or can you actually think for yourself? Because more and more you act like a sheep who will cower to the wolf."

Heat overwhelmed Oliver's head. He had the urge to slap Padmal, but he had restraint and he was not that type of boy. However, he was certain he couldn't take any more of her bitchy behavior. And he had something better than an assault using his hands to punish her with. He looked straight at her and said, "Dave didn't enslave you. He rescued you."

An abrupt laugh. "You are an out of touch idiot," she said.

Oliver suddenly felt full, like a vacuum that had sucked up enough hair and dirt and couldn't hold anything else. He could finally take no more. "Padmal, you and I are through," Oliver said, slicing his hand through the air.

Nabhi and Haady were doing a poor job of pretending their attention wasn't on the fighting couple.

"No," she said, in one long word, her voice rising an octave, "we aren't. You don't get to make that call, Oliver. I tell you when we're done."

"No, you don't."

"Oliver, you can't leave me."

He turned, putting his back to her. "Oh, but I can."

"Do it and I will make your life hell," Padmal said, her eyes on the place between his shoulder blades.

Oliver turned back to her, a sadistic grin on his usually sweet face. "You already do."

"How dare you," Padmal said and raised her hand to slap him. But behind her Nabhi caught it in mid-slap using his telekinesis. "What the hell. Let me go, Nabhi," she almost screamed, feeling her brother's energy restrict her. The triplets were attuned to each other's specific energy related to their telekinesis, having worked together all these years. Nabhi's energy felt like charcoal. Haady's had the sensation of sand against ones skin. And Padmal's was sharp like granite.

"No. Not until you promise not to assault Oliver. We don't hurt each other," Nabhi said to his sister.

"Oliver deserves it," she said, her hand held in the air, unmoving.

The illusionist shook his head. "You know, Padmal," he said, nearing her, realizing she was frozen under her brother's telekinesis. "Your brothers forged the death certificate about your mother."

"Oliver," Haady said, suddenly shocked by this admission and unaware of how Oliver knew that since the brothers hadn't told anyone.

"It's okay, Haady," Oliver said, his eyes still on Padmal. "Ian gave me some interesting information. Guess what, Padmal, your mother isn't dead."

"What?" she said, able to move her lips and eyes but nothing else. Nabhi had her body restricted, so strong was his telekinetic lock on her.

"Dave did save you," Oliver said, his raspy voice carrying strength. "He knew, based on Ian's vision, that if you stayed at the orphanage you'd be cursed and heartbroken. That's why he adopted you when he did. Because your mother came the next day."

"No," she said.

"Oh yes, but she didn't want you. She wanted her first-born son, Haady. Your mother could only afford him. And if Dave hadn't adopted you then you would have rotted away with resentment at that orphanage. Instead you came here where you've become a rotten little bitch." Then Oliver stood back two feet. He brought his face up to Nabhi and Haady. "Now you *all* know the truth."

The brothers' eyes watered slightly, a sweet fondness for Dave who always gave people what they needed even if they were like Padmal and hated him for it.

"Padmal, don't ever come near me again," Oliver said. "If you do then I will haunt you with illusions of your mother telling you what a horrid person you are. We are through." Then he looked at Nabhi. "Release her."

Chapter Fifty-Nine

*N*abhi pulled his telekinesis off his sister's limbs but stepped in closer in case she decided to attack Oliver, who he thought was standing too close to Padmal.

"You're going to regret this, Oliver," she said, spit flicking from her angry mouth. "I'm the best thing that ever happened to you."

"I'm sure you think so," Oliver said, lowering his pinned up shoulders. He felt like a barbell loaded with too much weight had been lifted off him.

Padmal spun around, ready to charge off. Then she saw the perfect instrument for revenge. The fight had earned her the attention of almost every person in the big top. Even Knight was regarding the scene with a mild interest. The one person who wasn't paying attention was the one who had been picked by Padmal for retribution. Sebastian was passing by her and the group of freaks, his head down, thoughts circling with plans of sabotage. Padmal turned and stalked in his direction, cutting off his path. He almost ran straight into Padmal, but halted just in time, two inches from her. Sebastian's gift, which to most resembled more of a curse, made him all too aware of his proximity to people.

He regarded Padmal with an irritated curiosity, but she didn't notice it. She was too busy flipping her head over her shoulder to shout back to Oliver.

"This is what you're missing out on, you stupid asshole," she said. And then before anyone could stop her, including Sebastian, she whipped back around and threw her arms around the boy's neck, pulling his lips to hers. Sebastian hesitated, his arms out wide with shock and indecision. But after feeling the urgent pressure of the arms around him and the incredible force of her lips pushed into his, he caved and yanked the girl into him. Sebastian had never been kissed. He actually hadn't been hugged, since the surrogates weren't the hugging type. They did direct the children sometimes by holding their hands. And when he was eleven, a surrogate named Brittany grabbed his hand. A few seconds later she fell to the floor dead.

Since that moment, no one had willingly embraced Sebastian. He'd touched hundreds of people, but only enemies of Knight's. And they were all dead now.

Intent on enjoying his first kiss and embrace, Sebastian grabbed Padmal's face, tangled his fingers in her silky hair, and covered her mouth more with his own.

Finley, seeing the exchange, jerked into a standing position.

Knight held out a hand to halt his son. "Nothing you can do about it now," he said flatly. "She's gone."

Oliver, beside Padmal, turned away, disgusted by how pathetic and diabolical the girl he once loved was acting. And just then, when Sebastian was about to deepen the kiss, Padmal collapsed in his arms. Her mouth didn't kiss his. Her arms fell slack by her side. The girl's head lobbed back at a weird angle.

Finley did move then, but not to save Padmal, but rather others. Sebastian let her slide from his arms until she lay on the dirt floor of the big top. As soon as she was down, Sebastian stepped over her body and simply strolled toward Knight. Oliver, who had been turning away when the girl went limp, rushed for her, as did her brothers. Finley switched on his turbo speed and cleared the big top in half a second. He halted in front of Padmal's outstretched body, blocking the three boys from it.

"Don't touch her. She's been poisoned and if you do you will be too," he said, not out of breath at all.

They squinted at him and then to the lifeless body of the beautiful girl.

"Is she okay?" Haady asked, kneeling down and studying his sister for clues to her sudden state. "How do we help her if we can't touch her?"

"You can't," Finley said. Then his head revolved over his shoulder and his eyes connected with Sebastian, who stood beside Knight. "Sebastian is poisonous. The oils he secretes are lethal."

"Wait! What are you saying?" Oliver said, looking at the body and then at the acrobat he firmly trusted, but who was also blocking him from Padmal.

"She's dead. Sebastian killed her," Finley said.

Nabhi and Haady in unison took shallow gasps of air. Tears prickled Haady's eyes. Nabhi retreated into a tunnel in his mind where the current reality was something he was watching on a screen.

"No, this is a mistake—" Haady said.

"It's no mistake," Knight said from across the big top.

Everyone in the tent was now focused on the scene.

"Leave her. She got what she deserved and I won't have her derailing our schedule any longer," Knight said, and then turned to Sebastian. "I think you've accidentally done me a favor. Padmal was obnoxious and ungrateful. Remove her from the big top. Call the authorities. You know the drill."

Sebastian smiled slightly, walking toward the girl whose lips were minutes ago on his. It hadn't been a good kiss but he had nothing to compare it to.

"You have poison in you?" Oliver asked when Sebastian stopped by Padmal's body. Finley stood like a wall between the two boys.

"On my skin. Want to shake?" Sebastian said, holding out a hand.

Oliver shook his head and took a step back.

"You're calling the authorities. Are you going to tell them you just killed her?" Oliver said, his voice bordering on irate.

"No, I'm going to tell them I found her like this. And they are going to examine her using gloves because they're coroners who know best and they will determine she died of cardiac arrest. It appears that the business of being in the circus is very taxing on the heart," Sebastian said, a sadistic smile in his voice.

"You..." Oliver said, connecting the pieces that had finally been overturned. Finley stepped back and clamped a hand on the illusionist's shoulder to restrain him if necessary.

"Yes, me," Sebastian said, his voice riddled with prideful glee. He then grabbed both Padmal's limp hands, lifted them, and dragged the girl's body out of the big top. Her dragged body made a path that looked like a giant snake had slithered through the tent. Everyone watched, powerless to protest, and too dumbstruck by the weirdness and wrongness to do anything but shrink inside themselves. It was right then that most of Vagabond Circus singularly made up their minds. *Knight had to be stopped.*

Chapter Sixty

*N*abhi and Haady remained frozen, staring at the entrance where Padmal was dragged through. For a solid ten minutes neither brother moved. Oliver, on the other hand, ran for the practice tent to find solace. He was more shaken by the bizarre events that had transpired than by the fact that Padmal was dead. Neither her brothers nor Oliver would admit that they had thought of the possibility. Thought things would be better without her around. Usually in this fantasy, Padmal left the circus, but death provided the same result, only made it more permanent.

Now that Padmal was gone there wouldn't be peace, as Nabhi had longed for. Unfortunately, her death brought a new level of animosity that would grow under the surface of the circus like hidden mold. Now that Padmal was dead, there were more problems. Her death brought so much to light, like the fact that a boy with the ability to murder was in their midst, but that shouldn't have been a concern. Everyone's skills at Vagabond Circus could be deadly in the wrong hands. Oliver could deceive with illusions. Zuma could read people's thoughts. Sunshine could roast a person. And Jasmine could have broken someone's neck with no effort. But Sebastian had a skill, and *had* used it to kill.

And now everyone was ready to finally make their own assumptions about Jasmine's mysterious death. If most hadn't questioned Jasmine's cause of death before, then they did after these events. Jasmine had been murdered. Dave, who was in good health as well, had died of the same causes. Cardiac arrest. The exact same report that would come out on Padmal. The Vagabond Circus members moved quietly, getting ready for their roles. But all of them now knew that Knight wasn't just the bad man they suspected who had inherited a circus. He was the worst man, and an extremely dangerous one, and he'd stolen the circus.

Chapter Sixty-One

*T*he show the night Padmal was killed was the darkest one yet. The brothers had less trouble performing than most would have thought. They had a routine ready, having performed it without her when she was recovering from the knife injury. And that night their tricks were faster than ever before. Nabhi moved with a grace he'd never owned, spinning his hands in perfect rotation with the knives that weren't really touching him, but rather moving telekinetically through the air. Haady's knives soared higher, reaching up to over twenty feet in the air. Then, when the brothers switched to juggling the knives between each other, the crowd gasped at the flawless transition. The boys dared to separate, both backing up to the opposite side of the ring. The knives flew across the neon green rug at a distance none had ever seen before. They weren't performing like they had before, when Padmal was injured. They were performing like they were finally free, their genius allowed to soar out of them. It was important for everyone at Vagabond Circus to witness this act and realize that tolerating abusive people will always have far-reaching effects. People do themselves little favor by allowing a toxic person a place within their life.

After the show the crew worked as they never had before, disassembling the big top. No one said a word or made a comment about Ian, who sat still, not helping his crew. His eyes were strangely focused, moving side to side at times like he was watching the flight path of a fly. The crew, knowing the drive wasn't far to the next performance spot, hauled the trailers and semis down the 101 the night of the last show. It was like they all feared the ghost of Padmal would soon rise from the earth and haunt the people of Vagabond Circus.

As soon as Finley parked his trailer on the new grounds, he was surprised to hear a knock at his door, as though the person calling had been riding on his bumper over the last forty miles. Finley hesitated before finally unlocking the flimsy metal door and pulling it back. And again he was surprised. This time it was by who stood at his door. He found Titus there, waiting for him. And then he was even more shocked when the creative director encouraged Finley back into his trailer, going with him as he did. Titus shut the door behind him after swinging his gaze over his shoulder, like he was afraid to be spied there.

"We've got to talk, but we don't have long," he said in a rush.

"Titus, what's wrong?" Finley said, studying the man before him.

"What isn't wrong, don't you mean?"

"I mean, is there something new? Is Zuma okay?"

Titus nodded. "Yes, I've ordered her to stay in her trailer and call me or Oliver if she needs to leave for any reason. She isn't safe by herself anymore."

Finley clenched his fist until his nails bit into the skin. Sebastian shouldn't have this type of rule, but he did and the circus was growing more powerless to stop it. Padmal's death was proof of that.

Titus stared down, a deliberate speculation in his eyes. "I didn't know you were Knight's son," he said, shaking his head like the news still hadn't sunk in properly.

"Yeah, apparently Fanny held on to that secret alone." Finley had questioned the healer at length since finding out the news. She kept her answers brief and strangely clinical.

"I had to know for myself and so I dream traveled into the past and followed the baby Fanny saved. She in fact took him to an orphanage," Titus said, his eyes to the right of Finley like he couldn't bear to look directly at the acrobat.

"Yes…" Finley said, daring to hope the story had a new ending.

"And I visited the child for the month he was at the orphanage and I can confirm that child was adopted by Knight," Titus said.

"But did the child grow up to be me?"

Titus looked at Finley, his eyes overflowing with remorse. "I'm afraid you are his son."

Finley gave a slow nod, one full of heavy emotion but already a growing acceptance.

"And when I confirmed that I couldn't have been happier about the news," Titus said, his voice growing with positive emotion.

Finley jerked his head up. "You what? Excuse me?"

Titus held up his hand to try to pause the series of confused thoughts streaming through Finley's mind. "I'm truly sorry for what you've been put through. That your mother died. That you have a deeper connection with that wretched man."

"But…?" Finley asked, realizing there had to be a *but*.

"Finley, I've been searching for a way to stop Knight. A way to get ahead of him. I'll admit that at times I wanted to give up, firmly believing that we were already defeated. I have been at such a loss. And then Jasmine died and I almost thought it was time to make you all leave, but Fanny wouldn't let me do it…because that brilliant woman knew we still had hope." Titus's eyes beamed with a pride he usually only showed when watching his circus.

"Hope?" Finley said, almost like that was a foreign word he used to know, but forgot its meaning.

"Yes, we have you," Titus said, and he sounded light for the first time in months.

"And you think I offer hope because I'm Knight's son? You may be disappointed then," Finley said. "Knight won't do anything I say. I'm more obligated to him than ever before."

Titus shook his head. "It's not about getting Knight to do anything. It's about stopping him."

Finley almost laughed at this. "And you think I can do that?"

"I know you can. Finley, you have his blood. You have Dave's blood," Titus said, and now there was pride in his tone. "It will still take work on our part. We will all have to work together and stealthily, but Zuma has a pretty good plan and so far it sounds like it could work. And now that we have you, we have the final ingredient. We have a chance."

"Why does my relation to Knight make any difference? I'm still powerless. I'm still under his influence or otherwise he'll punish you all," the acrobat said.

"Finley, the ability to curse, it's a craft, yes. It must be learned." Titus spoke slowly, giving each of his words time to sink in. "But it can only be learned by a select few. There are only certain lineages who can produce curses. Lineages of Dream Travelers with pure blood. You see, there are only a few founder families left. And…" Titus left the word hanging in the air, knowing Finley was smart enough to piece this all together.

"Knight and Dave were from founder families?" Finley said.

"Yes, they had pure blood and more importantly they are from the family with the gift to curse."

Finley's eyes shifted back and forth on the carpet as he put it all together. "Which means…"

"Here," Titus said, pulling a leather notebook from behind the waistband at his back. It had been covered by his shirt. He handed it to Finley. "This was Dave's." He smiled. "Your uncle. It's his notes on his ancestry, but more importantly it has the laws on curses and how to produce them. It's tricky and there's much you need to understand first before you attempt one, so you must be really well versed on the subject. I don't want you to even think about producing a curse until you've thoroughly studied this information."

"Why? What's the big deal?"

"Finley, a curse at the very least will steal years off your life as the caster, but if you don't do it the right way it also has the power to kill you."

Chapter Sixty-Two

𝓕or a whole week the Vagabond Circus members did something they had rarely done. They kept their heads down and their mouths shut. There were whispered conversations in private. Zuma spent a lot of time in other people's heads, relaying information. And she was rarely allowed to be alone, especially since too often Sebastian could be found in the shadows watching her, waiting for his turn. Finley could usually be found somewhere in the distance watching the girl he couldn't have, but could protect. And when he wasn't protecting her, he was by Knight's side doing an impeccable job of acting in the ringmaster's prescribed manner. Finley was the model son, doing everything his father asked, and usually anticipating his requests.

Knight had finally done it, he thought, and in a shorter amount of time than he believed it would take. He had full control over the circus. The people followed him blindly. Maybe some even would grow to admire him like Gwendolyn and Sebastian did. And the shows they put on for the people of Oxnard were the best yet. They were creepy and dark enough to make kids scream. To send grown women running from the big top. And it left everyone who exited the tent with haunted expressions and a dark door opened up in their minds. One where their repressed demons could finally surface. One that opened pits of deception in the world around these patrons.

And even though the employees of Vagabond Circus were compliant, that didn't mean there wasn't still abuse. Knight thrived on drama. Even if he couldn't instigate fights amongst the crew he found ways to create pain. A performer who did everything on cue would still be tortured with an awful headache just to create a problem in their reliability and then they'd be really punished. Belittled. Yelled at. Pay docked. And still everyone sucked in shallow breaths and took the punishment with their eyes low. No one left, abandoning the circus to seek peace. Everyone stayed and pretended that they were Knight's soldiers. But behind closed doors people were planning. Plotting. Taking on extra duties to cover for those who had to practice.

Fanny took care of the kids full time to give Jack and Sunshine unending hours for him to practice, not just walking but also drawing out his other skill. Nabhi and Haady covered for Oliver when he was missing, busy resting up. Zuma spent her spare hours working with Benjamin, going over his part until he rambled about it in his sleep. Titus worked behind the scenes doing a job he'd never been good at. He led. He quietly encouraged people the way Dave had. He counseled people. He sat straight behind his desk, his chin held up high, hands relaxed on his table top. He looked everyone in the eye and confidently expressed his faith in them. And Finley never slept. He dream traveled every single night, spending those hours studying his uncle's notes. Memorizing them.

There was more than Finley thought possible to the craft of cursing. Not only was it incredibly dangerous, but it was likened to producing a planetary law. It was elemental magic. And the precision to pull from these elements had to be extremely accurate. If too much energy was pulled from one then it would overpower the others. The curse would crush the caster. Furthermore, the law had to work in accordance with the existing laws of the universe. If they defied a single universal law then the curse wouldn't work. It would fail and as it did it would drain the power from the caster until he was no more. Literally only ashes.

The universe is energy, and mistakes to the fabric of the universe zap the commanding power in an effort to preserve the system. If someone tries to mess with a universal law then they are gunned down at once by the all-powerful universe. Dave's notes spanned forty years. That's how long it took the man to understand and master curses. And he had only cast one curse and it was the one that protected Vagabond Circus from Knight for all those years. Finley had less than a fortnight to do something it took the greatest man he ever knew to do in forty years. However, the acrobat never showed this doubt when Titus checked on his progress. Everyone was relying on him. Ian often caught Finley's eye during meals and the look he gave him was clear. He was counting on Finley. Everyone was. If he failed then not only would they continue in their circus of doom, but they would be so severely punished most would not survive the wrath of Knight. Maybe only Finley. But he wouldn't want to live after his failure and his punishment.

Chapter Sixty-Three

*T*he Vagabond Circus caravanned to Thousand Oaks after a week of shows in Oxnard. Although the show frightened most, every performance was still sold out. The press continued to encourage those with strong hearts to patronize the circus. Winter was making promises to surrender to spring, and Los Angeles was gearing up to greet the circus with open arms and large wallets.

"We won't make it to Los Angeles," Titus said, tapping his ballpoint pen on a piece of paper, making several useless dots. The pen had been a gift from his best friend. On the silver pen were words Dave said to Titus constantly: "Do what you think you can't."

Titus stared at those words which lay vertically on the upright pen.

"So what are you saying?" Fanny asked from her place on the other side of the desk, her hands clasped in front of her, her eyes on the dots as they multiplied on the paper.

"I'm saying we need to proceed with the plan *now*," Titus said, not like he dreaded the idea but rather with unstoppable conviction.

"What? Titus, we aren't ready," Fanny said, and then she brought her blue eyes up to his.

"We *will* be ready."

"There's so many risks though. I'm not sure that rushing things is wise. People's lives are at stake here," Fanny said in a rushed whisper, always afraid someone could be listening.

"All our lives are at stake, Fanny," Titus said.

"Exactly."

Titus stood from the desk. He walked around it and leaned on the surface, sitting on it slightly, much closer to Fanny. "Look, this is Dave's circus. These people have done extraordinary things. They have done them because they are incredible, but that's only part of the reason. You know what makes this circus what it is?"

Fanny nodded, looking almost nervous. "Belief. It was Dave's belief in others that encouraged their true genius."

"Yes," Titus said. "And I'm not proud to say he was able to maintain that belief with me constantly barking doubts at him. I'm not proud to say I've been a coward not wanting to stake my livelihood and life on faith. But I am proud to say I'm ready to do that *now*."

"You believe we can do this?" Fanny said.

"I know we can. I see it so clearly in my mind that the end result is tangible."

"You sound like Dave," Fanny said.

Titus laughed coldly. "Oh, minus the belly and shorter stature, I always wished I was that man."

Fanny smiled at him. "I don't think you should want such things. I like you for who you were, and even more so for who you've become," she said and placed her hand on Titus's, which lay beside him on the table.

Titus looked down at the embrace and didn't pull away like he would have done before. He simply smiled back at her.

"Titus, it takes a good man to admit when he's been wrong, but it takes a great man to become the person who would no longer make such mistakes," she said and then patted his hand as she rose. At her full height she didn't have to look up much to gaze into Titus's eyes. There was a pause. A silent exchange. And then the healer turned and strolled for the door, her long skirt swishing back and forth. At the door to the miniature big top office she paused. "I'll go prepare."

"Thank you. And Fanny?" Titus said, a question in his voice.

And when the woman looked at him he was flashing her a half smile, a discerning look on his face. "Yes, Titus?"

"I can't help but get the feeling that you're still hiding something, like that major secret about Finley that you kept from me for all these years."

She smiled back at him, no remorse on her face. "Yes, about that. I really hope you know I was trying to protect you by keeping that secret. Just like me, you wouldn't have been able to reveal it, and I didn't want you to have the burden on you."

"I appreciate that you had altruistic reasons," he said, his eyes lighting up, but only slightly, as they fell to the ground.

"And you're right, Titus," Fanny said. "I'm keeping two secrets from you."

He jerked his gaze up at that admission. "Are you planning on sharing soon or do I have to wait another twenty years?"

She touched her hand to her chest. "Warms my heart to think of us still acquainted in another twenty years."

"Me too," he said, nodding.

"And yes, I'll tell you sooner rather than later. But the timing for revealing these secrets has to be perfect."

"Okay, I trust you," Titus said, and it was a pure statement.

"As I do you," Fanny said and offered him one last smile before leaving.

Chapter Sixty-Four

"*I* can't do this," Jack said, blowing out a frustrated breath. "What am I missing?" He looked straight at Sunshine, who sat on the couch next to him.

"Usually I hate the word 'can't' but in this circumstance I kind of think it's the right one. I don't think you can do this," she said.

Jack dropped the hand he had outstretched. "Wow…thanks for your vote of confidence."

"Do you want me to help you or inflate your ego so you waste both our time and screw up this whole thing? I mean, an entire twenty-year venture that brings joy to thousands is resting on you, so your call." Sunshine said this whole thing in an unaffected voice.

"Vagabond Circus isn't resting on my shoulders," Jack said, a bitter edge to his voice.

"It's resting on all of our shoulders. One of us flops and this whole thing fails. This is our most important performance ever." And again the girl's tone betrayed her words. It was bored and matter-of-fact.

"Well, I don't think I'm electrokinetic. Is it possible Dave was wrong?" For days the couple had been practicing, trying to help Jack draw out the skill the dead ringmaster once said he thought lay dormant in him.

"Of course it isn't possible that Dave was wrong," Sunshine said, sounding insulted by the idea. "But I think it is probable that things have changed. You're still healing and that takes energy and what do you think electricity is?"

Jack rolled his eyes and shook his head at the girl. "I know what electricity is. It's a type of energy. You know you don't have to talk to me like I'm an idiot?"

"No, I definitely don't have to, but it sure makes this whole thing more fun."

Despite his frustration Jack found himself smiling at the girl.

"Don't look at me like that," she said.

Jack complied by sticking his tongue out and mock grimacing at Sunshine.

"Much better," she said and then she almost smiled but stopped herself.

"So if I can't use my electrokinesis then how am I going to complete my part of the plan?"

"Hmmm..." Sunshine said, lifting her eyes to the ceiling as she thought. "Maybe consider a more *hands-on* approach."

"Uhh, what?" Jack said.

"You know? Instead of using boring old electricity, which could fail if things don't go right, revert to just doing the job with your bare hands."

Jack's face went white as he gulped. "I'm not sure I can do that, Sunshine."

"I'm not saying it will be easy, but Jack, she *is* the reason that you fell. She's the reason that you were paralyzed."

Jack stared off and released a nod with little conviction. "I'll think about it."

"I, for one, don't think I'll have any problem with my job," she said and then rubbed her hands together, a look in her eye like she was imagining a decadent feast.

"Sunshine, your taste for vengeance kind of scares me."

The girl slid her sinister eyes on Jack. "Oh, does it? Well, then stay on my good side," she said and stood, taking the position in front of Jack and extending her hands to him.

He laid both his in hers, leaned forward, and pressed his weight into his feet. Most people just moved, but Jack had to think about each movement. It wasn't automatic yet, which was the other barrier to his success with the circus retaliation plan. Twice he tried to push up to a standing position and twice he failed, but on the third attempt Sunshine leaned back, pulling him up with some of her weight. When he stood properly he pulled his hands from her.

"Thanks," he said, only inches from the girl. "And I intend to stay on your good side." Feeling steady, he pressed a piece of her curtain of black hair back behind one ear. The movement made him sway on his unsteady feet, but Sunshine, sensing this, pressed her hands onto Jack's hips.

She wasn't smiling as she looked at him, but if he had her empathesis then he'd know she was happy in that moment. Jack's hand moved until it was just under her chin, barely touching her, but she felt his heat. And when Jack leaned down close to her upturned face she felt his breath. His lips almost grazed hers when at their back someone coughed loudly. Jack smiled and lifted his head to look over Sunshine's shoulder at the entrance to his trailer, which he'd moved back into permanently.

"So, I guess the wedding is off?" Zuma said, leaning in the doorway.

Sunshine turned with a cat's expression on her face. As she did she grabbed Jack's hand and wrapped it around her shoulder to keep him steady on his feet and also for the simple fact that she wanted to be near him, close.

"Yeah, about that," Jack said, a laugh in his voice. "I've been meaning to tell you, I don't think it's going to work between us."

"Well, I'm simply devastated," Zuma said dryly, strolling into the room. She plucked an apple from the gift basket a fan had sent to Jack with well wishes. Zuma took a colossal bite from the shiny red apple with her big mouth, then as she chewed she said, "Seriously heartbroken."

"You'll mend," Jack said, leaning a bit more weight on Sunshine than he'd like, but not wanting to sit again. Standing felt good.

Zuma took another bite and with the apple between her fingers she pointed to the pair. "So this happened? Congrats."

"You teach a boy to walk again and he becomes infatuated with you, what can I say?" Sunshine said.

"Hmm," Zuma said. "I'll remember that."

"You don't need to go find a paralyzed victim though, Z," Sunshine said.

The acrobat paused. It was the friendly tone in Sunshine's voice that struck her oddly. "Yeah, why is that?"

Sunshine tossed her long hair over her shoulder as she shook her head. "Oh, you know why."

"Did you come over here on your own?" Jack suddenly asked, his eyes changing with worry.

"It's two trailers down," Zuma said, rolling her eyes. "I'm tired of being caged and supervised."

"You know it's for your own good. You aren't safe by yourself," Jack said.

"I'm fine, Jack. I was coming to check in on you and your progress with the plan," Zuma said, chucking the half-eaten apple in the trash.

"Well, we need to make a change, but I'm hopeful," he said, looking down at Sunshine.

She looked up at him briefly before directing a sincere gaze back at Zuma. "Great circus retaliation plan, Z. It's pretty impressive that you came up with all this."

"Thanks. Titus and I hammered it out together," Zuma said.

"And if we pull it off…" Sunshine said, trailing off with a hopeful expression.

"Then we will be free. We can save Dave's circus," Zuma said, completing the thought.

"Exactly," Sunshine said. "Thanks for that, Z. For working so hard to save us all. You actually have somewhere to go and you stayed instead." Zuma's home was ten minutes away. She could have been in the safety of her mansion and had the comfort of her loving family. But she remained at Vagabond Circus, enduring the dangers.

"You know that I'm as willing to leave this circus as you are, Sunny," Zuma said.

The empath nodded, a look of pure respect on her face. "I know."

Chapter Sixty-Five

A hopefulness Zuma hadn't felt since before Dave died dared to enter her chest. It was a result of so many things: Oliver's freedom, Titus's confidence, Jack's happiness, and now Sunshine's friendliness. No, things were not all right at Vagabond Circus, but they felt like they had a potential to be…one day.

Zuma turned down the narrow row that separated the performers' trailers from sleeper row. Now she had to find out if Ian's vision had shifted. Was the one where the curse was broken and she experienced happiness a future reality? That was also the reality where Jack and Titus and so many others had the best possible futures. It was the one Dave died to protect.

Jack had tried to stop Zuma from leaving his trailer alone, but she'd been unkind and sprinted out the door, knowing he couldn't chase after her. Besides, she hadn't seen Sebastian all day and guessed he was busy doing some errand or other for Knight. And Zuma needed to get things done. Everyone at Vagabond Circus was following her coordinated plans and that meant she had to ensure everything was perfect. She had to talk to Ian one last time before everything fell into place. Zuma knew that she couldn't pull the trigger on the plan unless the future spoke the right message. Something clunked in the bottom of Zuma's stomach. What if the future wasn't right yet? What would she do then? Feeling suddenly panicked by the thought Zuma sped up, and just then her combat sense caught the movement.

She halted just in time to avoid colliding with Sebastian as he stepped out, blocking the space between two semis.

"Hey there, sweetheart," he said, his hands pressed into the pockets of his black jeans.

Zuma had been stupid. Careless. She flipped her head over her shoulder and gulped. She'd been an idiot. There, standing behind her, blocking the opening between the semis, was Gwendolyn. The girl, using her super speed, had blurred into the spot and now stood with her arms crossed in front of her tiny chest. Gwendolyn was smaller than Zuma. Not really a match. But the time and energy she took to fight the girl, to push her out of place, would give Sebastian the time he needed to put his hands on her. It had been their plan all along. Sebastian had been biding his time, waiting until Zuma was too reckless and went off on her own.

Zuma whipped back around to face Sebastian, only three feet in front of her. Gwendolyn at her back stood at the end of the semi, some forty feet away. She had seen the proud look in the girl's eyes. It was no secret that the girl once named Power-Stopper despised Zuma. Her eyes were constantly narrowed at her and then they'd shift to Finley with pure adoration.

"So, you caught me," Zuma said to Sebastian, her eyes on him, but actually studying the place under the trailers on either side of her. Were the spaces big enough for her to slide through easily before he touched her?

"It appears I have," he said and pulled his long-fingered hands from his pockets. They hung by his side, like guns in holsters, ready to be whipped out and shot.

"What is your deal?" Zuma said, and it was obvious she was stalling, but Sebastian didn't seem to mind as he trailed his cold eyes over her, not hiding their up and down path. "Why do you hate me? Why do you want me dead?"

He clicked his tongue and shook his head. "I don't hate you. Not at all. I want you," he said and like his master there was a hiss to his words. Sebastian shrugged, almost looking remorseful. "Wished when I touched you it only paralyzed you, instead of giving you a cardiac arrest."

"What?" Zuma said, her heart hammering wildly in her chest. Behind Sebastian she couldn't make out much, only empty circus grounds and more trailers in the back.

"Well, then I could do what I want to you over and over again," Sebastian said, and then there was the regretful shrug again. "But unfortunately once I touch you, you'll die. Then you'll grow cold. And cold bodies aren't as much fun."

Zuma thought she was going to hurl right then. Her hands hugged her stomach. Stalling wasn't helping. Soon she'd have to charge at Gwendolyn or dive under the trailer. She had to do something. Try and escape somehow. She dared to turn sideways. This was to give her a way to scope her options, but she directed her voice to Gwendolyn. "And what, are you just going to watch? Are you a sicko too?"

Zuma's combat sense told her Sebastian flinched on the other side of her. And Gwendolyn flexed with a new anger. Pissing them off was a part of the strategy. People didn't react as fast when angry. What most didn't know was that hostility fills a body with heat and cool bodies move faster. Zuma knew this though.

"I'm not a sicko," Sebastian said and took a step forward. "I'm misunderstood."

Zuma copied his step, backing up. "No, you misunderstand. I've read your thoughts and you are the grossest of humans and completely out of touch." Then she flicked her eyes at Gwendolyn. "And you're just as out of touch to think *he* would ever want you."

"I don't know what you're talking about," Gwendolyn said, her face flushing with both anger and embarrassment.

"Who? Who does she want?" Sebastian said, looking at Zuma. He looked a little amused, like this secret was of great interest to him. In truth, Sebastian's only friend was Gwendolyn and he thought he knew her.

"Gwendolyn wants the guy standing behind you," Zuma said and the words stole her breath, both due to fear and also exhilaration.

"I'm not turning around," Sebastian said with a laugh. "Nice try though."

"It's better if you don't," said Finley, who had materialized like a bullet. Quick and then frozen, like he hit an invisible wall.

He's standing too far away, Zuma thought. But he still stood there. His eyes were on Sebastian's back, his fists clenched, making the veins in his arms bulge. Inside her head she felt Finley there, a presence she hadn't felt for too long. It was like a fire on a cold night. His thoughts everywhere and then also nowhere in her mind. Intangible as smoke. *You're mine, Zuma. Think and know you're mine,* he said over the telepathic link.

Sebastian's eyes widened in shock when he heard Finley's voice. He shot forward, his poisonous hands reaching for Zuma. She didn't race backward as he would have expected. Instead, she closed her eyes and thought something very real. *I belong to Finley.* And just before Sebastian closed the gap between them, Zuma was suddenly wrapped in something, but it was too much of a blur to catch. And then she was gone. Vanished. Sebastian turned, thinking she was behind him, as Finley had been. But the space was empty. No Finley. No Zuma. He turned back, only to find Gwendolyn standing in between the trailers, shaking her head, repulsion on her face.

"He got away with her," she said.

"Why didn't you stop him, Gwendolyn?" Sebastian said, realizing Finley had teleported Zuma away. "You could have stopped his power."

"I know, but it happened too fast," she said. And in truth, it had happened fast, the series of recent events, but not too fast for Gwendolyn. It had merely been that she'd been distracted at the sudden sight of Finley. He had that effect on her. Made her heart pause. Her pulse gallop.

***

Finley and Zuma appeared quite suddenly in his trailer, his arms firmly locked around Zuma. She had her head pressed to his chest, eyes closed. The last time she'd teleported with Finley, when they were in Knight's compound, she'd almost thrown up all over him. It was a disgusting thought right then, because the last thing she wanted to do was be sick. The girl found that her arms were tight into her chest, having barely a second to register what was going to happen when Finley popped into her thoughts. He'd simply said in her head, *You're mine, Zuma. Think and know you're mine.* She knew instantly that this meant he was going to rescue her from Sebastian by way of teleporting. That's what she had to do for him to teleport with her. He had to hold her and believe she was his to take. And she had to believe she belonged to him. It wasn't a hard thought for her to think. It had been a forbidden one, but usually those kinds are the easiest to feel. The forbidden ones.

And Finley had rescued Zuma, who was seconds away from being Sebastian's victim. But Finley had teleported in front of her, using his super speed he'd wrapped his arms around her, and then he'd teleported them both away. Sebastian had lunged for the girl and Finley nearly was touched by the outstretched hand. Nearly. But he was fast and every movement precise, as his father had taught him.

211

For a long minute Zuma didn't open her eyes, although she knew they were safe in Finley's trailer. It smelled of him, a warm smell. It felt like him, safe and comforting. She pulled in a long breath and with it the smell of Finley, his arms and body all around her. The girl knew that soon she'd have to open her eyes. To look up at the guy in front of her. Then he'd back up and push her away with his tortured gaze. And because she didn't beg and couldn't force him, she'd leave the trailer. He'd follow her, only to ensure she didn't have another run-in with Sebastian, but he'd follow her as he always did, at a distance.

"Are you all right?" Finley said, his mouth close to her ear, his breath brushing her hair.

Zuma nodded, her head still down, her eyes still closed. And then as she'd been expecting, he pulled his arms off her. It was a fast movement, like she suddenly burned him with her skin. His arms had only been the device he'd used to transport her. Even though she wasn't Ian she had read the future well, because as soon as she lifted her head and opened her eyes she saw him backing away, giving her *that* look. The tortured one.

"God, Zuma!" he said, his tone punishing, his mouth tight. "What were you thinking?"

The sudden rush of adrenaline from her near death experience had left Zuma feeling zapped of energy now that she was safe and alone with Finley. "I don't know," she said and dropped her chin. She'd put up with so much since Knight had come to Vagabond Circus. Been strong for so long. Pretended not to feel the pain of losing Dave and Jasmine. But as Finley had suspected, her spirit was suffering. The girl of stone was being tarnished by the hot winds that Knight produced and the constant headaches. "I just..." She shook her head, feeling more haunted by the memory of Finley's arms protectively around her than Sebastian's recent threat. "Never mind. I'm sorry," she said and turned her back to him.

Finley cleared his throat, but found he couldn't speak. He hadn't been alone with Zuma in a very long time. It felt like an indulgent pleasure right then, and that was the worst thing ever for a guy who didn't allow himself to have such things. Again he cleared his throat and in a voice that wasn't quite his he said, "Where were you going? I'll take you there now."

While Zuma's back was still to him, he saw her shake her head. "No," she said, and there were tears in her voice.

Is she crying? he worried. Was it because she'd almost died or because he was hurting her, as he had so much over the last few months? Hardly speaking to her. Leaving without acknowledging her. Pushing her away.

Zuma reached into her pocket and he noticed then she was shaking as she pulled out her cell phone. "I'll have Ian come and get me," she said, and her voice cracked then with what Finley knew for certain were tears.

"Stop." The word jumped out of Finley's mouth. He hadn't even known he was going to say it. "I'll take you to Ian."

She shook her head again, this time more furiously, her whitish blonde hair swaying with the movement. Zuma's hand was still shaking, Finley observed. He stepped until he was in front of her, a series of graceful movements. She had been crying, a tear hanging on the edge of her jaw. Finley made to reach for her but stopped himself. She had been broken so many times since he met her and he was responsible for all of it. With the back of her sleeve she pushed away the heavy tear that still clung to her skin.

"You're safe now. I won't let Sebastian hurt you," Finley said.

Zuma didn't bring her eyes up to Finley's, although she wanted to. "He can't hurt me. He can only kill me," she said, and knew that was right. The death he delivered was probably quick and almost painless. And then her mouth opened and the rest of what she was thinking fell out. "The only one who really hurts me anymore is you."

Slowly Finley's eyes fell shut as his chin tensed. She was right and he had zero response. Even his father hadn't punished Zuma with headaches in a while. She had been able to avoid him since Santa Barbara, spending all her time coordinating in the shadows.

Again Zuma brought the cell phone up, her hands shaking. She swiped through the phone, finding Ian's number. Zuma knew what she'd just said was hurting Finley, since he was still frozen, his eyes closed, his chest tense. She turned from him to give him space. To give him the privacy to wear the hurt on his face. She pressed the phone to her head. It rang once. Twice. Three times. Zuma blew out a frustrated breath when it went to voice mail.

Ian had gotten the call. Knew what Zuma wanted. But he wasn't going to help her. She needed to stay where she was.

"Damn it," she said and ended the call, not leaving a message. Then Zuma found Titus's number. Before she could call a hand reached over her shoulder, taking the phone from her. She froze. The girl didn't turn to Finley to ask him why he'd taken her phone. She pulled in a steadying breath, trying to figure out what she should say now that they were locked in that tiny space alone. But before she could she felt the most unexpected thing. Arms belonging to Finley wrapped around her from behind. His arms slid over hers. His chest pressed into her back. And he didn't stop until he was locked around her, his head pressed up next to hers.

"I'm sorry, Zuma," he said. Those three words carried more meaning than anything he'd said all his life. They said he loved her. That he wanted her. That he pushed her away and that it hurt him. That not being able to be with her was *his* curse. And that he didn't like it, but he didn't know how to change it. And then he said what he knew he had to, to keep her safe. "But we can't do this."

Zuma laid her hand over his forearm, but didn't hug into him. She wrapped her fingers around his arm and tugged, ever so gently, but still the intent was clear. The movement said, "Don't."

Defeated in almost every way that mattered, Finley dropped his arms and stepped back as Zuma turned to face him. For many months these two had left so much unsaid. All their words were sealed inside hearts they had almost forgotten were locked, keys lost. Zuma looked at Finley now, giving him a cautious stare. She slid another set of tears away, off her cheeks. Her expression shifted into one he couldn't quite figure out. It was one of pain, but also something else. *Emptiness,* he thought.

"I can't," Zuma started, her words slow, painful. "I can't keep reaching out for you. I'm not as strong as you are, Finley. And every time you pull me in tight and then push me away it tears at a part of my soul. Not having you is worse than my curse, because I've never known what happiness feels like. I don't know what I'm missing. But with you, I've felt your love and not having it now is agony."

Feeling a sudden weight from Zuma's words, Finley pinned his hands behind his head trying to force oxygen into his lungs. He wanted to lean over to stop the pounding in his head. Finley would have left then but this was his trailer and he didn't have anywhere

214

else to go that felt safe. So instead he said, "What do you want me to do?" And it was a serious question that he really needed an answer to. He was forced to work side by side with the girl before him, to hold her in their acts. To carry her. To pretend they were in love and that they weren't. He was forced to be with her constantly and forced himself hardly to look at her, afraid his father would be jealous of the devotion he felt for her. That his father would punish Zuma for owning his son's attention.

"Finley, I almost died earlier. You pushing me away isn't keeping me safe anymore. All you're doing is punishing the both of us," Zuma said. "And if you hadn't shown up earlier and rescued me, then I would have died and all our months of depriving each other of each other would have been a waste."

He brought his hands down off his head. Again he said, "What do you want me to do?"

"Don't push me away. Not now. Not tomorrow. And no matter who is around."

He looked at her like she was asking him to throw her off a cliff. "Zuma—"

"You asked, that's what I want," she said.

He closed his eyes and pictured this strange reality where they didn't hide their affection for one another. Maybe they were discreet, but they didn't hide it. They were prisoners at the circus, but they were free about their feelings. It felt like he was imagining living on another planet. Finley opened his eyes and looked at the girl before him, the one he hardly ever looked away from and hardly allowed himself to really study.

"Well?" she said, and her voice sounded so tired.

"Zuma, if I lose you—"

"Then at least you had me," she said, and the most poetic smile laced itself on her pained face. And that expression simultaneously hurt Finley and made him feel that he could breathe again.

Come here, he said in her head as he extended his hand to her.

Zuma's face shifted into a tentative look as her feet brought her to him. She didn't take his hand, but rather slid her arms around his waist, tucking herself into him.

And this, to Finley, was proof that she owned him because that very action lifted a pain so searing out of him. Her arms. Her affection could heal him. And the absence of it *had* been killing him.

Literally putting a strain on his physical heart. Pushing his body to a dangerous capacity. Finley let out a long weighted sigh. He squeezed her into him before peeling back from her a few inches. Zuma's face looked up at him, smileless, but seemingly satisfied. Finley was about to lean over and kiss her when she pulled her hand up and placed her finger to his lips, pausing him. "Finley, I love you."

And he didn't know until that moment that words had that kind of power. The power to transport. To make him feel like he was floating. To make him feel strong and weak at the same time. Finley leaned down and rested his forehead on Zuma's. He had said those words to her. Maybe too many times. But to hear them... Only an inch away, she smiled at him. A nervous one. It was in response to the strange, almost cynical look that had just touched Finley's face.

"Do you mean that?" he said, his tone even.

"Of course I do," she said, pulling back from him, jumping into defensive mode. "I have never said that to a guy. Never felt it for anyone like this." Her emotions were all over the place. The beautiful, healing moment now felt strangled by him questioning her love. She backed up another step, growing with frustration. But Finley was already pulling her back from where she retreated. His skeptical expression was replaced by an endearing one.

"Shhh, don't be mad at my question, Zuma," he said, both hands gently resting on either side of her neck holding her face, directing it at him. "I've just never been told that. By anyone."

She blinked back a wallop of tears that shot through her being trying to escape. His words assaulted her insides. "No?" she said in disbelief and wanted to take it back instantly.

Finley simply nodded.

Zuma slid in close to him and angled her mouth next to his ear, standing up on her tiptoes. "I love you, Finley. I love you. I love you. I love you," she said over and over and over, feeling his chest rise and fall rapidly against hers. His hands were now around her back, her arms around his neck. The two pulling each closer, trying to crawl into the other person. Finley slipped back enough to find Zuma's mouth and kissed her, a gracious affection in his every move. He pulled her up until her feet came off the ground and she laughed against his mouth, a freeing feeling taking over them both.

***

The next morning Finley was awoken by the sunlight streaming through a crack in the curtains. The warm beam of sun streaked across his face and gave light to the best sight in his whole life. Lying curled beside him was Zuma, already awake and staring at him. She lay on her stomach, her head rested on her hands. Finley reached out and pushed a piece of tangled hair from her face so he could see her better.

"So it wasn't a dream," he said.

"Definitely not," she said, sliding in closer to him, a slight smile on her face. She slid her nose against his and then her mouth kissed his once. "I love you, Finley."

He blinked down at her with a tamed look.

"Is this what normal people do?" he asked. "Do they wake up every day next to someone they love and receive affection?"

"I wouldn't know what normal people do," she said, and curled her head down until it was resting on his chest, his heartbeat music to her ears.

Chapter Sixty-Six

*E*verything is about timing. Everything. Dave knew that. Ian had been taught that early on. And he had made it his mission to find the right timing for the events at Vagabond Circus.

Things have to happen now, he thought to himself as he crossed his meaty arms in front of his chest. Then he waited for the figure he knew was about to appear to walk out in front of the big top. From Ian's vantage point, twenty yards away, he could barely make out the details of the man. However, Knight's features were unique enough that he was recognizable from twenty stories up or twenty yards away.

Okay, Ian thought, *I've orchestrated this. Now I sit back and watch. My job is done.* He then slipped his eyes closed, to watch the events of the near future as they played in his head.

***

Knight approached Gwendolyn, who was surprised to see her master. She halted on her path between the big top and the trailers. In her hand she held a Styrofoam container. It was hot on the bottom and she used her hand under it for extra support even though it was slightly burning her skin. Gwendolyn, who was always by Knight's side lately, had stepped away to grab his dinner since Bill, the circus chef, was strangely too busy to deliver the meal as he usually did for the owner of Vagabond Circus. The red-headed girl dropped her eyes to the straw-strewn ground.

"Master, was I not quick enough? I hurried as fast as I could," she said, vibrating with anxiety. The idea of disappointing her master was tantamount to cutting off one of her limbs. Gwendolyn had only suffered from the headaches a few times. Her skill as a power stopper didn't work on Knight, which was typical of skills like that. Gwendolyn couldn't stop powers like Sebastian's, since his skill resided in the physical makeup of his body, and she also couldn't stop clairvoyance, telepathy, or empathy. Her ability worked on skills that were physical, like blocking people with telekinesis, levitation, super speed, pyrokinesis, and teleporting. If it affected the user's body then she could stop it but if it affected the mind then she was powerless.

"No, you weren't quick enough," Knight said, his hands clasped behind his back. "Toss that in the trash. I don't want cold food."

"But Master, it isn't—"

"Throw it away," Knight said in a quiet voice. Gwendolyn would have expected him to yell one of those words but he didn't. Still she stepped three feet and deposited the steaming box of rice and vegetables into the trash can. She then turned, head down to her master. Gwendolyn expected to be punished with a headache but instead Knight said, "I actually need you for a job."

"Oh, yes, Master. Thank you, Master," Gwendolyn said, realizing the mind-stabbing pain wasn't about to riddle her brain.

"Open the flap of the tent," he said and from Gwendolyn's peripheral she noticed Knight pointing at the big top which stood beside them.

She didn't question this odd request, only took off at once, pulling one of the two flaps of the entrance back. The big top was dark and empty since they were in between shows. Knight marched through at once and as dutiful as ever, Gwendolyn took the position behind her master. She stayed three paces behind him, her eyes on his long back, watching for the sign that he was about to stop. The young girl didn't want to run into him since he always stopped so abruptly. The man she'd known all her life, who had bestowed incredible wisdom and discipline on her, whom she'd follow through fire, led her to the curtain at the back of the ring. He didn't stop abruptly as usual, but rather slowed a degree before halting. She arched a suspecting eyebrow at him but halted in her mark, three feet beside him. They stood staring at the teal blue velvet curtain. She wondered what this job would include. Knight had such an impressive hold on the people of Vagabond Circus that her help hadn't been as necessary as it was in the beginning. She longed to block someone's power again, and watch the aftermath like she did when she stopped Padmal's telekinesis, sending the sharp blade into her foot, pinning her to the ground. Her master always came up with the craftiest ways to use her skill, like when she blocked Jack's levitation skill, making him fall to what should have been his death.

"Go and stand by the curtain," Knight said.

"Yes, Master," Gwendolyn said, her stomach giddy with anticipation.

He was positioning her so she was in place for his next stunt. She couldn't wait to find out what it was and what insubordinate would suffer for not complying with her master's every demand. She kept her eyes low once in place, the curtain barely brushing her back.

"Move two feet to the right, so you are in front of the seam," Knight ordered, his words not alternating between slow and an urgent rush, like they usually were. He spoke with an even pace. Gwendolyn almost jerked her eyes up to look directly at her master.

"Don't you dare look at me. You move into place now or suffer," Knight said and this time his voice was right, fast at first and then slow. And he, who knew how to study people, knew she was raising her eyes. All paranoia skipped out of her as she sidestepped to the right, directly in front of the curtain's seam.

"Good. Now close your eyes and remain completely still. This won't take long," Knight said.

Close my eyes? she wondered, but did as she was told. Her blood drummed in her head as a smile wrapped around her mouth. Gwendolyn could hardly wait to find out who would be punished, and how. She felt the curtain behind her swish softly against her head. Her eyes popped open and Knight stood still in front of her.

"I said keep your eyes closed. Now you'll be punished," he said, in that same way she was used to. Quick then slow words.

Gwendolyn expected her head to explode with blood vessels threatening to split. Instead there was a different horrible threat. From behind her, hands clapped down on her throat, cutting off her esophagus and therefore her air supply. Her first reaction was to grab the hands. She tried to rip them off her but they were strong. Calloused. Unrelenting. She dropped her knees, hoping to use her body weight to pull the force off her. But the strong arms didn't give up. This actually made the cinch around her neck worse. Her head felt like it was about to erupt and still she could see the feet of her master in front of her, not caring about the punishment. She'd never looked directly at him, not since she was a baby and had learned not to. Now she raised her eyes, intent on finding a solution to this mystery. From her oxygen-deprived state she could still make out the sharp features of his pale face. Crooked nose. Thin lips. Small dark eyes. And a forehead that stretched up a long way to a pointy bald head. And although he was standing, watching her struggle and die, he was still beautiful.

Spots popped into her vision. Bright spots. Black spots. So many they took over. Her head was hot with blood. Her heart slowing. And still the hands tightened, and wrung slightly. Gwendolyn pressed her fingernails into the hands but she knew that was doing little damage. She had little left. Her feet were now not under her because she couldn't hold herself up. The person behind her was strong though. Steady. And held her up by her neck, choking out her air, unaffected by any of her attempts to fight. She hardly even questioned her master but her last thought was, *Why? Why are you doing this?*

"I'm sorry, Gwendolyn," Knight said. And she could barely hear him over the beating in her head. "If there was another way. But we can't win with you alive."

We? she thought and then her eyes slipped shut and her last remaining oxygen reserves depleted, making her heart go out, never to beat again.

Knight's form flickered and then disappeared.

From the side of the curtain Oliver stepped out. He looked at the girl's limp figure hanging loosely in the hands protruding through the curtain. He flinched from the sight of the dead girl, but didn't look away. Zuma stepped out beside him but didn't flinch. Her expression remained stone.

"It's done. She's dead. No more consciousness," she said, having stolen a link into the girl's head. It was how she'd been able to make corrections and communicate suspicions Gwendolyn had when interacting with Oliver's illusion of Knight.

The hands dropped the girl and she crumpled to the ground. Then the curtain pulled back and Jack looked down at the girl, the one he'd strangled. He didn't kneel but he did drop his head slightly.

"I forgive you, Gwendolyn." And then he stepped around the body and with a confidence Zuma had never witnessed before, he walked forward. He didn't hesitate. Every step was strong. Deliberate. Full of grace only Jack possessed. One unique to him. He walked until he was just in front of Oliver and her. "It is done. Good work."

Zuma slid up next to him. She looked up at her friend. Cupped his face. "You, Jack Fuller, did the right thing. Thank you."

He nodded, his head in her hands. The burden of taking a life already lay across his heart. "I know you're right," he said.

She stood up on her tiptoes and kissed his cheek. "I'm so proud of you."

He smiled at her. "Thank you."

And at their back they heard the two crew members picking up the girl's body. She would be deposited in a respectful manner, but no reports made. She was one of Knight's kids and they, as far as the government knew, didn't exist. Zuma hooked her arm through Jack's and with Oliver in the lead the three walked out of the big top.

Chapter Sixty-Seven

"*I* thought I might find you here." Knight's voice made Sebastian jump to attention. The boy had been leaning against the trailer beside Zuma's, which was empty because it used to belong to Jasmine and no one wanted a dead girl's trailer.

Knight always moved with a silent grace so Sebastian wasn't surprised that he snuck up on him from behind. What surprised the boy was that Knight was there at all. His master was regimented. He always ate meals at the same time. This was his dinner time, which was why the boy had taken the hour to stalk his favorite prey. Zuma had gotten away but next time Finley wouldn't save her. Hell, next time Finley would go down with her. He was looking forward to the things he'd do to Zuma when she was dead. He didn't mind dead bodies. Actually, before his kiss from Padmal, dead bodies were the extent of his knowledge when it came to intimate experiences.

"Yes, Master. Here I am. Is everything all right? Do you need me for something?" Sebastian said, snapping to attention, jerking his eyes to the ground.

"Of course I need you. Why else would I come and find you?"

"Right, Master. My apologies. What can I do for you?"

"Follow me, Sebastian," Knight said and pivoted at once and walked through the space between the trailers. Nestled behind that row of trailers sat a strip of forest. It was unmanaged since the city of Thousand Oaks had strict regulations regarding interfering with the wild agriculture. Knight marched through the thicket of trees, having to duck several times due to low-hanging branches or curtains of vines. Twice he almost tripped on thick roots camouflaged by clumps of leaves. On Knight's second stumble Sebastian watched his master with a renewed interest. Yes, managing the forest was hard for even Sebastian, who was close to two feet shorter than Knight. However, Knight was used to his stature and also moved without error, no matter what. Sebastian's master was not a clumsy man. Not ever.

"Master, are you all right?" Sebastian said the third time a hard-to-see vine caught Knight up. They were deep into the thick trees now. The Vagabond Circus couldn't be seen behind them.

Knight whipped around and Sebastian darted his eyes away so he wouldn't be caught looking at the man. "How dare you ask me a question of that sort. Of course I'm all right."

"It's just that you—"

"Do you want a chance at Zuma or not?" Knight said, cutting off the boy.

Sebastian paused. Was Knight going to give him a gift? He had said that he was on his way to earning something. Sebastian thought that meant more money or more freedoms. More of a rein, like the opportunity to actually leave the circus at night and put his hands on people out late. Knight had always forbidden this but he was giving Sebastian more privileges since he showed him so much loyalty.

"Yes, that's right," Knight said, his voice that unmistakable tone, like a record scratching. "I've ordered Gwendolyn to detain her out here. Zuma thinks she's meeting with Finley. He told me she scheduled the meeting to figure out how to take me out. Can you believe she was so naive to not realize my son would turn her in?"

"Yes, that's very noble of Finley, Master," Sebastian said. *Too loyal,* Sebastian thought. It was hard to believe the guy who had just saved Zuma from his touch a few days ago would turn the girl in. That didn't sound in accordance with Finley's past behavior. What was more likely was Knight was being set up.

"Master, I don't think this is a good idea," Sebastian said and again Knight, who had continued the trek through the forest, stopped and turned, making the boy drop his eyes.

"Are you telling me you don't trust my judgment?" Knight said.

"No, not at all. I don't trust the people at Vagabond Circus, Master."

"What is it that you want to do? I'm offering you full access to Zuma. Touch her. Take her off my hands. Get her away from my son."

"I'll do it. But I don't think you should accompany me. What if it's a trap, Master?" Sebastian said.

Knight narrowed his eyes with satisfaction, but Sebastian didn't see it since his gaze was averted. "And if it is a trap?"

"Well, then I'll take down the attacker. None of them can beat me. They can run but then at least we will know who you should punish."

From Sebastian's peripheral he spied Knight nod. "Very well. You will walk to the end of this forest. There's a clearing there. Cross it and you will find Zuma waiting for you. The trees are too dense in that spot so she'll be trapped. And Gwendolyn is stationed close by so Zuma won't be able to use her combat sense on you."

"Okay, I've got this," Sebastian said, his eyes a little higher than usual when facing Knight. "I'll go now."

"Very good." And Knight turned and walked back the way they'd come a few paces.

Sebastian hadn't moved off yet. "Oh, and one more thing," the boy said, feet apart, head held high.

Knight turned and Sebastian was looking at him directly. "You've always punished me for not calling you Master in every address. Which means you aren't my master."

The fake Knight stumbled back, his large feet catching on a root again. Sebastian lurched forward, hands out.

Because the shape shifter was granted all the skills of the person he took on, Benjamin shot Knight's cognitive torture at Sebastian and the boy dropped to a crouch, the intense pressure making him cradle his head. Seizing his opportunity, Benjamin pulled Knight's oversized frame back up and ran for the clearing where they'd been headed. He had only one more opportunity to fix this but he'd have to move without error. He leapt over logs and knocked Knight's wide shoulders into unseen twigs. Then to his horror he heard another set of footsteps behind him. He dared to look and realized that his focus on getting away had released Sebastian from the headache he'd hit him with. Benjamin considered giving him another one but the adrenaline racing through him made it impossible to focus enough to be successful. All his efforts were on getting away. Sebastian was now just behind him. He could feel the boy reaching out for him and in his large body he moved so much slower than the boy. Sebastian's hand was almost on Benjamin when he made the impromptu decision and morphed instantly back into his ten-year-old figure. Suddenly he was sprinting at twice his previous speed.

"What the hell?" Sebastian said behind him.

Benjamin dared to look over his shoulder. Sebastian was still after him but the shock of watching his master's form slide into Benjamin's tiny body had slowed him considerably. Benjamin raced until he was on the other side of the clearing, hidden back inside a thicket of trees, and only then did he turn and see Sebastian halt.

The boy laughed. "Nice try, Benjamin. And nice trick. Now that I know you're a traitor you're really dead. You'll have to come out of there and when you do I'll be waiting."

Benjamin looked up at the figure beside him and nodded. Her hair made it hard to really see her but he could make out her pale face nod back. "I've got this now, Benny," Sunshine said. "You may want to look away."

"No, I want to watch," the boy said.

She nodded and then stepped out into the clearing. The empath was dressed all in black as usual, which made it hard to see her standing in the woods. "You won't be waiting, Sebastian," she called across the clearing. Sebastian was twenty yards away, closer to the other side of the opposite forest.

"What are you doing here, freak?" he yelled.

"I'm convicting and sentencing you," she said and walked forward, her combat boots mashing down the long grass under her feet.

Another laugh. "Of what?" Sebastian said.

"Are you or are you not responsible for Dr. Dave Raydon's death?" she said, still moving forward.

"Oh, is that what this is about?" he said, his hands on his hips and his black hair hanging in his face. "Yeah, so what? I was following orders."

"And what about Jasmine Reynolds-Underwood?" Sunshine said, her long black skirt taking pieces of grass with it as she walked. She was now fifteen yards away.

"I was bored," Sebastian said with a sneer. "Look, I don't really have the time for this. You and Benjamin should leave the circus now that I know you're traitors. But even then I *will* hunt you down and kill you."

"Not if I kill you first," Sunshine said in a playful tone.

The boy's laugh sounded cold in the clearing as it echoed with no joy. "What are you going to do? Set me on fire? I'm pretty certain

I can stop, drop, and roll. And you're too far away. I'll be in that forest and gone in no time."

"I'm closing in on you," Sunshine said, moving forward, now ten yards from him.

"Well, how about we end this then?" Sebastian said. And he took off at the girl, hand outstretched and aimed at her bare arm.

Sunshine stopped, raised her own hand, and shot a neat bit of fire at the boy, but it missed. He laughed, continuing to close the distance. When he was almost ten feet from the girl he halted.

"Looks like we get to have a showdown," Sebastian said. "One ball of flame from you will burn me, but one touch from me will kill you. How about we count to three and take our best shots."

And he was right. The odds were in his favor, but they were also in the favor of the person who had planned for this disadvantage.

"That sounds great, 'Bastian. Oh, and also notice your clothes are a bit stiff today. I took the liberty of doing your laundry. I used a solvent known as chlordane. It's odorless and also highly flammable. Thank me for it while you burn in hell," Sunshine said.

Sebastian's eyes widened. He lurched forward to close the distance but that only gave Sunshine a better shot. She aimed and hit him square in the chest with a large ball of fire. It knocked the boy back several feet, and what would have scorched him but disappeared, suddenly spread with vengeance. Fire ran over the surface of the boy, covering him like a suit. It licked up to his face where it paused as he screamed for mercy. He then threw himself to the dry earth but that only added kindling to the fire, which spread through the grass, smoking and growing hotter. Sunshine watched, feeling the pain and torture in the boy. She thought it was only fair to feel the emotions of the first person she'd ever killed. Then she looked up to the sky, closing her eyes against the bright fire in front of her. A tear slipped down her cheek, tasting of salt as it fell into her mouth. It was a welcome taste over the smoke and burning flesh.

"I love you, Dave. And now you have the retribution you never would have asked for, but I needed to give you," she said and then felt the warm hand slip into hers and squeeze. She didn't look at the figure melting before her, only pulled her gaze down to the boy beside her. Sunshine slipped her hand from Benjamin's and put her arm around his shoulder, turning him back toward Vagabond Circus.

"Let's get out of here, what do you say?"

227

He nodded up at her, his lip pressed firmly between his teeth.

Chapter Sixty-Eight

Knight's fingers drummed on the desk he had set up in his semi. The place was quite cozy and didn't resemble a truck at all. That's what money and unlimited man hours did for a person. He swiveled his eyes to the antique clock on the far wall. Gwendolyn was late with his food by exactly thirteen minutes and twenty-six seconds. That was unacceptable. She would be punished severely for the incompetence. And still, it was so unlike her. She met expectations, or rather exceeded them, most of the time. Knight threw down the pen he'd just had in his other hand. He couldn't focus knowing the girl had tarnished her almost perfect record. It made him livid enough to upturn the desk in front of him which once belonged to FDR.

Knight slid back from the desk, his hands gripping it. He had pretty much made up his mind to overturn the piece of furniture, even though that would most likely leave it in an irreparable state. But just then something bright flew by the door at the back of the truck, the one he left partially ajar to encourage air flow. Knight stood, his eyes pinned on the open door. Again an orb of sorts flew past the open space, but it paused and hovered just in the doorway before zooming off.

"What the hell?" Knight said, wondering who was daring to disturb his dinner schedule. They should all know better. Then the orb returned, flying straight into Knight's chamber and pausing just inside the space. It was a bright ball of light. No discerning curves or details, it was like the sun, too bright to see properly.

"What are you?" he said to the extraterrestrial object.

In answer it zoomed out of the semi and out into the grounds. Knight bolted forward and ripped the door back at once. The orb of light hovered just in front of his truck and then flew to the right. Knight's eyes followed it and then it disappeared between two rows of trailers. He squinted, his gaze blurred by the setting sun.

"Damn fools and their tricks," he said, thinking it was one of the crew members playing with their lame gifts. That's why they were all crew members, because they didn't have a useful skill for performing, like his son, Finley.

Knight was just about to turn back to his desk when someone impossible happened out from between the rows of trailers. Not only was it impossible for this man to be walking around the grounds of Vagabond Circus, but he was strolling casually, whistling and twirling his top hat around one finger. Knight blinked at the figure draped in evening sunlight. It had to be one of Oliver's illusions. He would make the boy pay. And then the figure of Dave Raydon knelt and picked up something from the ground. The dead ringmaster held up the shiny penny between his gloved fingers as if inspecting it. Then he pocketed the found money. Illusions couldn't pick up objects in the physical realm. But Dave was dead. Knight knew that.

His brother strolled through the grounds until he disappeared into the big top, a little ways off. Knight didn't believe for a second that his dead brother was ambling around the grounds of his circus. And still he had to believe his eyes. And then two other figures stepped out from the same spot where Dave had originated. One with red hair and the other with a head full of black hair. The two looked at the semi where Knight stood, but they were looking straight into the bright setting sun. They squinted. Gwendolyn even put her hand over her eyes like a visor and then shook her head at Sebastian. The two, as though deciding Knight wasn't watching them, darted across the grounds in the direction of the big top. Knight guessed they couldn't see him standing there in the doorway because of the direction of the sun.

They both checked over their shoulders before disappearing into the big top. Knight shook his head. He didn't know what was going on but he was going to get to the bottom of this damn mystery and he was going to do it right then. He only wished Finley was there, but he'd sent his son on an "errand" to take care of some patrons who had disgraced the side of the big top with graffiti. Knight stepped down from the semi easily and stalked east toward the big top.

Chapter Sixty-Nine

*F*rom Titus's vantage point, located behind Knight's semi-truck, he knew they had been successful. The ringmaster had taken the bait and was now crossing the grounds, headed in the direction of the big top. It had been Titus who produced the ball of light. He'd always hated that he had such a lame skill, the ability to illuminate. He was in essence a walking flashlight. While some Dream Travelers could read minds or teleport, Titus was only really useful in a power outage. Dave didn't think the creative director's gift was lame at all and mentioned it on several occasions.

"Don't you see, old friend, that you have the ability to illuminate because that's what you do in other people's lives?" Dave had said to Titus multiple times. "You produce light in the physical world as your Dream Traveler gift, but your gift as a human is that you bring that light out of people."

Titus always thought Dave must be projecting himself onto him, because he didn't think he brought out much in most people. That was what Titus *had* thought, but presently he was thinking that Dave was right. Titus had swelled with pride when he watched Benjamin do the perfect impersonation of Dave a few minutes prior. He had worked with the boy for hours, ensuring that the ten-year-old didn't just look the part of the dead ringmaster, but also acted the part, using Dave's true mannerisms and flashing Dave's easy smile. And Oliver, who had trouble crafting real people to detail, was able to create two exact replicas of Gwendolyn and Sebastian. Titus had helped with this. The creative director held out his hand and made a sphere of light appear there and smiled at it. *My job is to illuminate, and for now my job is done,* he thought to himself.

Everyone at Vagabond Circus had done their job that day, except for one. He would be the only employee in the big top when Knight entered it. And everyone was ordered to stay out of the big top no matter what. That had been Finley's one request. "This war will end between father and son," he had said during the final planning meeting. "I want no one there to be used against me. I want no one hurt in this final battle."

Titus had thought that Finley sounded much like his uncle saying those words. Finley had always reminded Titus of Dave in a way, and now he knew why.

Titus watched as Knight paused momentarily before entering the big top. Now Finley would have to do something that his uncle was never prepared to do. He'd have to risk his life by taking Knight's. Two men were in the big top and only one would walk out.

Chapter Seventy

*T*he big top was dark when Knight entered. He paused in the entrance, but not because his eyes had to adjust. He could see fine in the dark, just like everyone in his family. It was a gift they all shared, like the ability to curse. He paused to take in his surroundings, since he suspected he had just been led into a trick. Still, anyone foolish enough to trick him would only find themselves defeated, he thought.

Nothing was out of place in the big top. The seats were set up. The performance equipment stowed away in the practice tent, and the curtain pulled as it always was. *And Dave? Where is he?* Knight had seen him enter the big top, but it was empty now. Knight's ability to torture through cognition made it so he could feel the minds around him, pick up on their energies. However, he felt no presence in the big top.

"Gwendolyn? Sebastian?" Knight said, his voice loud and clear.

Only silence met his ears. He stepped forward, his head held high. The man didn't care for games. Had never played them as a child. Knight didn't actually believe in the luxury of playing. It corrupted people's minds. Made them soft and chipped away at the opportunity for discipline.

In truth, the big top wasn't empty. Benjamin had already cleared the space and exited through the practice tent at the back. However, hovering just inside the big top was Finley, but his father couldn't feel the presence of his mind. The acrobat pressed his eyes closed and said a final prayer before teleporting.

***

Knight was about to turn around and storm out of the big top when an unmistakable figure appeared in the middle of the ring. He could clearly see the features of his son's face, which were much more proportionate than his own. His nose the right fit for his face. His chin the right degree of roundedness. His eyes not small, like

Knight's, but wide and unmistakably the greenish hazel shade of his mother Cynthia's. Thankfully, Knight thought, his son took after his mother in appearance; otherwise he would have been more a freak than an acrobat.

"Finley," Knight said, not a question in his voice, although it was too dark for most to see in the big top. "What are you doing here? You shouldn't be done with the job I sent you on yet."

"I didn't do it," Finley said, his chest held tall, his chin high too. He could see his father without issue, as well. Knight's snow white skin seemed to glow in the darkened big top. His long face and its features told Finley what he already knew. Knight was pissed. Pissed that he'd been led to the big top. Pissed that Gwendolyn and Sebastian appeared to be acting insubordinately. And pissed that he, Finley, had not done the job he was assigned.

"You what?" Knight said, his voice rising.

"I. Didn't. Do. It." Finley said each word deliberately. "I haven't done any of the jobs you've assigned to me recently."

Knight marched forward until he was only a few feet from Finley. "Why?" He hissed out the word.

"Because hurting people is wrong," Finley said and crossed his arms in front of his chest.

"That's not for you to decide, SON!" Knight said, yelling the last word.

"How I live my life is *my* decision."

"That has never been the way things are. You are mine. You were mine when I adopted you. And you are mine now that I know you're my son. You don't have the liberty of making your own decisions unless you want others to suffer," Knight said, racing through parts of some sentences and deliberately slowing on others.

"You aren't going to hurt anyone anymore, Father," Finley said, and the last word had a bite to it.

"You don't get it, do you, Finley? You think that people shouldn't be hurt? You've always had that wrong notion. I watched you flinch when the kids in your set growing up were hit with headaches. You didn't understand then, and you don't comprehend it now, that I was disciplining them."

"You were killing them. That's what happened to the kids in my set. All of them," Finley said, allowing his emotions to spill out of him as he flung his arms out wide.

"The weak die from discipline. That's the natural order of things, Finley. That's why you survived. You are my son. You are strong. But you are also flawed in your ability to see things clearly."

"It is not for you to decide who gets punished. You aren't God. You don't control the natural order of things. That's not your job," Finley said.

"So you didn't punish the kids who disgraced the side of my big top? Or punish any of the other kids I've assigned you to go after? Don't you get that you're allowing chaos when I'm trying to stop it?" Knight said.

"There was never chaos or theft or violence by our patrons before you were the ringmaster. When Dave led this circus, he inspired good behavior by being good."

"Don't you dare speak to me about my BROTHER!" Knight said and he raised his hand as if to strike Finley. However, Finley teleported back several feet just as Knight's long arm swung through the air. He was quick, like Finley, and the movement barely missed his son.

"You always had no issue striking me," Finley said through gritted teeth. Too often he'd felt Knight's oversized hand and heard the speech about how he was making him stronger.

"What are you doing, Finley? Are you acting out? Are you having doubts about your role in this family?"

"This is not a family. And what I'm doing is putting a stop to you and your demonic rule. It's gone on too long, Father."

Knight laughed, one so loud that Finley could have sworn it made the support beams of the big top vibrate. "You are naïve. You are as diluted as the people you try and protect. Gwendolyn! Sebastian!" Knight yelled his kids' names loud enough that Finley was sure the circus members who were no doubt stationed outside the tent could hear it. Actually he was fairly certain his father's yells could be heard at the edge of the circus. "Gwendolyn! Sebastian!" Knight called again a few seconds later.

"They won't be coming," Finley said plainly.

"What did you do with them? Where are they?" And there was a hint of worry in Knight's eyes. He was strong, but without the ability to stop others' powers or kill them with touch he was at a significant disadvantage.

"They won't *ever* be coming to help you. Father, you're on your own."

"What did you do with my KIDS?"

"They were punished for helping you," Finley said. "I didn't like it, but that's what had to happen."

"Why?" Knight's voice actually vibrated with something akin to pain. "You killed them? Why would you do that?"

"Because you can't be stopped as long as they are around. And they blindly follow you, no matter what you ask. There's no reasoning with them. They are exactly what you intended them to be. Soldiers. And the worst kind. Unquestioning ones."

"Finley, you will pay for this," Knight said. And if Finley had Zuma's combat skill then he would have seen his father lunging for him before he did. But his father's long frame and fast actions made it so he didn't move before Knight wrapped his hand around Finley's shirt, and launched him into the air so Finley's feet flew off the ground. "How dare you try and stop me," Knight said, spit flew and hit his son in the face.

Finley wrapped his hand around the arm holding him up off the ground. His father's skin was cold and tight. He took a steadying breath, knowing Knight was about to throw him through the air. He couldn't give him a headache, but he could beat him until he couldn't breathe and had done it on many occasions. Finley let out the breath and then disappeared.

Knight dropped his hand to his side, looking around the big top for his son who had teleported away. "Oh where, oh where are you going this time?" Knight said, in a demonic sing-song voice.

On the far side of the ring, next to the curtain, Finley appeared.

"Why are you doing this?" Knight turned and faced his son straight on.

"Because I'm tired of watching you abuse. I'm tired of being your pawn. I would rather die than allow you one more day to spread cruelty."

"Finley, you are asking to die then. You realize that, right?" And Knight raised his hand up and the movement that followed was quick. A single jerk. His hand moved less than a foot through the air, but the result was immediate. The metal scaffolding that held up the large spotlight bent with a rush. The light on the end of it flew loose and raced overhead, straight down at Finley. The acrobat looked up just in time. Instantly he discerned the safest path out of the overhead assault and using his super speed he sprinted to the other side of the ring. But Knight, sensing the direction his son would take, raced, knocking into him, tackling him to the ground. Knight weighed significantly more than his son due to his superior height.

Metal and glass from the spotlight rained from the trigger effect Knight had caused using his gift to pull down the light support. It dragged down the curtain when it fell on it and this encouraged the other scaffolding on the other side to crash down.

Father and son rolled. Finley struggled to free himself from the hands seeking to pin him in place. Knight sought to maintain a hold on the guy who could outmaneuver him using his super speed. Knight brought his hand up and before Finley could move, a rain of broken glass stole the acrobat's attention, which caused him to hesitate. His father's fist made his teeth shake in his mouth, like they were all loosened at once. His head exploded with white burning pain. The scene in front of him turned black and that's when he realized he couldn't fight his way out of this anymore. Finley disappeared.

It took Knight a second to realize his son wasn't under him. His arm swung out, catching only air. The movement, so hard and meant to be fatal, made the man throw himself in the opposite direction. The domino effects of his earlier actions were still occurring, metal and pieces of the support scaffolding shredding apart, unlacing in pieces. The big top was built like a pyramid and any piece out of place created a shift in the balance. Knight had knocked out one of the principle support mechanisms without knowing it. He rolled over, startled by the screeching of metal above and just then, the side of the big top fell, cutting the space in half. Knight was covered in part of the tent and stumbled out to the other side of the ring, just as another beam flew sideways, crashing down and knocking the man to the ground. It lay oddly across his legs, pinning them in place. The big top shifted all around him, falling down in places, tearing in others. Billowing from the force of the rush of air.

"Ahhhh!!!" Knight screamed, looking at his pinned legs. The beam had cracked his femur, of that he was positive, but what burned more was his anger. Knight actually loved pain. It made him feel alive, but he hated being trapped. He could manipulate the heavy beam pinning him, but he couldn't move it. To release himself from that position would take time. He scanned the dark tent. He didn't know where Finley was and was certain he didn't have much time.

The big top was half deflated when it finally stabilized. The remaining support beams had done their job and stayed up, although two of their brethren fell. The scaffolding and beams that fell had finally stopped creating further destruction in their wake. Knight could hardly see this due to the dust clouding the air around him. He could see in the dark, but he couldn't see through dust particles.

Knight blinked several times and a figure coated in dust and dark appeared. His son's unmistakable figure. "Finley," Knight croaked out, his voice more scratchy than usual. "Help me."

Finley stepped forward until he stood only feet from his father. The dust had started to settle, but still his eyes watered from the assault of dirt. "I will help you, Father. I will give you a choice."

"A choice!" Knight boomed. "You let me up now and when you do I won't kill you. How about that?"

"No," Finley said, his one word almost too quiet to be heard.

"Well, I'm not going to do whatever it is you want. And we both know you don't have it in you to kill me. You could never harm anyone easily. There's no way you're going to kill your father."

"I have other ways," Finley said, and then the dust in the half big top settled at once like it had all been sucked to the earth where it originated. The ambient light that slid around the cracks made by the crash of support beams brightened. All noises, those heard and those unheard, intensified. And the temperature in the tent rose suddenly, making Knight's long forehead bead with sweat.

"What are you doing?" Knight asked, although he knew. He'd felt these elemental changes enough times to know what was going to follow.

"I'm giving you a choice," Finley said, his chin low, but his eyes on his father who lay before him. The acrobat narrowed his gaze and drew in a long breath. He felt the power, the one granted to him by pulling on the energy of the universe. He hadn't practiced this enough, but felt that he needed a few more seconds to establish the foundation for the curse that would follow.

"Don't you do this, Finley," Knight said, real terror in his eyes.

"You've made me do this," Finley said, and just then he felt a tug in his core, like the most startling gut feeling ever. It was now or never. When Finley spoke his voice was different. It was louder than he intended, like it was being projected from speakers all over the big top. It made the rug under his feet vibrate. And it burned his lungs. However, he still spoke, each word a deliberate part of his curse. Each word a critical ingredient. Each one spoken with the same amount of power. "As long as you, Charles Knight, have ill will towards others then your heart will not beat. Lungs will not breathe. I give you every chance to live. All you must do is let go of the evil within you if you want to survive," Finley said and then stopped, holding the force and intention inside his heart and mind, directing all the power he'd borrowed from the elements to them.

Knight didn't do anything. Just remained frozen. Finley watched, continuing to hold the focus. The seconds following a curse were the most crucial. His lungs began to burn. His heart began to hurt and he suddenly feared that the curse had backfired. A real repercussion he was aware of. Finley kept the intention of the curse central in his thoughts even as something seemed to shift in his body. He could feel himself degrading, as though years of his life were being stripped out in a few single seconds. The acrobat wanted to crumple to the earth, suddenly feeling the worst exhaustion ever, but forced himself to stay standing.

And then Knight gasped for breath. His hand flew to his throat, as his eyes widened with pure horror. The man's mouth hung open wide enough he could have swallowed a golf ball. One of his hands jerked to his chest. He convulsed three times, his head ripping forward with each one. Then he looked up to his son and reached for him, his long arm crossing a large distance. His eyes pleaded. His mouth remained open, unable to pull any oxygen into his lungs. Every part of him was begging to his son who stood before him.

"You know how to stop this curse," Finley said, again his voice not his. It was like a voice sung from the heavens. One that made changes. Created laws. Shook the earth. "No ill will towards others, and you live. It is a choice."

Knight's hand flew to his chest, pure grief in his creased face. Finley knew that his father's heart wasn't beating and he could only sustain that for a few more seconds. It was a law of the universe that one would live until their brain was too oxygen deprived. And that was the law he had based his curse on, knowing that its construction had to be perfect. He stared down at the man he'd known all his life. The one he'd watched in dream travel form try to murder him when he was a baby. This man was a demon. This was Finley's father and he was the worst human being ever.

"Goodbye, Father," Finley said. "May you rest in peace as I know the world will when you are gone."

Knight lay back, his dark eyes blinking up at his son. Then he closed them slowly, and his head fell to the side.

Chapter Seventy-One

The exit to the big top was partially obscured by a portion of the tent that had sunken in. Titus had to hold Zuma back when an internal assault threatened the integrity of the big top and it deflated gradually on one side. She could have fought him but then he whispered, "He didn't want anyone in there. Especially you. You are his greatest weakness, Zuma."

She looked up at the creative director and realized he knew that Finley and Zuma were in love. Titus had grown so much over the last few months. He'd matured, but he'd also become intuitive, something she guessed he never allowed himself to be in the past.

All of Vagabond Circus was watching when the flap to the exit shifted. This was the moment. The moment where they would learn their fate. If Knight exited then they were doomed. They wouldn't be able to run fast enough. He would curse all of them. More than half a dozen would fall dead with aneurysms. They would die or if they lived, they'd wish they were dead.

Whoever was fumbling with the extra portion of tent blocking the exit was having trouble determining the way out. The big top was in such a sorry state that it didn't look like itself anymore. Finally, a hand reached through, finding a path to the outside. Everyone sucked in a collective breath. Everyone's hearts skipped, like a rock over water. Three long beats followed by two short and then a pause before gravity pulled the stone down to the earth.

The circus members had made this gamble for themselves, knowing they would rather die than be defeated and lose the circus. The hand pushed the tent flap back, sliding through a small opening. One hand was over his figure covered in dust and dirt and his own blood. Finley's eyes took a second to adjust to the bright setting sun, which was a stark contrast to the dark tent. Then he dropped his arm from his face and looked out at the sea of people. No one moved. No one made a single sound. No one's expression changed for several seconds. They all just stared in disbelief at the guy who didn't look like the one they expected to leave the big top. He was older. Matured. And elegantly beautiful.

Finley regarded his people, his eyes taking in their expressions of incredulity. He raised his chin and stared straight at Titus. "We are free! Knight is dead," he said, and his voice was his own again. It came out of him filled with a purity. One that wrapped itself around the people of Vagabond Circus, embracing them. Healing their wounds.

The entire crowd erupted in an applause bigger than they had ever received at any show. It could be heard miles away. And it went on for longer than any applause had ever lasted at the circus.

Finley marched forward, the crowd parting for him. Clapping for him. Slapping his shoulder. But the acrobat had his chin down and his eyes on only one person. He reached Zuma in only a few strides. "Your curse will have been lifted now," he said and stood in front of her, like he was presenting himself. Once the caster was dead, then the curse they created was too.

With everyone's eyes on Zuma, she stepped forward and held her hand up, pausing it just before his face. Finley's lip was bleeding from where Knight had punched him. His skin was flecked with blood from where shards of tiny glass had rained down from the lights. But Zuma didn't see his injuries as she touched his face which she could hardly believe was before her, and she could hardly understand what she was seeing in his features.

"What?" he said, reading the confused expression in her eyes. "What is it?"

Her hand paused at his hairline, her eyes running over the part of it owning her attention. Then she ran her fingers through the top left side of his hair. "You have a white streak through your hair," she said, in awe of it. It was two inches wide and raced from the left of his hairline all the way to the back. Even covered in dust, it contrasted beautifully against his dark brown hair.

"Oh, yeah," Finley said, his eyes dropping. "I felt myself aging when I cast the curse. I probably don't look nineteen anymore."

Zuma read the shame and disappointment in Finley. Her hand dropped to his chin, pulling it up so his eyes were on her. They were still a strange greenish hazel, but now they'd matured. "You, Finley, are more handsome than ever before."

Finley smiled at her and glided his hand over the side of her head, where the pink lay among whitish strands. "I guess we match now, huh, Pink-Streak?"

"I think that means we're meant to be together," Zuma said, aware that all eyes were on them. No one seemed interested in giving the couple any privacy. They were the final act, the finale to the torturous show they'd watched all these months. Watching the two acrobats look at each other with unabashed love was a gift they all deserved.

"I'm glad you think so," Finley said, leaning down low, wiping the blood from his mouth. "Because I don't plan on ever leaving your side."

Zuma smiled, one so pure, so beautiful, the crowd around them was accosted by the small gesture. It wasn't a smile they'd ever seen, not on her face or anyone else's. It was an expression that radiated a force. It was an expression of a freed girl. Eighteen years of suppressed happiness poured out of Zuma in that one moment, making her eyes sparkle, her face light up, and her elegance made everyone watching suck in tears of joy. "Nothing in the world would make me happier, Finley, than to be yours."

A tear slipped from the face of the warrior. The one who had battled his entire life. Been deprived. Been abused. Been neglected. And now Finley had something he never, ever thought possible, the gift to bring happiness to someone he loved. He closed the rest of the space between them, laying his lips on Zuma's. She sucked him in with her mouth, pulled him in closer with her arms, breathed him in with each kiss. Her lips smiled against his as he kissed her, a kiss so beautiful and full of grace that no one dared look away. Love really is the most beautiful show. It can't be rehearsed. It can't be planned. It is the product of magic. It is what Vagabond Circus is all about.

Chapter Seventy-Two

"Well, I dare say, Titus," Fanny said at his side as she watched the two acrobats embrace. "I think we are going to have to throw out that rule about no dating."

Titus, who was smiling at the couple as well, said, "Yes, I think so. And since the curse is lifted, I think there's no reason for it anyway."

"Yes, and that means one day we might have babies here at the circus," Fanny said, hope in her tone.

"I think at the rate these two are going we might have babies sooner than later," Titus said with a laugh.

Fanny playfully slapped the creative director's arm. "Oh, would you stop that. They have much to celebrate. Freedom. Happiness. Each other."

"Yes, and they are quite sweet," Titus said.

Finley and Zuma were no longer kissing, but rather holding on to each other with a quiet need. Her head lay on his chest, his arms wrapped tightly around her.

Only Fanny would dare interrupt the two lovers who were finally granted the opportunity to love each other openly. She stepped forward and cleared her throat.

Finley raised his head, opening his wise eyes at the woman in front of them.

"I think I should look over your injuries," Fanny said, holding out a hand to him.

He nodded, squeezing Zuma into him once before releasing her.

***

Inside Fanny's trailer, Finley sought the mirror first thing. She was busy gathering supplies to clean his wounds. The streak of white was exactly the width of the pink one in Zuma's hair. And it did give him a rebellious look. He liked it. The slight wrinkles on his face were met with a different response. He didn't like or dislike them.

They were strange to see on his young face, but he figured in time he'd come to appreciate what they represented. That would take time though. He had never killed someone, and now alone, away from the crowd, the guilt prickled to the surface. Yes, Knight needed to be stopped. And Finley as his son was the only one to do it. He had felt that stopping Knight was his responsibility. And yes, the only way to do that was to kill the unstoppable demon. But Finley had now done it and it lay across his heart like a burden.

"Okay, let's see you," Fanny said, calling Finley out of the bathroom.

He exited, his head down and his worries covering his face like freckles.

"Uh-oh," Fanny said. "I've seen that look before. That's the look of guilt and shame."

"I killed my own father. Cursed him. Killed him with a fast-acting curse. What kind of devil does that? I'm worse than him, aren't I?" Finley said. His usually cool demeanor was gone and replaced with a slow-growing worry. Only with Fanny would he speak so openly, exposing his real fears.

"What you did was kill an evil man," Fanny said.

"I'm not God. I don't get to decide who lives or dies. And I did. I took someone's life. I did something I've always hated *him* for. I've become him, my father."

"God works through us, Finley." Fanny approached him and held out an open hand. "And I don't actually think you killed your father."

Finley's eyes went wide. "You think he'll come back? That he isn't gone?"

She shook her head. "Take my hand and come sit with me, and I'll try to explain what I've done. And I hope that God grants you the peace to forgive an old woman for playing games that only Ian should dare to play. I took some risk and I must blame faith for that."

Finley closed his fingers around the older woman's. Her hands were soft and plush in his. She led him to the bench outside, the same one where he sat and learned to read all those months ago. The same one where she shared the news of the curse on Zuma, which he later discovered to be true. The curse that connected her to him, because he was the child whom Knight was trying to avenge by cursing any child born at Vagabond Circus.

Fanny settled herself down next to Finley, smoothing down her skirt before looking up to the sky. She always believed the best place to reveal or learn information was outdoors. It made the process easier somehow, as though the open air gave the person recording the information a new capacity.

"Do you know what Dave's gift was?" Fanny finally said, her eyes back on the boy beside her.

Finley thought for a minute and then shook his head.

"I thought so. You see, after Cynthia died and the child that he had thought was his was murdered, Dave went into a depression. He suffered a great deal of pain, but he had a circus to run and he was more motivated than ever after that tragedy befell him. His brother had sought to ruin his life. Dave finally pulled out of the depression, but still held on to the pain. He suffered nightmares and was only able to rest while dream traveling or using a concoction I made that stole his dreams away." Fanny shook her head, her tight curls only swaying slightly. "He was a tortured soul after that. And he gave up much that day. He gave up years of his life and also his powers. You see, a person cannot use their dream travel gifts if their heart is too weighted with sadness. It steals their power. Dave knew this, and yet he never let go of the pain. And therefore he was never able to use his Dream Traveler skills after the day his wife, and supposedly you, died."

"What was his gift?" Finley said, thinking he knew the answer, and then shaking his head at himself because that was impossible. He hardly knew anything about Dr. Dave Raydon.

"He had a few actually," Fanny said, and there was a surprisingly sneaky grin tucked behind her words. "He had the gift of super speed and he was a teleporter."

"Wait. What? So I inherited my uncle's gifts? How is that possible? Does that ever happen?" Finley said, knowing that gifts were shared in families. All of Zuma's immediate family shared the gift of telepathy.

"It hardly ever happens that a nephew inherits a gift from an uncle," Fanny said.

"Then why do I have Dave's gifts?" Finley asked.

And Fanny, dear sweet Fanny, actually raised a challenging eyebrow to the young man. She knew he was smart enough to figure this out. Knew it would be more powerful if he did. She wasn't playing a game, but she was enjoying dismantling a secret she'd held onto for all those months.

"What? Why are you just looking at me like that?" Finley asked.

"You didn't inherit your uncle's gifts, Finley," Fanny said, and then she reached out and touched his chin with her fingers. Held it up a little higher so she could see those eyes, the ones that reminded her of the man who saved her life. "You inherited your father's gifts, sweetheart."

"What? Dave...you think...are you trying to tell me..." Finley couldn't construct a sentence because his mind couldn't assimilate this new information.

"Yes, I believe Dave Raydon was actually your father," she said, dropping her hand back to her lap.

"But I time traveled. I saw my mother, Cynthia, tell Knight that he had killed his own son when he'd confessed what he'd done," Finley said.

"Oh, yes," Fanny said, with a knowing look. "And what would be the worst punishment you could think of for a lover who had killed your child, the one from another man?"

"To reveal to him that the child was actually his," Finley said slowly, in awe. "But still, this doesn't make any sense."

"Finley, from my perspective it makes perfect sense, since I knew your mother. From your perspective it's a strange reality that's not easy to digest."

"What are you implying about my mother?" Finley asked, but there wasn't any offense in the question, only a sincere curiosity.

Fanny pulled her mouth to the side as she considered how to phrase what she needed to say. "Your mother, Cynthia, she was the type of woman who would have an affair with her husband's brother. She—"

"You're saying she was a bad person," Finley said, wondering if he was destined to be evil if he came from two dishonest parents. *Maybe it would have been better to be born from the surrogates,* he thought.

Fanny's head shook. "Life isn't black and white. There aren't bad and good people and no one knew that better than Dave. He loved your mother because she was incredible. She had an essence about her that drew people in. Cynthia was stunning to look at and also had a brilliant mind to impress. But all of this gave her too much power over people, and made her a bit greedy at times." Fanny said this all matter-of-factly, not a hint of judgment in her tone.

"And that's why she had an affair with Knight?" Finley asked.

"I believe so," Fanny said. "I think she was also punishing Dave when he wouldn't abandon the circus."

"I hear what you're saying about the world not being black and white, but I think my mother was a bad person. She definitely sounds manipulative," Finley said.

Fanny teetered her head side to side, her lips puckered slightly with a look that said, "who are we to judge." Then she reached out and patted Finley's knee. "I believe people do bad things. If I recall, you were not always nice to Zuma and she punished you for a long time, as well."

"But that was different. I was protecting Zuma by being mean to her. And she punished me because I was culpable for Dave's death," Finley said in an urgent rush.

"Exactly," Fanny said with a triumphant smile. "Everyone has reasons and we do ourselves many favors when we don't judge others for their decisions. There are all types of people in the world who were molded by all different experiences and have different motives for their actions. For whatever reason, your mother was the type who punished people who didn't act in the way she wanted. And you, Finley, are the type who will punish yourself to protect people."

"So based on your knowledge of my mother, you think that she told Knight I was his child to punish him? To make him regret murdering me?" Finley said.

"That's right," Fanny said. "It feels like something she'd do, and then everything else about you would make more sense too. It would explain your abilities, features, and personality, which resemble Dave much more than Knight."

"But then I don't understand why you told Knight, and me, and the rest of the circus that he was my father? Why would you mislead us?"

The calm smile on Fanny's face fell away. "I know. I don't like to play games or mess with people's lives. Lies are not something I've ever been comfortable with. However, this situation was unique and dangerous. I knew I was in a special position since I was the only one who possessed the knowledge of your birth. And I prayed and prayed and God granted me an idea one morning. He told me that the solution to rid the circus of Knight was only possible if he thought you were his son. And after thinking about it that made perfect sense. I think if he would have found out you were Dave's son then you'd be dead already. And he probably hesitated killing you today because he thought you were his son. And then also, I think you were more motivated to rid the world of him because of the connection he held to you." She then shrugged like this was all conjecture. "It is hard to know how and why God works the way he does, but Knight is gone and that's because of you, so there you are."

"Well, is there any way to determine if Dave is in fact my father?" Finley asked.

"I figured you'd say that, and yes, there is. As you know, I care for and monitor the health of everyone at Vagabond Circus. I saved a sample of Dave's blood from his last physical. Ironically I was going to do the DNA test the very day I found out Dave was dead." Fanny then sighed like she was trying to relieve a heavy burden from her chest. "I never had the opportunity to perform the test while Dave was living. I never got the opportunity to tell him who you were and my suspicions about Cynthia's lie. God decided Dave would never meet you for who you were, his blood relative, but I also believe, his son. You see, Finley, Dave and Knight were related, but you take after our founder. I've been observing it since the day I met you. And there's one thing that makes me certain my inkling is right." The healer smiled now, but there was a great sadness to the gesture, as a memory surfaced in her eyes. "You have Dave's heart."

Finley found that swallowing wasn't really an option after all this news. Instead, he attempted his own weak smile.

"Now," Fanny said, pulling confidence into the word as she shook off the sentimentality. "What I need from you is a sample. If I can have that, then inside my trailer I have the equipment to determine who your real father is."

Chapter Seventy-Three

*F*inley waited outside Fanny's trailer. He couldn't stand the idea of watching her perform the DNA test. After she'd taken his sample, he stayed in the trailer, but not for long. The waiting was worse when he watched her measuring chemicals and shaking test tubes. He had taken back up the spot on the picnic table where the kids usually did their lessons, out in front of the trailer.

"Hey." It was Zuma's voice.

Finley looked up at her and tried to smile. The grin on his face made his heart feel heavy.

"What are you doing out here? I came to check on you," she said, studying the cuts on his face. "It doesn't look like Fanny has treated you yet."

He shook his head. Bit his lip.

"What is it?" she asked, reading the worry in his face.

"Zuma, Fanny believes that my mother lied to punish Knight." The words spilled out of Finley too fast, like something he would explode from if he didn't share.

Zuma's face contorted with confusion. "What?"

He nodded. "Fanny thinks Cynthia told Knight he'd killed his son to punish him. Or maybe she thought I was Knight's son. But Fanny doesn't."

"What? Why?" Zuma asked, the full implications not dawning on her yet.

"Did you know what Dave's gifts were?" Finley said.

She nodded. He had never used them around her since he couldn't, but from being in his head she knew. "Yeah, he had super sp…" Her words trailed away as her mouth hung open. "Dave? Fanny thinks Dave is your father?" And now a bright smile sprung to her face. It was so wide it hurt her lips. Being happy would take getting used to. Again her sudden happiness made the space seem brighter, better. Zuma sat beside Finley with an exuberant thud.

"But there's a chance he's not. That Knight is my father. That I killed *my* father," Finley said, that same shame from before in his voice.

Zuma turned to Finley and grabbed his hand. "It doesn't matter to me who your father is. I love you no matter what."

He brought his tortured gaze up to meet her eyes. "But you'd probably love me more if I was Dave's son."

She pulled his hand locked in hers to her chest and held it there like a prize. "That's impossible, because I couldn't conceivably love you any more than I do."

The door to Fanny's trailer swung open, grabbing both the acrobats' attention. They stood in unison. Finley looked down at Zuma and he read the question in her eyes. "Yes, I want you to stay. Hear the news with me," he said.

She grabbed his hand again and squeezed it once. Together the pair walked forward, meeting Fanny halfway. The trip seemed double the distance Finley remembered. And the whole time he studied Fanny's face, trying to discern if she was holding onto good or bad news. For a woman with such a usually expressive face, her features were all neutral. No smile, nor frown. Eyes set in a clinical gaze. Jaw relaxed. Even Zuma, using her combat sense, had difficulty picking up any information by studying the woman.

When Finley and Zuma halted in front of the healer there were a few seconds of silence. This was a moment full of weight. Fanny seemed to know it shouldn't be rushed. That's why she stalled, sucking in a steadying breath before meeting Finley's eyes.

"Tell me," Finley said, his tone bordering on demanding.

And just then Fanny's eyes betrayed the cover-up she'd been attempting. She was so overwhelmed with emotions that it took everything she had to pretend to have the unaffected bedside manner. Even in the darkening grounds the sparkle of excitement radiated from her blue eyes.

"I tested fifteen genetic markers and there was a one-hundred-percent match for your and Dave's samples," Fanny said, and then every wrinkle on her face punctuated the wide smile she adorned. "It is my great honor to inform you that Dr. Dave Raydon, the illustrious founder of this circus, was your father. And that means you are now the *rightful* owner of Vagabond Circus. Congratulations, Finley Raydon."

Chapter Seventy-Four

*T*itus and Fanny stood side by side watching the crew working side by side to take down the big top. It would be loaded up and have to be repaired once they set up in Los Angeles. Ian called orders and each of his crew members responded with a quick attentiveness. They worked like a machine, everyone supporting each other. Some whistled or hummed as they disassembled the various parts of the big top. Knight's body had already been removed and would join Gwendolyn's and Sebastian's ashes.

"This circus has seen much the last few months," Fanny said, her hands on her hips as she watched the crew.

"We've lost much too," Titus said.

"But we have bonded together to overcome a great evil."

"True," Titus said.

"And I think we are better off for this."

"You do?" Titus said, raising his light-colored eyebrows at the woman.

"I do," she said with a proud smile. "Jack has healed and you know, Titus, he has a confidence that's to impress. That look of shame is gone from his eyes. He's the man that Dave thought he could become."

"And you think being paralyzed brought him all that?"

She shook her head, a smile in her eyes. "No, I think getting rid of the pity so he could make himself walk again did. And I dare say I don't think he'd have found love without being paralyzed."

Titus laughed easily. "Yes, we will definitely be getting rid of Rule Two."

"And Finley, he has a legacy to be proud of."

"Yes, his father's," Titus said, his eyes lighting up. "Finley Raydon, the new owner of Vagabond Circus." Titus liked the idea of sharing his co-ownership with the acrobat. He loved the idea actually. "Poor Dave, he never knew," Titus said. "His son was here. And he was so very proud of him, knowing he was his star performer. Imagine if he knew that star who saved Vagabond Circus financially was his son. And then he went on to save Vagabond Circus from Knight and his curses."

Fanny lifted her chin and looked at the sky that was just starting to wink with bright stars. "Oh, I don't know, Titus, I feel Dave knows. I feel that he's proud of his son. God would gift that man with that knowledge."

Titus smiled at Fanny. He'd always admired her faith. It amazed him actually. There were many things about the woman that amazed him.

She caught him staring at her. "And then there's Zuma," she said.

"Yes, she can finally be happy. The curse is lifted."

Fanny slid her hand into Titus's and squeezed. It surprised him at first but then he relaxed. "You know, Titus, we can all be happy now."

He nodded, knowing exactly what she meant. Then the creative director raised her hand in his and brought the back of hers to his lips where he kissed it once. "Yes, I think it's overdue," he said and allowed his lips to linger on her hand for a long few seconds, a passionate smile on his face.

Chapter Seventy-Five

*T*he big top was loaded in record speed the night Charles Knight died. Again the crew was intent on escaping a place where death had happened. Ian requested that they all rest and leave first thing the next morning. He saw all the trucks off. Then he continued to sit on the back of his teal Chevy pickup as the caravan took their lineup. Zuma's trailer pulled out last, just after Finley's. Sunshine was in the lead, Jack behind her. And as was usually the case, Titus and Fanny had the middle position. They were in essence the parents of Vagabond Circus. And the people of the circus were all their kids.

They will do well now, Ian thought. Over the last few months he'd played a dangerous game, messing with the futures he saw. He didn't just intervene, he instigated change. He stopped futures, prevented Finley's death. Allowed Jasmine's to happen. Created the likelihood of Padmal's death. And he watched like a prisoner as the futures changed. He kept tweaking things until he saw this one. The future where everything was tied up in a beautiful oversized bow. And now he was living that reality. It was all he wanted.

Ian's eyes were glazed over. The visions were unrelenting now, but they were mostly good. Zuma would be happy. She'd go on to love the life she never even knew was a possibility. And so would Finley. He'd hold his soulmate every single night, only to be parted from Zuma on the three separate nights where she needed space after childbirth. Jack would not only walk until the day he died, but he would run, run after the girl who dared to leave the circus because she was afraid of the emotions in her own heart. Sunshine was afraid of love, of being loved. She'd read that emotion in other people, but never thought she could feel it. Jack would convince her not to run from him. And there would also be loss at Vagabond Circus. Titus wouldn't live forever, and Fanny would feel extremely alone when she couldn't save him. But they would have many decades of love and companionship before that.

Ian saw these futures. He saw hundreds of futures. So many people affected Ian and therefore their futures were a part of his visions. The day before, due to the unrelenting flashes of the future, he could hardly help to take down the big top so he gave orders. Ian had gone blind. A doctor would say his eyes worked fine but his mind wouldn't allow them to see. All that flashed in front of his retinas was the future. Ian couldn't drive his truck. He knew that. And for too long he'd seen this future. It came at the end whether Vagabond Circus had a happy or sad ending. He'd known that and was grateful things had indeed ended happily. But he wasn't an optimist and knew that not everything ends with a pretty little bow on it.

Ian smiled, looking at nothing in his physical world. And still this was the perfect ending for him. He'd done what he set out to do. He'd saved Zuma from the curse, the girl who was the key to saving the circus.

The clairvoyant felt around for the pistol. His fingers finally knocked into it. He placed it in his hand and brought it into position. Ian's fate was always to follow his mother's. And he was grateful he left no offspring, cursed with the visions of the future. Ian's wasn't a happy life, but he had helped others achieve happiness. This was his last thought before he pulled back the hammer and released the trigger.

A flock of birds sprung into the air, startled by the loud bang.

Epilogue

LA Times

Summer Time, Circus Time

Summer is here and that means that the Vagabond Circus is gearing up for another season. The circus is celebrating its 21st year and there've been many changes. For one, there are new owners, Finley Raydon and Titus Rogers. The two have really set the bar high, promising to bring the circus to more cities this year, and thereby spreading more magic. They've also hired a few new performers who will definitely bring more awe-inspiring moments to the show. And even though Dave Raydon has passed the circus on to his son, he won't be absent from the venture he started twenty-one years ago. Last year he was replaced as ringmaster by Charles Knight, but Rogers stated in an interview that Knight wasn't the right fit for the circus. The Vagabond Circus and Knight mutually agreed that his time with the circus should be short. They had tried something new to switch things up but have decided to return the circus to a dreamier feel. So if you're like me and prefer the whimsical circus to the nightmarish one, then you're in luck. Check out the show, which promises to have some new and old stars returning.

***

"You're going to do great," Zuma said, placing a hand on the young boy's shoulder. She leaned down and kissed Benjamin on the cheek, making him blush. "You were born for this role."

He smiled so wide at the acrobat that his eyes could hardly see. "Okay," he agreed and turned for the curtain.

Zuma felt the hand in hers and turned to find Finley behind her. "If you're giving out kisses, I would take one."

She rose on her tiptoes to plant a kiss on his cheek but using his super speed he whipped his head forward so the kiss landed on his mouth. Zuma giggled against his lips, loving the free feeling happiness gave her. The lovers were so engrossed in each other that they didn't realize that the show had started until the music boomed overhead. The lights dimmed as a single spotlight shone down in the middle of the ring.

"Gadies and lentlemen," the voice of Dave Raydon said and was immediately followed by deafening applause.

"He's back!" people in the crowd yelled.

"Woohoo!" a boy screamed, jumping up and down in his seat.

Not until that first show did the public know that Dave Raydon had returned as the ringmaster.

Zuma turned to peek through the crack in the curtain, Finley's arm around her shoulders, holding her into him. There in the middle of the ring stood a man who no one would ever suspect wasn't Dr. Dave Raydon. He wore the same teal blue suit and top hat. The same broad grin, and the same easy manner. And most importantly, Benjamin had in his heart the purpose of bringing magic to life and that exuded from the performance. "Welcome to Vagabond Zoo," he said and the crowd exploded with laughter.

"Why are you laughing at me?" he said in the voice of Dr. Dave Raydon.

"It's not a zoo!" people shouted.

"It isn't?" he said, pulling his hat off his head and scratching his smooshed down hair.

Zuma smiled and turned to Finley. "He's doing a brilliant job."

Finley's fond eyes were on the man in the center of the ring. The one who was his father and also wasn't. "Yeah," he said, attempting to swallow. Zuma placed her hands on his chest to borrow his attention.

"Mr. Raydon, are you ready for our first act?" she said to him.

He brought his eyes to hers. "Yes, Ms. Zanders," Finley said and kissed her once on the cheek. His gaze was over her shoulder at the man he would never truly know, but would love with all his heart.

***

Zuma and Finley stood on the platform for the flying trapeze. They wore their matching teal blue and neon green leotards. Hers was cut high like a one-piece swimsuit. His was a full suit covered in brilliant gems. The pair held onto the scaffolding with one hand, leaning out over the platform, waving out to the crowd.

"There they are!" people yelled.

"He's back!" someone in the crowd said.

"Woohoo!" the crowd chorused.

Finley stepped up, taking the bar Zuma handed to him. With a "hup" the trick started. Finley jumped off the platform with an incredible height, swung forward and then back, clearing the platform and rising fifteen feet above it. That was the height he needed for the trick to be successful. He flew forward and at precisely the perfect moment he released off the bar and spun once, twice, three times and then when the crowd thought that was it, he soared in a tight ball at super speed a fourth time. Finley laid himself out and there was a bit of a distance from his catcher so he teleported a foot to ensure he was caught.

Jack swung forward and clapped his hands around Finley's outstretched arms completing the quadruple. The pair of acrobats swung back as the crowd stood with applause. Jack looked down from his upturned position into the eyes of his friend.

"Nice catch," Finley mouthed up to him. He couldn't be heard over the applause.

"Anytime," Jack said and released Finley, who dropped down to the net. After he dismounted Jack pulled his legs off the bar and dropped to the net as well. And then he joined Finley on the ground where they both bowed to a crowd who had bright eyes and a renewed belief in magic.

The End.

To stay up-to-date with Sarah Noffke and receive fun news and freebies, subscribe to her newsletter.
http://www.sarahnoffke.com/connect/

Acknowledgements:

*W*hen I was a little girl I didn't dream of being a writer. That was a preposterous idea. I grew up reading Kahlil Gibran, Emily Dickinson, and Judy Blume. I knew who good writers were, and that wasn't me. I set my sights on something more realistic. I was going to be an Olympic gymnast. Makes sense, right? And as fate had it, my pride got the best of me and I quit gymnastic and became a super huge nerd…and later a writer. I still have callouses, but they're from typing my books on my phone. Did I forget that this is the acknowledgement page and mistake this as a blog entry? No. I'm still coherent…mostly. Anyway, I became a writer because of awesome supporters. People who believed in me. Who pushed me. Nurse Fanny is named after a freshman English professor who did this for me. I remember Trudy Swedlund calling me a tiger on my first day of college. Then later on she praised me for my papers, again and again. And it's because of people like her and many others that I have the confidence to write. So thank you to those who in the past and in the present gave me encouraging words. It made me start and keeps me going. Thank you to my readers. You're my Trudy Swedlunds now.

Thank you to my friends. You're my first readers. My biggest supporters. Where would I be without you all? I'd be sad. A little lonely. And laugh a lot less. But also I wouldn't have the encouragement I need to write. For some of you, I write just to keep you entertained.

Thank you to Christine LePorte, my editor. I love that we have this long standing writer/editor relationship. And I love even more when you offer me praise, because I know you are one of the few objective people who read my books. That's why you're great at your job.

Thank you to my cover designer, Andrei Bat. When we completed this cover, I actually held my breath. It only lasted a few seconds, because I can't spare any brain cells, but it was really that good. Your designs take my breath away. There, I said it.

Thank you to Dominic and Maja who run the Goodreads fan group. You amaze me with your support and encouragement. I feel so lucky that you picked up my books in the first place, and continue to do so. Thank you for the bookmarks, Dominic. They are simply marvelous.

Thank you to BOD and all the supporters there. I could fill up another book listing all the people from that group who amaze me with their support. Best group ever, run by amazing ladies. Thank you.

Thank you to my family for all the support and encouragement. To my Texas family, thank you for reading and the lovely praise. Thank you to my sister, Anne. You've always been my biggest supporter in everything. To my nieces and nephews, thank you for all your kind words. Thank you to my sister, Bea. I hope to make you proud. Thank you to my parents and in-laws.

Thank you to my beta readers: Heidi, Colleen, and Melinda. Thank you to ARC readers. OMG, there's so many of you now!!! Do you know how happy that makes me? I love you all. I might forget someone so forgive me in advance. Thank you to Katie, Katy, Kimberly, Dominic, Maja, Tamika, Anna, Christine, Elizabeth, Lesley, Heidi, Kelly, Kit, Kira, Tiffany, Nicole and Karen. Thank you to my devoted readers. Kathy, Stephanie, Christine, Cheree, Cheryl, Elizabeth, Katy, Vikki, Alicia, Shelah, Jennifer, Diane and April. I know no matter how crappy my post are you'll Like and Share. You're so good to me. Don't stop. Seriously. Ever. ☺

I want to say a giant thank you to my author friends. I firmly believe that when we support each other that we all do better. And you all continue to inspire me with your stories, your journeys, and your relentless passion. I love that I can share my ideas with you and that you in turn give me great ideas. I've learned so much from other authors. I'm constantly humbled by the people I get to work with. Thank you!

Thank you to Luke. And you know why. Because you're awesome and encouraging. And you keep supporting me while I do what I do. Which the more and more that I do it, it feels like a real profession. That's thanks to you.

This is my tenth novel. I will not be breaking tradition here. The final thank, as always, goes to my daughter Lydia. In your eyes I see so much of the strength in my characters. In your smile I see the magic that inspired this circus. And in your words, I feel the passion that became this book. Forever and always, my muse. I love you.

Love,
Sarah

About the Author:

Sarah is the author of the Lucidites, Reverians, Vagabond Circus and Ren series. She's been everything from a corporate manager to a hippie. Her taste for adventure has taken her all over the world. If you can't find her at the gym, then she's probably at the frozen yogurt shop. If you can't find her there then she probably doesn't want to be found. She is a self-proclaimed hermit, with spontaneous urges to socialize during full moons and when Mercury is in retrograde. Sarah lives in Central California with her family. To learn more about Sarah please visit: http://www.sarahnoffke.com

Check out other work by this author:

The Lucidites Series:
Awoken, **#1**:
Around the world humans are hallucinating after sleepless nights.

In a sterile, underground institute the forecasters keep reporting the same events.

And in the backwoods of Texas, a sixteen-year-old girl is about to be caught up in a fierce, ethereal battle.

Meet Roya Stark. She drowns every night in her dreams, spends her hours reading classic literature to avoid her family's ridicule, and is prone to premonitions—which are becoming more frequent. And now her dreams are filled with strangers offering to reveal what she has always wanted to know: Who is she? That's the question that haunts her, and she's about to find out. But will Roya live to regret learning the truth?

Stunned, #2
Revived, #3

The Reverians Series:
Defects, #1:
In the happy, clean community of Austin Valley, everything appears to be perfect. Seventeen-year-old Em Fuller, however, fears something is askew. Em is one of the new generation of Dream Travelers. For some reason, the gods have not seen fit to gift all of them with their expected special abilities. Em is a Defect—one of the unfortunate Dream Travelers not gifted with a psychic power. Desperate to do whatever it takes to earn her gift, she endures painful daily injections along with commands from her overbearing, loveless father. One of the few bright spots in her life is the return of a friend she had thought dead—but with his return comes the knowledge of a shocking, unforgivable truth. The society Em thought was protecting her has actually been betraying her, but she has no idea how to break away from its authority without hurting everyone she loves.

Rebels, #2
Warriors, #3

Ren: The Man Behind the Monster:
Born with the power to control minds, hypnotize others, and read thoughts, Ren Lewis, is certain of one thing: God made a mistake. No one should be born with so much power. A monster awoke in him the same year he received his gifts. At ten years old. A prepubescent boy with the ability to control others might merely abuse his powers, but Ren allowed it to corrupt him. And since he can have and do anything he wants, Ren should be happy. However, his journey teaches him that harboring so much power doesn't bring happiness, it steals it. Once this realization sets in, Ren makes up his mind to do the one thing that can bring his tortured soul some peace. He must kill the monster. *Note* This book is NA and has strong language, violence and sexual references.

Spanish version of The Lucidites Series:
Awoken: *Despertada*
Stunned: *Atonita*

Sneak Peek of Defects

(The Reverians Series, #1):

Prologue

My fingers tremble as I assemble the pieces.

He'll be back in a few minutes.

I blink away the sweat dripping into my eyes. I can't afford to swipe it away.

The two ceramic pieces chip at the edges as I try to match them up to how they should align. I know he keeps glue in his front desk drawer. Everyone does. *We fix things that are broken.* I slip the tube from the drawer and dab a glob of adhesive on the center of one of the broken pieces and then press it against its counterpart. I'm so used to fixing things, but now I'm not doing it because it's the law. I'm doing it because if he finds out I was here he'll punish me with night terrors again.

The pieces slip just as the glue is setting. Ragged breath hitches in my parched throat. *If he finds out I was here, that there was a trespassing...* I press the pieces together so firmly the glue seeps out and threatens to cement my fingers to the statue. Footsteps in the hallway. Soft-soled shoes. His. I know *his* gait.

I release my fingers from the statue. It teeters but stands, looking unmarked by the fall it recently experienced. But will it stay up?

The envelope still sits neatly on the mahogany desk. It was my own nervous reaction to it that shook the statue down from its high place on the shelf. I knew I should come here and look first. Knew I'd find information. My father always told me, "Instinct is the gods tapping you on the head." Still, I wish I knew what lay inside the folds of that envelope that bears my name.

The key slides into the lock, a sound like a reluctant bell. I close my eyes and dream travel back to my body, pulling my consciousness out of its current location.

Chapter One

My house is haunted. I've never seen a ghost in it, but Tutu, whose gift is seeing the dead, says there are many who reside in our home. I haven't received my gift yet. At age seventeen that's rare. My sister, Dee, teases me that this is a sure sign our mother had an affair with Ed, the mailman, who's a Middling—a person who can't dream travel, has no gifts. I pretend this is a joke but with each passing year I believe it could be a possibility. My family is pureblooded Dream Travelers and they're all gifted with strong talents since puberty. And although I dream travel I have no other talents, which is a first in the Fuller family. My grandmother, who I call Tutu, has three abilities. My mother, two. Even my older sister, Dee, has her gift— which she spends every single opportunity rubbing in my face. Since I have no super power I've reverted to spreading false rumors about her all over Austin Valley.

"You're going to be late again," Dee says, sounding pleased by the prospect.

"Thanks for the reminder," I say, not meaning it.

I slip my favorite organic bamboo blouse over my head and hurry out of the room I share with my sister. With one hand I smooth my hair and the other guides me down the banister as I take the stairs two at a time.

"I'm sure his mother would love the opportunity to be interviewed," my mother says to a visitor in her usual subdued tone. I don't even chance a glance at her as I scurry to the entryway, head low. Maybe this visitor will actually save me from being scolded. The brass doorknob is cold under my palm. I wrench the door open and pull it back, a rush of warm June air greeting me at once.

"Not so fast there, Em," my mother says.

I freeze. Push the door closed. Turn and face her.

My mother stands in the threshold of the sitting room, her hands firmly pinned to her hips. "You're late for your meeting with your father."

"Which is why I'm rushing to get out of here," I say, sweeping my eyes to the person my mother was talking to. Zack. He's giving me a curious expression, arms crossed in front of his suit jacket.

"Have I not instilled in you the proper manners to know you should greet and say farewell to everyone you come in contact with?" she says, shaking her head at me.

"Hi, Mother. Hi, Zack. I'm leaving before Father kills me for being late. Goodbye," I say, turning on my toes. I slip my hand onto the door handle again, but don't even dare to open it.

"Em?"

I turn and stare at my mother. Her red hair is pulled back into a tight low bun. Her sleeveless black turtleneck must be stifling in this heat. "Yes, Mother?" I say, working hard to keep the irritation out of my voice.

"You weren't planning on leaving the house like that, were you?" she asks with a disappointed glare as she sizes up my appearance.

"I was—"

"Looking for your blazer, right?" Zack plucks my black blazer from underneath a cushion on the settee behind him and holds it out for me.

Reluctantly I eye it and then him. He's wearing his most encouraging look. It partners well with his slick blond hair and winning smile. He's right, politics is the right career for him.

I take my blazer from him and slip it on. "Thanks," I say, pulling my tangled blonde curls out from underneath the jacket.

"Oh, you're still here?" Dee says, tromping down the stairs behind me. "You really take advantage of our father's unending patience, don't you?" Her black heels make note of each of her steps. When she meets me at the landing she pushes my hair behind my ears. "And really, if you're not going to at least dress like an upper-class Reverian you could brush your hair once in a while."

I bat her hand away and clench my teeth together. Insulting my sister will not release me from my mother's wrath, which seeks to make me even later for my appointment. Still, someone should say something about how my sister looks more and more like an obsessed Goth whose only mission in life is to give the Catholic clergymen a heart attack. She wouldn't understand that reference though. Most people in Austin Valley wouldn't. My sister is wearing her usual get-up: short pleated skirt, starched black button-up shirt open to reveal too much, heels, and an assortment of gold jewelry.

Instead of commenting on how she looks like a confused Catholic schoolgirl I lick my finger and press it to a flyaway by her hair line. "You have a hair out of place. Here you go, dear."

She steps back, grotesque horror written on her face. "Eww, don't touch me." My sister turns to our mother. They don't just share the same disapproving scowl, but also the same straight red hair, which they wear similarly. "Oh, Zack, you're here," my sister says, strolling in his direction. "I had no idea."

"Are you blind?" I say dully.

She throws me a contemptuous glare over her shoulder before turning back in Zack's direction. "You could obviously teach my sister something about dress, couldn't you?"

He coughs nervously, flicking his eyes over her shoulder to me. I know Dee makes him nervous. Hell, she makes the devil nervous, probably because she's soulless. I shrug and sling my bag over my shoulder.

"Well...I..." Zack begins.

"There are not many students who choose to wear a suit before they're chosen for positions," Dee says, having cleared the space between them. Her long pointy fingernail has found his shoulder and is now tracing its way down his pinstriped sleeve until she finds his hands. She pulls his fingertips up close to her face and inspects. "And such clean nails. This says so very much about you. Obviously you take a great deal of pride in your appearance."

"I'm merely tryin—"

"Zack is actually here because he'd like to interview your tutu in order to better understand cultural changes which have transpired within our society over the generations," my mother informs Dee, pride evident in her tone.

"Impeccable dresser and ambitious," Dee says, her hand still gripping Zack's.

"Yes, I dare say that if you stay on this track then you'll make great contributions for the Reverians once released from your studies," my mother says, her stare not on Zack, but rather on my sister.

Although I realize I'll be punished later for interrupting this crafty attempt at mating I dare say something. I have other punishments way worse I'd rather avoid. "Well, I really must take my leave," I say, injecting pleasantry into my voice. "I don't want to keep Father waiting any longer than I already have. Goodbye." Again the brass knob greets the palm of my hand.

"Yes, you are *so* late," my sister says, eyeing the ancient grandfather clock in the entryway. "He's going to be livid."

"I'm going that way too," Zack says, taking hurried steps in my direction. "I'll walk with you."

Just over his shoulder I catch a fiery glare flash in my sister's eyes.

"Sure," I say with a shrug and turn at once and hurry out the door.

The humid breeze is a welcome relief from the frigid air in my house. Sunlight greets my eyes with a quiet satisfaction and I smile at the blue sky like it's an old friend.

"You always do that, don't you?" Zack says, hurrying to keep up with me.

"Make my mother and sister furious? Yes."

"Well, yes, that, but I was referring to your reaction to the outdoors. You always break into a relieved smile when you walk outside."

I snuggle my shoulders up high, enjoying the warm sun on my cheeks. "I do love it," I say, pausing to allow a group of elderly Reverians to pass in front of us. Zack pauses with me but gives an irritated expression while we wait. "I'm already late," I finally say to him when they've moved on and we continue down Central Boulevard.

"I don't get you, Em," he says, shaking his head. "Why do you make your life harder when you know what they want you to do?"

"I just find it difficult to conform to their standards. I mean, why in the hell should I have to wear a blazer in the middle of the summer?" I say, scratching at my forearms which are already sweating under the tight-fitting jacket.

"It's just customs. If you followed them then they'd leave you alone and let you do what you want."

"Somehow I doubt that," I say, raising an eyebrow at Zack.

"It seems you're looking to get in trouble: being late when it's easy to be early, dressing inappropriately when they supply you the right clothes, and not following etiquette."

"And may I point out that you seem to only notice my shortcomings," I say, taking an early turn. It's a shortcut down a less than desirable neighborhood, but still completely safe and will save us an extra minute on the commute.

Zack's hand clamps down on my shoulder. I stop and look at him, ready to defend the route I've chosen. His denim blue eyes lock on mine. "That's not all I notice," he says, a firmness in his voice.

"Mmm…" I say, gauging his expression which is so familiar and also year by year growing indistinct, like my father's. "Yeah, what else do you notice?" I say, turning and continuing our trek. The alleyway here is a little more crowded, but only because this is a Middling street where they build the houses too close together and the insides are too small for the families who are forced to reside within them.

"It doesn't matter," Zack says, eyeing a man leaning in his doorway up ahead. "We can finish this conversation later. Let's just get you to Chief Fuller's office quickly."

"Right," I say, kicking the contents of a puddle, which is no doubt a result of poor drainage from the sprinkler system. It splatters droplets on my shoes and bare legs, but doesn't irritate me in the least.

At my father's office Zack stops, eyeing the door and then me with an uncertain expression. "You know I'm just trying to help, right?"

"Then you shouldn't have offered to escort me here," I say, pushing him playfully in the chest. "Dee will probably set fire to my bed while I'm sleeping tonight as retribution." Literally she's done that a time or two. I have no idea why the most hostile Dream Traveler born to the gods was given the gift of pyrokinesis.

Zack doesn't respond, but instead gives me his usual commiserative expression. He doesn't know what to say. I get that. "Yeah, I know you're trying to help," I finally say. "You may want to consider there's no help for me. I'm a Dream Traveler whose only talent is I disappoint my family."

271

"Oh, Em, I've told you that your gift is delayed. It will come on soon and when it does you'll blow all of them away."

"Thanks, Zack," I say, reaching out and straightening his tie. It isn't even that crooked, but I know he likes when I do it because it sharpens his appearance. "Are you off to go take over Austin Valley?"

"Not quite yet," he says with a wink. "I've got a thing or two to learn still."

"Don't we all," I say, returning the wink and then dismissing him by facing my father's ornately carved door. I've stalled long enough. Now I must face that which is certain to be extremely unpleasant.

To continue reading, please purchase Defects (The Reverians, #1)

Sneak Peek of Awoken

(The Lucidites Series, #1):

Prologue

The howling wind always marks his arrival. Tonight I'm not sleeping when it shakes the trees and sends debris flying around outside. The recurring nightmare woke me an hour ago. I wipe away the sweat beading my hairline and steal a glance out my window. The figure lurks in the shadows. He's never any closer than the old oak tree, but that's near enough. A chill shakes my core. I can't do this one single night more. Shaking fingers scroll through my phone contacts until I find the right one.

"Hello," a groggy voice says on the other end.

I speak in a whisper. "I'm not sure I believe what's happening, but I'm ready to let them protect me."

"Good," the voice says with relief. "You'll be glad you did."

"What do I do now?"

"They want you to meet someone. He'll explain what happens next."

Chapter One
Forty-eight hours later

I wouldn't believe any of this was real if it wasn't for the two-inch gash in my arm. Still, denial has rented a room in my head and frequently stomps around slamming doors. I have never considered myself normal, but only now do I fully realize how extremely abnormal I am. That's not the part I'm denying anymore. It's my potential fate.

Now I have to do the one thing that feels impossible: focus. It's difficult when my life has quickly turned into a mass of confusion. I force myself to shake off the distractions. The answers I seek reside in a place I can only get to if I let go.

With immense effort, I relax enough to concentrate. In my head, I see the dam. The concrete stretches out like a barrier, pushing the water away. I pay attention to the water, how it voyages down the spillway. Slow breaths intensify the meditation, giving it color and sound. I continue to visualize until I sense the change. It's polarizing, in a good way. My body remains planted in the comfy bed while my consciousness dream travels. Now I'm racing through the silver tunnel—my transport to the other dimension. Adrenaline tastes like salt water in my mouth. And too quickly the journey is over, leaving me panting as I'm tossed into a vast space.

The tunnel deposits me at the edge of the spillway on a concrete embankment. A cursory glance behind reveals a calm lake reservoir; ahead the spillway plummets for a hundred feet or more before cascading into the lake. The moon overhead is full. Beside me is a woman.

"I was beginning to think you were lost again," she says.

"It's nice to meet you too," I say.

"I assumed you already knew my name."

Apparently the Lucidites don't believe in greetings. "Well, some ID wouldn't hurt."

Shuman's black hair resembles strands of silk. She wears a leather vest and blue jeans. I straighten, feeling smaller than usual next to her.

"Did you decipher the riddle on your own?" Shuman says, ignoring my comment. The moon reflects off her high cheekbones, making her appear angular.

"No," I admit, "Bob and Steve helped."

I'm confused why Shuman gave me a riddle instead of just telling me where to dream travel to meet her. I guess as the Head Mentalist for the Lucidites she has to make everything as perplexing as possible. She must be great at her job.

"Yes, it was forecast that they would assist you," she says.

"Right, of course," I say, not masking the irritation in my voice. It isn't Bob's and Steve's help I resent, it's that the Lucidites are privy to my life through psychic means.

"And we are here because of a different prediction."

"Yes, I've heard about it."

"Have you also heard that it involves you?"

"Well, I know there's a *potential* I'll be involved."

"We have new information. Your name is the only one in the forecast now."

"What?" I breathe with quiet disbelief. "No, that's impossible."

"It is possible and I assure you it is true. The speculation of predictions solidifies as the approaching event draws closer. Now forecasters see you as the true challenger."

"No," I say too fast, denial evident in my tone. "And I'm not here because of the forecast; I'm here because they said you'd help me."

"They are correct. The first way I can help is by getting you to accept what has been predicted."

"Predictions are just guesses though. What if they're wrong?" I say.

Shuman raises her eyebrow in disapproval, shakes her head. "Roya, do you doubt it because it involves you?"

"Mostly I doubt it because it's absurd. None of it makes sense."

"Maybe not yet, but it will," Shuman says. "Unfortunately we are running out of time. The forecasters have determined the static moment to be twenty-one hundred hours on June thirteenth."

That's in a month. My throat closes and my chest shrinks in on itself. "What? I can't…There's no way…" I trail off, lost in morbid thoughts of my impending death. "Why not you or someone else more qualified?"

"If I was chosen I would be honored, but I was not. You were." Shuman gazes at the full moon, her silver earrings highlighted by its white light. "I have tracked Zhuang for decades without success. Many of us have." She turns and looks at me for the first time. Her dark eyes resemble amethysts. "This fixed point in time is the only chance anyone will have the opportunity to challenge him. And the forecast states you are the person with the best opportunity to end his brutal reign."

"That's ridiculous. I'm not a threat to anyone."

275

"A few days ago you saw yourself very differently than you do now, is that right?"

"Well, yes, but—"

"Then consider it possible that in a month you will be a deadly force."

After what I've learned, I'm almost willing to believe this might be true. I sigh. "So what do you really want from me?" I ask.

"Make a choice," Shuman says at once. "You must decide whether you accept this role. If you do, then I can give you the help you asked for."

"If everything you've said is true then I *don't* have a choice."

"It is all true," she says through clenched teeth. "And in waking life and dreams, you *always* have a choice. This is what makes Dream Travelers different from Middlings. We do not sleep and fall into dreams that happen to us. We create our dreams. We choose where we travel."

I rub my eyes, frustrated and strangely tired. "It's just facing Zhuang sounds like a death sentence. I don't want to go through all this just to die in June."

"If you make the choice to be the challenger then you will face many dangers. You may not even make it to June. You may die tonight." Shuman's face lacks any compassion.

"If you're trying to convince me to do this then you're not doing a very good job," I say.

Shuman stares at the moon for a minute as if she's calculating something. "I will need your answer."

"What? Now!?" My voice echoes over the spillway. "Just like that? I don't get a minute to think it over or go home and weigh out my options?"

"You do not have a home," she reminds.

My foot connects with the concrete curb in front of me. I want to throw an all-out tantrum. Running and hiding also sounds like a good idea. Shuman's oppressive demeanor, indifferent to my predicament, makes it tough to think. I wait for her to say something, but she just stands motionless watching the moon. She's starting to creep me out.

"What's going to happen to my family?" I ask, the last word sounding strange as it tumbles out of my mouth.

"I suspect Zhuang will maintain his hold on them, but who he really wants is you," Shuman says indifferently. "Your family is officially classified as hallucinators. He has the ability to keep them like this for a long time. Or he could finish them rather quickly."

Finish them? Does that mean what I think it does? This man, this parasite, is stealing my family's ability to dream, causing them to fall into hallucinatory states. And I'm powerless to stop Zhuang if he decides to drain them of their consciousness. Then they'd be shells, sleepwalkers. Dead in no time. A shiver runs down my spine.

Shuman continues, "Zhuang's plan was to make you panic and surrender to him. It is fortunate we found you first. My guess is your family will hang in limbo. Zhuang's attention will be on finding you. If you want to help your family then stay away, otherwise he will use them against you. And if you want to release them then you need to fight Zhuang."

"And win," I say, doubt oozing all over the words.

"Well, of course."

"This whole thing makes no sense." I rub my head with a shaky hand. "Why me? I'm barely old enough to drive. I've only known about this mess for a few days. How was I chosen? How am I the best person to face him?"

"I do not know the answers to these questions," she says, still fixated on the moon.

"Then why should I do this!? Why should I jeopardize my life without knowing why I've been chosen?"

Shuman takes one long blink as though contemplating or meditating. Her words are airy and quiet when she finally speaks. "The great Buddha once said, 'Three things cannot be long hidden: the sun, the moon, and the truth.'"

I bite down hard on my lip. So this is the way it is? Either I live my life alone on the streets and watch as Zhuang ransacks humanity's dreams. Or, option two, I volunteer to kill him and most likely die trying, but my consolation prize will be I'll know why I'd been chosen. I'll know who I was and where I could have belonged…if I hadn't died in Zhuang's hands. This seems like a scam, although an ingenious one.

A sincere part of me wants to return to my family and shake them until they're released from their hallucinations. Then we can go on living our lives where the most interesting things that happen are football, church, and barbeques. It's not a great life for an agnostic vegetarian, but is it better than death? I may be a product of the East Texas soil, but the winds here have never agreed with me. I've been looking for a way out of this town, but not like this.

"I cannot grant you any more time," Shuman says. "I need your answer."

I scan the surface of the water, looking for nothing in particular. She *can* wait for my answer. She will.

I push my fingers into my eyes and inhale deeply. This duel is inevitable. Zhuang and his challenger's futures are intertwined. Any attempt to evade the other person will only bring the two together. And somehow I was elected by people I don't know, for a danger I only recently knew existed. Still none of this makes sense, which is why I know I have to rely on instinct. It's all I have left. "Fine," I say a bit pathetically. "I'll do it."

A smile would be nice, or maybe a "good for you." Instead Shuman, who appears to be all business, all the time, begins spouting instructions. "Your next step is to find the Lucidite Institute. Since you are relatively new to dream traveling there are many risks you face."

No big surprises there.

Shuman continues, "You must dream travel to the Institute while fully submerged in water."

Um, what? "Are you serious? I'll drown."

"There is that risk, yes, but the only way to enter the Institute is through water. To travel there you must return to your body and then immerse yourself in water. I advise you to *know* you are one with it. It is through this knowledge that you overcome the fear of drowning and focus on the higher task of dream traveling. If you remain calm and focus properly then you will travel and arrive at the Institute. If you are unsuccessful, then yes, you will drown."

"Oh, is that all? Sounds like a piece of cake." I'm wondering now if I made the right decision.

Shuman narrows her eyes, but doesn't respond otherwise.

I rub my temples as an overwhelming pressure erupts behind my eyes. "This is all so strange, it sounds like a recurring dream I've been…" My words fall away as the inevitable truth dawns on me. "You put those dreams in my head, didn't you?" I accuse, staring at her rigid persona.

"The Lucidites are responsible, yes," she says, her tone matter-of-fact.

"What! That's insane! That's awful. Night after night I dreamed I was drowning myself. Do you know how horrifying that is?"

"You should be grateful. We have prepared you for the journey you are about to take. Your subconscious mind has already practiced much of what you are going to do."

"Grateful!?" I shake my head in disbelief. "I thought I was losing my mind. I didn't sleep well for weeks. No. I'm not the least bit grateful. You invaded my subconscious," I spew, more frustrated now than frightened.

Shuman takes a long inhale and says, "Everything that has been done was to protect you and the future."

How do I argue with that statement? How do I argue with any of this? I want to run, to abandon this farce which has become my life. However, my instinct is concrete around my legs, pinning me in place, assuring me this is where I belong.

"Roya, we are running out of time," Shuman says, breaking the silence. "Do you have any questions?"

"Why does it have to be so complicated to dream travel to the Institute? Isn't there an alternative?" *Like a spaceship or a drug?*

"No, there is not," Shuman says. "The Institute is heavily protected by water. The difficulty it takes to travel there is what makes it the safest place on earth."

The idea settles over me like a down comforter. Safety. What would that feel like? Every moment has been cloaked with a hidden threat for so long. When the recurring dreams weren't plaguing me, the paranoia lurked in the shadows and was all but incapacitating. It was almost enough to make me take the pills the therapist kept pushing. Almost.

"If I do all this"—the words drip out of my mouth— "if I don't drown, then I'll be at the Institute? I'll be safe? At least for a little while, right?"

Her eyes jerk away from their focal point. There's a twitch at her mouth. "Yes."

I sigh. It's the first one of relief in a while. "All right then, I'll do it," I say halfheartedly.

She turns and faces me, resting her arms across her chest. Around one of her forearms is a tattoo of a rattlesnake. The serpent's tail lies on her elbow and its head on the back of her hand.

"There is one last thing," she says, a warning in her voice. "Only Lucidites can enter the Institute. You must want to be one of us, or you will be forbidden from entering."

I blink in surprise. My mouth opens to voice hesitation, but she disappears, leaving me alone and feeling as though I'm standing on the edge of the earth.

To continue reading, please purchase: Awoken (The Lucidites, #1)

Sneak Peek of Ren:

The Man Behind the Monster:

Prologue

*W*hen I was born the doctor said I wouldn't live the night through. I had a problem with a valve in my heart. My pops called a secret healer who lived a few towns away. And now I write this to you as a grown man. I'm not spoiling anything for you from the tale you're about to read. It isn't a spoiler that all these years I've survived. The true secret is that I lived at all. Actually I lived on an edge, one so dangerous most don't even know it's there. I didn't sell my soul to the devil or dance with her on a clear night. I ran up to the devil and I stole the mask she wore and I wore it comfortably for quite some time. But then I met an angel and she made me want to die. I didn't though. My secret isn't even that I lived. It's that I lived pretending to be the devil, wishing God would save my soul. I knew this was a wasted wish. I have no soul left to save. It's why I could steal the devil's persona. It's why I lived when I should have died too many times.

I don't hold babies or pause for the elderly. It's not because I'm unkind. I'm kind. I'm kind enough to never put myself close to anyone vulnerable. I'm afraid I might break them. I'm afraid of myself. I live alone or with the strong and arrogant. But I don't live close to those who are vulnerable. I don't live close to those who might dare to love me. I don't trust myself otherwise.

When I was born God made an awful error. He allowed a healer to save me. He allowed me to live. I'm a mistake. Not because my parents didn't intend to have me and God failed to kill me. I'm a mistake because of what I can do. I'm a mistake because people like me aren't destined for happiness. We are the miserable. The lonely. The people you warn your children not to become. The ones you warn your children to stay away from.

I'm Ren Lewis and I was born with too much power.

Chapter One

April 1985

The antique clock on the wall had the most irritating tick. It seemed extraordinarily loud. Probably because the old grandfather was a knockoff. It most likely was manufactured the year before in some backyard by a wanker who failed clock-making school and decided to go into forgery. I instantly liked the clock a lot more.

Snap. Snap.

The middle-aged Middling therapist dared to snap his dried fingertips in front of my face. Sure, I wasn't paying attention to him. Sure, he'd asked his question to me repeatedly, and without answering I continued to stare at the clock which had too much lacquer and the detail work was a bit rough in places. How much did this shrink shell out for such a phony piece of furniture?

Unhurried, I pulled my gaze around to face the irritated therapist. I had to give him credit. He almost appeared in control of this situation. Bravo. This is the only thing I think he had control of, since I was guessing his overweight wife probably bossed his skinny ass around all day and his three kids owned the parts of him that she didn't. But this guy had a mock sense of authority over me; at least he had been trying to make a show of it.

I blinked at him blankly. "What was the question?" I said.

"Ren, are you paying the least bit of attention during this session?" Dr. Simon said, pushing his wiry glasses up the thin bridge of his nose.

I took a deliberate moment to actually think about the question. Should I answer honestly or should I save his ego and make him as the poor therapist feel better about himself? Yeah, saving egos is someone else's job, for sure.

"Not really," I said, stretching out my arms with a long yawn. "But if it will make this whole mess go along a tad faster then I'll give it a bit more of my attention. How's that, doc?"

He bristled, pulling his yellow pad of notes closer to him as he crossed a skinny ankle over his bony knee. "What do you have to say for your actions? Are you the least bit remorseful about what you did to poor Widow Johnson?"

I felt my eyebrows rise with surprise. Yeah, I was remorseful, but not about what I did to the old bag. I was remorseful that I'd been so foolish. Still new to my gifts, I had a lot to learn about limitations. Using my mind control, I convinced the old lady to give me her husband's old Bentley. Give it to me. No questions asked.

"Here you are," she said, her Scottish accent much fainter than I remembered in years past. "It's all yours." Old Mrs. Johnson handed me the keys to the Bentley Continental, which had only been driven on Sundays. Then she gave me one little bit of advice. "Be careful around the corners. Henry didn't like the tires to get dirty."

I'm sure he didn't. But this car had only one destiny in my hands. It was going to get dirty. Inside and out. I was going to drive it to London. Park it in front of the finest clubs and tempt the finest of women to join me inside it. And my plan would have worked and I would have been laid by a model at the early age of fifteen years old. *However*, it didn't work because I didn't have a license to drive or the know-how to do so.

Instead of driving that sleek ride to London, I crashed it into old man Miller's stack of hay bundles on the other side of Mrs. Johnson's farm. I knew then I'd never see a pretty lady undressing herself in that backseat. I had the know-how without all the actual "know-how." I could control minds, but didn't know how to do things…simple little things like driving. I needed to learn how to do these small tasks. But being fifteen provided all sorts of disadvantages. And namely, the first disadvantage was sitting squarely in front of me, fidgeting with his note pad.

"The last time you were in here was because you let all of Mr. Gretchen's sheep loose," Dr. Simon said, reading from his file on the side table. He needed to have his orderly notes. Needed to be able to refer back to them. He didn't have the advantage of a flawless, photographic memory, like me. Poor soul with his weaknesses and many shortcomings. How he made it through graduate school is ever a wonder to me.

My green eyes narrowed at the accusation. It was all wrong. As usual. Just like with the Bentley. They thought I stole it, when it was actually given to me. And I didn't let the sheep loose. I made Mr. Gretchen do it using a bit of hypnosis, partnered with mind control. However, I made silly errors in the process. Firstly, I'd hung around to watch the mayhem of sheep patrolling through our muddy streets. I'd also done a sloppy job of mind control on the dumb farmer. He remembered me. Didn't know what I did to him, but there was enough suspicion that the whole thing was pinned on me. They thought I just let the sheep out, which is a lot more innocent a crime than what I really did.

"Tell me, Ren, why is it that you keep acting out?" Dr. Simon said, almost looking a little afraid of me, but bent on acting his part as the parish therapist. The church wasn't just paying him to sign off on the health and well-being of most of its members. They also expected him to fix the lot of us who were intent on the devil's rule.

I sized the guy up. We'd had at least half a dozen sessions. None of my usual lies had worked, so I decided he was ready for the truth. The truth I always saved until I was in the most amount of trouble. The truth invariably set me free, but not because people believed me. Rather because they thought I was crazy, which I probably am.

"I keep acting out because," I began in a rehearsed voice, "well, it's complicated, and it's actually a secret. I'm not sure if I should tell you. You may get mad at my parents since it was their insistence that I keep this private."

"Ren, I won't get mad at your parents," Dr. Simon said in his soothing therapist tone. "You can tell me anything and we will work through it together. Your parents will suffer no harm by your truths."

I nodded. Inside I smiled with glee. "The truth is that I was born half Dream Traveler, and not only can I travel through space and time using my dreams, but as this special race of humans I'm also gifted with a skill. Some Dream Travelers have one or maybe even two gifts. I can control people using my mind, hypnotize people with movements, *and* if I touch someone I can hear their thoughts." I scuffed some imaginary dirt off my shoe. "That's the truth. The big secret. Don't be mad at me or my parents for it."

The therapist took in a long annoyed breath. "Until you, Ren, are ready to actually talk about your crimes in a real manner then these sessions are futile."

A slow smile formed on my face. The truth was always the better option in these situations. No one believed it and therefore just assumed I was a no-good teen. A troublemaker. A pathological liar. The truth was I kept telling the truth over and over again and no one believed me. My father, who had spent his life hiding the fact that he carried Dream Traveler blood in him, hadn't especially liked that I did this. But he was smart enough to realize no one was ever going to believe me. I was Ren. The boy who had been there when my teacher pulled her knickers down during my solo detention last year. The boy who had been the one to call authorities when my entire church group, including our teacher, fell into inexplicable comas. I was the strange boy. The one who things happened around. But people thought it was because I was a troublemaker branded with the word "cursed" across my head. They had no idea it was because since I was ten years old I'd come into my gifts and could control most using my mind and hypnotize anyone I dared. I told them to hold my hand so I could read their thoughts, but they'd totally shrugged me off most of the time. Even though I kept telling the truth, I was dismissed. And that's what made the whole thing even more fun. What fools they all were. Utter, stupid fools.

But my mum saw through it and knew I was manipulating the lot of them. And her look of heartbreak did cause me a bit of stress. She kept professing her faith in me though. She thought that a heavy hand would never make me see my awful ways, but rather the hand of our Lord and Savior. That's why she kept convincing the church to take me in after each of my crimes. Counsel me. Absolve my sins. Steer me in the right direction.

However, my mother was as short-sighted as the rest. As a Middling, those who are without gifts or the power to dream travel, she'd never see how much fun it was to manipulate. My mother didn't see a lot. Mostly because her life was so limited. And I wasted too many years of her life with my antics when I could have been with her, learning the lessons only she could teach me. The ones I only now realize Middlings can teach. Those of the heart. Dream Travelers are too distracted by our minds, by our gifts, to fully

285

understand how love works. However, Middlings aren't complicated in that way.

"Ren, we've been doing this regularly," Dr. Simon said to me that evening. He was thoroughly done with my shenanigans, and soon the poor chap would sod off to his meager dwelling on the outskirts of Peavey, where his family would abuse him with neglect and pesky remarks about his feeble appearance. He sighed deeply. "Ren, when you get caught, your mother makes her case to the vicar and somehow you end up seeing me instead of the constable. These opportunities for you to have rehabilitation instead of punishment are running out. I suggest you be real with me. I want you to tell me why you act out. Many of your teachers describe you as having a chip on your shoulder. Of being hostile. Do you want to tell me why? This is your last chance."

More than once throughout my life I've been asked what it is that made me so hard, so hostile. Why would something have to make me the way I am? I've known dozens of happy people who have nothing to be happy about and still they plaster stupid grins on their faces every bloody day. There are those who are all scared and tortured and they've got no good reason for the self-pity. Nothing more than a few trivial things have ever happened to them. Forgetting their lunch. Missing an exam. Not getting the girl. And yet these lowlifes go through life like they were given a curse at birth.

It's mostly just a choice. Life doesn't make most of us any certain way. We wake up, and usually without knowing it, act in a way that fits our personality. Nothing made me the way I am. Not really. Things colored me. Persuaded me. But no experience is responsible for making me hostile. It's just the way I prefer to be. Also, who I am is a result of something inside my bones. Probably a monster who feeds off my unhealthy behavior. I'm not a victim of circumstance. I'm a man who believes that the best strategy involves being extremely cynical and even more conniving. And if there's one thing I'm more excellent at than all the other things, it's strategy. I'm a bloody master at it. Hell, I'm fairly certain God takes notes out of *my* book. He should. If he knows what's good for him.

I brought my eyes up to meet the therapist's gaze. I'd made a great show of putting real emotions on my face. My bottom lip quivered a bit. My eyes were filled to the brim with fake tears. And when I opened my mouth an actual croak happened out. "It's my sister, Lyza," I wailed. "She abuses me. She abuses me badly," I sang.

"Your older sister, Lyza?" Dr. Simon said, sitting forward, almost knocking the pad off his thin lap.

"That's right," I said, furiously nodding my head. "The one due to graduate early this year and with an acceptance to Oxford. That one. But what you don't know is she does things to me," I said, putting a look of shameful hurt on my face.

"Don't you worry, Ren," Dr. Simon said, leaning forward, placing a hand on my shaking arm. "We won't let her hurt you any longer."

Truth be told, Lyza only hurt me with dirty remarks and cold stares. But Lyza had told our mother since she was thirteen that our mum was no better than a servant in our house. She had despised our mum for being a Middling and I in turn despised Lyza. And now I was going to make her pay for every hurtful thing she did to our mum. See, the thing is, when Ren gets in trouble, so do other people.

I allowed the doctor's hand to linger on my forearm. Now was probably not the time to tell this homosexual that I didn't quite enjoy his touch, but definitely go and cart my sister away for abusing her little brother. I grabbed one more thought out of the doctor's head before he slipped his hand away. That one thought was enough for me to know that the punishment Dr. Simon saw for Lyza would fit the bill until I could up the ante.

To continue reading, please purchase: Ren: The Man Behind the Monster (Ren Series, #1)

For more books by this author or to learn more about
Sarah Noffke, please visit:
http://www.sarahnoffke.com

Made in the USA
Charleston, SC
16 March 2016